PRIMAL DEITY

1

the
CHAOS ENGINE

ALLEN OZARK

Edited by Bella Fox

Published by Sumner House Publishing

a division of Wisemen Multimedia, LLC

www.sumnerhousepublishing.com

ISBN: 9781733465601

Experience the Primal Deity Series…

~ 1 THE CHAOS ENGINE ~

2 CRISIS MANAGEMENT

3 CONTAINMENT

4 EARLY DETECTION

5 ONE FEDERAL PARKWAY

www.primaldeity.com

Acknowledgements

I would like to give a heartfelt thank you to:

My family and friends, who are in no small part the foundation for my success and the formula for my happiness;

My publisher, Sumner House, and everyone, who worked so hard to launch the Primal Deity Series and ensure its success;

First responders, who risk their lives to make the world a better place;

Members of the intelligence community, homeland security and defense industry, and our military men and women and their families, who know freedom is not free; and

Last, but definitely not least, I thank God for his thoughtful kindness and generosity in designing a Universe where anything is possible.

Dedication

Growing up, I always knew what I wanted to be: a writer, a movie director, or some equally entertaining professional. Throughout my years working in homeland security and defense, I never lost focus on my goal. However, in recent years, I've come to realize all I ever wanted to be is a good dad. This book is dedicated to my son, Victor Ethan. If ever there's doubt that God exists, I need only to look into his eyes for a surefire reminder. With all my heart, I truly believe I am the luckiest dad in the world. Thank you, son.

PRIMAL DEITY

the CHAOS ENGINE

Chapter 1

I'm so bored. I can't take much more of this. Cranky artists—and I use the term loosely—computer geeks, and drooling politicians have become the highlight of my day. Anti-Piracy sucks. I feel like I'm taking crazy pills. Sure, it's a job, but it's not what I signed up for. I've got knowledge, skills and abilities. Plus, I've been through enough for my country to have a holiday named in my honor, or at the very least a promotion. I'm still waiting on both. I just feel like I need more, something bigger, you know a real exciting career. Unfortunately, there's no such thing as excitement around here. When I walk through the door at the office every morning, I just wanna turn my black-ass around and go right back home.

The sad part is I actually had an exciting job, key word being *had*. Soon as my tour of duty was up, the United States Navy got rid of me so fast my head spun. I think those are the rules. If you like your job a little too much, some idiot at the top will kick you out on your butt at their earliest convenience.

In the service, I had the best of both worlds, I'm talking training, field experience, the whole nine yards. I was stationed in the sexiest place on planet earth, South America, Brazil. I spent four years in Rio. Aside from all the random drug cartel violence, it was like a tropical paradise. I worked counternarcotics with the best of the best. Now, I'm stuck behind a stupid desk. I'm not complaining—okay, maybe I am a little—but I'm not feeling this job at all.

Rio de Janeiro, Brazil. What a way to put in 40 hours a week. I loved every minute of it but being the only woman in my unit was no walk in the park. They pissed on me with zero remorse more than I care to admit. I could have complained, but I sucked it up and actually got a chance to do some real fieldwork. True, most of it involved dodging bullets, or blending in with the local working girls, but I'd take that any day over sitting around in a stuffy, dusty office.

The sheer boredom of normality is getting down right unbearable. I used to do meaningful work. Every day was some kind of new adventure. Nowadays, the only excitement I see involves paper clips and number two pencils. Everything that makes me who I am seems to be withering away, slowly but surely.

If I were a lesser woman, I'd complain, but no one cares. The government needs team players, which at this point I'm convinced is just agency jargon for shut your mouth and be lucky you have a job. Maybe that's not true, but I play it smart just in case. I keep all my opinions to myself because even though my paycheck is more of a bi-weekly gag reel than a payday, the rent keeps on coming.

Even if I had the nerve to speak my mind at work, it wouldn't make a difference. My colleagues act like life can't get any better, and there's no convincing them otherwise. I see them every day, running around, smiling and sucking Starbucks coffee up a straw like it's a controlled substance. Let them tell it, working for the FBI is great. I think they're all a sandwich short of a sack lunch, but again I don't say a single word. I keep it all to myself.

Whenever I get the urge to complain, I bite my tongue because I know they don't want to hear the truth from ole Denise Alexandria Southerland. Their little caffeine pumping hearts can't handle it. I have no clue why I rub them the wrong way. I'm shy, nice, caring and sweet ... and if you believe that, I have a bridge in Brooklyn I'd like to sell you real cheap. Honestly, I'm not a very nice person at all. I'm a firecracker. I have a *Handle with Care* warning label stamped across my ass. Mess with me and I will put you in the hurt locker, one way or another, sooner than later.

My personal life has not been a walk in the park either. I've been fighting family, friends, coworkers and anybody else brave enough to go a few rounds with me since I crawled out the womb. I never back down, and I maintain a constant state of readiness because you just never know when someone in arms-reach might need a personality adjustment. People who think my bark is bigger than my bite, I got news for them. I'm committed, and I don't like to lose, ever.

Most people I come into contact with conspire against me, so I have to keep a sharp eye on others, particularly while negotiating the dregs of the illustrious Federal Bureau of Investigations. Working in this dump, I have to be prepared for the worst at all times. If you ask me, FBI really stands for *Female Bashing Imbeciles*.

People around me say I have a cold heart. They whisper behind my back and say things like I am self-loathing, but I don't think so. In fact, I happen to love everything about me, unconditionally I might add, everything except my name. It's not a terribly bad one as names go, and I guess I should thank my lucky stars I didn't get stuck with some weird hippy shit. I imagine that was due to either a freak occurrence or divine intervention. I've seen the old family photos from the 70's, and I can definitely see Dad going for Sky, Starbright, or Autumn Flowers. Thankfully, my folks left those names where they belong back in the sixties with the Volkswagen vans and colorful peace signs.

I didn't get scarred for life with a screwed-up name, but my parents didn't put much effort into coming up with a good one either. Denise sounds like somebody's grandmamma. Don't get me wrong, I ain't down with names like LaShundra or Shaqwana. Can you imagine that at the top of my resume? I'd never get a job. Nah, I'm fortunate in that respect, but Denise? To me it's just too plain.

Evidently others share my pain because everybody and their momma takes it upon themselves to rewrite my birth certificate. I've been called every name in the book, some good, some bad, and some I'm too embarrassed to mention, but I've embraced them all. They're all part of me. Back in the service, my C.O. called me a goddamn pain in the fuckin' ass, and he actually took the time to say it just like that, in its entirety, every single time. On the other hand, my subordinates respectfully called me Lieutenant, or Sir. Nowadays, I'm known by most as Special Agent

Southerland, which I think suits me well. I've had many names, and I've been many things to a lot of people, but to my closest friends—the people I love—they all call me Alex.

So, who am I? I think I'm a simple girl. My boyfriend Bill would argue otherwise though. He says I'm as difficult as a jigsaw puzzle without the box cover, but what does he know? I don't have a single problem with myself. I totally get me, but to everyone else, I'm an enigma and a magnet for problems. I have no idea why people think I have so many issues, but whatever they are, I can't take all the credit.

It's no secret my family was dysfunctional to say the least. To sum it all up, we're a big batch of chaos, wrapped up in a crunchy, destructive shell. I'm not joking either. If it weren't for Dad all those years, we would've probably killed each other.

I'm a daddy's girl all the way, and I truly adored mine. To me, he's the real Superman, indestructible, helpful and caring, I mean Christopher Reeves ain't got nothing on him. I never cared what anybody had to say about him either. To me he could do no wrong. I used to hang around him all the time too. My mother hated we were so close, but I didn't care, and neither did he. Growing up, he was the biggest part of my life, and he remains a source of strength that helps me get through the day.

Unfortunately, Daddy's no longer with us, rest his soul. He died on the job. He's been gone for a while, but he stays on my mind. I get depressed a lot during the high points in my life—high school graduation and college, pretty much all the times you wanna hug your dad's neck like everybody else, but you can't. That's when I miss him most. It may sound weird, but no man has ever taken his place. One almost got close, and boy was he wild, but I'll never let anybody penetrate my defenses like that again. When they leave, and trust me they always do, it hurts way too much.

I think about the way Daddy died, and I get so pissed off. It didn't make any sense whatsoever. He was a Major with the Fulton County Sheriff's Department. Now everybody knows being a cop can be dangerous, but the thing is, he didn't die in any kind of dramatic act of bravery, which makes it even harder for me. To this day, I still haven't gotten a straight answer, but from what I was told, the whole thing was just a freak accident.

Daddy planned a big raid. When they got on site, his team cleared the drug house, but somehow, they managed to overlook a damn crackhead hiding in the back. This kid was a real piece of work too, completely doped up and out of his mind. I guess for him, going out like a dishonored samurai made more sense than spending a night in the lockup. Just when everybody let their guard down, the kid popped out, waving a fully automatic pistol. I don't think he was even eighteen years old. Despite Dad's best efforts to talk him down, the boy spazzed out and went suicidal. He held the gun up to his temple and pulled the trigger. If he'd just shot himself, Daddy would still be alive, but the gun was still going off as his body dropped to the floor. Bullets flew all across the room in every direction. Everybody ducked and scattered, but as close as Daddy was to the boy, he just couldn't get out of the way fast enough. That's the story my Dad's partner told me.

Daddy's funeral was closed-casket. We never even got a chance to see him and say goodbye, or anything. The sick part about it is the kid survived. I guess life's funny that way. Sometimes I think it's poetic justice he turned out to be a vegetable, but it's not. Truth is he'll be a burden on the system for the rest of his uneventful life all because he wanted to play Kingpin. I've tried not hating that kid, but I just can't let it go. Because of him, Daddy's never coming back home.

I still love my dad with all my heart. I really enjoyed listening to him talk too. He had a way with words. I hated asking him stuff sometimes though because, instead of just answering, he'd go into this long-winded story that had some kind of remote, related meaning. I swear that man spoke in parables, but I'd give anything to hear another just one last time.

Daddy was more than just a good man. The way I see it, he was the glue that held the family together and kept us all sane. We took him for granted, but after he died, it was clear how much we actually needed him. With him gone, it didn't take long for our family to rip apart at the seams. Before his body settled in the ground, we were at each other's throats. The littlest things set us off. After years of explosive battles, the family just fell to pieces. I don't talk to my people much anymore, but I wish things were different. It's like I say, we need Dad now more than ever. I miss him so much. Not a day goes by without me wishing he were here.

My Dad took a huge piece of my heart, but I'll always have enough for my younger sister Theresa and my baby brother Chris. I don't get a chance to see them much, but when we're together, for me it's like taking a long stroll down the streets of heaven. Now that Theresa's older and starting to think for herself, instead of being a mindless puppet for Momma, we've started talking a lot more. Matter of fact, we talk just about every day.

Theresa's one of the few people, who really gets me. We still have little fights here and there but linking back up with her is probably the best thing that could've happened when I got back from the service. Don't get me wrong, I love my brother. Chris is an angel, but there's nothing in the world like being tight with your sister.

Oh yeah, I almost forgot about my mother—well, I guess she's my mother. I always got the distinct impression she didn't like me very much. Since day one, she talked to me like a dog and made such a big deal about my complexion. She said I looked like a dingy bed sheet. What kind of person says that about their own daughter?

Mom was born in Jamaica. She's very proud, extremely old fashioned, stubborn as a mule, and as it turns out, a bit of a psychotic racist too. I know I shouldn't call my own mother crazy, but I swear she is. With Momma, black folks—especially islanders—have an all-purpose Get Out of Jail Free card no matter the circumstances. But, if you're light-skinned, like me, beware! Oh, and don't even have stringy hair because you're automatically a blond-haired, blue-eyed devil, whether you've got blue eyes or not. I'm serious. White people beware. One false move and she'll unleash hell and pound you into puppy chow. This is all strange and ironic in more ways than one.

My sister and brother are both gorgeous, brown-skinned angels, so they managed to escape Momma's vengeful wrath. Not me. I took after Daddy, and I was a terrible looking little thing when I came out. Anyone, who sees my baby pictures would agree, but they'd have to pry them from my cold, dead hands. It was more than just my bright skin—I was four different shades of white. I had spots all over my face too, and I was completely baldheaded. I looked like a little hairless alien rat. Daddy said Momma had a fit in the hospital. She thought the staff had swapped me out with some other "white folk's baby." Honestly, sometimes she makes me wish I was somebody else's daughter.

I found out the hard way just how much skin color meant to the sophisticated Mrs. Ezola Southerland. Since I seemed to have been birthed out of a vat of bleach, I ranked pretty low on a scale of one to ten in her book. Daddy didn't care what I looked like though. No matter what I did, he was always so happy and proud of his little girl. Naturally, this caused a ton of problems at home.

When my parents argued, it was usually over me, or something I'd allegedly done to offend Momma. Daddy never liked the way Momma fussed and kicked me around the house every day. At the same time though, he never did anything to stop it. I guess I understand because every time he said something to her about the abuse, World War III broke out.

I remember when I was seven, I told Daddy just to give me up for adoption, so they could finally be happy together. Ever since then, he made a point every other day to tell me it wasn't my fault. He'd claim they just had some "minor" issues to iron out, but I knew he was lying. Everybody knew the real reason they were fighting.

Early on, I felt the need to shoulder the blame for all the drama in the house, but I'm not sure how any of it was actually my fault— I mean, Momma's the one who married a white man. What exactly did she expect? How oddly ironic is it when a black woman, who for whatever reason hates and distrusts white people, ends up marrying a white man and having his kids—three of them? It just doesn't make any sense to me.

So, do I actually believe my mom's racist? I really do, and she'd be wasting her time trying to refute my claim. She's as racist as a hooded Klansman. Daddy on the other hand was the exact opposite. He hung around any and everybody, black, white, red, or green for that matter. And you know what, who cares? I mean, he was a nice guy, and he took care of his family. If you got a good man, who cares if he's white or black? Unfortunately, Momma didn't see it that way. She always seemed embarrassed to be with him. Now that I think about it, she acted the same way when it came to me.

I don't think I really ever understood the whole racism thing until recently. I started putting the pieces together for myself a few years back. I can definitely see it almost everywhere I go, but even now that I'm more aware, I still don't really get it. Like I say, if two people love each other, race shouldn't matter, but try convincing my mother of that. You'd have a better chance surviving a game of "run across the busy freeway," wearing all black at midnight.

With the way things went down and how she acted after Daddy died, I came to the conclusion she married him just to get to America. I know it sounds shallow, but I wouldn't put it past her. That woman wakes up evil for no reason whatsoever. Sometimes, I remember the few good times we had together, and I start to think maybe she does love me in her own way, but then reality kicks in and I come to my senses.

Without exaggerating, I can honestly say my mother has nothing but disdain for me, especially after I foiled her master plan. I may not have been much of a looker, but I was smart as a whip, so naturally I was her little star child. Since before I could remember, she spent the majority of her time grooming me to be the greatest attorney on planet earth. Even by marginal standards, that was one hell of a task because I just wasn't interested.

I didn't know what I wanted to be when I grew up. I was just a kid, and like all kids, I wanted to play and have fun. None of that mattered though. By third grade, Mom knew exactly what I would do for the rest of my life, or at least she thought she did. It must've been around the time I started middle school when she realized her wants and mine didn't quite match up. To keep me from straying from the path, she turned up the heat and rode me like a rodeo bull. It was ridiculous to say the least. She acted like one of those showbiz moms, who work their kids like dogs. She was always yelling at me too no matter where we were. We could be in church, at my school, or anywhere—hell everywhere—and she would go crazy and yell at me. It was so embarrassing. After a while, I just stopped trying to have any friends whatsoever. Maybe that was her plan.

School was just as screwed up as my home life. Well, up through the 11th grade it wasn't too bad because I just kept to myself, but my senior year was a real nightmare. I was only 15-years-old in a class full of kids ages 17 to 20. The other kids treated me like a freak because I was younger and smarter than them, but they all came to me for help with their homework. It never really mattered what I did either. Their opinion of me never changed. I could've gone to school topless with spinning nipple rings and I still would've just been the little freckle-faced geek, who didn't belong. Kids can be really stupid and mean sometimes, but just go to your high school reunion, and I guarantee the cool kids from your class will be the ones saying, *uh, yeah, I'm between jobs right now.*

It's funny because my classmates had cars and designer clothes, fly shoes and jewelry, and they skipped class like graduating was just a suggestion. For them, it was party time, but not me. I had to buckle down and finish at the top of my class. If I didn't make valedictorian, according to Mommy Dearest, I was a nobody.

Aside from school and church, I had no social life. The only exciting thing in high school was I got myself a real live boyfriend. It was serious too. His name was William, but I affectionately called him Bill or Slick Willy when appropriate. Bill was all that and a bag of chips. He talked to me like he actually cared about what I thought. He was my knight in shining armor, and I was counting on him to show up, slay the evil dragon, and rescue me from the zoo I called home. Unfortunately, that never actually happened. Bill didn't save me from anything. To my dismay, he was drawn in by the dragon's cheap parlor tricks, just like everybody else. Even now, he gives Momma a pass no matter what sick brand of demonic shit she does to me. I guess I'm the only one who can see what a sick bitch she is.

Momma always kept an eye on me in school. She was relentless about it too. It's amazing how I pulled off the whole boyfriend thing because every move I made she was on me like a hawk on a squirrel. Bill and I had precious little time together, but the moments we shared alone were among my few good teenage memories. We stuck it out even through college. We're still together now, so I guess that means we're doing something right. Can you imagine that? High school sweethearts? How 'bout that.

Other than being with Bill, I can't say much positive about that time in my life. All I remember is my mother worked me from sunup to sundown, pushing and drilling, all the while acting a complete fool with me. She was determined to whip me into shape for college. I'd go to school, focus hard all day, and then come back home for night school.

I guess all Mom's antics paid off though. I graduated at the tender age of sixteen—no, I didn't turn sixteen until the December after graduation. Oh, and yes, I am a December Capricorn and proud of it. Just wanted to put that on the table so you know.

Graduating as young as I did, I thought I'd made history. Turns out, nobody cared, well, nobody except Momma, and she wasn't exactly ecstatic about the whole thing.

I remember graduation night after we got home, I just sat quiet in my room, holding my diploma and wondering if all of the sacrifice was worth it. I started thinking about all the times I had to choose wisely between studying like a bookworm and sneaking out to play. Sometimes, I chose poorly. Soon as Momma wasn't paying attention, I'd sneak out and play as long as I could, because I knew what would happen once I walked back through the door.

Momma wasn't a very big woman, but she had iron fists and no remorse when it came to using them on me. I could tell whenever she was gettin' all riled up because she'd start speaking Patois. Of course, I didn't understand it, but whatever she said would always end in *kill mi dead!* Well, you don't have to be much of a linguist to figure that one out.

I'd retaliate by calling her Daddy's *island-booty* and screaming that she needs to "go back to Africa." Yes, I know it doesn't make sense, but it was enough to push her over the edge, so that was good enough for me. At that point, Daddy would just back up and stand clear. He always seemed too afraid to get between us.

Daddy was a big bad cop. He trained most of the SWAT team and was over a lot of men, but I think he would've rather taken on every inmate in the detention center before tasting Momma's wrath. She was that big a fool. Whenever she rose up at me, he'd turn his back or go in the other room, which seemed to give her the green light to pulverize me. I resented him for it, but I remember he always came back afterwards to help pick up the pieces. Somehow, in my young mind, that small gesture set the two of them apart. I guess a little bit of love beats a bucket of hate any day.

Now, don't think for a moment I'm exaggerating here. I got punched so much you would've thought I was an Everlast heavy bag. After a while, it was sort of a Southerland household ritual. Momma would smack me around like a disobedient slave, Theresa would watch and snicker, and Daddy would pretend like he didn't know what was going on. We were one big happy family. If a day went by and I didn't get in trouble, well things just didn't seem right.

I think in a lot of ways, Momma was just determined to live her life through me. Note to parents: *Please get all the stuff you want to do with your life out of the way before you have kids.* She had high hopes and dreams, but never got around to doing any of it. By the time she got the nerve up, she was pregnant with me, and at that point, her ship had sailed.

Whenever anyone asks why she didn't really go for it, she always answers, "Kids got in the way." I was the oldest, so most of the blame fell on my shoulders. I guess she figured sacrificing her dreams and carrying me around for nine months left a hefty bill to pay. She made it clear I'd be picking up the tab. Bottom line, I had to do exactly as she instructed, to the letter, even if it killed us both.

I trip a lot about it, but I don't think she completely hated me. I just think she was counting on me to make her life mean something. Like I say, I was her star child, and she was going to make me a successful attorney come hell or high water.

Everything leading up to graduation was fucked up beyond repair, but college was a major improvement. Compared to high school, it was as different as night and day. After a major knockdown drag-out fight over colleges, I ended up compromising by doing exactly what Momma told me to. I went to Georgia Tech in Atlanta. It was close to home, so she could still keep an eye on me around the clock, but after a while, things changed.

It didn't take long for me to realize I'd lived a sheltered life. Those kids on that campus opened my eyes to a new world, the real world of alcohol, frat parties, sororities, and ... well, let's just say I went through a serious period of adjustment. Oh, and talk about peer pressure—I had a crazy roommate. For the most part, we were cool, but she had some strange ways. The good news is she loved to party, and when Momma wasn't hovering over me or calling my room every five minutes, we had a helluva time.

I always wondered where my wild side came from. If I had to guess, I'd probably say my dad. I never heard much about Momma growing up in Jamaica. That's like some big secret, but from what I hear, my dad was a bad boy back in the day. My uncle, Johnny, used to sit around, get drunk and tell me story after story about the two of them. Man, the things white people do when they're intoxicated!

My dad was handsome. He had blonde hair, deep blue eyes, and arm-to-arm tattoos. I only remember him with his standard mustache and buzz cut, but I've seen his scrapbook. He used to wear his hair long, down to his shoulders, and he had a full scruffy beard. Johnny says he was a superfreak too, cool like a brother, and of course, he had a special place in his heart for the sisters. Johnny said there wasn't much on this planet Daddy wasn't willing to take on either. He regaled tales of bar brawls, crazy women, and drugs. Basically, anything that life wanted to throw Daddy's way, he was down for whatever. Obviously, I didn't get the blonde hair and blue eyes, but I think I got a little piece of his spirit.

Up on the Tech campus, there were cuties and hotties poppin' up out of the woodwork. The first time I walked into the student center and saw all that eye candy, the untamed blonde chick inside me took over like Hyde did Doctor Jekyll. Blondie had me totally out of control, but you never caught me complaining. I was finally in my element. I was finally happy.

I'm not sure how I managed to get out and party all the time, especially since Momma all but had a GPS tracker stuck up my ass. I guess I just never really got much sleep. When the lights went out at night in the dorm, so did my roommate and me. There wasn't a party we didn't show up at, and nobody seemed to care I was underage. We had a blast.

With my "mom-jockey" riding hard, I double-timed a criminal justice degree in two and a half years. I would've done it in two, but I took some time out to run track and do some other things for myself. I was so proud I'd graduated, and, for once, I was happy Momma was standing by my side. Despite how I feel about her, I probably would've never made it without her constantly pushing and prodding.

Fresh out of college, I felt like I'd conquered the world, but nobody cared. As far as my mother was concerned, it was just the pre-game show. She was more interested in the next episode—law school.

Mom had her heart set on me attending a prestigious school, Harvard, Columbia, or Yale. I had the grades, and she wanted it more than anything in the world. I'd already taken the LSAT and done well. At that point, all I had to do was get accepted somewhere. I remember Momma spending all day gathering applications, contacting people for letters of recommendation, and cursing up a storm, but I hardly shared her passion. Of course, I knew how important attending law school was to her, and I kinda felt the need to repay her for all the horrible things she'd done to me up to that point, so I did what any good girl would. I joined the Navy the second I turned eighteen.

Mom did not approve, and that's saying it nicely. She was pissed off and just plain hateful about the whole thing. For the first time in my life though, I'd made a real decision on my own. By the time Momma found out what happened, I'd already signed the contract.

I remember walking into her room, proud and bold as ever. I stood at attention right in her face and told her the news, finishing my announcement to the tune of, "There's nothing anyone can do to stop me from serving my country." Momma responded in kind.

That was the worst beating I'd ever gotten. As if a one-sided ass whooping wasn't enough, Momma completely disowned me. I'm sure by now she's written me out of her will too. How's that for a mother's love?

So anyway, I ended up reporting for duty with two black eyes and a busted lip, but I was smiling big. Despite all the drama, I think everything worked out just fine, but as far as Momma's concerned ... well, let's just say I won't be invited to Thanksgiving anytime soon.

To this very day, I still love Momma very much. I also believe I got some of my best qualities from her like persistence, strong will and boatloads of spunk. I miss her a lot, but I don't see us ever talking again. She's as stubborn as I am. The difference is though, with that woman, once you're on her shit list, you're done, forever.

Enough about my stupid family and back to work. You know, I'm not at all opposed to some good old-fashioned hard labor but working for the government can hardly be considered an honest day's work. I've never seen so many ill-tempered sissies in my entire life. *Talk about underachievement. Jeez!* I hate my job with a passion and I'm not too fond of my co-workers either. It's hard to get up every morning and drag myself in to work, but then again, it's better than being broke and hungry.

Before I started with the Bureau, things were rough. Hot out of the service, I was pumped up and ready to start a career in the real world. I just knew I would pick up a high paying job. I was counting on it. Hell, I figured companies would be busting down my door, begging me to grace them with my presence, but it didn't go down like that. In fact, nobody wanted to hire me. It was as if my military experience didn't even count. Hey, no worries, right? I had a backup plan. I thought surely, my degree would count for something. A sharp academic superstar like myself should be able to get a job easy. So, I toned down the Navy stuff on my resume and went for round two. What a waste of time. Most of the hiring managers said I was too academic and didn't have any "real business experience." What exactly does that mean? I know I'm smart, I got the transcripts to prove it, but hearing that, interview after interview, made me feel like a complete dummy.

Employers were not feeling my skills at all. See, the thing is, most people hear the words "Navy Officer" and they instantly get juiced-up, fantasizing about Seals, Admirals, and big nuclear submarines. Here's a reality check people. Forget what you see in those big Hollywood movies like G.I. Jane. Women are never allowed in combat, and I shouldn't even have to mention getting promoted is like pulling teeth from a hungry killer shark.

Even if females could qualify, we're forbidden to try out for Seal team selection. More than that, it's against the law. We are, wait how does the Navy put it...? Oh yes, we're "encouraged" to be a diver or go into bomb disposal. Now, you know black people and explosives don't mix. I would've ended up blowing myself into itty-bitty pieces. And, who in the hell wants to be a diver? Hi there, you should hire me ... oh you didn't know...? Well, I'm a diver! Yeah, like that's a useful office skill. I didn't like my options, so I ended up going into Intelligence, which is a whole nother story.

After I came off deployment in South America, things were a trip back home. The real tragedy was people were only interested in hearing about all the drama, you know, posttraumatic war syndrome from Desert Storm and Afghanistan. They wanted heroes, not sidekicks, and I was definitely a sidekick. Hell, I wasn't even in Desert Storm. It didn't matter I'd been in the field working right alongside a Navy Seal team commander and his unit. Bottom line, I'm no Seal, and despite my best sales pitch, I never blew any skirts up saying, "Hi there, I'm a former Naval Intelligence Officer." Most people don't even know what that means.

So, there I was, back home, restless, jobless, hopeless and about to be homeless. I'd gone from the top shelf to rock bottom in almost no time at all. Still, no matter how bad it got, I'd starve to death before groveling back to Momma. When Dad died, she made out like a bandit with all the life insurance money. I found out later she had a few policies he didn't even know about. I know for a fact she got paid something fierce, but her undeserved new wealth did absolutely nothing for me.

I remember Dad would always tell Momma, "Baby, these streets are dangerous out here. If I take a dirt-nap, you take care of my little man and both my girls too." Amazing how he had to emphasize *both my girls* with her. I thought that would've been one of those common-sense things, but I guess if he didn't specify, she just might find herself a convenient loophole.

Daddy died right before I went off to college, which is when all the real dough came rolling in. Momma claimed she was saving everything for me, but I never saw a dime. Turns out, she didn't need a loophole after all. I've come to the conclusion she'd feed a filthy, stinking, rabid stray before she gave me a crumb.

After I joined the Navy, Momma did everything in her power to alienate me from family on both sides. She told them all types of stories, none that were true of course, but they were convincing enough for everyone to turn their noses up at me. The rumors spread fast how I mistreated her and Daddy and stole from them, how I was a drunk, hooked on drugs, and all kinds of mess she knew wasn't true. After that, I couldn't go to family for help. I was pretty much on my own.

One way or another, I had to get a job, that or rob a bank. I actually had a gun at the time, but I couldn't afford to buy a ski mask, and if I sold the gun, well then how could I shoot people? Besides, armed robbery is a Federal offense, and I'm too skinny to go to jail. Those big bitches in orange jump suits would eat me alive. It took less than a millisecond to decide doing hard time wasn't such a good idea after all, so I buckled down and diligently hunted for a job.

I sent my resume out to potential employers nearly every day. I actually went out on several interviews, each time thinking I'd finally hear the words, *you're hired*. I came close a few times, but no cigar.

Weeks passed, and then months. Eventually my money ran out completely. I was getting more desperate by the day and started thinking maybe Momma was right after all—I should've gone to law school. Funny thing is, I really am a hard worker, and I don't mind dirty jobs, but McDonald's wouldn't even hire me. Guess I was too old to be the girl working the goddamn fry basket. I'm sorry, but that's degrading.

Everything kept spiraling downward, until something unexpected happened. One day, I got a magazine in the mail, I forget which one. The damn thing wasn't even addressed to me, so I'm not sure how I got it, but I figured I'd read it anyway. What else did I have to do, right? Inside the magazine was a story about an FBI agent—a black woman at that. Man, that sister was doing it big. She really blew me away, and suddenly I got very curious about the Bureau. I never thought about going into law enforcement before, but my dad was a sheriff, and I had a few other relatives who were law too. *How hard could it be?*

I toyed with the idea for a few days before I got up the nerve to make a phone call. Finally, I called the local FBI field office, and after a few transfers, spoke with someone in recruiting. Turns out, all I needed was a four-year degree and, of course, be in good physical shape. In fact, the recruiter seemed to think I had the perfect background to be an FBI agent. The job offered paid training, full benefits, 401K, paid vacation, everything. It all sounded good to me. The problem was the pay. The salary was so low I felt somewhat insulted, but I didn't have a lot of other options, so I applied for the job, and the rest is, as they say, history.

I remember the day I arrived in Quantico, Virginia. Training was brutal, nearly six months of grueling, rigorous mental and physical abuse. It was horrible, but I toughed it out and made some good connections in the process. After graduating from the Academy, I was officially sworn in as an FBI Agent, and man was I hyped-up. I'd stand in the mirror for hours flashing my badge and yelling, *SPECIAL AGENT SOUTHERLAND!* I liked the sound of it, and I loved how being an agent made me feel. After college and the military, I finally had a sense of accomplishment and serious aspirations too. I imagined being the H.N.I.C., out in the field, taking down terrorists. I'd be the meanest, baddest, lowdown mofo in all of counterterrorism. If there was a towel-head in the vicinity, I'd be knee-deep in his ass before sunrise.

I had my little bag packed, ready to go, and I was waiting to get the call. Unfortunately, I never got that call. As a matter of fact, I got passed over for that promotion and several others too. The FBI made it clear my future would not involve counterterrorism, ever. Instead, my first assignment was right here in Atlanta, GA. It was one of the greatest challenges of all time—Federal Anti-Piracy. Now, you should know, this is the deadliest of assignments, one that could render me mentally disabled and riddled with paper cuts with a bitching case of carpel tunnel.

Like all agents, I started on a 90-day probation, which I passed with flying-colors. I worked hard, closing case after case like a machine. After a few years of service, I'd learned a lot and amassed one hell of a record. I figured I was a shoo-in for promotion, but it didn't quite work out that way.

I qualified for several other assignments and put in for transfer three more times—THREE TIMES! What did I get? Zip, bupkis, nada, absolutely nothing at all. I soon realized I was stuck in Anti-Piracy, unlike several of my colleagues, who went on to extremely rewarding posts. It felt like there was a twisted little demon hovering over me, pulling my strings and laughing a hearty evil laugh as I suffered all the way to my death. Honestly, I don't think that's far from the truth. I couldn't imagine a single reason why I didn't get promoted, but I tried to keep calm about the situation.

Maybe there was some social or political reason for the rejections like keeping women off the battlefield. Personally, I like to think all the big boys in the Bureau were just intimidated, you know scared a little girl like me would show them up? Who knows the real story? I gave up thinking about it.

I played my last card a few months back when I requested a transfer to Counterintelligence. I'm still waiting to get word. I figure with my background, I'll get it, but as always, I have my doubts. Whenever I used to say things like that, Daddy would claim I was being negative, but I call it being cautiously optimistic. Daddy used to say, "Pork Chop, when the odds are stacked up against you, be patient, stay positive, and keep an open mind." Well Daddy, I'm trying to be positive, but my patience is evaporating. My boss, the infamous Tony Crane, always says, "Alex, it's just a stepping-stone", but hell that's easy for him to say when he's the fuckin' poster boy for the FBI. Unlike me, every one of his stepping-stones forms a neat, easy path all the way to the top. I keep getting screwed over, over and over again. Something's gotta change. I'm so over it. Every single day is just like the one before, boring as hell.

My job is just the worst. The term *Anti-Piracy* itself sounds complicated as if it's exciting work, but it's not. Allow me to give you the D. A. Southerland crash course on it...

Say an artist or developer makes something like a video, movie, music CD, or software, whatever. They copyright their work and proceed to sell it for what exact reason, I don't know, but I doubt it's because they need the money. Most are already rich. No, I suspect it's because they aspire to share all their creative bullshit with the rest of us common folks. Anyway, the new media hits the market and the artist starts clocking big dollars, so it's all good, right? Wrong! Out of nowhere, some smartass kid in Idaho, who by the way has nothing better to do, cracks it, rips it, and posts the whole thing on the web. Then, voila! All his friends get a free copy.

So, basically, this kid, a.k.a. the "Pirate," just broke U.S. Copyright law, statutes on trademark counterfeiting and the anti-bootlegging statute. It doesn't matter if he made a single penny off what he did or not, it's still highly illegal. Next thing you know, the stolen goods spread like wildfire on the net, and the greedy owner of the associated label or production company, who wipes his ass with a million dollars, loses potential money on every illegal download. Of course, the Bureau assures me these pirates threaten the very fabric of this great Nation, so I must do my duty and spring into action. I launch an investigation, write everything up, get a judge to issue a warrant, and then a couple of hardcore Robocop type field agents bust down the kid's door and lock him up. To top it all off, they sentence him to five years in prison or a $250,000 fine, which if he had all that money in the first place, he probably wouldn't have engaged in his felonious caper.

Okay, so maybe it doesn't go down exactly like that, but you get the point. And, the point is, my job is boring, it's going nowhere, and I hate it with a passion! Don't get me wrong, I'm good. I've helped crack several high-profile cases. I guess in a way I was doing something worthwhile, but I promised myself, if I ever got the chance to get out on the streets, you know really fight crime, I'd die before I took another desk job. At least that's how I felt back then, when I was young. Technically, I'm still young, but that's not the point. The point is, back then I wasn't exactly the sharpest knife in the drawer. Since then, I think I've grown a little and learned a lot. Now, I'm a bit wiser. I no longer have a morbid desire to chase the action, glamour and fame. It took me a while to figure it out, but I finally realized all great people achieve most by being humble. Unfortunately, I learned this the hard way.

Turns out, a big part of being humble involves controlling your raging desires. See, it's not love, hate, or any other emotion that destroys you—it's ambition, pure unadulterated ambition. It infects you like a virus, killing you off just a little at a time. Before you know it, you spend the day trying to be more than you really are. You start to change from deep down inside. The change is always gradual. You barely even notice it at first, and when you do, you try to cover it up. Everybody denies it, but when you give in to ambition, you change, for better or worse, whether you want to or not.

Some say the choices you make change you faster than anything else in the world. With every lie, every fake smile, and every time you show something opposite of what's genuinely in your heart, you change. It's only near the end, after something tragic happens, when you realize just how different you've become. For me, this is no new revelation. Daddy always warned me to be true to myself. He constantly talked about the pain you experience if you don't. With all his years as a sheriff, all the things he saw, he was definitely qualified to speak on the subject. He told me that, as long as I live, all I should ever aspire to be is just me, plain old Alex, nothing more and nothing less. I wish I'd listened to him.

Chapter 2

You ever tell a lie? Yeah, right, me neither. Seriously, I think lies are truly incredible. It's like they have a life force of their own. I believe nothing in this world happens without them. All major change starts with a lie. Just think about it for a minute. Thing is, it doesn't even have to be a big deal. In fact, usually it's just a little white lie. *Sure, I can handle that. No, it doesn't look that bad. I'll do anything for you. I just had to have it.* See, it's those first little harmless, significant white lies that get people every time.

My significant lie was one of those itsy bitsy, teeny weenie ones that ended up costing a lot more than it was worth. I don't think it was intentional, it just sort of happened. I'm not sure how or why, but it did. Maybe I wanted it to. It's hard to know for sure why I started lying to myself, but even today, I wonder how differently things might've turned out if I hadn't. Would I still have headed down the same road? Truth is, I'll never really know, but what I do know is from that moment on, soon as I told that little stupid lie, my life mutated into something I'd never seen before.

So, what was my lie? That's simple. I told myself I was ready for more, and when I say more, I mean more of everything. Despite my inexperience, immaturity and complete disregard for both authority and proper procedure, I decided I was ready for more money, more excitement and more exposure. I'm talking the whole thing here, baby. The second that thought popped into my head, the danger switch flipped to the *on* position. Suddenly, I was on a collision course with a Mack truck of violence and deceit. People always talk about getting rid of their 800-pound gorilla in the corner, but it would seem mine is here to stay. He's more punctual than I'll ever be too. He shows up everywhere I go, breathing down the back of my neck, ready to pounce at a moment's notice. Every time I get myself into a jam, I think back to the day I invited that big hairy fucker into my life. I remember it like it just happened this morning.

It was noon on a Friday, and I was in the office. The case I was working was fairly complicated, but as usual, I already had a plan to get the job done. So, there I was, sitting at my desk, flipping through all the evidence and sorting out the details on the best way to bait and hook the crook. By then, I'd finished all the preliminary work and was looking for that small piece of crucial evidence that makes a case—a note, an email, account transfer, anything that incriminates the bad guy beyond a shadow of a doubt. I call this my *gotcha bitch scenario* because whenever I get my hands on that kind of evidence, I always yell, "Gotcha bitch!" What can I say? It makes me feel empowered.

I started the morning thinking clear, my objective in sight, but the more time passed, the worse things got. After 30 minutes of staring at the same screen, I thought maybe I was losing my touch, but no, my game wasn't slipping, I was changing, fast. I didn't realize it, but that moment marked the beginning of a series of major changes, twists and turns in my life. By the time I finally understood how bad my situation had become, it was too late.

That day, things were just beginning to go south, but the situation escalated rapidly, and I had only myself to blame. See, once you let that first lie slip, it's like a snowball effect. It starts small, but before you know it, everything's rolled up into this big, uncontrollable ball of crap. You can save yourself a ton of heartache by just stopping at that first lie, but no one ever does. They keep right on lying, and that harmless little spark of a fib ignites a flame that spreads like wildfire. Sad part about it is I understood the consequences if I didn't stop lying, but I kept right on feeding the fire. More like I threw a bucket of gasoline on it and blew hard, but who's keeping score anyway?

Once I started down my ridiculously arrogant path, it was nearly impossible to concentrate on anything, especially work. I tried hard to focus, but my mind was elsewhere. No, I tell it like it is, I was full of ambition. I knew the truth, and I should've just shut up and got back to work. At the end of the day, I was a hard worker, not James Bond, but I was feeling almost embarrassed about my job. Out of the blue, I was fed up with being stuck behind a desk. I figured before long I'd be kicking a pair of those thick-rimmed glasses and a matching pocket protector. I felt like I was going insane. Something had to change.

Despite my half-assed attempts to get back on the clock, I couldn't focus. After a while, my computer screen was just an endless sea of nothingness. I knew what had to be done, but I was going through some kind of moral, spiritual warfare. Ever heard of a place in the Bible called Lodebar? Okay, you know, I'm not the complete heathen everybody makes me out to be. I do go to church sometimes, thank you very much! Anyway, Lodebar's a place. The name itself means *no bread, no pasture, no hope.* I know it sounds a little dramacidal, but that's how I felt. I was totally in Lodebar. My outlook on life had changed, and my case suffered the consequences. I was getting nowhere fast. I knew beating myself up about it wasn't going to help, so I took a break to try and regroup.

I stood up and stretched. Then, I grabbed my coffee mug and headed towards the break room. I only got a few steps away from my desk when my phone rang. I was going to ignore it at first and just let it go to voicemail, but I was still waiting to hear about my transfer. So, I swiftly backtracked and checked the caller ID. It was an intraoffice call, which meant still no word on the transfer, but hey, I was there, so I figured I might as well answer. I set my mug back down on the desk and picked up the phone.

"This is Southerland."

"Southerland," came a voice over the phone. "Agent Crane would like to see you in his office."

"I'll be right in." I hung up the phone and whipped my head around. I stood there for a moment, looking across the floor over all my fellow agents, who at the time, were sitting at their government issued metal desks, trying their damnedest to look busy. I knew they weren't doing shit. They never are.

Crane was in the big glass office all the way in the back corner, pacing around waving his hands. It looked like he was on the phone. There was no telling what I'd done, but I'm not like those other sniveling jackasses. If you're going to fire me, I'm going out with my head held high. That said, I prepared myself. After a nice deep breath, I put my jacket on, kicked up the attitude, and strutted back towards Crane's office. The door was open, but he was actually on the phone, so I waited outside for him to finish up.

Crane's assistant, Lisa, ended her call and cut her eyes at me. I instinctively returned the favor. She and I never had any kind of altercation, but for whatever reason, she didn't like me, and let's just say I wasn't too concerned for her wellbeing either. She flung her long blond hair back and, with a flick of her wrist, waved me into Crane's office. She gave me a few more looks as if to suggest I was an idiot for waiting outside. Of course, I took offense, but I dismissed her and went on in.

My gut told me I was in for another disciplinary meeting, so I shut the door to keep all the nosey bastards I call coworkers out of my business. I turned around and waved to get Crane's attention. He casually smiled.

I watched the boss man carefully as he continued his call. I study him every chance I get. I'm not sure why. He's just fascinating to me. Mr. Assistant Special Agent in Charge, Anthony Crane, a farm-town boy from Wisconsin, but don't get it twisted, he's no slouch. He finished top of his class in the Academy. Crane stands about 6' 2" and has dark brown hair, which he wears in kind of a Clark Kent style. He's got very distinct facial features too, a long straight nose, sleepy eyes, thick eyebrows, and a chiseled chin. Yeah, he's kinda hot for a white boy. He keeps his face clean as a whistle, and he has this smile that says, *don't worry, just trust me.*

If Crane wasn't a Bureau man, you might mistake him for one of those models in the black and white underwear ads. He's quite the clotheshorse too. He always shows up at work fly from head-to-toe. Even when he comes in on his off days, he's still sharp. I think I like him most because he's one of the few genuine nice guys still on the planet. He has a great personality and is overly friendly, but you never want to get on his bad side because at the drop of a hat, he'll switch up out of that nice guy routine and turn a bad guy into mincemeat. Mr. Crane is quite stealthy and wily, which probably explains how he fits in so well with the good-ole-boy network.

I stood in the middle of his office, waiting impatiently for him to finish his call. I just wanted to get it over and done with. Go ahead, suspend me, fire me, just get it done and let me go home. Hell, he could've called me that morning, so I didn't have to waste my fuel coming into the office. Bosses think they're so clever. They'll make you work all day and then fire you right at 5 p.m. They need they ass whooped.

Crane didn't have his speakerphone on. He was wearing a remote headset, but I couldn't help overhearing the call anyway. I made out several voices, but none I recognized. They were discussing some big screw-up. I prayed it wasn't mine, but reality kicked in. It didn't take a rocket scientist to figure it all out. They were pissed, and I just got called into the office. Since I started with the Bureau, the only time I ever get called into the office is when the powers-to-be have a bug up their ass and a hard-on for me. I'm amazed I still have a job. And, don't get me started on the Office of Professional Responsibility. OPR is the worst.

Crane pointed to one of the guest chairs neatly positioned in front of his desk, so I walked over and sat down.

"Gentlemen, I have to go offline," said Crane. "Wrap up and send me your report."

He hung up his headset and sat down in his black leather executive high-back chair. He put his hands together in front of his face and sighed. I figured he was trying to cover up a disgusted look. Like I say, there's no telling what I'd done or not done for that matter.

"You wanted to see me, Sir?" I asked, softly.

"Yes, Alex," he replied, "about your transfer...."

"Sir?"

"Counterintelligence passed. I'm sorry."

I'm sure he could see the surprise on my face, but it wasn't because I got rejected again. I was just glad I wasn't in trouble. I gave him the best smile I could, based on the situation and replied, "All the same, Sir, I enjoy working here, and I'm still learning a lot."

"I doubt that," Crane said, rubbing his head with both hands. "Let me ask you something Alex...."

"Sir?"

"You believe in teamwork, you know getting along with your peers, right?"

"Absolutely, Sir."

"And, the chain of command?"

"I try to do what I'm asked, Sir."

"Then, why after a year of me repeatedly asking you to call me Tony do you continue to address me as Sir?"

I grinned a little. I wasn't sure if he was serious or not. "Respect I guess, Sir," I answered.

"I see," he responded. He rubbed his head again and sat up straight in his chair. "Go back to your desk and grab your gear, you've been reassigned."

"What?"

He raised an eyebrow.

"But, Sir...." I cleared my throat and continued saying, "I mean, Tony, I don't understand."

"Alex, you're a good agent." Tony put his hands up for a second, and then said, "I have to say a little unorthodox, but a good agent nevertheless. I know guys with half your abilities who transferred out a long time ago. I can't beat the politics here, but I can give you a fighting chance in another area. I've made arrangements for you to go to David Chandler's unit."

I nearly jumped out of my seat. "You mean Zombie Squad?"

"That a problem?" Tony asked.

"Honestly, I don't do the dead people slash serial killer thing," I said, frowning and shaking my head. "Those bodies stink like shit—pardon my French. Thanks, but no thanks. I'll stay right here for-"

"Fortunately for you, you don't have a choice," Tony explained. "I gave out more favors than I had in order to make this happen. David's expecting you. In fact, he personally requested you be assigned to his team once he heard you were available. If memory serves me, he said your skills and experience will add value to an ongoing investigation."

I crossed my arms and sat back in my chair. I wanted to flip him off or at least roll my eyes, but that wouldn't have been smart, all things considered. True, I wanted to hit the streets, but not like that. I said I wanted to kick terrorist asses not smell their dead carcasses. Tony sensed I wasn't feeling it, so he didn't hesitate to go for the hard sell.

"Listen, I know it's not C.T., but it's a start. Besides, technically, you'll just be on loan. Look, spend some time over there and show David what a good agent you can be. Get some field experience under your belt, and I promise I'll personally push for a proper promotion ASAP ... you have my word."

"We're talking about the guy, who works serials, right?" I asked.

"Yeah, David Chandler. Hands down, he's the best. Man's solved a lot of tough cases, and he's well respected throughout the Bureau. It'll do you some good to hang around him and pick up whatever you can."

"But, Tony, I don't know anything about catching serial killers."

"Chandler thinks you're a good match. So do I."

"Fine, but I'm not field authorized, so I can't-"

"You are now!" Tony held my file in the air. "Look, stop making excuses Alex. It's not as bad as you think. Now, run over, grab your things and report to Chandler. Trust me, you'll be fine."

"I've heard a lot of stories Tony. Seriously, what's the deal with this guy?" I ask.

"He's a good man. And ... well, he likes you. He feels strong about your work ethic and case history. I will warn you though, he's pretty particular about his name, so don't screw around, just stick to the basics."

"And, what about the case I'm working right now? I have to-"

"I'll have Bruce pick up your case load, just leave him your notes and...." Tony halted at the sound of his phone ringing. He leaned over and checked the caller ID. "I've got to take this, Alex. Lisa has your paperwork." He picked up the phone. "You straight?"

I gave him a fake smile and a double thumbs-up.

"Good luck!" Tony said. Then, he turned his attention to his caller. "Jim, what's up buddy?"

I walked out and stopped by Lisa's desk.

"Agent Southerland," said Lisa.

"Lisa...?" By then, there was a whole lot of eye-cutting going on.

"I have some paperwork for you," she snapped.

She grabbed a folder from her drawer and dropped it on the edge of her desk. Then, she looked up and smiled. It was one of those "glad you're never coming back bitch" type smiles.

"Thank you, Lisa," I said, a proud frown on my face. I took the papers back to my desk, sat down and shot Bruce a quick email with a summary of the work I'd done so far. After that, I was ready to go. I didn't have much to do in terms of packing. I never clutter my desk with a bunch of personal items just in case they feel the need to fire me unexpectedly. No sense fumbling around trying to put a bunch of pictures in a box while everyone pretends not to notice you've just been given the axe. When you see two federal police officers escorting someone off the premises, I think it's safe to say they're not going on holiday. I'd just as soon avoid all that drama. Only thing I keep in my desk is my purse. I grabbed it from the drawer and took a moment to look around at my peers.

"So long assholes," I mumbled. And, that's exactly how I felt about them. They were all a bunch of assholes. None of us were close, and the only time we talked was when we were collaborating on a case. For the most part, everybody kept to themselves. I didn't mind it one bit either, no love lost for me. Most of those turkeys gave me nothing but attitude from the very beginning, so I wasn't compelled to give a heartfelt goodbye to anyone. They weren't going to miss me, and I sure as hell wasn't going to miss them.

I left the area and walked down the hall, speculating on the real reason Tony loaned me out to Z-Squad. After being rejected several times by other teams, the whole thing just didn't sit right with me. I'm a sailor, paranoid and suspicious at all times. If I could sleep with both eyes open, you bet your ass I would. My gut told me it was all some kind of new form of trickery. A way for OPR to finally sink their filthy claws in me. At the same time, if Tony says he stuck his neck out, then that's exactly what happened. He was among the few who ever lifted a finger to help me around that place. Everybody else tried to chop me down one way or another, but not Tony. He was a good man, and I trusted him—no, I owed him, big time.

I had my reservations, but at the same time, I was a little excited. Whether Z-Squad was the right move or not, being out in the field was just what the doctor ordered. Guess I should've just let my paranoia go and appreciate the situation, but I had a feeling I'd regret it all later.

I walked to the other side of the office looking for Chandler's area. I had an idea where it was, but that place was like a labyrinth. I searched and searched but came up with nothing. I kept wandering around, thinking maybe there wasn't a Z-Squad after all. Maybe Tony was just pulling my leg, and when I show back up to my team, they'll all be standing around, pointing and laughing, playing a cruel, unusual practical joke on poor ole Alex.

It should be hard to lose your way in a single office suite, but I definitely had wandered off the beaten path. As much as I give my boyfriend a hard time about driving around lost and not asking for directions, I figured I'd take my own advice and solicit some assistance.

I reached up to knock on the door of a nearby office when I bumped into an old friend, Joe. I hadn't seen him in a while. We met when I was in the Academy. Back then, he'd been with the Bureau since—well I don't know how long he'd been there, but from what I hear, it was a long time. Joe was a cool dude, black guy, average height with a thick mustache and a great big toothy grin. His hair was about an inch long, but he kept it perfectly trimmed. He was kinda heavyset, but you could tell he played ball or something back in the day. Joe had the gift of gab too, he could talk to anyone, and man was he a flirt. His wife had her hands full keeping up with that guy.

Joe really got around. He knew just about everyone in the office, and when I say everyone, I mean everyone. As soon as he saw me coming up the hall, he broke out laughing. I ran up to him and gave him a big ol' teddy bear hug.

"Long time no see, Alex," he said, still chuckling.

"What's up Joe? I see you still down here doing yo' thang."

"Wouldn't trade it for all the oil in the Kingdom," he replied.

"The Kingdom?" I giggled. "You're outta control, Joe."

He smiled really big. "One does what one can."

"Listen, I'm looking for-"

"Z-Squad, right?" he said.

I squinted at him and cocked my head to the side. "Damn Joe, how the hell you know that?"

He pointed to his ear. "I keep my ear to the ground ... you know, actually you're not that far off the mark. See this hallway right here?"

I turned around to see where he was pointing.

"You just go all the way down there," he said, "hang a right at the end, go straight through the double doors, and you're all good."

"Oh, okay ... thanks Joe, you're the man."

"No problem," he replied. "So, what's the deal Alex? I hear they're transferring you. Finally got promoted, huh?"

I rolled my eyes. "You know something I don't? Come on Joe, in this place? Nah, I told my boss a while ago I'd help other teams just to get more experience under my belt. For whatever reason, I guess he thought it was a good idea to stick me with Chandler's group."

"Awe, hotshot like you should be able to handle it, right?"

"You think so?"

"Hell yeah." Joe said, grinning and slapping my shoulder. He actually did seem to know something I didn't.

I batted my eyelashes. "Thanks Joe ... I think."

"Hey, what are friends for." He laughed, loudly.

"Exactly." Seeing Joe just made me smile. "Well hey look man, it's good seeing you. I guess let me get down here before I'm back in trouble again."

"You take it easy Alex ... stay outta trouble!" He laughed again.

"Okay smartass, make sure you say hi to the wife for me."

"Will do," he said, "Don't forget you owe us a dinner. Bring your skinny ass over and let's break some bread and get some chicken in you."

"Absolutely ... wait no, who's cooking? You right?"

"Alex, you better not let her hear you say that! Don't be wrecking my happy home."

I laughed. "Just kidding. Name the time Joe, and I'll be there."

"Better!" He smiled again, waved and walked off.

I followed Joe's directions but ended up on the far side of the moon. I was beginning to wonder if they had stuck Chandler back in the storage area. The hallway was dusty, and it smelled odd like the inside of a tire factory, whatever that smells like. I finally rolled up on the double doors, which turned out to be a lot nicer than the hallway—clean even. I paused for a second, collected my thoughts and then walked in. The hallway on the way in was busted, so I was expecting the office inside to be a pigsty, but surprisingly, the place was not bad, not bad at all.

The office inside looked completely normal, everything you'd expect to find on a typical FBI floor. There were a few rooms in the back, but for the most part, it was just one big open space with rows of desks lined up perfectly. Each desk was equipped with a phone, lamp and computer with a big ass monitor, which of course had the FBI logo floating around on it. I think they're under the impression we might forget who signs our paycheck if they don't keep burning that image into our minds. Folders, coffee mugs, t-shirts, pens and more. They stick that logo on the side of everything that doesn't move, and I mean everything.

Government computers are a trip and our IT group's like a bunch of techno-Nazis. I remember the time I tried to change my screen resolution. Boy did I get in trouble. You would've thought I'd committed a capital crime. I had to spend the next hour or so listening to some geek jerk-off talk about how important maintaining the COE image is and how I threatened the integrity of the network, blah-blah-blah. Really? Who gives a shit?

I walked around to get the lay of the land. Nobody was in. The place was like a ghost town. They must've all been in the field, everybody but Chandler. His office door was wide open, and he was sitting at his desk. I walked back and stuck my head in the doorway, but he didn't even have the decency to acknowledge me. Now, it wasn't like I was sneaking around or anything. I'm not exactly light-footed, so I know he had to hear me walk up. Then again, maybe he didn't hear me after all. I was trippin'. I took a second and cooled my temper, and then I knocked on the door to get his attention.

"Excuse me, Agent Chandler, I'm-"

"It's either David or Sir," he interrupted without looking up.

I walked on into the office.

"Sir, I-"

"Bad choice," he snapped. He kept writing with his head down. "Sit down! I'll get to you in a moment."

He mumbled something under his breath. I couldn't make out what he said, but it sounded like he called me a dumb split-tail, the typical sexist bullshit I've come to expect from the average Bureau boy. I just had to smile because I had no idea what was going on. It would've been nice if Tony had been more specific when he said Chandler was particular about his name. Greetings aside, I was somewhat confused. All I could think about was Tony telling me that Chandler requested me for his team, so what's with the old man's attitude? I wanted to ask, but I dared not utter a word. I just slowly walked over and took a seat. And, take a seat I did. I sat for the longest, staring across his desk, watching and waiting for him to say something, but he never did. He just kept mumbling under his breath. Maybe he was humming to himself. Hell, I don't know. I doubt he knew. I just assumed he was a penny short of a nickel. After a few minutes, he finally put his pen down. Then, he sat straight up in his chair, took off his glasses and stared at me. I wasn't sure how to approach this man, but when in doubt, direct is always the way to go. I leaned over to give him my paperwork, offer a handshake, and introduce myself.

"David, I'm Agent-"

"Quiet!" He snatched the folder and slammed it down on the desk.

I still had my hand out, but he refused to shake it. I thought my head was going to pop off from all the pressure building up. All I could do was sit back down, bite my tongue, and try to remain calm. After a few more moments of uncomfortable silence, Chandler finally addressed me.

"Denise Alexandria Southerland ... Anti-Piracy drama queen ... highly recommended by soon-to-be big shot SAC Anthony Crane..."

"I was under the impression you requested-"

"Let me tell you something," he interrupted. "All that don't mean jack-shit around here. I don't know how you pulled this off, or why Crane thinks you'll make the cut, but you better learn how things work around here and get on board fast, or you'll be out on your ass...."

He kept rambling on and on about what I'd better do and how I needed to fit in. I couldn't get a word in edgewise. Just when I thought it had gotten as bad as it could get, it got worse.

"I didn't realize you were black," David said. "All those pasty photos in your file, you looked a little like tornado-bait to me, you know?" He laughed, slapping his knee hard. "Well, black or not, no such thing as affirmative action on my watch. You wanna be on my squad, you gotta put some points on the board, and you're not off to a good start...." He checked his watch. "You're only about two hours late."

"But-"

"Look, far as I'm concerned, you've gone from terrible to worse in less time than it takes me to watch a bad movie on HBO."

"Sir, I-"

"Look, get your shit and go home, I'll call you."

"What? Wait, no-"

"Southerland!" he yelled.

"Sir?"

"You have a government issued cell phone?" asked Chandler.

"Yes, but I-"

"Go home!" he snapped. "When your phone rings, I'll be on the other end telling you what to do and how to do it. I think fast, I work fast, so you better find a way to deal with it or I'll deal with you, and you won't like it one bit. Not gonna be any handholding for you 'round here. By the way kid, next time you walk on my floor, make sure you cover up. I got enough to worry about without being distracted by your cleavage. Captivating it may be, there's no place for that around here. This may be a foreign concept to you coming from Crane's group, but sometimes we catch the bad guy, and when we do, we like to look the part. Got it?"

"Excuse me, but I-"

"Look kid, I like you," he interrupted, "so I'll help you just this once … don't make the same mistake your predecessors did. Pick your chin up off the floor and get the hell out of my office!"

He turned his attention back to his work.

Somehow, furious just doesn't say it. I was mad as fuckin' hell. I couldn't decide whether to leave or jump up on his desk and mule kick his ass in the forehead.

Chandler looked back up at me as if to ask, "Why are you still here?", but he didn't say anything. After about a minute of staring each other down, I backed off and headed for the door.

"By the way, kid…."

I glanced back over my shoulder.

"Welcome to the team."

I stormed out and slammed the door as hard as I could swing it. I was so pissed. I marched right back down to Mr. soon-to-be SAC's office. I was going to give Tony whatever little piece of my mind I had left, but then I tried to slow my roll a little. I took a few deep breaths and thought about just going outside to blow off some steam. Unfortunately for Tony, that idea didn't last very long. It would've been pointless anyway. I stopped smoking years ago, and besides I couldn't let that son-of-a-bitch get off the hook that easy.

I ran back down to my area in a rage like never seen before. It's funny, you can always tell when white people think you're about to go off because they act like you got explosives strapped to your chest. In my case, I'm light and bright, so my face turns beet red, a sure sign of a mushroom cloud waiting to happen.

Tony was in his office, right in the middle of a meeting, but I didn't care. Whatever they were talking about wasn't nearly as important as what I had to say, at least that's how I felt. No way in hell I'd wait an hour for them to finish jacking' each other off. I was going in full speed. I blew right past Crane's little arrogant assistant.

"You can't go in there!" yelled Lisa. She leaped across her desk to stop me, but I didn't even look in her direction.

I busted through Tony's door and stood right in the middle of his office, legs spread wide with my hands on my hips. Everybody in the meeting stopped and turned around.

"Wow Alex, that was quick." Tony said smiling.

I gave him my cold-hearted, "kiss of death" stare.

Lisa ran in behind me. "Sir, I tried to stop her!"

"Guys, can you give us a few minutes?" Tony asked casually.

Lisa sighed and reluctantly directed everyone outside. As soon as she shut the door, I unloaded on Tony.

"Is this some kind of a joke?"

He looked confused. "What's up Alex?"

"I don't like being made a fool. Is that what's going down?"

"Not at all." He chuckled, still seemingly confused. "Listen, calm down and tell me what happened."

He got up and walked over.

"Chandler sent me home! Said my tits distracted him, and I was two hours late, but I just found out about this shit and-"

"Alex," he interrupted, "calm down, it's okay. David can be a little rough around the edges, but-"

"Rough? That's a helluva understatement!"

"Okay, so he's got a unique management style," said Tony, "but I'm telling you he likes you. I wouldn't lie to you."

"This is bullshit Tony ... is this supposed to make me quit?"

"No, it's just the opposite," he replied. "Look, it's the only way you're getting out of here. You wanna spend the rest of your life down here or back up in Quantico?"

I gazed up at the ceiling for a second and dropped my hands down by my sides. Then, I took another deep breath and shook my head. "No, but I'm not sure I can deal with all that-"

"Look, he told you to go home, so take a break," said Tony. "Go home. Trust me, everything will work out."

I rolled my eyes. "Whatever." Then, I turned around and headed towards the door.

Tony took off right behind me. "Wait Alex, I'm going to D.C."

I turned back, crossing my arms and shifting my weight to one side. "Really...?"

"Yeah, imagine that." He laughed.

"Special Agent in Charge, huh?"

"How'd you know?" he asked.

"Chandler and his big mouth," I replied.

Tony frowned.

"I'm sorry, but that guy's a fuckin' asshole! I'm just saying Tony, you move on to a big shining career, and I get slapped around down here? I've done my time."

"Alex, you're not the only one who's had trouble moving up in this office. Sometimes, when you want to get ahead, the universe conspires against you, and you end up taking a fall, but as long as you fall forward, when you get back on your feet you'll be pointed in the right direction."

"What...? Tony, that's the dumbest thing I ever heard!"

He grinned really big. "Look, all I'm saying is ... let me put it this way I've already taken my nosedive, so now it's your turn. It may look bad on the way down, but you're going to get through the other side in good shape. Trust me."

"Have I ever told you how much I hate it when you say, "Trust me"?"

"No, but I'm pretty sure I can see it on your face."

I smiled and cocked my head to the side a bit. "So, you'll be working out of Headquarters?"

"Just for a while until a vacancy opens up. I think I can finally make something materialize up there. It'll be good for everybody, you included."

I frowned. "Well, I hope so. I guess congratulations are in order," I said, humbly. I was proud of Tony, but I still had to give him some attitude for throwing me to the wolves yet again.

"Thanks," he said. "Listen, don't worry about anything, you're a good agent. Once I get settled up north, I'll touch base and we can talk about a few things."

My left eyebrow shot up instantly. "Talk about what?"

He tossed his hands up. "Have a little patience, will you. We have some other things to talk about—personal stuff— but it's not life threatening, so it can wait. In the interim, do the best you can to get along with David, okay?"

"Okay, Tony."

"Promise?"

"I promise. Seriously, thanks for your help ... I mean it's not that I don't appreciate what you do for me ... that Chandler guy just rubbed me the wrong way."

"He actually said he had a problem with your tits?" Tony laughed loudly.

"Yeah, not in so many words, but yeah." I chuckled a little too and shook my head.

Tony gave me that famous smile of his and touched my shoulder. "Just do what you can, alright?"

"Copy that, Sir!"

"Oh, and remember, if you need anything, anything at all, you call me first, got it?"

"I got it. You take care of yourself up there, boss." I leaned in and gave him a hug.

"Get out of here, Alex. Go get some R&R, you deserve it."

I walked out of his office feeling a heck of a lot better. Tony always did a good job of calming me down and refocusing my energy, Lord knows I need it from time-to-time. As I canvass my shining career with the Bureau, I think he's about the only thing standing between me and the unemployment line.

After our little chat, I felt so good, I didn't even respond to Lisa, who was busy playing to the crowd with her typical bullshit.

"Looks like we can go back in everyone," said Lisa. "Sorry for the inconvenience." She rolled her eyes at me.

I just smiled and said, "Pardon the intrusion."

It was a half-assed apology, but at least it was somewhat polite. Mother would be proud.

I left the office and took the elevator down to the parking garage.

"See you next week, Alex," said one of the guards, waving goodbye.

"Later, John."

I walked out to my car, a 1989 Ford Mustang 5.0 LX hatchback, black with grey interior. She was my pride and joy, sexy, sleek and fast as hell. I put a lot of work into that little pony, so she was special to me. And, between you, me, and the walls, I felt like a superhero behind the wheel. All I needed was a cape and maybe a golden lasso or a big glowing hammer.

I love cars. My dad taught me how to work on them, and I'm never afraid to get dirty either. I can change the oil, check my tire pressure and even do a tune-up, spark plugs and all. My boyfriend Bill hates it. He's around cars all day long on his job. He works for the GM plant up in Doraville. Bill thinks being a grease monkey is degrading, but I absolutely love it. I remember he used to always complain about my Stang. "Why don't you put that piece of junk in the shop?" he'd whine. "You spend more time on it than it's worth!" I think he was just jealous because I wasn't paying him that much attention.

Bill gets huge discounts on GM cars, so of course when I got back from the service, he tried to get me to buy something new. I was already broke, so I couldn't afford a car note, and I don't believe in no man taking care of me. I didn't want a handout. I wanted to stand on my own two feet. Besides, if he gave me a car, I knew I'd never hear the end of it, so I fought his ass tooth and nail.

One time, Bill caught me by surprise though. He brought a new car over to my shitty little apartment without telling me. He just showed up with it one day. By the way, I complain about where we stay now, but it's a French chateau compared to what I called home back then. That place was a dump. When it rained, little squirmy, squiggly bugs came in under the front and back doors. It was a nightmare. Basically, the car Bill brought over was nicer than the inside of my apartment. I would've been better off living in the car, but I couldn't accept it. To me, it was the principle of the whole thing.

I called Bill and told him I hadn't driven the car and asked him to come pick it back up. He said he'd pay the note if I took care of the insurance, but without thinking, I blurted out, "Nigga I'd rather take the bus!" I didn't mean to say it the way I did, it just kind of happened. Boy was Bill pissed. Looking back, I know I handled the entire situation like a juvenile, but what's new, right?

I got on Bill's nerves so bad about that car he almost broke up with me. He was just trying to take care of his girl, you know make sure I got around safely, but keeping that car was like signing my life away, and I wasn't having that. Hell, we weren't even living together at the time, so having him pay my bills—even one—just made me feel like a gold-digger.

I gave the new car back to Bill and kept looking for a used one on my own. After months of searching, I finally found my Stang. An old lady in Jasper, Georgia, one of my Uncle Johnny's acquaintances, sold it to me. It was her husband's, but he'd passed away. The car had been up there, parked in the backyard in a patch of weeds for years. The second I looked at it, I knew it was mine—well, maybe not immediately. Honestly, at first it looked like a junkyard heap, but the lady told me they'd bought it brand new, so I gave it a closer look. I think what got me was she still had the owner's manual and window sticker. That got me past the condition of the exterior. Looking at the body, you'd think it had survived a flood, but the inside was clean, and the mileage was low. According to the woman, the car had never been wrecked. Obviously, people say anything to make a sale. It's always hard to believe what they tell you, but she seemed genuine.

The way it was backed up in the yard, I thought it might've been rusted out, so I took my time and checked it over from bumper-to-bumper. I looked underneath the body and inside the hood too. Then, I checked all the lines where the doors and the trunk meet the body. I know that lady probably thought I was crazy, but if a car's been wrecked, you can usually tell. Something will be slightly misaligned. Once they get smacked around, it's hard to put them back together the same.

After a long, drawn-out nose-to-paint inspection, far as I could see, the old lady was telling the truth—that or she had the best repairman in the world. Aside from a few scratches and a small dent, the car was damn near perfect—no rust or nothing. It was really just dirty. Once I put a little soap and water and some wax on it, it was all good. I was lucky to find that car. I've had her ever since.

I remember the day I towed it home. I was so excited, but that evening, Bill came over after work. He all but fell on the ground laughing at me. He told me I should've spent my four-thousand dollars on bus fare for the next five years. I didn't care what he thought about it though. I had a plan and a friend named Patrick, who owned a repair shop a few miles up the road. Unbeknownst to Bill's smartass, Patrick always wanted to sleep with me, so he was more than happy to help with my ride. All I had to do was show up in some little booty shorts and a tight t-shirt and he did anything I asked. If I were a better woman, I may have felt bad about it, but you know how it goes. Together we completely restored my car. After buying a few parts and putting some serious elbow grease in, that little stallion was running strong.

With a reconditioned motor and everything back to factory specs on the inside, it was time to get her pretty on the outside. I had it repainted all over. Even the inside of the doors, trunk, and hood got a fresh coat. Then, I put some nice big racing wheels with razor thin tires on it, and I was good to go. It pains me to think that car had just been sitting up there in Jasper all that time, rotting away. Granny looked like she almost forgot it was back there. I guess one old lady's trash is another sexy, hot, young vixen's treasure. *Okay, let me stop now.*

I'm still completely fanatical about that car. Every time I see it, it's just like the first time. After thousands of miles and damn near a new motor, I still love it. Every day, I leave for work early so I can back into a space right up front. You'd think I drive a Bentley or Jag the way I act, but don't trip,

I'm proud of my babygirl. She's fully loaded with a V-8, a 5-speed transmission, power everything, and a popup sunroof.

Patrick and I finally got all the kinks worked out about a year after I bought my Stang. Then, he took it and souped it up big time. After that, she was faster than lightning. I never knew much about how to install all those performance parts—some of that shit's complicated—but I know what each one is called, and I know exactly what they do. I'm an auto-enthusiast.

Yep, my Stang's hot. Only problem is the damn sunroof, if you can call it that. It leaks like crazy. I had a dealership and at least two glass companies look at that thing, but it keeps right on leaking every time it rains hard. I have to push my ass all the way into the left corner of the seat and drive crooked over to the side in order to stay dry when it's pouring down. What can I say? Buying a used car and making repairs can cost, but it's a small price to pay for having reliable transportation with no car payment.

Sometimes, I stand in the parking garage at work looking at my car, and I just have to smile. The garage is dim, but the light right above my space makes the metal flakes in the paint sparkle and stand out. I can spend hours hanging out, properly appreciating her, but not that day. After my brief encounter with Chandler, I needed to get out of there fast.

I unlocked the car and threw my bag on the passenger seat. I hopped in the driver seat, stuck the key in the ignition, and shut the door. Then, I stepped on the clutch and turned the key forward. The starter squeaked and whined until the motor roared. She was nice and noisy even while idling just the way an American muscle car should be. The engine rumbled deep and low. I smiled big, gripping the steering wheel and gearshift. "Let's go baby," I said softly. Then, I strapped on my seatbelt, rolled down both windows and blasted the stereo. I bet the Bureau would've thought twice about hiring me if they knew how ghetto I could be. With Rakim's *Don't Sweat the Technique* bumping from my 10-inch woofers, I shifted into first gear and peeled out of the parking deck.

One of my natural born purposes in life is to drive like a maniac every second I'm behind the wheel. That day was no different. I sped down the street, cutting off other drivers on Clairmont Road all the way to I-85. Then, I jumped onto the highway, shifted into fifth gear, and it was 95 MPH all the way home.

My apartment was down I-75 off Northside Drive. It wasn't much, but it was home, and we had everything we needed. I pulled up about 3:30, a little surprised to see Bill's pickup truck in the parking lot. "What's up with this?" I said. "He should have his black-ass at work." I pulled into the space right beside his bright red gas-guzzler. Bill's funny to me. I think he had every tool he owned right there in that big metal box on the back of his Z-71 4x4. That's my boo though.

It was a rare occasion for us to be together while the sun was still out, so I was eager to see him. I hopped out and ran upstairs to surprise him. I was just about to put my key in the door when I noticed it was already cracked open. I walked in, closed the door, and dropped my keys on the table.

"Babe, you here?"

I walked around the apartment looking for him, but the place was empty. Evidently, he'd left, and the damn fool forgot to close and lock the door.

I crept around the corner, and just as soon as I stepped foot into the kitchen, the front door swung open. I turned around, and what do you know, it was Bill. He didn't notice me at first, but then he looked up and almost jumped up out of his skin.

"Shit, Alex, you scared the hell outta me!" he said.

I just looked at him for a second. Long as we been together, Bill can't hide anything from me. I could tell by the look on his face something was up.

"You're home early babe," he said.

"Likewise, Bill."

I walked over and tried to kiss him, but he hugged me instead. I pushed him away. I didn't know what was going through his head, but he had a big guilty sign around his neck.

"Bill, I thought you'd left and forgot to turn the alarm on and close the door. It was wide open."

"Come on, you know me babe," he said, grinning.

I rolled my eyes. "Yeah, I know you alright. You left the door wide open. What are you doing home anyway?"

"Well babe, I finished early at work and ... I just came on in you know. I got here a few minutes ago, must've just missed you ... yeah, I ... I ran out to the mailbox."

"No mail?"

"Nah, just a bunch of junk advertisements and stuff," he replied, shrugging his shoulders. "I threw 'em away."

I crossed my arms. I didn't believe him, but I also didn't feel like playing Cagney and Lacey.

"I'm 'bout to take a shower," Bill said. "You wanna grab some dinner and catch a movie?"

"Take your shower and give me a minute," I replied. "I'll let you know."

"Okay babe ... love you," said Bill.

"Love you too." I stood and watched him walk back to the bedroom. Bill's never been the most truthful negro on the planet, but he was usually honest with me. That day, he was acting strange as hell. I could tell he was hiding something. I wanted to run down and check the mailbox, but that would've been too obvious, and besides I was tired, so I just chilled out.

I executed a near acrobatic move, simultaneously kicking off my shoes and jumping into my favorite spot on the sofa. I grabbed the remote and turned on the Smooth R&B channel. Of all the things in the world, I may love cable the most. I closed my eyes to kick back to some serious tunes. I was planning on just laying there for a second but ended up dozing off after a few minutes. I woke up a half hour later to Bill's lips pressed tightly against mine.

"Oh, now you wanna kiss me?" I mumbled, sucking his bottom lip.

"Wake up sleepy head."

"I'm up." I sat up.

"There's a six o'clock downtown ... some scary demonic movie." He continued kissing me. "Figured you might wanna check it out."

"No, not tonight."

He pulled back. "Okay, why you trippin', Alex?"

"I'm not baby. I'm just tired, and I haven't even taken a shower yet. Why don't we grab some food and stay in tonight?"

"That's cool," Bill said. "If that's what you want, I'm down with that. Let me guess, Chinese, right?"

"Yeah, but don't get that shit you got the last time. Oh, you know what would be good?"

"What?" he asked.

"Greenbriar."

"Hell nah Alex, I ain't driving that far."

"Come on baby," I begged, pulling him down on top of me and tongue kissing him slowly. "Get me some Mongolian beef, and I'll make some tea, okay?"

"And, what do I get out of it?"

I kissed him again and rubbed the front of his pants.

"Oh, you must really be hungry," he snapped.

I pushed him off of me. "You know what, kiss my ass Bill! God, you can fuckup a wet dream! You gonna get the food, or what?"

"Of course, your highness!" He bowed like a geisha.

"Move boy, I ain't even got out my clothes yet." I got up and stomped back to the bedroom. Bill had already pissed me off, lying about the mail. I was just waiting for him to give me attitude, so I could break his punk-ass off somethin'.

"I'll be back," he shouted.

Wait, he didn't give me any attitude. That's unlike him. I couldn't believe he didn't give me attitude.

"Hang on, baby!" I yelled, running out of the bedroom to make nice. "Drive carefully Bill ... hey babe?" But he didn't answer. Bill was already out the door. I never seen him move that fast. Like I said, something was up.

I ran to the window and watched him climb up into his truck. The situation presented the perfect opportunity for me to follow up on my earlier suspicion, and so I did. As soon as he backed out of his parking space, I crept out of the apartment into the breezeway. I ran barefoot full speed down the hall around to the other side of the building. Then, I crouched down near the wall in front of the rail, being careful to stay out of sight. I watched impatiently, hoping Bill would just drive off, but he didn't. He stopped at the mailbox.

"Bastard!" I slammed my fist against the wall. "Fuck that hurt, mothafucka!" I yelled, rubbing the edge of my hand. I didn't want to jump to conclusions, but Bill left me no choice. He definitely lied to me, and now he was trying to cover his tracks. "Stupid ass, I work for the FBI, I mean come on!" I said aloud.

At that point, I had to make a decision. I needed to either just confront him, or put him on a wait list, you know, wait 'till he really fucked up, and then clinch his nuts in the wringer. I chose the latter.

I calmed down, walked back into the apartment, locked up and went into the kitchen to make the tea. I put a pot of water on the stove and tossed in a couple of tea bags. Then, I got the big pitcher down from the cabinet and filled it with ice cubes and a few cups of sugar. I don't like being idle, so I wiped down the countertops while I waited for the water to boil. Once the tea got nice and dark, I poured it over the ice cubes and sugar in the pitcher. Then, I stirred my concoction with a ladle until the ice melted and the sugar completely dissolved. As always, I did my little taste test.

"Damn, that's good!"

I'm from the south. I love sweet tea, but you gotta make it right. Men, if you got yourself a southern girl, who can't make sweet tea properly, she may be defective, and you probably wanna try and get a refund. As for me, I'm the sweet tea master. My Tea-Fu is strong, and no one can defeat me.

I put the top on the container and put the tea in the fridge. Then, it was time to get comfortable. I walked back into the bedroom to clean up. I hung up my clothes, put on my shower cap and turned the water on. My body was aching for soap and hot water. I stood under the showerhead for a while and cranked up the heat. My day had been a trip, dealing with Chandler's stupid, rude ass, but by then I was in 100% relaxation mode.

I got out the shower, dried off, and put my pajamas on, a silk short set, which I absolutely love, mostly because I hate wearing clothes and they're pretty unnoticeable. If I had my way, I'd be in a nudist colony, so I'm not the one for long ridiculous baggy pj's, but the shorts aren't bad. Of course, they're very thin and sexy, but they're also extremely comfortable. So, there it is. That's my story and I'm sticking to it.

I grabbed the remote from the nightstand and stretched out across the bed. I watched Cops while I waited for Bill to get back with the food. It's sad to watch the perps on that show, but I'll be dammed if they ain't entertaining.

Now, I'm not stupid. Greenbriar Mall ain't that damn far away—30 minutes tops. How 'bout it took Bill's ass nearly two hours to get back home with the food. When he walked through the door, he had this look on his face like I was about to trip, but I didn't give him any shit. The food was still hot, so I figured he'd run into some traffic on the way—that or he stopped at a nearby 711 to use the microwave. Girls pay attention now because these boys can be tricky little devils. Trust 'em but keep your eyes sharp and protect yourself at all times.

Even though Bill took forever to get back, I didn't wanna fuss about it. I just wanted us to have a nice, peaceful evening at home. Whatever the problem, another woman, stress at work, or whatever, I was confident we'd sort it out later, we always did.

We sat down, ate dinner and watched a replay of a boxing match from the week before. Bill loves boxing and so do I. I probably enjoy it more than him. I actually like the real thing better than watching it though. Whenever I get a chance, I strap on some headgear and hop into the ring.

One time I came home with a black eye after sparring with this big dude. When I say big, I'm not exaggerating either. This guy looked like Rocky Balboa on steroids. The trainer kept saying, "Watch your contact!" but did I listen? 'Course not. I kept sluggin' that big bastard right in the head. After a while, he got sick of my shit, so he reached around my guard and landed a solid right. It was so quick I never even saw it coming. All it took was that one hit. He damn near knocked me through the ropes. My feet went up in the air and everything. I thought it was funny as hell, but Bill didn't. When he saw my face all swollen up, he wasn't laughing one bit. I thought he was going to have a cow. He acted like he wanted to go do something, but I knew his little sniveling ass was just trying to play big man. I think his pride was hurt.

I always loved sports. I wanted to play basketball but was never any good at it. Running and boxing's always been my thing. When I run, I take my worries out on the blacktop, and when I box, I take my anger out on my sparring partner's chin.

Bill and I finished checking out the fight, and then watched the first part of the news. After that, I started getting ready for bed, but Bill stayed up.

All while I was brushing my teeth, I was starting to trip again. I kept staring at myself in the bathroom mirror, getting angrier with each passing moment. I wanted to go back in the living room and pick a fight with Bill. I guess I was still pissed he lied to me, but we'd had a good night, so I didn't want to ruin things over what could turn out to be a misunderstanding.

I yelled from the bathroom, "What you doing tomorrow babe?"

"Gotta work," he replied callously. "Probably hit the gym 'round 7:30 before I go in."

I walked back into the living room. "You building cars on a Saturday?"

"We're behind on everything," Bill replied. "Gotta get caught up."

"Well ... okay." I kissed him on his forehead. "Goodnight."

"Night baby," he replied.

I went into the bedroom and shut the door. Even with my 30-minute nap earlier that evening, I was still tired, so it was time to get some serious sleep.

Unlike normal people, I wear my pajamas around the house, but not to bed. Like I say, I hate clothes, so I stripped off my pj's and put them back in the drawer. Then, I turned off the lights and slid under the covers.

I love the way sheets feel against my skin, I find it strangely erotic and very soothing all at the same time—well, maybe soothing isn't the right word. Either way, when it comes to bedtime, I absolutely cannot sleep in clothes for any reason. It drives my sister nuts, but I can't help it. Last time we went out of town, she got so pissed with me she ended up sleeping on the sofa. Why? Well, because she refused to let me sleep on it. She was like, "People gotta sit on that couch, bitch!" To which I kindly replied, "Fuck you, I'm clean from head-to-toe, ho!" For whatever reason, she couldn't, or wouldn't follow my logic on the issue. I hardly cared because I slept soundly in the bed. Unfortunately, I can't say the same for Theresa. Her shit was all fucked up the next morning after sleeping on that hard couch. Then all of a sudden, she's asking me to crack her back for her. "Fuck that shit! Crack your own back, dumbass!" She could've just slept with me with her stuck-up butt, but no.

Seriously, if I have to wear clothes to bed, I'm up all night. But, when the pj's are off, it's sleepy time the minute I pull the covers up to my neck. I tell you I really am a simple girl. It doesn't take much to please me. Give me some nice bed sheets with a high thread count and put the air conditioning on blast—hell, I'm feeling rather submissive just thinking about it. I'd be putty in anyone's hands.

"Okay Alex, it's sleepy time," I said softly.

I turned off the light on my nightstand, said a quick prayer and that was all she wrote. Once my head hit the pillow, I shut my eyes and fell fast asleep.

Chapter 3

Normally, I sleep like a baby. When I can't, which sadly happens more than not nowadays, I play Beer Chess with myself until I pass out. One way or another, I make it a point not to wake up until the morning. However, that night something got my attention. I kept hearing this loud buzzing noise close to my head, right in my ear. At first, I thought I was dreaming, but it was too real to be a figment of my imagination, so I opened my eyes and rolled over. The room was pitch-black, all except the alarm clock, and my cell phone, which turned out to be the culprit. There it was pulsating around on top of my nightstand. The little indigo blue disco display illuminated my side of the room, flicking on and off like a miniature disco show. I picked up the phone and checked the caller ID but didn't recognize the number. I was about to ignore it, but then I figured, whoever it was would just call back.

I yawned. *This better be good.* "Southerland," I answered in my deep, sleepy voice.

"Alright kid, it's time," came a voice over the phone.

"Chandler?"

He laughed. "Get up off your boyfriend or girlfriend or whatever you got over there and get dressed. I need you on Roswell Road."

"What the hell are you talking about?"

"We got a DB," said Chandler. "I'll send the address to your phone."

I rubbed my eyes. "DB...? What, n ... no ... it's after midnight, and I-"

"Come on kid, get the shit out your ears," he interrupted. "I'll meet you there, now move it!"

I turned my nightstand lamp on. The clock said 2:30 am. I lay there for a moment with my cell phone pressed against the side of my head.

"Southerland, you there?" Chandler asked.

"Yeah ... I'm here," I replied. I dropped my head down and stared off the edge of the bed into the darkness.

"WELL, GET THE LEAD OUT YOUR ASS!" he exclaimed. "Tell you what, I'll send a car for you."

"No ... No, I'll be there." I glanced back up at the clock. "Be there in 45."

"Make it 30," he snapped. Then, he hung up on me.

I pulled the phone back away from my ear and just looked at it. "I don't care how good Chandler is," I mumbled, "he needs to learn how to talk to people—nah, fuck that, he just need to learn how to talk to me, especially when he wakes me up in the middle of the night."

I sat up and put both feet on the floor, running my fingers through my hair and scratching my scalp with my nails. I stayed there slumped over the edge of the bed for at least five minutes before getting up. Finally, I was up on my feet. I stretched for a while, and then walked into the closet to grab something to wear.

Looking through my clothes, all I could think about was how Chandler tripped earlier about me showing a little chest. I've never been much of a conformist, so I grabbed the lowest cut blouse I could find. "You think Chandler's terrorized by cleavage?" I whispered in my best Jack Nicholson, Joker voice. "Wait'll they get a load of me!" I laughed out loud. Apparently, I'm witty and funny even in the middle of the night, at least to myself.

I put on my scandalous blouse along with some slacks, my trouser duty belt, and a pair of boots. I clipped my cell phone and badge on the belt. Then, I put on my jacket. I grabbed my keys and headed for the door but stopped short. "Shoot! Almost forgot my gun." I turned on the lights and started rummaging through my drawers, but my gun wasn't in the dresser. I sat down on the edge of the bed, trying to remember where I'd put it. After a few minutes, I was beginning to wonder if it was even still in the apartment. Maybe I'd lost it. Wherever it was, I had to find it. God knows if I actually lost my gun, OPR would have a field day with my black-ass. I'd never hear the end of it. "Wait a minute ... I remember..." I ran back into the closet and pushed my shoeboxes around. "Thank you, God!" There it was, my little gun case, all the way in the back.

I cracked opened the gun box. Inside was my Glock, a tactical holster and two magazines. I grabbed the plastic molded holster and clipped it onto my belt. Then, I checked the gun, loaded it and slid it into the holster until it clicked into place. I walked out of the closet and stood for a minute in front of our full-length mirror. With my jacket pulled back, I definitely looked the part, and believe it or not, I was wide-awake without coffee or booze. I guess I was just excited about my first crime scene. You know what, forget the crime scene. With my gun on my hip, I felt like Shaft or Magnum PI. I hadn't worn that thing in years, but all of a sudden, I couldn't imagine going to work another day without it. Z-Squad was already paying off.

I walked out of the bedroom floating on cloud nine, high as a kite, but then I saw Bill, curled all up on the sofa, dead to the world. There were three empty beer bottles on the table and the TV was blasting. I thought about waking him up to tell him I was leaving, but I was still pissed with him, so I just left.

By the time I pulled out of the apartment, I got a text message on my cell phone. As promised, Chandler sent me information on the target location. I took I-75 North to 285, circled the perimeter heading east, and then exited Roswell Road. I made a right off the exit and another onto Mt. Paran. A few miles down the road, my cell phone rang again.

"Southerland," I answered.

"What the hell are you waiting for, Easter?" asked an angry David Chandler. "Dammit I told you-"

"I'm here Chandler. I can see the lights flashing."

He hung up on me again. That man was really working my last goddamn nerve.

I followed the dance of flashing lights from all the emergency vehicles, and it led me straight to the house, which was up on the right. I pulled over and parked in front of the house on the street just ahead of the driveway. I got out and just gazed at the property. That place was off the hook. That's the only way I could describe it. It was like no home I'd ever seen before in real life. I walked slowly through the main gates and down the driveway towards the front. With my head tilted all the way back, I still couldn't see the top of the house. That place looked like the Taj Mahal, like it belonged in Saudi Arabia or on the Vegas strip. There were giant stone pillars out front, lights everywhere and more marble than I could afford if I worked for the Bureau for two lifetimes. From the looks of it, the footprint of the home was more than ten thousand square feet.

"Fuckin' rich people," I mumbled under my breath, "and they wonder why they be gettin' robbed and killed and shit … house is bigger than a goddamn skyscraper. I guarantee they some white folks."

Fulton County police were on the scene. The yellow caution tape was already up, and the CSI guys were parked out front, waiting for a chance to get inside. There was an officer posted at the front, controlling access. Chandler's impatient ass called me yet again, but I didn't answer. There was no point in me wasting any more time outside talking to him. I was on the scene, ready to get in there and solve the case so we could all go home.

I walked up to the officer at the door with confidence. I pulled my jacket back, and he glanced down at the badge on my belt.

"Agent Southerland, FBI." I said it seriously, but deep inside, I was just giggling. This was cool.

"They're already upstairs," said the officer. "Top floor."

"Thank you." I walked inside and looked around a bit. The interior of the mansion was more lavish than the outside. There was a fountain right in the middle of the entryway—A FUCKIN' FOUNTAIN. I'm not bullshittin' either. It had little statues of naked people with water spilling out of their mouths, and the whole thing was as big as—well, it looked bigger than my living room. Everything was meticulously clean too. The lights were dim, but I could still see my reflection on the marble floor. Nothing seemed out of place, which made the whole ambiance kinda spooky.

I must admit, I was in awe of the home. It was a sheer architectural wonder. Who knew people lived like that in Georgia? I scavenged around and found a box of latex gloves on the table near the stairs. I put on a pair and looked around a little more before going up. Some detectives were hovering on the other side of the floor near the elevator. I wondered what they were up to, but figured I'd fooled around enough. Chandler was probably livid by then, so I just headed upstairs.

I jogged all the way up. My legs were a little stiff at first, but by the time I got to the top, my blood was circulating, and I was feeling good. I took a quick glance over the banister. The top level was so high up, the men down on the first floor looked like insects. *I apologize in advance if I come off as ghetto, but goddamn that place was off the mothafuckin' chain!* Every step I took I saw something even more impressive and expensive than before. I could've just loaded one of those Persian rugs in the back of the Stang and probably took the rest of the year off.

I stopped trippin' and walked down the hall towards the master bedroom. There was a man in an FBI jacket standing in the doorway. Like the first floor, the entire upstairs was marble, so he heard me coming and turned around.

"You must be Southerland," he deduced.

"Yes."

"Hey, I'm Mack."

"What's going on, Mack?" I shook his hand.

"Well, we got a-"

"Is that Southerland?" yelled a grumpy sounding Chandler.

Mack just rolled his eyes.

Chandler popped his head around the corner. "You're late again!" he exclaimed. "Hurry up and get your ass in here. You can make friends later."

"Yes, sir." I smiled, but Chandler frowned big time. He knew I was trying to push his buttons, and of course, he didn't appreciate it one bit. He retreated into the room. Chandler was a big man, well built, and in his late-fifties. He had a serious southern drawl too, which if you could get past all his bullshit, actually made him kinda cute. From what I'd heard, he'd been in the Bureau since he was in his twenties and ended up working all the cases nobody dared to touch. They said he's some kind of legend, but I had my doubts. I heard the rumors and how other agents talked about him— never in a good way. His reputation preceded him, and it wasn't exactly stellar. Obviously, Chandler commanded serious respect, but I doubted any sane person could stand his ass for more than a minute. Far as I was concerned, he was just a rude old bastard in a suit.

I guess that fool Chandler figured since no one's willing to do his job, he could say and do whatever he wanted and get away with it. *Mothafucka needs to check that shit at the door*. Then again, it was my first case and I felt a little grumpy myself. After all, it was the middle of the night. After 20 years of that, I'd probably be a bitter old hag too. The way I felt, I wasn't sure I could add much value to the situation anyway. I was in one of those moods where I was just hell-bent on pissing somebody off that night. *You think my car's fast? I go zero to bitchy in five seconds flat.*

Chandler was steadily running his mouth. I couldn't make out exactly what he said, probably because I was temporarily ignoring him. I just stood there staring at him for a second, thinking of a clever way to pay him back for lashing out at me earlier in the office. I was working up the nerve, but then I got to thinking maybe it wasn't such a good idea after all. Tony claimed Chandler's the best. So far, Tony had never lied to me, not that I know of. Yes, Chandler was a prick, but looking at the bright side, how many times do you get to work with a legend? It was definitely a first for me. If David Chandler was half the investigator Tony claimed, then I needed to drop my pride and get to learning. Of course, that translated into *cut the bullshit Alex and go make nice,* and so I did.

"I'm sorry for calling you Sir... it's Dave, right?" I moved in closer and smiled.

"David," he snapped. He looked down at my blouse and frowned. "You're stuck with me now, so you better start sucking up fast."

"I know exactly what you mean," I said. Then, I grabbed his hand and gave him a firm handshake. I had to keep myself from laughing because his eyes were glued to my tits the whole time. I honestly don't know how he made it 30 years without catching a sexual harassment case. By then, I'd reluctantly accepted which side my bread was buttered on, so I sucked it up and got right to stroking his little wrinkled ego.

I continued working my fake smile. "David, I hear you're the best, and I wanna learn everything I can from you and the rest of the team."

He smiled really big. "That's more like it, kid. My butts a little hairy though. You need some Chap Stick?"

His crass comment wasn't funny to me, but I laughed loudly anyway. Turns out it was just enough to get him to let his guard down. He just kept right on smiling. Believe me when I tell you flattery got you everywhere with that nut.

"Come on kid," he grumbled.

We walked into the bedroom, which as you can imagine was like the rest of the house, massive. By my estimates, that room alone was bigger than a small ranch-style home. Our footsteps echoed as we made our way across the floor. The room was decorated with beautiful, expensive furniture too. There were rugs and art all over. The marble floor was exquisite, and all along the walls were solid gold accents and extras like door handles, fireplace tools, and other doodads. It was a trip. There was also an elaborate crystal light fixture hanging down from far above. If all that doesn't bring a smile to your face, everything was integrated with all the latest gadgets, screens and remote controls. Seeing that place made me feel like I lived in some third-world country without running water.

"I know what you're thinking," David said as we moved further into the room. "You probably want to crack me over the head, right? Show me who's boss?"

"Absolutely not, I-"

"Come on kid," he interrupted. "I wasn't born this morning. I know you want to, but I also know you won't."

"And you're sure of this because what?"

Chandler laughed a little. "Look, here's the deal ... I'm an old cranky son-of-a-bitch, but you're nothing like me. You're one of those cute little nice girls, and I bet a dollar to a doughnut your bark is way bigger than your bite. Plus, the fact I'll fire your ass doesn't help your case much. Our deal is simple ... you do what I say and that's it. Now, you can either accept our little arrangement and move on, or you can get on my bad side and, well just ask around. You can hate me all ya like, but we gotta work together, and I'm too old to change. You get what I'm saying through that thick skull of yours?"

"I believe I do. And, since we're on the subject of working together David ... you don't suppose you might be able to refrain from calling me kid, do you?"

"Get the fuck outta here, kid," he replied, laughing loudly.

We circled around the sofa in the sitting area. I guess that's what it was. That place came right out of Lifestyles of the Rich and Famous.

"Here kid, have a look," said David, pointing to the floor.

"Holy shit!" I covered my nose and mouth with both hands and jumped back.

"You okay?" David asked, grinning like an idiot.

I put a hand up, "Give me a second," I said, my words muffled by the palms of my hands. There on the floor was a horrible, horrible sight. I wasn't spiritually prepared for that shit. I felt like I was going to topple over. I tried to compose myself, but it was like my heart was full of acid. My chest was burning, and suddenly I was short of breath. I turned away for a second and closed my eyes tight.

"Southerland!" yelled David, standing right beside me.

I held up a finger. "I'm okay...."

By then, everyone in the room was staring, so I cowboyed-the-fuck-up and turned back around.

"Jesus Christ David, what the hell is that?"

"Some people like to call it a crime scene," he replied, sarcastically. "Welcome to victim number four. Here, check this out." He leaned down over the body. He wasn't wearing a mask or anything. None of them were.

I got as close as I could without throwing up. It felt like a big gob of green slime was building up in the back of my throat. I reluctantly crouched down around the body next to David.

"See this?" He pointed to the palms of the woman's hands.

"Stigmata?" I guessed.

"Well, yeah, but not exactly," he replied. "Killer did this with a power drill."

"Oh, God!" The smell was indescribable. I wanted to ask, *don't you people smell that,* but I held my peace. I'm sure I've smelled worse, but that shit was weird and distinctive. It was the type of smell that could only come from a big heap of road-kill on a hot, smoldering summer day. It was intoxicating and not in a good way. I put my finger under my nose to seal off my nostrils, but somehow, I could still taste the smell.

"What's the deal with the cross?" I asked.

"We believe he assembles the crucifixes onsite," said another agent, who'd been taking crime scene photos. He lowered his digital camera and introduced himself. "I'm Frank." He had a slight New Jersey accent.

"Alex." I waved.

"Killer doesn't nail 'em to it," Frank said. "Too much noise I guess ... don't want to wake the neighbors, you know? Look, he used zip-ties to strap the boards together and secure the victim. Once that's done, boom, he drills into the hands and feet to make the marks."

"Zip ties? I would've thought he'd put the cross together with rope or something more-"

"Medieval?" Frank interrupted. "No, our guy's way too smart for that. Tox on the others came back negative too. He doesn't drug them, and you're not talking about serious wood here. With a rope, you'd have to tie a special knot to restrain her and keep the boards together. Zip-ties are a lot easier. Just loop 'em, zip, and you're done."

I shook my head. "How could anybody do this?"

"Yeah, he did a job on her," Frank said, pointing at her midsection with his ballpoint pen. "Stomach, womb, everything below the navel's been carved up. You can tell by the upper wounds ... see these long ones up and down here? Killer most likely used a serrated knife."

"Postmortem?" I asked.

"Check out the rookie with the proper crime scene terminology," Frank said, sarcastically, looking back at David.

David rolled his eyes.

"Yeah, well I stayed at a Holiday Inn Express last night," I joked.

Frank chuckled. "No, I doubt they're postmortem. Here, take a look at this..." He shined a light to her left side where there was a large puncture wound and a ton of blood. "This was most likely COD-"

"COD?" I asked.

Frank paused for a moment. He had this weird look on his face like I'd just said the dumbest thing on earth.

"Cause ... of ... death," he said slowly.

"Right," I nodded. "Gotcha."

Frank said, "We'll know more once the autopsy comes back."

I swallowed hard and shook my head.

"Yeah, this one's a sick bastard," Frank said, solemnly.

I just sat there on the floor, crouched over the victim's body. I wanted to get up, but I couldn't move. It looked like she was gorgeous at one point, but tied up there on that makeshift cross, you could barely see her facial features. She was all twisted and swollen, and her entire body was way beyond mutilated.

"Is all that her blood?" I asked, still struggling to adjust to the gruesome sight of cold, hard murder.

"Yeah, we found blood in the elevator too," Frank said.

I looked up. "So, what, he beat her unconscious first?"

"Yeah, there's no sign of a struggle," he replied. "Must've knocked her out when she wasn't looking."

I almost felt like crying. "Who is she?" I asked.

"Don't know we're still working on that. Hopefully we can ID her."

"Hey Boss," yelled a rather tall woman from the other side of the room. She must've been at least six feet. She wasn't thin either she had some size on her. She was definitely big boned. Her hair was long and brown, and she was wearing the standard Bureau getup—khaki pants, a white shirt, and an FBI jacket.

"Yeah, whatcha got?" asked David. He stood up and ran over to her.

While David was off talking to the big girl in the corner, I tried to get my stomach together. I had to grab hold with both hands and say a prayer to keep from adding my own special evidence to the scene.

David finished talking to the tall woman and came back over to us. "It's definitely not her house," he said.

"I doubt it's her neighborhood," Frank replied.

"House belongs to Jason and Mary Ritchers."

"So, where the hell are the Ritchers?" asked Frank.

"Karen's trying to track 'em down now."

Frank scratched his head. "So, killer meets girl ... somehow, he knows the house is empty, and he brings her back here for a midnight thrill?"

"You mean drill, right!" David laughed, slapping me on the back and clapping like he'd made a funny. Then, suddenly, he got very serious. "Hey, how'd he know the house was empty?"

"I think it's for sale," I replied.

They both looked at me.

"No sign out front," said Frank.

"Yeah, but I'm pretty sure I saw a flyer on a table downstairs," I replied. "Maybe the killer's a contractor or real estate agent?"

"Maybe he knows the Ritchers," David speculated. "Hey Frank, make sure you talk to the Rockefellers once Karen gets a hold of 'em. Maybe they can point us in the right direction."

"What about fingerprints?" I asked.

"Doubt we'll get any," Frank said. "Look at the barbwire on her head. Guy had to be wearing gloves to handle that. We found three others just like this, but only the vic's blood was present and we didn't find any prints. Usually, with an amateur stabbing, we'll get some of the perp's blood too."

"Really?" I asked.

"Yeah," Frank confirms. "Most times with a violent knife attack, the killer end ups cutting himself too. That wound there would take a lot of effort to punch through. We didn't find any prints or foreign blood at the other crime scenes, which means he's probably using gloves, and I'm guessing our boy's not without some skill."

"Souther ... wait, I can call you Alex, right?" asked David.

"Please."

"So, Alex, what do you see here?" asked David.

"I don't know. For a serial killer this guy takes a lot of shortcuts. Aren't most serial killers devoted to producing some kind of perfect ritualistic effect? I mean, isn't that important to them, to get all the little details, right?"

"What's your point?" he asked.

"My point is this guy ... I'm just saying he seems completely detached from the crime. Almost like..."

David crossed his arms. "Go on."

"Well, it's like ... I'm not sure how to explain it. It's almost like when you tell a kid to clean his room and he does just enough to say he cleaned it. Maybe somebody else is pulling his strings, telling him how to kill and how to make everything look."

"Interesting," said David.

He and Frank stared at each other for a moment as if I'd said something profound. Then, David started barking orders again.

"Okay, that's all folks," said David. "We're done here. Get the CSI guys up. Frank, stay with 'em till they get everything processed. We need to be sure this is the real deal and not some idiot copycat."

"You really think it's a copycat?" Frank asked.

"Hard to tell," David replied, "just don't feel right, Chief. Other vics were killed at home with the shades drawn. This one's out in the open. No window coverings, house is wide open and unlocked. Either our guy's getting sloppy or he's getting really smart. Hey Karen, get over here!"

The same tall woman from earlier ran over.

"What's up David?"

"Listen, I want you to go back to the office. You and Dimitri get plugged in. See what's new out there, got it?"

"I'm on it." She hurried out.

"Plugged in to what?" I asked.

"Take it easy kid," David warned. "It's a lot to absorb in one night, and you're looking kinda green. Go home, I'll see you Monday."

I didn't argue at all. I still felt like I was going to hurl, so I was more than ready to go. Being around that girl's dead body had me all messed up. It infected my soul with some kind of evil, joy-killing virus. Even today, I still can't get the image or even the smell of that poor girl out of my head. No matter how much I blink, squint or try to drink myself into a comatose state, the smell of that dead body's forever burned into my memory. It's like I was smelling death itself. I know it sounds crazy, but I promise you, whenever I'm around a body or danger's close, I swear I smell that exact same smell.

I darted out of the master suite in a daze, stumbling down the stairs and out the front door. I made my way up the driveway, dragging my feet the entire time. It felt like they weighed a ton each. I got to the car as fast as I could. I was drained mentally and physically. I couldn't focus at all. I got in the car and collapsed over on the steering wheel. I sat there for a moment with my head down and my eyes closed. I had to compose myself before cranking up. Finally, I got it together and pulled out of the neighborhood.

I took I-285 around to I-75. It was after 4 a.m., and I was tired as hell, but I couldn't bring myself to go home, so I stopped at a local Waffle House. I walked in and looked around for a decent spot to sit, which was stupid since the place was empty, but I was all messed up and indecisive. I just stood there with my hands on my hips looking lost.

"What can I help you with, officer?" asked the girl behind the counter.

I looked at her wondering how she knew, but then I realized my jacket was pulled back on both sides. The waitress noticed my badge.

"Yes, I'd like a coffee please."

"A coffee?" she said smiling. "Gurl where you from?"

"Atlanta, born and raised," I replied, proudly.

She giggled. "I ain't never heard nobody black say they want a coffee before, all proper and stuff ... uh yes I'd like a spot of tea!"

I smiled. "Well, how do you know I'm black?"

"I can't remember the last time somebody white came in here. Not this part of town. You either crazy or you got some black in you."

"Fair enough ... then, how about some coffee? Is that better?"

"That's more like it baby. Just have a seat right ova here." She pointed to a stool at the bar.

I walked over and sat down. The waitress placed a small white coffee mug on the counter and filled it up.

"Still on duty?" she asked.

"No, I just got off," I slurred.

"It'll be alright, gurl."

I shook my head. "It's been a long day. I got pissed on at work, I can never seem to get enough sleep, and to top it all off, I think my man's creepin' on me."

"Gurl, they all do," she said. "They just think we stupid. Cream and sugar?"

"No thanks, I'm good." I picked up the cup with both hands and sipped. It was good, I think. You know, I'm not really sure whether to hate Waffle House coffee or love it. It's cheap as hell, but better than a lot of the expensive stuff. I don't know, it's truly one of life's little mysteries.

I heard the door open behind me but didn't even bother to turn around. I was enjoying my caffeine rush too much. They could've been robbing the damn place, and I wouldn't have budged out of my seat or even looked up.

"Excuse me beautiful ... hey, excuse me miss," came a voice from behind.

I peeked back over my right shoulder. There was a man standing a few feet behind me with his buddies on each side of him.

"Can I interest you in a candle lit breakfast?" he asked.

"You've got to be kidding me, right?" I responded.

"Nope ... mind if I join you?" he asked.

"It's a free country, and there's plenty of bar boys, knock yourselves out."

He strolled up with confidence. He was a sight to see too because he was wearing a red velour track suit, unzipped just enough to show off a lonely little nappy patch of chest hair. Oh, and he was accessorized from head to toe. He wore several gold chains, a Kangol hat, and had penny loafers on with dress socks.

"Hey, I'm Johnny, gorgeous," he said, moving up close as if we were old friends.

His ridiculous getup was enough to make you snicker, but the minute I noticed his gold tooth, I quickly gave him the hand to keep from laughing in his face.

"Not in the mood, man!" I said, shaking my head.

"Yo, she trippin', dog!" hollered one of his boys. "Come on man, let's get a table." Another whispered, "She probably gay anyway," before they all walked off, everyone but Johnny.

"Come on, I'm buying," said Johnny.

"Of course, you are ... listen, thanks, but no thanks Johnny I'm not hungry. I got my coffee." I held my cup up a little.

"It's all good sweetness. I'll be at the table in the back, waiting for you to change your mind 'cause I know you will."

"Bye Johnny."

"Okay lovely, I'mo see you fo' show."

It would seem Johnny just didn't get it.   The   waitress looked him up and down as he walked away. She rolled her eyes and said, "Yeah, they always buyin' till they get some ass. You'd think he'd at least ask your name first, old dumbass," she giggled. "Oh shit, pardon my language." She hardly seemed embarrassed.

"Nah, you said it right." I stood up. "Tell you what, I'll take this to go. How much I owe you?"

"On the house," she said, waving me off. She poured some fresh coffee into a Styrofoam cup, put a top on it and handed it to me. "You be safe out there, okay?"

I gave her a nod. "Thanks for the coffee."

She was sweet. I dropped a few dollars on the bar and then walked towards the door. Johnny noticed I was leaving, and he darted in front of me, blocking the door. That was his first mistake. He kept right on working his charm, leaning in and talking as smooth as he could.

"So, I got this boat down in Miami, right ... yo, I ain't trippin' baby, but I can see you out there on deck in a bikini, ridin' the waves, know what I'm saying?"

"You're in my way."

"Nah baby, I'm trying to give you a better way out," he said snickering like an idiot and looking back to his buddies, who were all but videotaping him in action.

That was mistake number two. I planned to let it all fly until he put his hand on my shoulder. Then, I snapped.

"You want me to ride your waves little Johnny?" I asked, softly and seductively.

"It's all on you baby." He kept grinning big and laughing. "Shit, you can ride whatever you want wit' me, you know what I'm sayin'?"

"Oh Johnny, I know exactly what you mean baby."

I raised my coffee cup up and took the little plastic lid off. I held it up to my lips and licked it. Johnny's eyes got big and he looked back over to his friends, which by my count was his third and final mistake of the morning. Before he could turn his head back to me, I took my cup and smashed it right up into his balls. I swung so hard, all the coffee stayed inside the cup until the moment of impact.

"Motherfucker!" Johnny yelled, grabbing his crotch with both hands.

Hell, I wanted to scream too. That coffee was burning hot. It damn near scalded my hand. It hurt, but I shook it off. Talk about showing your horns. Mine were fully erect and pointy on the tip with sparks developing right over my head. By then, he was damn near on the floor, so I leaned over and yelled in his ear, "Sorry Johnny, I was aiming for the trash, but you were in my way. You take care of those balls, okay baby. Know what I'm saying baby, huh? Dickhead!"

"Crazy bitch!" exclaimed Johnny.

By then his boys had circled around us, moving in and mean muggin' me like they were going to do something. I pulled my jacket back, so they could see my badge and gun. They stopped dead in their tracks and stood with their mouths open.

"Yeah, that's what I thought!"

"Don't worry 'bout it gurl," yelled the waitress from behind the counter. She was laughing her ass off. "Go on, I gotta mop up the floor anyway! You need another one?"

"No thanks," I replied. "I'm good." I rolled my eyes, pushed Johnny out of the way and rushed out to the car.

Usually, after a stunt like that, I'd be instantly feeling better about myself, but not that time. Believe it or not, I actually drove under the speed limit all the way home. You know I was trippin'. For whatever reason, I was still in a foul mood. I had a serious headache too, but that's not why I was driving so slowly. I kept seeing that dead girl's face in every pair of headlights and on every street sign. She had one helluva day. And, to think I spent most of my time complaining about my so-called problems. Compared to her, my issues seemed trivial.

I got back home just before 5 a.m. Bill was still sprawled out on the sofa in the same spot. I just stood there and stared at him for a while. He was so gorgeous to me. I remember when we first met back in high school in the cafeteria. Bill was standing around watching and laughing as I cursed out his best friend, who at the time was completely convinced I was his woman. I guess his friend and I was sort of an item. We'd hang out after school while I waited for my mom to pick me up. I tell you what, if she knew I was kissing boys behind the bleachers, she would've had my head on a platter. Lucky for me, she never found out.

Anyway, Bill's buddy was constantly all over me, every single day he'd be waiting outside my classes like I was his property. Truthfully, he irritated me. At the same time though, the kids in my class thought I was strange, so having a pseudo boyfriend gave me a few cool points. Far as I'm concerned, it's better to have a man and not need him than need a man and not have one.

So, how'd Slick Will get into the picture? Well, I guess there's no honor amongst thieves. Bill set his eyes on the prize, and the day after I saw him in the cafeteria, he started pushing up on me behind his boy's back. Bill was cold about it too, like he didn't even care about that other fool. We started talking a lot. Eventually we kissed, and that was all she wrote.

Bill and I dated behind my mother's back all through high school. By the time she found out, it was too late. It didn't matter anyway because she really liked Bill believe it or not, which completely amazes me. That bitch hates my guts, but she wants to hang around my man like he's her own son. What kind of fuckery is that? After school, Bill went to college out of state. He didn't finish. He dropped out, but by the time he moved back home, I'd already joined the Navy. We still stayed in touch though and managed to hook up again years later. We been together ever since. *I know he loves me. I love him too, but if I find out he's fucking around on me, I'll kill his ass.*

I went into the bedroom to get undressed. I took off all my clothes, but was too tired to hang them up, so I threw them in the corner chair along with my gun, cuffs and other gear. Then, I crawled into bed. I was exhausted, but I couldn't manage to fall asleep. In my mind, all I kept seeing was that dead girl.

I thought I was ready for anything David could dish out, but I was wrong. It's hard to explain. It was just too much like there was never any life in her body at all. Her face was completely blank, and her stomach was shredded to pieces. You have to really hate someone to do that to them. I've seen a few dead bodies, but not like that. There's a big difference between a dead rebel in the jungle and a mutilated girl off I-285 in Atlanta. No reason she should've died like that.

I just lay there in the bed, looking up at a dark ceiling, sleepless, angry and confused. Bill got up around 6 a.m., but I played possum. I watched as he stumbled around trying to get into the bathroom. He must've been a little hungover. He can never hold his liquor. After a few beers, he's done for.

After scratching around on the wall for a while, he finally found the light switch. Then, he went on in the bathroom and shut the door. I rolled over onto my right side and pulled the covers up to my neck. As soon as Bill turned the shower on, I started imagining him with another woman and got pissed off again. I wanted to dress up in a ghillie suit, kick down the bathroom door and waterboard him until he begged for mercy. I tried not to obsess over it, but I couldn't help myself. And yes, I know you're not supposed to go to bed upset, but torturing Bill in my mind helped me get over my newfound case of insomnia. I yawned a few times, and then just dozed off.

Chapter 4

Under normal circumstances, I only need a good three to four hours of sleep, but that morning I was out for eight hours straight. I must've been really tired. When I finally woke up, I didn't feel like going anywhere, so I just hung around the apartment and watched TV. I had breakfast for lunch, oatmeal with raisins, toast and some OJ to wash it all down. Around 2 p.m., I got a call on my cell. It was my little sister Theresa. I didn't have much of a normal social life, at least not one I was comfortable sharing with anyone, so talking to her was the highlight of my day.

"Hey girl, what's up?" I answered.

"What' up big sis?"

"Not too much," I replied. "Whatcha got goin' on today?"

"Trying to stay out of trouble," she said. "You know how it be."

"Yes ma'am, I do."

"And, how's work, Miss Alex?"

"Good ... good ... it's goin' great."

"That bad, huh?" She laughed and giggled. "I know that voice when I hear it."

"Nah, it's cool, I'm just going through some changes up in there."

"Well, if you need to talk, you know I'm here for ya gurl ... I mean, that's what sisters are for, right?"

"Thanks T. Where's Momma?"

"Oh, she went to the store," Theresa said. "Throwin' some kinda stupid ass party for all her little friends today ... I can't stand it when they get together, cackling and shit. I'm tellin' you, I gotta get the fuck out this bitch."

"Wanna come over?" I asked.

"Girl, it's Saturday, I ain't tryin' to get between you and yo' man. I think I'm gonna check out a movie tonight. I got this new brotha ... yeah, I'mo hook up with him later."

"Damn T., every time we talk, you goin' on and on about some new dude. You going for a world record or sumthin'?"

"Like you're one to talk Jezebel!" she exclaimed. "You couldn't keep it in your pants if it meant world peace. Fuck you, and I mean that with love bitch!"

We both laughed.

"Uh huh, that's right, I know you laughin' Alex. Shit, it'd take me years to catch up with yo' ass. By the way, where's that fine Mr. Bill of yours?"

"He's working today."

"So, you home alone, huh?" asked Theresa.

"Yep, guess a girl gotta do what a girl gotta do."

"Wanna hit the mall?" she asked.

"Shit, I ain't got no money, Theresa. I'll have to get wit' you next week when I get paid."

"I ain't got no money either," she said, "but you know I don't pay for shit anyway."

I chuckled a little. "Yeah, you don't, but you be leavin' a sister hangin'."

She laughed loudly into the phone. "You just gotta learn how to work these jokers. You too bossy, Alex!"

"Whatever. I'm about to do some cleaning, I'll hit you up later."

"So, you gone be in all day?" she asked.

"Yeah, I think so. I don't feel like venturing out."

Theresa replied, "Okay, well maybe I'll see you later."

"Just give me a call if you decide to head this way, T."

"I will," she responded.

"Alright then, bye girl."

I hung up and started surveying the apartment, making a to-do-list for the rest of the day in my head. I had a ton of things I should've done days ago like cleaning the kitchen, and I don't mean just washing the dishes. I needed to do the fridge, sweep and mop the floor, clean out the cabinets and everything. After that, I figured I'd wash some clothes, vacuum, dust the apartment and finally do something with my hair. Oh, and I was still disgusted with the way I handled myself back at the crime scene, so I needed to add some detective style research to the list. Bottom line, there's no way in hell David Chandler was running me out of the Bureau.

I knew all the blood and guts would take some getting used to, but the least I could do is spend some time getting smarter about serial killers. Like it or not, I was Z-Squad, so I had to get a grip fast before David tried to give me the boot.

I spent the next few hours doing my chores. I figured Bill would check in on me at some point, but he never called. I kept an eye on my cell phone too. I checked it several times, but there were no missed calls and no new voice messages.

I got done with everything around 6 p.m. I'd just finished washing my hair but didn't feel like melting my skull under the dryer, so I just wrapped a towel around my head. Despite popular belief in the black community, looking like a—as my sister says, a lily-white cracker—yes, looking the way I do has its advantages. I can practically towel-dry my hair and it's all good, but that nappy-headed Theresa be up in the hairdresser from sunup to sundown trying her damnedest to work the kinks out. It's amazing how two kids from the same parents can be so different.

I breathed a sigh of relief. All the housework was done. My hair was done, and I was feeling good, so it was time to do some serious serial killer studying.

I set my laptop up on the coffee table and sat down on the floor. I powered it on, logged in and opened a new web browser. I navigated to Yahoo, but honestly, I wasn't sure what to look for. I thought about it for a minute, but then I found myself face-to-face with the mother of all questions, *what makes a serial killer kill?* It was a good question, but one I had no answer for, so I decided to start with the basics. I typed *serial killers* in the search field and pressed the *Enter* key.

The search returned a ton of results. I scrolled through the page slowly, line-by-line, looking for a good place to dig in. The first link that caught my eye read, "Stories About Famous Serial Killers and Murder Cases." I clicked the link and glanced over the home page. The website had detailed information from a crime lab library, so I knew I was in the right place. I scanned the page a while and then clicked on the link, "Most Notorious Serial Killers." The next page had a quote from Edmund Kemper:

"It was an urge... A strong urge, and the longer I let it go the stronger it got, to where I was taking risks to go out and kill people, risks that normally, according to my little rules of operation, I wouldn't take because they could lead to arrest."

Now, that was scary. I guess even savvy FBI agents believe what they see on TV. I always pegged serial killers to be raging animals, you know oddities of nature, completely out of control and killing off pure instinct, but not Kemper. He said he had "little rules of operation", rules he followed to avoid capture. "Not so primal after all," I said to myself.

I read on. After a while, I was completely immersed in this strange but intriguing world of vicious, relentless killers. I wanted to know more about these psychos. I read about Wayne Williams, Son of Sam, and Ted Bundy. Now Bundy, well he was just a sick mothafucka, but at the same time, he seemed to have his shit together, so I focused my attention on him.

I backtracked to Yahoo and did another search, but this time just on the name "Ted Bundy." I found several good websites with a lot of information on him. Theodore Robert Bundy. According to the reports, he was one of the most infamous serial killers in U.S. history. Nobody knows how many people he actually killed, but evidently, he was a necrophiliac too. Seems old Teddy liked to fuck corpses. *Yeesh!* I can't even begin to imagine that.

No matter what you may think about Ted Bundy, one thing's for sure, he was smart, maybe even brilliant. The thing that stands out in my mind is how normal people say he seemed. I mean, he went to college on a scholarship and worked at a grocery store. *How's that for normal?* I say he seemed to be normal, but the truth is he'd already been killing as early as his teenage years. Bundy was quite stealthy too. He lived out his life, probably with all the normal elements that define a good one, family, friendship, even love. However, all while he was living this so-called normal life, he operated in complete secret as an evil, cold-blooded murderer.

Bundy had a degree in psychology and a PhD in killing from Backyard University. He was a busy little bastard, but he was methodical. He had a process for scoping out victims and gaining their trust. He'd be patient, play the game, stick to the plan and at just the right moment, BOOM, he'd crack his prey right over the head and get to work. His methods were full of design and purpose, and he was consistent. However, after four victims, our killer seemed amateur at best for one of three reasons. Either he's too stupid to get the job done right, he's still evolving despite the fact he's had enough practice to know better, or he just doesn't give a damn about his work, you know, poor craftsmanship. No matter the situation, even an inexperienced rookie like me could see something was wrong with this picture. My gut told me he really wasn't a serial killer at all, but somebody wanted us to think he was. On the other hand, what if we're facing a young, emerging yet bolder Ted Bundy? Was this the closest we'll ever get to him? Would he continue to outsmart us? Would we be watching a wrinkled old man on trial 30 years from now after he's killed dozens more people saying, *Damn, we almost had him?* Could the FBI even catch this guy? Did we have what it takes? I didn't have an answer to any of those questions. I don't think anybody did.

That trip down serial killer lane, informative as it may have been, actually did absolutely nothing for me. For all intents and purposes, I was back at square one. So again, what makes a serial killer kill? Is it obsession? A conscious decision, or some uncontrollable urge? A primal instinct? Are we all victims of uncontrollable urges? Does this mean I'm a serial alcoholic sex-fiend? Getting sloppy drunk and screwing around in no way compares to decapitating a woman, fucking the rest of her body, and keeping the head in your apartment like Mr. Bundy. Or does it?

I read on, but then I stopped dead in my tracks. I'm not sure where I was going with that, but I rewound the last conversation I had in my mind and realized I just compared myself to a filthy, evil, remorseless demon. I don't like the thought of comparing myself to them, but I think I'm finally on to something. See, I don't kill people, but I do hurt them one way or another. Even if they never find out, does it really make a difference? I know I have a problem. Question is, are my urges the same as serial killers'? I wanna say no, but what if I'm wrong?

Let's face it, I'm not one of those people in denial. I know without a doubt I got serious issues, and drinking only makes it worse, but I can't control myself. It's like I gotta have it. At least I'm discrete with it, nobody knows. Correction, Theresa knows, but she'd never rat me out with Bill. T's loyal, a true sister and a friend. It's a good thing too because I think it would break Bill's heart if he knew half of the shit I've done since we been together. I really have to laugh about all this. It's rather complicated and hard to explain. See, even though I haven't been exactly faithful, I'd be ready to stab Bill if I found out he was screwing around on me. Yeah, it's a double standard, and I'm somethin' like a bitch for how I act about it, but I'm sorry, that's how I feel. I'd fuck him up.

See what happened just then? I went from being pissed at Bill to stabbing and fucking him up all in an instant. Do I have killer instincts too? If we all have the ability to kill ... I dunno, maybe it's just a question of how far we're willing to go. When I say I'll fuck Bill up, do I really mean I'd hurt him? Do I want to just hurt him, or do I actually want to kill him? What stops me from crossing the line? I imagine it'd be troubling work for the average person to hack up a little girl. But what happens if you have an urge, the same way I need to feel good all the time? What if you just have an appetite for murder? How hard would it be for you to give in to the urges?

Don't get me wrong, I'm not a crazed maniac killer, but in a way, I think I was starting to understand them. There's a razor thin line between sane and insane. So, what does it take to push you over the edge? What does it take for you to wanna make others pay with their life for some kind of pain in yours? More than that, what motivates you? A tragic childhood experience? Hate, lust, or jealousy? Who knows? Clearly, it differs for each individual. For me, it's not about stabbing, raping, or eating people. I'm more of a booze, sex, and lies kinda gal ... probably more sex than anything, but I don't think I ever met a bottle I didn't like.

Maybe it's just payback for the pain you feel. What's your idea of payback? That's easy for me. When Bill pisses me off, which happens more than not, I go out looking for a total stranger in the deepest, darkest corner of the earth I can find. I get in the car and find myself a real hole in the ground, I'm talking a place the average Joe thinks twice about stepping foot in after sundown. It's never hard to find a partner in crime. Men'll fuck anything. As sexy as I am, I don't have no trouble at all. I walk right up to the finest nigga in the joint and give him that look like, *come get this pussy!* Next thing you know, we're fucking like goddamn jungle animals. All the while, I close my eyes and imagine Bill chained up in the corner, watching us like an angry jealous husband. The thought alone makes me feel better no matter the situation.

Afterwards, I go home to Bill and have this feeling of complete superiority, knowing another man's been deep in this sweet, black pussy, and his lame ass don't have a fuckin' clue. I used to write it all off as my way of punishing Bill, but honestly, I'm starting to rethink the whole thing.

There was a time I could resist the promiscuous voice inside my head, but things are more complicated now. My urges have morphed into something more like a reflex. No matter how hard I fight, I get in this mood where I'm about to bust, like I just wanna rip somebody's head off with my bare hands, and few things can snap me out of it, a stiff drink and a hard cock, or hard cocks based on the severity of my condition.

I continue to struggle with it all. At one point, it got so out of hand. I kid you not I was making arrangements to have myself committed. But then I became aware of her, or perhaps she revealed herself to me. She's a powerful, wise creator of all things amazing, my primal deity, a god of gods, which of course makes sense because I'm a goddess, who should be worshiped by all mankind. I call her Blondie because no mortal name captures her true spirit. She's devoted, vicious, and hateful, spawned from pure, unadulterated evil. I soon learned I was created to obey her every command, and she finds delight in forcing me to do things that appeal to her sick sense of superiority. With her, what is is not, and what is not is. But, despite her trickery, she's always on my side. She helps me get through the rough times.

Now, it may sound stupid and utterly reckless to blame all my shortcomings on a figment of my imagination, but it helps me make sense out of life, and that's worth ten imaginary ancient demons alone. I used to sit around for hours tormenting myself about the hunger and thirst, but not anymore. Now, when faced with situations that cause me to do something Denise Alexandria Southerland can't stomach, Blondie steps right up to the plate, and suddenly I'm back on target. She and I are forever bound, for better or worse. She made me from her own mold. She is my master, and I am her humble servant.

Look, I'm not crazy and I don't suffer from multiple personality disorder, I don't think. It's just that, simply put, Blondie takes all the pain away. Like I say, I'm not crazy. I'm just being honest about the situation.

I hate to self-analyze, but I think the key to understanding someone else's life is to find common ground within your own. It's not hard to see similarities between my behavior and serial killers'—the duality, the secrecy, the urges. Like Bundy, I'm dastardly in one part of my life, but manage to keep people from finding all the skeletons in my closet. True, I don't kill people, but is the underlying behavior really different? I've lost count on the number of times I hurt Bill. "Speaking of Bill, where the fuck is he?" No sooner than the words came out of my mouth, my cell phone rang. I squinted at the display. "Speak of the devil." I pressed the answer button and put the phone up to my ear.

"Hey, where you at baby?" I asked.

"Oh yeah, I'm up in Marietta with a couple of guys from work."

I checked my watch. It was 7:30.

"Alex...? Babe, can you hear me?" he asked.

"I'm here Bill."

Bill cleared his throat. "Okay, I thought I lost you for a minute there ... hey, look I'm gone be out for a while, that cool with you?"

"Whatever."

"Hold on, why you trippin', Alex?" he asked.

"Bill, you know what...? Forget it, don't even worry about it."

"Alright then, I'll talk to you-"

"All I'm saying Bill is it's Saturday night, you been gone all day, and you ain't even called to see if I was still alive."

"So, now I gotta check on the big badass Navy Seal?" he snapped. "Some shit pop off and you'll kick my ass and everybody else's too, right?"

"FUCK YOU, NIGGA!" I exclaimed.

"See what I'm talkin' about?" he yelled.

"You're such a pussy Bill, always bitchin' about somethin'. What's the matter lil Billy, your shriveled-up baby nuts okay?" I taunted in a peculiarly high-pitched voice.

"See, you got a problem," Bill said. "I don't have time for this I gotta go. I'll be home late, so don't wait up."

"So, what am I supposed to do for dinner?" I asked.

"Man, you kiddin' me!" he said, chuckling, "I know you gotta be kiddin' me!"

"You know what, fuck you lil Billy, you can stay out all night for all I care, but you can forget about stickin' your little pencil dick up in this-" The phone clicked, and I heard a dial tone. "Oh snap, this nigga hung up! How the fuck he gone hang up on me?"

I was instantly pissed off. I called him back, but he didn't answer, so I tried Theresa. She didn't pick up at home, so I hung up and called her cell.

"Hey gurl!" she answered. There was a lot of noise in the background.

"Theresa, I need to talk to you!"

"So, talk whitey," she teased.

"Cut the shit, I'm serious!" I exclaimed.

"I was just kiddin'," she responded. "What's wrong, Alex?"

"It's Bill, T., I can't' stand his ass, and I can't trust him either. I'm just confused ... It's like when I see him sleep on the sofa or he's got his shit thrown all over the place, I want to kick his ass, but then other times, I could just eat him up. He keeps doing a bunch of stupid ass shit too. Like today, now he been gone all day, right?"

Theresa was quiet.

"Theresa?"

"I'm here gurl," she said.

"All I'm saying is, we hardly see each other during the week, and all of a sudden, out of the fuckin' blue, he's working on the weekend? Now after he been at work all goddamn day, instead of him coming home, this nigga hanging out with his punk-ass friends all night long?"

"B, get me a cosmo," she whispered.

"B...? Cosmo...? Theresa, who you out with? T.! Are you listening to me?"

"Yeah yeah gurl, I gotcha." she replied. "You mad at Bill again, right?" She was all but snickering.

"You make it sound like it's an everyday occurrence."

"Well...?"

"Well, what Theresa?"

"Alex, all I'm saying is Bill's a man. You know how they are. It ain't like you go out of your way to make him feel like one. You always-"

"The fuck's that supposed to mean?" I asked. "Is he with you now?"

"Nigga please ... look Alex, you keep a padlock on the coochie, like he stay on punishment, but then you go pass it out like a Chick-fil-A sample at the mall."

"What are you talking about? Bill don't know shit, and I don't do that anymore."

"You mean you don't do it as much anymore," Theresa said. "But I know you still be puttin' out 'cause you always tellin' me about this nigga and that nigga. Shit, you need to check yo'self 'because you got a good man. You don't even deserve him. I tell you what, if he was my man, I wouldn't be sittin' on the phone trippin' like a little bitch ova some trivial bullshit. I'd be lovin' his fine ass down and fryin' him some chicken. I mean goddamn, Alex, niggas want home cooking and pussy not a bunch of bullshit games like you play all the goddamn time."

I frowned. We sat in silence for nearly a minute.

"Dammit T, work is hard, and he doesn't even care about-"

"Now you sound like the victim," she interrupted. "Alex, you know what, you always gotta have everything your way. You're a fuckin' control freak, and I hate you for that. You never did what Momma told you to, you got me in trouble all the time, and now you're fuckin' up your relationship 'cause you wanna act like a stuck-up ho. Bottom line is, we reap what we sow!"

"What? Hey, you don't know shit about what happened between me and Momma, so don't run your mouth about shit you don't ... wait, did Bill say somethin' to you?"

"What are you talking about?" she yelled. "Shit, I don't even talk to Bill."

"Yeah, right Theresa, you be up in church with him every five damn minutes. Sunday, Wednesday, Friday ... did he say something or what?"

"Even if he did, Alex, I'd tell him it was none of my business. Look, I don't want your man. I'm trying to have a good time. I gotta live my life, so I can get my own man. I keep trying to walk a higher path and shit, but you keep bringin' me down to the gutter every goddamn five minutes. You make me sick."

"You know what you don't give a shit about me, Theresa!"

"Alex, how you gonna say some stupid shit like that? You're such a whiny stuck up ass!"

"Fuck you, Theresa!"

She laughed. "I knew that was coming ... look I gotta go."

"No, no, wait," I said, sighing heavily. "Where are you?"

"Dave and Busters up in Marietta, wanna come? I'll let you cry on my shoulder." She laughed again.

"You're an asshole ... I pour my heart out to you, and all you do is make fun of me."

"I don't know why you trippin' anyway," Theresa said. "It ain't like you walkin' the straight and narrow. So, maybe he's just like you. Maybe he's having a tough time at work."

"He's a foreman at a car factory, how hard could his job be? I'm sure sitting around on his ass all day, telling grease-monkeys what to do really wears him out."

"Then, maybe he just needs a little space to grow his balls back, I dunno."

We both laughed.

"You okay?" she asked.

I could hear her sipping her drink, loudly. "Damn, that's a good cosmo!" she exclaimed.

"Yeah, don't worry about me T, go enjoy yourself, I'll be fine."

"Cool, I'll see you tomorrow," she said.

"Nah, I'll have to check you later. I'm not going to church."

"Shit, you need to, heathen!" yelled Theresa. "It's all good though. I'll call you after, alright?"

"Alright T, talk to you later."

"Bye, Babe."

I hung up and closed the lid on my laptop, suspending it. I turned the TV on and stretched out across the sofa. After watching a few shows, I eventually fell asleep.

Later, I woke up feeling energized, but by then it was already dark outside. I stretched and yawned, shaking myself awake. The TV was blasting. I'm not sure how I slept through all that noise, but I did quite peacefully I might add. All and all, I felt nice and recharged.

I turned off the TV and got up to put a CD in the changer, Sade's greatest hits. I love Sade, but sometimes she can be depressing as hell. I guess it was the thing to listen to based on my day. It was almost 11 at night, Bill still wasn't home, and I felt like everybody was lining up against me yet again. I walked back over to the table to grab the CD remote and press play, but then I noticed a missed call on my cell. I pulled up the recent calls list, but didn't recognize the number, so I dialed it to see who it was.

"Yeah," answered a man.

"Bill?"

"Ain't no wackass Bill up in dis joint Red," the man said.

"What?"

"I said ain't no punk ass nigga Bill here goddammit."

"Malik? Oh, shit! How the fuck you get this number?"

"What, you think the FBI the only one can find somebody?" he asked.

"Oh, Mr. Malik," I teased, "your resourcefulness is overwhelming."

He chuckled. "Yeah, whateva, nigga. Hey, come see me," he commanded.

"What? No hello, Alex? How ya been the past two years, Alex? Dang!"

"Whateva," he said, "come holla at a playa."

I sat back down on the sofa. "I can't, I'm seeing somebody right now."

"You mean that punk-ass nigga you met back in middle school?"

"It was high school," I replied, "and while you trippin' I met your tired black-ass in high school too."

"True dat Red, but I guarantee he don't put this thang down like I do, do he?"

I shut my eyes and moaned softly, licking my lips. "I thought you were in California, boy."

"Back for the weekend," Malik said. "But you know I can't hit the ATL without hittin' that fat pussy ... you know that, right?"

I rubbed between my thighs. "Mmm, she misses you."

Malik laughed. "So, what' up, you gone shake that square to the left or what?"

I got silent for a minute. "You here on business?"

"No," he snapped. "Yo, you trippin' man, gone and bring that badge and them cuffs down here, I'll chain yo ass up fo' show. Shit, you know how we do it."

"You so silly." I put the phone on speaker and laid it on the coffee table, so my hands were free to roam.

"Shit, you know you want it. Remember the last time, Red?" he asked.

I squeezed and rubbed my breasts. "Just thinking about it makes me wet, Baby."

"Yo, I'm tryin' to put this thang together right now," Malik said. "Stop actin' like you ain't wit' it. I got some cognac and shit."

"Damn, you got that good shit, baby?"

"Hell naw man, fuck that, it's cheap than a mufucka, but you can't tell the difference after a few. So, what's up?"

I sighed. "Where you at?"

"Marriott," he replied, quickly.

"Downtown?" I ask.

"Shit, again, who you talkin' to?" he brags.

"Whatever nut, what room?"

"You the detective." He laughed loudly. "Fuck I'm posed to know what room?"

"How 'bout 'cause you sittin' yo' black ass in there, fool."

He laughed again. "Hold on ... uh, yeah it's ... it's room 1214."

"Well, I might stop by."

"Might? Shit, you betta bring that big booty ova here. You coming or what?"

"You'll just have to wait and see."

"Well, if not, I'll be back in town in a few weeks. I'mo get at you Red, one way or another."

"I'll call before I come 'cause I know how you do it Mr. Malik. I don't want all them jealous ass hood-rats keyin' up my car."

"What about that square ass nigga you fuckin' wit?" he asked. "He probably gone be stalkin' me and shit."

"Bye fool!" I hung up.

Every inch of my body was tingling with desire just from the sound of Malik's voice. I met him at a homecoming game I snuck off to back in the day. I went to Benjamin Mays High School, but Malik was at Tri-Cities. At the time, Bill and I were kind of off and on. Yeah, even back then, Bill was constantly doing shit to piss me off. Anyway, Malik walked up to me at that football game, and needless to say, his game was strong. He was arrogant as hell, but I soon found out why. His dick's bigger than my forearm, long as hell and thick too. Most importantly, he knows how to work it. Malik's one of those dedicated brothers. He'll find that spot and hit it all night long. When we're together, it's never a bunch of kissing and foreplay either. He goes straight to the main course every single time.

I stopped reminiscing about Malik and me for a moment and thought about what Theresa said earlier, how I can't keep it in my pants. Well, she's right. I got a condition. Even when I force myself to go through all the drama, you know the whole *Bill deserves better* thing, it only lasts for about a minute. Then, I go right back to being the horniest bitch on the planet. This time the good girl bit only lasted 30 seconds before I started feeling the itch. Then, it was all over. "You know what," I said, "fuck this, I'm out!" I jumped up and started getting ready to go.

Once again, I'd given into my uncontrollable urges. But even though I was committed to the deed, I was still feeling a little guilty about it. I needed a boost, so I made the mistake of asking Blondie for her help. Unfortunately, she was up for the task.

"It's okay, Baby," said Blondie, slick-talking me like only a pimp or hustler knows how. "You're a woman, a woman with needs. I just wanna make you happy Baby 'cause a sexy thang like you shouldn't be walking around frowned up all the time with that sorry, poor excuse for a man, Bill. You know he's out fucking some bitch right now. Let me help you feel good too, Baby. I promise I won't make you do anything you don't want to."

God she was so convincing. Then again, she didn't have to be. She was honest. Blondie never lied to me. She was always straight up. Not everyone I know can say the same. She was the only real friend I had, the only one I could trust, and she never pushed me to do something deep down I didn't want to do. Besides, she was right. Bill was fucking somebody else. I could feel it in my bones. Two can play that game, only I'm a helluva lot better at it than him. And, as far as Theresa's concerned, I don't give a damn what she thinks, she ain't exactly a fucking saint herself. Matter of fact, who gives a shit what anybody thought about me? Morality was the last thing on my mind that night. I was going on safari, hunting for mind-blowing ecstasy between Malik's thighs.

After Blondie's pep talk, I was good to go. I skipped into the bathroom and smeared hair removal cream on to make my little Alex look presentable down there. I brushed my teeth, flossed and washed my face while I waited for the chemicals to work their magic. After about ten minutes, I rinsed all the goo off, and my kitty was so clean you could see your reflection in it.

I took a quick shower, dried off and sprayed on some deodorant. Then, I covered myself in this sweet-smelling body lotion from Victoria's Secret. I combed my hair and put on some perfume, Chanel No. 5, which just so happens to drive Malik crazy. I checked myself in the mirror. I was looking good in my birthday suit and smelling fantastic, so I walked into the closet to get dressed.

I had one thing on my mind, so I didn't need much in terms of clothes, just enough to cover up and keep it legal. I threw on a thin pink tank top with the word *delicious* written across the front and *yum* on the back in glittery letters. Then, I put on a tiny Ralph Lauren skirt, black with a big split up the side. I strapped on some high-heel sandals and my little gold anklet. Then, I gathered my things and left.

I locked up the apartment and took off running down the stairs. My top was barely enough to contain my breasts. They bounced all over the place as I skipped down the stairs and out to the car. By then, all the reasons I was about to cheat were a distant concern. I needed to get fucked bad, and Malik's timing was perfect. Bill was out actin' like a jackass, so as far as I was concerned, it was Malik's lucky day.

I'm always down for Malik, but don't get it twisted, I know his game. He's infatuated with white women. It's funny too because he's blacker than midnight, but if a girl ain't pale-skinned, or at least high-yellow with long stringy hair, that fool ain't trying to hear nothin' she got to say. Malik will act a straight fool with a black woman, but when he's with them white girls, his nose be wide open. *Typical negro.*

It's funny because it doesn't matter where we are or what's going on, Malik's mind stays in the gutter. I think that's what I like about him. He's the king of badass, always talking shit, and be steady trying to fuck as many white women as he can with that big amazing cock of his. Contrary to popular belief, Theresa's included, I'm only half white, but I guess I look close enough for Malik to make an exception. It's cool though, because even with all the racial issues and the illicit, deviant acts of sexual congress between man-king and goddess, we're still good friends. No matter what, we've stuck together, and I don't see that ever changing.

Despite how embarrassingly ghetto Malik can be, I put up with a fair amount of his shit because, truth be told, he really did it for me. When I got his call that night, all I could think about was the last time we were together, and I couldn't wait to feel every inch of him again.

I hopped in the car and took Northside Drive south into the city towards Peachtree Road, teasing myself the entire way.

I pulled up to the Marriott around midnight wet and horny. I grabbed the first parking space I saw. Then, I ran inside. I walked tall through the lobby, my strappy heels clicking and clacking rhythmically to the bounce of my big round natural breasts. I practically glided across the floor. The man at the front desk couldn't take his eyes off me, and I made a point to let him know I knew what he was up to. I licked my lips and winked at him. I think I gave him a serious hard-on. He just gazed at me with his mouth wide-open, damn near drooling. He was watching me, and I enjoyed watching him watch me. That joker didn't have to say a word. I knew I was hot.

I got in the elevator and pushed the button for the 12th floor. The doors closed, and I caught a glimpse of my reflection. I couldn't wait for Malik. I leaned back against the rail, pinching my nipples, which were standing at attention and poking out through my top. I could feel the juices beginning to flow, so I hiked the front of my skirt up and slid a finger inside. It was so hot and wet. Whoever was monitoring the security cameras got one helluva show that night. I wanted them to watch me too. The thought of a bunch of men in uniform, standing around, eyes locked in on the security monitor, holding their dicks while they watch me play with myself, turned me on even more. I was horny as hell.

Up on Malik's floor, I hopped off the elevator, sucking and licking my fingers, carrying on like a nympho all the way to his room. I walked up to the door and knocked a few times. I waited a second, and then knocked again. Finally,

Malik opened the door wearing a robe and some black boxers.

"Come in," he said, holding the door open for me like the gentleman I knew he never was.

He took one look at my body and I thought he was going to start rubbing his hands together like he was at an all-you-can-eat buffet. As for Malik's body, well it seems he'd grown up big time because he was nothing like I remembered. He was cut something serious all over. His chest was on swole, and his six-pack looked like it'd been carved out of granite. He had a body like a top celebrity male model. It was obvious he'd been working out. His beautiful dark skin glistened under the lights. He was fine as ever, and I was ready to put his new rock-hard body to the test.

"You need some help with all that down there?" I asked, pointing to the front of his shorts. I posed for a second with my butt stuck out like a streetwalker. Then, I moved in close, pressing my body against his.

Malik let go of the door and properly greeted me, kissing my neck and grabbing a handful of everything. We were both breathing erratically.

I stuck my sticky wet middle finger right under his nose, "Taste my pussy juice!" I commanded, forcing it into his mouth. He licked and sucked the juice off my finger like a strawberry Popsicle in 90-degree heat. With that small gesture, I was already feeling the power. "You gonna fuck me right here against the wall?" I asked, teasing.

"Come 'ere girl, smelling all good and shit." He swooped me up off the floor by my waist. He was strong as hell and headed in the right direction, straight towards the bed. Like I say, Malik don't fuck around, he always goes right for the main course, and I could tell he was starvin' for some of this good stuff.

As we made our way across the room, I dropped my purse in the chair near the dresser. When we got to the bed, Malik manhandled me a little, and then tossed me down on my back. I deliberately bounced on the mattress a couple of times, giggling like a schoolgirl. I licked my lips and stuck a finger in my mouth. Malik dropped his robe onto the floor and walked over to the desk to pour me a drink. He filled a glass halfway with cognac and brought it over to me. "I know what you like," he said, swirling the liquor around in the glass, inches from my face.

That drink smelled so fucking good I could already taste it. I snatched the glass away from him and gulped down every last drop in about a second. Seductively, I licked the rim of the glass and whispered, "More please."

Malik was about to pour me another when I lifted up my top. He gazed at my body, and his jaw dropped as my big red-boned breasts popped out, one-by-one. I was surprised he didn't get down on all four and start howling like a wolf. I pulled my top over my head and tossed it across the room. Then, I squeezed my breasts and slowly rubbed both nipples with my fingertips. Malik's a sucker for big, dark-brown nipples. Mine stand up like erasers when they're hard, and he can't resist the sight of them. His eyes locked in on my tits and his cock grew instantly, poking out from the bottom of his boxer-briefs.

His hands shook as he poured my drink. This time, he filled the glass to the top. *Guess he learned his lesson.* I quickly swallowed the drink down, all except the last bit, which I poured on my left nipple. I cupped my breast and offered him a sip. I didn't have to ask twice. Malik jumped on top, still holding the bottle of cognac while he hungrily licked and sucked. It felt so fucking good. I rewarded him by gently caressing his shiny baldhead, pulling him down, and feeding him my double-D's.

"Uh ... mmm," he grunted, sucking and gently tugging on my big hard nipples with his teeth. "Damn, you taste so good!" he exclaimed.

"I'm still thirsty," I reminded him. I wrestled the cognac from him and turned the bottle straight up to my lips, gulping the liquor down until I damn near drowned in it. Malik was right, that shit was cheap as hell, but it was still strong. It burned my throat and made my eyes water, but to a seasoned drinker like myself, it was like manna from heaven.

After I got my buzz on, I leaned over and put the bottle on the floor by the bed. Malik continued licking and squeezing my perfect soft tits while slowly moving his hand up my skirt. I leaned my head back and spread my legs wide. Malik knew exactly what to do to get me wet. He rubbed between my thighs and teased me with two fingers, playing with my throbbing clit. I feared I would cum before we even got started, but I stopped him just in the nick of time.

"Fuck me," I moaned, my dripping snatch aching for deep penetration. I reached for his oversized love rod, and reeled it out the top of his draws, stroking it back and forth. It was long, smooth and hard just like a big steel pipe.

Malik responded graciously to the touch of my long skinny fingers up and down his shaft. He kissed me deeply, sucking my tongue and pushing his into my mouth, flicking it around all inside.

"I want it so bad baby. Give it to me Malik!" I pulled him between my legs and gripped his rock-hard penis, rubbing the tip of it up and down against my pussy lips. I was so wet you could hear each time I teased my kitty with his cock.

I toyed with him until he couldn't take it anymore. Then, he took control. He rolled his boxers all the way down to the floor, and then snatched off my skirt. He stood there and stared at my naked body, advancing his gaze from my ample breasts, to my smooth, hairless slit, and long, slender legs. He just took a moment to enjoy the sight of hot sex waiting to happen. Then, he got right back in his spot between my thighs.

I guided the head of his cock up to the entrance of my pussy. Malik's penis, fully erect, is something to behold. It's unusually thick and long, but I was so wet it slipped right in. I locked my legs together around his waist and pulled him deep inside me. Malik drew back till the tip was almost out. Then, he plunged back in hard and fast several times. Suddenly, my worries were a thing of the past. I quickly forgot about Bill and his bullshit. At that point, it was just me, Dr. Malik, and his intense sexual therapy.

Malik and I never make love. That night was no different. He pounded my throbbing kitty for 20 minutes nonstop like a convict fresh out of jail, his heavy balls slapping up against my ass with every thrust. I desperately wanted it from behind. Evidently, he can read minds too.

"Yeah, I know what you want," he whispered. "You a nasty white bitch, huh? Yeah ... let me show you what I do wit' a nasty lil white bitch like you." He grabbed my arm and flipped me over onto my tummy, forcing me face down, flat on the bed.

Then, he pushed my legs together and mounted me from behind. "Take this big black dick!" he commanded, stuffing every inch of it between my ass cheeks and into my hot wet love tunnel.

I nearly crawled up the headboard as he thrust his shaft deep. I closed my eyes, hoping our ecstasy would never end. I wanted to feel him in my ass too. I love anal, but I knew it was more than I could handle. All the same, I had no problem with him pumping my pussy exclusively with that massive Zulu anaconda. It was invigorating.

Malik kept calling me a nasty white bitch, getting more aggressive with each passing moment, but hell, I didn't care. By then, all my so-called "blackness" was long gone. I'd be his lil white bitch all night, long as he kept working that monster cock in me. I wanted him to fuck me hard and treat me like the slut I am. That's exactly what he did. He thrust deep, stroking like an animal with no regard for the mismatched size of his dick and my little tight pussy. Each stroke was a new experience. His hips moved like they were attached to a spring-loaded hinge or running along a smooth gliding track. That man was really working it. I believe Blondie must've slipped Malik a copy of my owner's manual, because he kept hitting my G-spot over and over and over again. I was about to lose my mind, and of course she was right there at ringside, instigating all the action.

The first time I came, my legs trembled uncontrollably. The pressure forced his cock out and I squirted all over him. He smiled, and then proceeded to fuck me like the big black stallion he is, working deep inside my swollen pussy for what seemed like hours until he couldn't hold it any longer.

"Oh shit, I'mo cum!" he yelled.

"Cum in me baby! Cum deep in this white pussy!" With my face pressed against the bed and my arms stretched above my head, I closed my eyes and clinched the sheets, holding on for dear life as if his orgasm might launch me off the bed through the wall and into the next room. Malik smacked my cheeks and pushed them together as he pumped in and out, harder and harder.

"Ooh, that shit feels so good," I whined. "Mmm, it's so deep in me ... come on you big, black nigger I want you to fill me up!" That did it. Soon as I called him a nigger, he just lost it.

"Fuck ... oh fuck ... goddammit, I'm cummin'!" he yelled as he exploded inside me. His penis pulsated as he pumped an amazing load of hot sticky love juice inside me. I tightened my grip around his cock with my pussy lips and we both moaned with pleasure as he filled me up, just like I told him to.

Now, most men would've called it quits, but not Malik. He rolled me over, pushing my right leg up and to the side in a half-circle so he stayed inside me the whole time, and then he continued thrusting.

"Get it daddy," I said.

Malik was still rock hard even though he'd just had a massive orgasm. It was all so wet and nasty, and he just kept pumping and pumping. I loved it, but I knew I couldn't keep up that pace for the rest of the night. He was way too big, so I climbed on top to finish him off.

I could feel our juices dripping down my inner thighs as I slid up and down his pole. Malik reached around and spread my cheeks wide, fingering my asshole as I bounced up and down and back and forth on his beast of a cock. I leaned down so he could bite my tits. I worked it on top until I could feel he was getting ready to blow his load for the second time. I can tell when a man's about to cum.

I pulled him up off the bed and dropped to my knees. I aimed straight for his balls, stuffing them in my mouth, sucking and blowing them one at a time while he stroked his pulsing man meat. I opened wide and nearly took both his balls in my mouth at the same time. Malik shrieked and shuttered, covering my face with his hot sticky cum.

I could barely see, but that didn't stop me from pleasuring him. I grabbed his member and stuffed it in my mouth. With both hands, he cupped the back of my head, forcing himself as far down my throat as possible. I couldn't believe he was still cumming. It tasted so good. I looked up and watched his eyes rollback as I swallowed every drop. Then, I pulled it back out my mouth, spitting on the tip and licking all around until he'd had enough.

He fell back on the bed, his big, wet shiny cock in hand. I got down on my back on the floor near the bed and started playing with the cum on my face, pushing some into my mouth and smearing the rest all over my tits and down into my vagina.

Malik sat up on the edge of the bed to watch me play. "Damn yo ... you ... you a bad m-mufucka," he stammered.

He was right. I was the baddest, low-down, filthiest slut in the city. Just so happens, I was also a clean freak, so the novelty of having cum all over my face wore thin fast. Bottom line that shit had to go!

I jumped off the floor and headed straight for the bathroom. Malik stretched out on the bed, his super-sized package finally defeated and limp. He watched as I strutted across the room.

"Damn girl, that booty gettin' thick, know what I'm talkin' bout?"

"Whatever nigga!" I yelled. "Pour me another drink."

I watched in the mirror. Malik sprung to his feet and grabbed the bottle of liquor off the floor. See, once you put some real good pussy on a man, I don't care who or how big and bad he is, he'll obey your every command.

Malik was an O.G., hard and cold-blooded, but my Kung Fu was strong, and I ain't like them other hoes all afraid to mess up their hair. I'm always prepared to go the distance. At that point, I had that man eating out of the palm of my hand, or so I thought.

I was feeling great until I stepped in the bathroom and took a look at myself in the mirror. I instantly hit an all-time low. I was sticky and nasty all over, and I had a big red guilty sign stamped on my forehead. See, when you're like me, when you got a condition, you never think about what you're doing until it's done. I was a poor excuse for a girlfriend.

I closed my eyes and washed my face, but all I could see was Bill making a few creampies of his own, and my heart sunk. I started feeling really bad. I felt so dirty I had to take a shower. My guilt was getting the better of me. I just wanted to clean up and get the hell out of there before something bad, or something worse happened.

I jumped in the shower and turned the hot water on full blast. I think I was trying to boil myself clean. Needless to say, it was the fastest shower ever taken by a human. When I stepped out of the shower, the mirror was completely fogged up. I used a hand towel to clear a spot on the mirror because I needed to try and fix my hair. It was a hot mess, sweaty and wild all over the place. I had to get it dry first, so I fired up the blow dryer and spent a few minutes working on it.

I thought maybe if I got my look back to normal, I wouldn't feel so guilty, but it was pointless. No matter how much I combed my hair, it still looked like I'd been fucking all night. Evidently, everybody and everything in the world knew I was a tramp, even my hair. If I had a set of trimmers handy, I think I would've shaved it all off. After a while, I just gave up. I sprayed on some of Malik's deodorant and went back into the room to look for my clothes.

"I gotta go," I said, pulling up my skirt.

"What? Yo, hold up Red." He jumped to his feet, grabbing me by the shoulders. "What, this a muthafuckin' booty call now?"

"Don't front, you know that's how you want it."

"Naw, fuck dat, Red ... come back wit' me to Cali."

I smacked his arms away and sat down on the edge of the bed to finish dressing. "Don't fuck with me, Malik!"

"No, I'm serious yo." He sounded so genuine it was sickening. "Red, I got this spot out in Long Beach now man. It ain't a whole lot, but a nigga tryin' to do it big, and-"

"What, weed? No, let me guess, you up to heroin or cocaine now?"

"Hell naw, Red!" he exclaimed. "I don't fuck wit that shit no mo'."

"So, what is it, Malik? I know it's sumthin' ... you runnin' hoes? Is that why you keep coming to Atlanta?"

"Red ... Red, look all I ever wanted-"

"Just answer my question Malik."

He refused to answer.

"Like I said, Malik, whatever it is, I know it's some bullshit. I work for the FBI I can't be fuckin' wit' you."

"Too late for that!" He grinned big as hell.

I rolled my eyes and pulled my top down over my head. As I stuck my arms through the sleeves, Malik's cell phone rang. I just sat there and watched him. He was so full of shit. See, I knew Malik's M.O., and I could tell he was talking out the side of his neck with all that *come home with me* bullshit. He checked the number on the caller ID and had to stop himself from answering the call.

"See ... gotta get that, right big baller? Shot caller!"

"You trippin', Red," he replied.

Suddenly, I heard a noise. It sounded like it came from the closet. "Fuck was that?" I gave him a strange look and immediately started speculating. "You got some hoe waiting in the closet for me to leave?"

"What? Shit, hell naw ... I don't know ... probably somebody next door."

"Look, I gotta go, fool ... peace!" I stood up and walked over to the dresser. "Tell that stanky bitch in the closet she can come out now ... I'm leaving."

"What, you runnin' back to that square ass nigga?" he asked.

"Hey, watch your mouth! I love him!"

"And, you don't love me?" he asked.

Right there, Malik hit a serious nerve. I didn't know how to respond, so I just ignored it. I checked myself in the mirror. My skirt was on a little crooked, so I straightened it out.

Malik didn't slow down one bit. He kept pushing the issue. "Look me in the eye and tell me you don't love me, Red!" he dared.

"You're full of shit, Malik I ain't paying you no attention. Plain and simple, you were my best fuck tonight! You weren't the first, and you won't be the last. Now bye boy!" I snatched my bag and headed for the door.

Malik rushed me from behind, pulling me back into him. He kissed my neck and shoulders. "Don't leave like this," he begged.

True, I had feelings for him, but he's trouble, always had been. I mean there's bad, there's worse and then there's Malik and me. I'd already stuck my neck out for him before and damn near lost my job. Truth is I couldn't imagine having to watch my own man get thrown in the back of a squad car. I had no clue what he was into, but as different as we are, he and I've always had one thing in common, ambition. In my heart, I knew he was into something much bigger than selling weed like before, something I didn't want any part of. Another stretch would kill Malik. Honestly, it would kill me too. He vowed never to be caged up again, and I never want to see him like that as long as I live.

"Come on Red, I just want to be with you, straight up, no bullshit. Spend the night wit' me. Stick around tonight. Yo' man ain't gone miss you. Besides, I want you to meet this real cool lady I been working this business opportunity with. She put me down with this situation and-"

"Stop it, okay!" I exclaimed.

I tried to turn around, but he grabbed me by the waist and held me close. I stared him right in the eye for a moment. All I could do was shake my head.

"Baby you don't have to worry about money, you hate that job anyway," he reasoned. "I'm telling you I'm down with this businessman and this lady who can put us into the big time, legit too for the most part. I'm already-"

"Malik, you're nothing but thug passion," I interrupted, "now let me go nigga ... I ain't got time for this fuckin' shit!"

"What?" He became angry.

"I said let me go nigga, now!"

"Fuck you bitch!" he yelled, pushing me onto the floor and tensing up like he was about to swing on me.

I could tell I'd hurt his feelings. He started pacing back and forth, pointing at me and rambling.

"I got shit to do," he yelled. "I ain't got time to be foolin' around wit' yo' ole fickle ass, stupid ass bitch. You wanna act like a hooker, I'mo treat yo' ass like a mufuckin' hooker. Here...!" Malik grabbed a wad of cash off the dresser and threw it down on me. "Ole dumbass hoe, wastin' my goddamn time ... shit, time is money bitch! I'm the man! I run shit up in here!"

I stood up and dusted the 100-dollar bills off me. "See, nigga you ain't no good," I said calmly. "Don't call me no more ... I'm through wit' you."

"Oh, you still here hoe?" He ran past me and flung the door wide open. He stood there, butt-naked in the doorway, dick just hanging all out in plain sight, acting a straight fool. "Get the fuck out bitch!" he yelled. "I said get yo' shit and get to steppin'!"

People walking by looked in at us like we were just a disgrace.

"Oh okay," I replied calmly, "so now you gone make a scene in front of all the white folks."

"Shawty, you know what's up, this big pimpin' ... you betta recognize. I ain't playin' wit' you, ole psycho trick. Get yo' blackass the fuck out my sanctuary!"

"So, now I'm black all of a sudden?" I pulled my purse up on my shoulder, walked over and stood right in front of him. I took a deep cleansing breath and shot him a bird about a centimeter from his nose. Then, I casually walked out.

"BITCH!" he yelled, slamming the door, which bumped me on out of the room from behind.

Everybody on the floor heard us. I noticed a few people with their heads stuck out of their door as I walked towards the elevators. I could still hear Malik cursing and shouting all the way down on the other side of the hall. If I didn't know better, I would've thought he was arguing with somebody back in there. That fool was completely out of control, but he was a good example of how quickly people change. One minute he's all but trying put a ring on my finger, and the next he wants to smack me around like Ike did Tina. In a split second, he morphed into a totally different person. I think if I hung around long enough, he might've actually tried to hit me, and I would've had to put that bastard through the window. Men always go violent when their pride gets stepped on. I think Bill would've tried some shit a long time ago if he had the balls. Deep down inside, men are just little girls frontin'.

Back at the car, my cell phone rang just as I was about to get in. It was after 1 a.m., so naturally I thought it was Bill, calling to pick a fight. I answered without even checking to see who it was.

"What is it Bill?"

"Uh ... yes, Alex Southerland please?" came a voice.

It wasn't Bill after all. It was a woman. She sounded confused, but I was definitely confused. Her voice wasn't familiar to me at all. I pulled the phone away from my ear and looked at the display but didn't recognize the number either. Maybe it was Bill's new woman calling for some late-night Jerry Springer action.

"Are you Alex Southerland?" asked the woman.

I cocked an attitude. "Yeah, speaking, who is this?"

"Hi, it's Pam," she said cautiously. "Is this a bad time?"

The name didn't register. "Pam who?"

"Pam Reece with the Crime Lab in Atlanta," she replied. "Frank had to leave, so he asked me to call you after we processed the body. If this is a bad time, I can-"

"Oh no, I'm sorry Pam, I didn't realize who you were. Umm ... well, did you find anything?"

"Maybe. We found a mark ... figured you guys might be interested."

"You say you found a mark?"

"Small of the back," said Pam, "and it's fresh. Looks like it may have been done within the past 24 hours."

"Done...? You mean a tattoo?"

"Yes. Would you like me to send a photo?"

I thought about it for a minute. I could've just gone home and had her email it to me, but I was sure Bill was already there waiting for me to get in, and I wasn't ready to have the big fight just yet. Besides, if Frank trusted me enough to have Pam call me, I might as well woman-up and earn my pay.

"You still there, hun?" Pam asked.

"Yeah Pam ... you know, actually ... I'm gonna come and see you. I'm on the way right now if you'll still be there."

Pam said, "Oh yes, that'd be fine. You know where I am?"

"Yes ma'am ... I'll see you soon."

"Alrighty then," she responded.

I hung up the phone and put it back in my purse. Then, I glanced at my reflection in the car door window. I was a mess. My hair was everywhere, and I could think of at least a dozen reasons why I didn't deserve to live. I fucked another man in the middle of the night when I should've been at home with Bill, and now I have to go to work, half-dressed with my tits out and tattoos on display. To top it all off, I'm not wearing any panties. *Real professional, huh?*

I should never have gone to see Malik in the first place. I'm such an idiot. I always try to be tough and act like I'm going to use someone else, but they just end up using me instead. Malik got what he wanted and then he put my ass to steppin'. As always, I walked away empty-handed. I should've taken his money, so I'd at least have something to show for me giving up all the goods. "Damn, wait ... do I even have my ID?" I checked my purse. Thankfully, I had enough sense to bring my credentials, and my gun was in the car. I may be crazy, but I ain't stupid. I stuck my gun in my purse and hopped in the car.

Earlier, I overheard Frank mention where the body was going, so I knew exactly where to find Pam. I cranked up and headed straight for the police station. I didn't know what was in store for me there, but it had to be better than dealing with Malik, or even Bill for that matter.

I left the Marriott, sinking deeper into my dark hole. I couldn't help but wonder about all the stupid things I do, the alcohol, drinking and driving, my indiscretions with Malik and a lot of other undeserving jerkoffs. Each devilish deed was probably the next layaway payment on my one-way ticket straight to hell. At the end of the day though, none of it mattered. People were counting on me. I had no choice but to put the heap of a mess I called my personal life to the side and get back on the clock.

Chapter 5

It was 1:30 in the morning when I got to the police station. I walked in and showed my badge to the officer at the front desk.

"FBI, how you doing?" I greeted. "Listen, I'm looking for Pam."

"Lady, we got a lot of folks here, so you-"

"Crime lab," I interrupted.

"Oh yeah," said the officer, "just take the elevator down to the basement. She's all the way down the hall in the morgue, you can't miss it."

"Thanks."

"No problem," he responded, sarcastically. "Always ready to help the F, B, I."

Smartass. I walked down the deserted hall, got in the elevator and pressed the button for the basement. The building was extremely old, but the elevator must've been built during prehistoric times. Taking the stairs probably would've been quicker. The elevator descended, slowly but surely, shuttering and creaking, floor by floor, until finally it hit the bottom. I got out and looked both ways. The hallway stretched forever in each direction. The officer said I couldn't miss the morgue, but it was nowhere to be found.

I took the right side of the hall first and wandered around for a while. I didn't find the morgue, so I doubled back. Finally, I found it all the way down on the other side of the basement on the left. I pushed the door open and walked in. There were rows of tables with cadavers lined up and down all over the room, some were covered, but others were in plain sight.

"Pam?" I yelled, but there was no answer. Turns out, I was the only thing still alive down in that room. It was creepy. There was no sign of Pam, so I figured I'd just look around for the body. I spotted a woman all the way in the back turned over on her stomach, so I put some gloves on and walked towards her table. I was trying my best to tiptoe around and not make too much noise with my shoes. I'm not sure why. It wasn't like I was going to wake them up. I guess I just thought since they were already dead, the least I could do was be a little considerate.

I walked up to the table and checked the toe tag on the body. The name on it was Jane Doe 33. Sure enough, there was a big tattoo on the small of her back. The skin around it was red and puffy. Pam was right. It looked like it'd just been done. I touched around the center and on the edges. Then, I leaned in for a closer look. The artwork was very detailed. I couldn't make out what it said, but I thought it might have been Middle Eastern, maybe Arabic.

"What are you doing in here?" came a voice.

I looked up and saw a little white-haired woman in a lab coat standing in the doorway. She was holding a sandwich and a Coke tighter than required as if I might try to steal it and sell it on the street for drugs. Yeah, it sounds funny, but that was the expression on her face. I knew why she was trippin'. She caught me red handed. I was up close and personal with Jane Doe's tattoo.

"Pam?" I stepped away from Jane and walked back up to the front.

"Yes, I'm Pam, but who are you? And, what are you doing down here?" She looked me up and down. "And, where's Ricky? He's not supposed to have any visitors in here, take those gloves off. You're going to have to wait upstairs."

"Ricky...? Umm, no ma'am I don't know Ricky. I'm Special Agent Alex Southerland, FBI. We spoke on the phone earlier."

I took off a glove to offer a handshake, but she still seemed unsure. Her eyes went up and to the left while she thought for a minute. Suddenly, it all clicked.

"Oh okay, I'm so sorry!" She laughed a bit. Then, she wedged her Coke bottle under her arm and grabbed my hand. "I don't see too many girls dressed like you still breathing down here."

"Doctor, are you hitting on me?" I smiled.

She burst out laughing. "Frank said you were a pistol ... come on."

I followed her back to Jane Doe's table. She put her drink and sandwich down next to the body. I've seen coroners do that in movies, but I had no idea people did it for real. I guess it's not too different from me eating at my desk.

"So, what do you think?" she asked.

"You mean about the tattoo?"

"Uh huh."

"Pam, I have to confess, this is my first time."

She smiled and shook her head. "He always makes rookies start down here. It's how he can tell if you're up for the job or not. Most folks run out with their tail between their legs."

"Yeah, I don't think I did very well myself at the crime scene."

Pam said, "Well, you're still here aren't you?"

I smiled and nodded. "Yes, I am ... is that a good thing?"

"Maybe," she replied, taking a moment to look me over from head to toe. She frowned in complete disapproval. I think if she had an extra lab coat or a blanket nearby, she would've wrapped it around me. "You sure have a lot of tattoos for an FBI Agent, Ms. Southerland."

"Please, call me Alex." I looked down at my arms, chest and legs. "Umm ... yeah, they're usually covered up," I said. "I'm sorry. I just ran right over."

She shook her head. "Young people. I guess I get it though, I had my day too, but that was a long time ago before you were born."

I didn't want to go there, so I quickly changed the subject. "So, how long have you known him?"

"Who, Frank or Davey?"

"Davey?" I asked, giggling. Surely, that had to be a top secret, classified designation.

Pam smiled. "Only I can get away with calling him that Alex. I've known that man for years. We were in the police academy together, and we actually ended up going to the same night school. When we finished, he moved on to the Bureau and left me down here in the basement to rot. Here baby, I've already got a good shot of that tattoo, help me turn her over."

I put my glove back on and, together, we flipped the girl's body right side up.

"I'm getting way too old for this though," Pam confessed. "It's about time for me to pass the torch on to somebody. Problem is there ain't nobody else to pass it to."

I looked the body over. I could tell from the Y-incision she'd already done the autopsy. She cleaned the body up pretty good too. The girl's face was still puffy, but she looked a lot more human than the last time I saw her. She was average height, kind of slender, and young. Now that I had a good look at her without all the makeup and blood, I could see she was definitely underage.

Laying there on that table, my Jane Doe looked peaceful and innocent. I wanted to know who she was. I felt like her momma needed to know her baby girl was dead on a slab in the county morgue. If she were my child, I'd want to know.

"So, was COD the side wound?" I asked.

"No, this one was tricky, Alex. All of the stab wounds were postmortem. We'll get the preliminary toxicology report soon, but I think this poor girl had an asthma attack."

"Asthma?"

"She only had about a minute without treatment, maybe two," said Pam. "Killer didn't get a chance to do much of anything before she died."

"What is she about 16, 17?"

"More like 14, 15," Pam replied.

"Hmm ... you think she's that young?"

"Definitely."

"Pam, David said he thought we might be dealing with a copycat ... what do you think?"

"I processed the other bodies," she said, sighing and shaking her head. "It's definitely our guy, only it's different this time around."

"What do you mean different, how?"

"I mean different," she repeated. "I think our man definitely killed her, but he wasn't himself—not like with the others. None of them were beaten and stabbed so badly. In fact, they looked like little princesses when he finished with them short of the wounds in the hands and feet. Something went wrong and he adjusted or improvised. I'm guessing, she had an asthma attack, but didn't have her medicine, and he just kind of lost it. But hey, what do I know, you're the detective. I'm just the old lady who looks after dead people."

Pam was quite witty. She made me smile. I thought for a second, and then told her, "Frank said they found blood in the elevator, so your theory definitely makes sense."

"Honestly, I don't think there's any way he would've killed her first. I think this killer likes to paint a perfect picture, and then watch them till the very last breath, watch the life just spill out of 'em. It breaks my heart."

"Pam, do you have any idea what her tattoo means?"

"I don't know," she replied. "It may not mean anything."

"I thought it may have been Arabic."

Pam took out a photo of the girl's back that she'd taken earlier. She put her glasses on and held the picture under the light. "It very well could be," she said.

"So, girl meets boy ... girl gets sick ... boy goes nuts when girl dies prematurely, and he takes it out on her?"

"Maybe," Pam said. "It usually takes a few days to do the final report, but I'll send you a copy of whatever we get as soon as we get it. You got a card?"

"Yeah, hang on...." I dug into my purse and pulled out a card. "The extension might change, but the email should stay the same and so will my cell phone number."

"If for some reason I can't reach you, I'll just call Frank or Davey."

Pam covered the body up and I helped her roll the table over into the corner.

She said, "I guess I'll just have lunch while I wait for Ricky to get back."

"Is there something I can help you with?" I asked.

Pam looked at me and smiled. "I don't think so. He's got to pull down the next body for me and do some tidying up. No offense, but I don't see you lugging around a 300-pound stiff."

I pointed at her with both hands like two six guns and smiled a cheesy grin. "It was nice meeting you Pam!"

She laughed hard and replied, "Same here ... you be safe out there, dear."

"Oh, one more thing Pam...."

"Yes?" she responded.

"I'm curious, why do they call it Zombie Squad? Because all the dead bodies?"

"No," she said, frowning, "it's the killers themselves. You know how in the Day of the Dead type movies, zombies have only one basic instinct, a simple function-"

"The need to feed?" I interrupted.

"That's right. Well, serial killers have a basic need too, the need to show superiority, and they keep going and going, until somebody stops them. Even then, they cling to it through the trial all the way to the death chamber, that is, of course, if they actually get caught. We've probably never even heard of most of the serials out there. They skate through the system and end up getting off scot-free."

"Well, I hope we can get this one soon ... look, I gotta go Pam, but thanks for the info, and I'll be looking for that email."

"You're welcome Alex, I'm sure we'll be seeing you again."

"Looking forward to it." I smiled.

"Next time be sure to cover up honey. It's freezing down here, and I don't want you catching cold."

"Yes ma'am." Pam sounded like my grandmother, very sweet and sincere. Funny thing is I think she somehow tricked me into having a brief moment of clarity. I'm not talking about what she said about the serial killers. Nah, I think it was the way she carried herself, that or all the dead bodies. I guess being around that much death makes you take a closer look at your life.

There's no way in hell I was getting back on that slow elevator, so I took the stairs up. I climbed floor after floor, thinking about my entire life—Bill, my family, Malik, pretty much everything and everybody. I'd been acting like a spoiled rotten brat, running around starting a bunch of mess with everybody. Most of the stuff I was trippin' on, it didn't even matter in the grand scheme of things. I couldn't remember the last time I actually made it home without somebody road raging me or vice versa. Thinking about it, I felt like a complete ass. I didn't like that at all.

By the time I made it up out the basement, I was comparing myself to Pam. Yes, I know it sounds a little weird, but the truth is, being around her was kind of intimidating. Honestly, I was totally out of my league. Yeah, she was pretty for an old lady, but that wasn't it. Of course, she was smart, she was the chief medical examiner for the county, but I'm smart too, so that wasn't it either. I think the thing that set us apart was she carried herself like she automatically had people's respect without demanding it, and without any of the drama I always attract into my life. Maybe it's time I took a serious look in the mirror.

Nothing seemed to be working out right in my life, not even the job I put so much effort and time into. I had to make a change, but where the hell should I start? How do you change your entire life, 20 plus years of habits and attitude, all in a single day? Maybe I should just start being nice. Is it really that easy? So, you just wake up one day and say, *I'm going to have a good day*, and boom that's it? I wish it was true, but I don't think it's that simple.

A woman in my line of work gets no respect if she's soft. I remember my first week on assignment in Brazil. Those ignorant bastards down there damn near ass-raped me with no remorse—not the bad guys, but my fellow Navy men. Did I just bend over? No, I fought like my life depended on it. I didn't bitch about it to my CO either. I just stood up for myself, and those men respected me for it. You can't just let anybody run over you like that. You have to be tough. You have to defend yourself. You can't be a pussy. You have to strike first, or at least fight back with all your might. But what if I'm looking at all this the wrong way? Maybe it's not about being tough. Maybe it's more about being well balanced. I put a lot of time into work, and at the office, despite not getting promoted, everything's in tiptop order. On the other hand, my personal life's in shambles like a broken record that just keeps on skipping. Enough is enough. I gotta fix it. Somehow, I've gotta get this thing back on track. Deep down, I knew if I didn't make a change, I might not live to see the age of 30.

It was a little after 3 a.m. when I finally got back home. The apartment was lit up like Turner Field. Bill was home, and he wasn't happy to see me. I opened the door and there he was in the living room, pacing back and forth. He'd been up waiting for me to get home, preparing his sermon and dusting off his soapbox. I could tell he had something serious to get off his chest, but one look at my outfit, and he forgot all about it. His jaw hit the floor. He was at a loss for words.

I casually pushed the door shut and locked it. Then, I took a deep breath and prepared for Bill's emotional rant. I knew it was coming.

"I can't believe this shit," he mumbled, "I can't fuckin' believe this mufuckin' shit."

I turned around and faced him.

Bill pointed a finger at me. "You know what Denise ... Something's wrong with yo' ass."

Bill always called me by my first name when he was upset with me. Now that I think about it, so did everybody else. I just stood there and let him get it out of his system.

"First, you try to embarrass me on the phone in front of my coworkers," he said, "and now you pull this bullshit? You got a fuckin' problem!"

"You're right," I said softly. "I'm sorry for giving you such a hard time all the time." I walked over and sat down on the sofa. I pulled the edges of my skirt down as far as I could, so I didn't look so much like a hooker.

"I was worried something happened to you," Bill said. "You didn't say you were going out, and damn, look what you got on! I mean shit do you even have any drawers on? Just look at this shit Denise, what the fuck you expect me to say?"

"Bill, I know you're mad, but-"

"But what...?" He threw his hands up. "But what, Denise?"

"I was working."

"What the fu...." Bill got so mad, a vein popped out in his forehead. "Where were you working on Stewart Avenue?"

"Actually, it's Metropolitan now," I replied, "they changed it because of-"

"The fuck you take me for?" He frowned up big time. "Oh, I guess I'm just some little punk ass nigga who 'posed to take what you say and that's it?"

"Believe it or not Bill, that's where I was, I was working. I got an emergency call, I just had something on around here and I had to leave fast."

Bill sighs, heavily. "So, you ain't have time to cover your ass up? Don't give me that shit ... you work for the F, B, muthafuckin' I ... I know you lyin' now."

Bill acted as if he just caught me on video with a dick in both hands.

"I'm not lying," I said calmly. "Bill, you can check my phone if you don't believe me." I offered it to him, same as always when we argued over my whereabouts. Usually, he refuses to take it, but this time he actually went for it. He scrolled through my recent calls list, and then he fixed in on a number and turned the phone around to me. He just knew he caught me red-handed.

"What's this number?" he asked.

"That's the Marriott."

I knew it wasn't the Marriott. It was actually Malik's cell, but I also knew Bill. It'd take a few more numbers and a couple of hardball questions before he actually got pissed enough to call one.

"Who the fuck you been calling at the Marriott?" he grumbled.

"If you look, it was an incoming call ... Wrong number."

He holds my phone up to my face. "Well, what about this one, huh?"

I rolled my eyes. "County morgue."

"You think I'm stupid?" He waved the phone around. "Bet you don't want me calling this number, do you?"

"Go ahead Bill. Call it since you don't trust me after all these years."

"Man, fuck this!" Bill pressed the send button and put the phone on speaker. After a few rings, someone answered.

"Fulton County Police Department," came a voice over the phone.

Bill hung up fast. Then, he started pacing around again, shaking his head and pointing at me. "You know what, I'm trippin." He chuckled. By then, he was behaving like a lunatic, walking around and hopping from one foot to the other.

"It's okay baby," I said. "I know I'm hard to be with."

"Yeah, I'm trippin'." He walked back over and dropped my phone on the coffee table.

"Sit down Bill." I grabbed him by the wrist and pulled him onto the sofa with me. "Look, I know I been actin' funny, but I've been thinking about a lot, and ... I know I've been giving you a hard time. I'm sorry. It doesn't have to be like this Bill. I love you. I know we can do better,"

"Are you fucking around on me?" Bill asked. "I wanna hear you say it!" Bill surprised me he was so direct and straight to the point.

I tilted my head to the side. "Who you been talking to, Bill?"

"Look, I ain't stupid, Denise. What, you think just 'cause I didn't finish college, I can't come up with an original thought?"

"Well Bill, I could think you're cheating on me. You change your schedule out the blue, so you're off during the week, you're never at home, and when you are here you don't pay me no attention."

"See that's what I'm talking about!" he exclaimed.

"Okay, I'm trippin', but all I'm trying to say is, it's just you and me baby. I don't care if you went out with somebody else tonight. I'm not jealous. Let's just make it you and me from now on ... can we do that?"

"I ain't been wit' nobody!" he yelled. "You might be, but I ain't tryin' to disrespect you like that."

"Bill, I'm here, here with you." I kissed his lips. He reluctantly kissed me back. "Baby, I'm sorry for actin' so stupid, okay?"

"Yeah..." He kissed me again. "Me too."

I could tell he was disappointed he didn't catch me red-handed, but them's the breaks.

Bill sighed and said, "I just don't understand what you were doing out. I mean, you work a desk, right? Why you gotta be out in the middle of the night like this?"

"I got promoted baby!" I exclaimed.

"What?" he asked.

"Yep." I smiled proudly and nodded, saying, "I'm field qualified now. Oh, and I'm working serial killer cases with-"

"Serial killer, what the...?" Bill interrupted. He pulled away from me.

"Bill don't be mad. You know I been trying to get out of Anti-Piracy for a long time. I thought you'd be proud of me."

He let his guard back down. "I am ... no, I mean, that's great ... I'm proud of you babe." He leaned in and gave me a half-ass hug.

"Thank you for supporting me Bill, I promise things will be different from now on."

Bill looked up to the ceiling for a quick second. "Well, we'll see what happens, Alex," he said.

I was glad he finally called me Alex. Obviously, he was beginning to calm down. I kissed him again. "You hungry or something? I know it's late, but I can fix you breakfast if you want, grits and bacon, maybe some cheese and eggs."

"Nah, I'm good," he said. "I'm just gonna hit it. You coming to bed? We gotta be at church early tomorrow."

"Yeah, um ... about that...."

"Not going I gather?" he responded.

I shook my head. "I had a long day. I don't feel like it."

"You wrong," he said, pointing his finger at me again.

"I know, but I-."

"Just 'cause you don't feel like it don't cut it," he preached. "God wakes you up in the morning whether he feels like it or not."

"Look, do you have to give me a sermon about everything? Gosh! I tell you what Bill, give me a break this week, and I'll make up for it, okay?"

"Whatever," Bill snapped. "So, you coming to bed or what?"

"In a minute."

He walked back to the bedroom. I waited until he'd turned the lights off, and then I walked in. I got undressed and crawled under the covers next to him. I curled up all around him and kissed his ear. "I love you," I whispered.

"Love you too," he mumbled.

We fell asleep together, peacefully, this time on the same side of the bed. For months, we'd slept in separate corners, but that night it was all good.

The next morning, I woke up around 9 a.m., but Bill was already gone. Guess he couldn't wait to run his "holier-than-thou" ass up in church with the rest of those hypocrites. He and Theresa seemed to be getting buddy-buddy all of a sudden. *Maybe they can start a church together and stay up each other's ass all day.* Okay, that wasn't the right thing to say, and it's Sunday too. I'll try to do better. "Dear Lord," I prayed aloud, "please help Bill's sorry ass and the rest of my hateful family to have a very productive time in church. And, I hope they find you soon, so I don't have to beat their asses." I giggled, completely amused with myself.

I had work to do, so I stopped thinking about my family and made coffee. I sat down at the table with a nice strong cup and powered up my laptop to check my email. As promised, I had a message from Pam. I double-clicked the touchpad and opened the email up in a new window. The preliminary coroner's report was attached to Pam's note. I opened it and carefully read each section.

Just as Frank suspected, the toxicology report came back negative. Cause of death was definitely bronchial asthma, although I'm sure the fracture of the right side of the skull and the presence of multiple stab wounds didn't help the situation either. There were over 30 deep, long stab wounds, some starting from the navel in the umbilical region all the way down to the womb. Other stabs were just punctures where the knife went straight in. The report said the absence of contusions around the wounds indicates the knife was sharp and precise. Blood type was A-Positive, and the time of death based on body temp, combined with rigor and liver mortis, was between 6 p.m. and 9 p.m. Friday night. Pam also included a close-up headshot of the girl.

"What's your name sweetheart, and who did this to you?" I asked, staring at the digital photo. "We're gonna find that son-of-a-bitch. I promise." It sounded like some good bullshit when I said it, but who the hell was I fooling, playing detective? I didn't know the first thing about catching a serial killer. Still, I had to find a way to get my arms around the case, find her name, and help her family put her to rest. I at least owed that much to my Jane Doe.

I logged onto the secure law enforcement portal and checked for the autopsies of the other victims. COD in each case was a single stab wound. The victims had abrasions to the head, obviously the barbwire, and a stab wound on the right side of the torso, approximately one-half inches long. The pathway of this particular wound was through the right fourth rib, about four inches deep. Unlike my Jane, this one was a fatal perimortem wound, resulting in the perforation of the right lung and a hemothorax, which is basically a lot of blood between the lungs and the walls of the chest. The victims also had abrasions on the wrist and ankles, and of course, the perimortem wounds in both hands and feet were from the power drill.

Who knew what was on our killer's mind, but I'm guessing, based on the crucifixes, he was some kind of Jesus freak. It was still hard to tell if he was giving in to the kill-voices or was just a pawn in someone else's sick game.

I couldn't believe I was wracking my brain over this case, but that's how I am. When I put my mind to something, it don't stop and it won't stop. I'm sure Chandler wasn't expecting me to give up my weekend, but my gut told me time was not on our side. Our killer had probably already scoped out the next victim. We had to act fast, or it might be too late for her, whoever she is.

I spent the rest of the day studying practitioners of death and destruction. I wanted to know what they were made of, but all I found is what other people think makes them kill. I'm beginning to think the shrinks who analyze these killers are just as sick in the head as the killers themselves. Unlike the serial killers, they can actually control their urges. Talk about a superiority complex. I mean who's really a danger to society, the crazies or the assholes writing their prescriptions?

I read a while longer, but I soon got my fill of psychos and shut my laptop down. I can only take so much of that stuff at a time, and then I have to just get away from it and breathe a little, try to feel human again. Unfortunately, my mind wouldn't let it go. Jane Doe was really working a number on me, so I switched on some music and tried to relax.

Bill came home later that evening with food from church. I thanked him and ate what I could. Some of that shit was just greasy and all fucked up. Black folks kill me cooking up a plate of heart attacks, smothered in bad cholesterol, but you gotta love it man because it damn-sure taste good going down. Church food makes me feel right at home.

I tried sparking up conversation with Bill, but he didn't have much to say to me at all. I guess he was still stewing about the night before. I figured he'd eventually get over it though. We sat in silence together and watched TV. After the news, we both went to bed. That night, we were back to our separate corners of the mattress.

I woke up early the next morning feeling excellent. It was Monday, and I was firing on all cylinders, ready to go out and take down King Kong if necessary. I got dressed and said goodbye to Bill before heading out. He was just waking up. I kissed him on the forehead, and he smiled.

"Hey beautiful," he whispered.

"Good morning dragon-breath." I frowned and kissed him again. "I gotta get to work early. I just wanted you to know how much I love you."

"I love you too babe." He moved my hair out of my face. "Be careful out there today, okay?"

"I will. Love you."

"Have a good day, Alex."

I gathered my things and left the apartment. I swear it was my lucky fuckin' day. Traffic was unusually light, so I got to the office around 7 a.m. The place was empty, all except for the guards. Usually, by the time I get in at 9 a.m., they're all tired out and cranky, but they were wide-awake and cheerful as ever.

"Good morning, may I please see your ID?" asked the guard at the front desk. I held up my badge. "Thank you. Have a nice day Agent Southerland."

"You too," I replied. I took the elevator up to my floor and went inside the office. I headed straight back to my new area without stopping. I wasn't going to wait for someone to tell me where to sit and what to do. I figured I'd make coffee, find a home, and get started.

I walked onto the floor, thinking I was all alone, but much to my surprise those punks, David and Frank, were already in, loitering around the coffee pot. They looked up at me at the same time and just broke out laughing.

"What?" I shrugged my shoulders.

They didn't say anything, they just continued to laugh.

"What...? What's so darn funny?"

"Yes," David replied.

"Yes what?" I put my hands on my hips.

"Yes, we sleep here," he replied.

They continued chuckling like college roommates. "Guess she thought she'd beat us in here, huh Frank?"

"Rookies!" Frank shook his head. He threw his little stirrer in the trash and walked off with his coffee mug in hand.

I walked over and put my stuff down on a nearby desk, then I came back to fix myself a coffee. David stood by, watching my every move. I flipped over a mug and washed it vigorously. I'm a bit of an obsessive compulsive when it comes to being clean, especially with something I plan to put my lips on. *Hey don't go there!*. Anyway, I didn't look up, but I could sense David standing behind me just hovering.

"You know, those mugs are already clean," he said, sipping his coffee.

"Good morning to you too," I replied. I dried my cup with a paper towel and filled it with coffee. David continued staring, so I turned and stared back at him. Suddenly, he started grinning like a goofy kid on a first trip to Disney World.

"What is it now, David?" I asked.

"Black coffee?" he teased, "what's a little girl like you doing drinking black coffee? Don't you want some cream and sugar, maybe one of those little fruit muffins or something?"

"Hey, it's the closest thing we got to Jack up in here. I take it any way I can get it."

He stepped back, seemingly shocked by my response. "You'll go far down here, smartass," he replied, laughing.

"Come on." He turned around and headed towards the back. "Frank, move your ass!"

I grabbed Jane Doe's file out from my bag and ran behind him. Frank jumped up and followed us into David's office. We sat down at the conference table and waited patiently while David took his jacket off and neatly hung it up on the coat rack.

"Okay," said David, walking over to join us at the table. He sat down, and pointed right at me, squinting his eyes. "You see Pam kid?"

"Yeah David, here's a copy of the preliminary coroner's report." I pulled a stack of stapled papers out of Jane Doe's file and slid them across the table.

Frank slammed his hand down and intercepted my pass. "Give me the cliff notes," he said, picking up the papers.

"Okay, COD was asthma."

"Seriously?" Frank seemed surprised. He started thumbing through the reports. "Didn't see that coming...."

"Yeah, all of the wounds were postmortem."

David scratched his head and rubbed his eyes. "So, it's a copycat?"

"I don't think so," I replied, "and neither does Pam. She thinks it's him."

David leaned back in his chair. "Okay Alex, lay it out for me."

"The girl's only about fifteen. Now, it's just speculation, but here's what I think happened ... the killer knows her, maybe hangs around her school or something. He gets real friendly and then convinces her to go out with him. He takes the time to gain her trust, but she's smart enough to figure he's up to something when they pull up to that mansion. By the time she realizes what's going on, it's too late, she's already out the car. She doesn't want to spook him, especially if he's cool and she's gonna get some thug-passion in that big beautiful palace, so she plays along. She doesn't put the pieces together until they get in the elevator. She tries to back out, but then boom, it happens...."

"What?"

"She has an asthma attack, a bad one. Her medicine's back in the car, so she starts breathing hard. Obviously, at this point, the killer doesn't realize what's going on, so he freaks out and clocks her. By then, she's still gasping for air. Genius probably thinks she's faking it, so he hits her a few more times before she's out. Once he realizes she just died on him, he's already beyond the point of no return, so he decides to go through with it anyway. He's got everything ready upstairs. He drags her into the bedroom and finishes the job, only he's still pissed she screwed up his masterpiece, so he ends up taking it out on her and cuts her up real bad."

David glanced over at Frank, who nodded in agreement.

"Thug passion?" David raised an eyebrow.

"Well...." I chuckled a bit and smiled.

"Okay, Frank, Alex ... your new mission in life is to ID this girl. Get a name and try to connect her to one of the other victims ... maybe there's something we're missing."

"Wait, I-"

"Look kid, Crane said you wanted field work," David reminded. "Well, now you got it. Bureau says you gotta work with a senior agent, Frank's not exactly a senior citizen yet, but he's your senior today. Would you rather it be me?"

"Uh ... well I-"

"Don't answer that!" David laughed loudly. "Now, both of you get the hell outta here. Bring me back something I can work with, or I'll show you what a mean bastard I can really be."

Frank and I got up and walked out of David's office together. We headed back to the floor to roll our sleeves up and dig in to the case.

Chapter 6

It was obvious Assistant Special Agent in Charge David Chandler had a serious problem showing common courtesy and respect to other people. Maybe Frank was used to the whole verbal abuse thing, but it was still rubbing me the wrong way. The only man I ever let talk to me like I was trailer-trash was Lieutenant Riggs, a high-ranking badass Navy Seal team leader out of Little Creek in Virginia Beach. Hell, G.I. Jane had a picnic compared to what I put up with that sick mothafucka. He woke up evil for no reason at all. I didn't even report to him, but from the very start, he had it in for me. At first, I thought he was cool because he let me in on a lot of missions and took it upon himself to give me some serious field training. After a while, I realized he was actually just trying to get me killed, surefire proof I shouldn't have been there in the first place.

Setting foot in South America can be a challenge in more ways than one, but for American troops in Brazil, it's downright unforgiving. My job down there as an Intelligence Officer was to provide direct support to the Seals for counternarcotic missions. We blew up crops, bribed and killed cartel members, and tried to give the people a fighting chance at a good life, at least that's why I thought we were down there. Turns out certain parties had other ideas in mind.

Lt. Riggs pretended to be a good guy at first, but quickly became my arch nemesis. He was a rotten bastard, right down to the core. I remember his favorite name for me was whore. After a while, he actually started his team briefings by saying, "The little crack-whore gathered some good intel." It was beyond inappropriate, maybe even against Navy regulations, but who would I ever tell? If I reported it, they would've pulled me out the field faster than I could say, *apology accepted*, which is exactly what that asshole, Riggs, wanted.

Honestly, I'm not sure Riggs actually hated me. Maybe he just hated the thought of a woman being anywhere near his prestigious, elite Seals. None of that meant anything to me though, because I would've ridden to hell with gasoline draws on before I let him force me out. I just sucked it up and did my job despite all the drama.

Riggs screwing me over back in the day is one thing. I was in the Navy, but the FBI ain't the Navy. The only reason I didn't throw a quick spin-kick to the back of David's neck is Tony asked me to be nice. Otherwise, that son-of-a-bitch would be face down on the floor with carpet burns on his forehead.

Frank and I had just walked out of a meeting with David's rude ass, so I took a few deep breaths and ignored every urge to go back in there and fuck David up. Back out on the floor, I calmed down and refocused my energy on the task at hand.

"You can set up camp at one of those desks over there," Frank said, pointing to a group of empty workstations. "Doesn't matter which one. Soon as I get a chance, I'll put in a ticket to have your phone moved up from Anti-Piracy. You ever run fingerprints?"

"Not recently, no."

He smiled. "Alright Rookie. Get settled in and then come back over to my station. I'll show you how it's done and refresh your memory. Okay?"

"That'll work Frank, thanks."

I took a few minutes to just throw my stuff on the best-looking desk available. There was no point taking time deciding where to sit. It's not like it made much difference because all the desks were the same. I chose a spot in the last row and dropped my gear. I logged in, checked my email, and then locked my workstation before heading back over to Frank's desk. I grabbed a nearby chair and rolled it over beside him.

"Frank, you ready for me?" I asked.

"Yeah." He opened a program on his computer. "See, Pam already sent the prints," he said, pointing to a set of latents on the monitor. "We can use the system to search for a match."

"But, the girl's only about fifteen," I said.

"Yeah, probably won't get anything, but we'll start there anyway."

Frank and I sat and waited while the search completed. I think we were both hoping for a match, but we didn't get anything at all.

"So, what's next juvenile records?" I asked.

Frank laughed. "Get out of here, Rookie. Nah, that's not a good option, especially if she's not in the system. It'd be a big waste of time."

"You mean if she's not a violent juvie?"

"There you go." Frank scratched his chin. "Best thing to do is probably just go public. Look, we know where we found the body ... hmm ... let's target the high schools in the area, see if we got any missing students. If that's no good, we'll check with the local tattoo shops and see what we get there."

"Just like that, huh?"

Frank laughed. "What, you expected some kind of high-tech CSI lab experiment?"

"You've been laughing at me a lot this morning, Frank."

"What can I say, I look for the humor in life," he replied, smirking. "Keeps me sane."

"Oh, I see, and so now you've found me, huh?"

"Man, you really are good Alex." Frank said still chuckling, "Seriously though we need to do everything we can to catch this joker before he kills again. Run the search, find the schools, and let's get rolling."

"I'm on it, Sir." I pushed the chair back to the desk I'd borrowed it from and ran back to my station. I didn't waste any time. I immediately ran a search on the high schools in the area. There were nearly 150 schools in a 15-mile radius, so I tried to narrow my search. There were quite a few private schools on the list, mostly religious. Based on the way the girl was dressed and the fact she was out so late, I figured I'd move them to the back of the line. I searched and sorted for almost two hours. By then, everybody was in— Karen, Mack, Bob, the whole crew. It's funny too because they didn't procrastinate like we did in Tony's group. Guess they couldn't afford to. They took their stations quietly and got right to work.

It didn't take long to figure out what everyone on that floor did. You may call it being nosey, but I call it good intelligence gathering. For the most part, everybody seemed to be doing what normal FBI agents do. The only suspect one was Karen, so I watched her carefully. As soon as she arrived that day, she locked herself in with the guy in the back. It had to be that Dimitri character David kept talking about. The room they were in looked like it used to be a conference room at some point. Now, it had computers lined up and down all over the walls, really high-tech stuff as far as I could tell.

The thing that gets me is I never see Dimitri go in or out of that computer room. Only time I see him is when I'm on my way to David's office, and even then, it's just the back of his head. The first time I saw him I was like, *damn, that's a lot of hair!* Naturally, I was extremely curious what they were up to, but I had more important things to worry about like Jane Doe #33's real name, rest her soul.

I kept searching, but unfortunately, I was struggling to come up with a good list of probables. Finally, I decided to look for public schools with a high number of students per teacher. The way I saw it, less teachers per student meant less attention and more opportunity to skip class or get into trouble. Clearly, my method wasn't scientific. I was just working my own little system. I took the top five schools with more than 19 students per teacher and started making phone calls.

I spoke to someone in the main office in all but one of those schools. The first four didn't have any unusual absences. The woman at the last school said she was extremely busy, but promised to call back, so I gave her my name and extension.

I didn't get very far with the first group, so I moved on to the next five schools. The first three were a bust, so I kept working the list. I was just about to pick up and dial the next school when I got an incoming call. The phone rang a couple of times before I noticed it, but I picked up before it went to voicemail.

"FBI, Southerland," I answered.

"Yes, Ms. Southerland, this is Ms. Hollis calling back from Douglass High."

"Yes, Ma'am."

"I checked and we didn't have any unusual absences today. I'm sorry."

"No problem, thanks for calling back."

Ms. Hollis replied, "You're welcome. Have a nice day."

"Wait, Ms. Hollis, don't hang up..."

"Yes?" she said.

"Let me ask you, did you have any absences at all?"

"Well, yes," she replied, "we always have a few."

"Any girls call out? Maybe a freshman or sophomore?"

"Hold on, let me check." I could hear her sifting through some papers. "Well, yes ... we actually have one student that hasn't showed yet ... looks like she was out Friday too."

"Can you describe her for me?"

"Yes ... um... let me see...." She paused for a moment. "She's sixteen years old, blonde hair and-"

"Do you know this girl?" I asked.

"No, not personally," she replied, "but I believe her mother's a teacher here."

"Really? She working today?"

"Yes, Ms. Charles is here today," she responded.

"Ms. Hollis, I think this may be the girl I'm looking for. What's her name?"

"Karla Charles," she replied. "Is something wrong?"

I avoided that question. I figured it'd be best to reply with some time-tested agency jargon. "It'd be helpful if I could come down and see you in person."

"Well, I'll be here all day, until about 4:30," said Ms. Hollis.

"Thanks for your help." I hung up the phone.

"Frank," I yelled, "I think we got something!" I ran over to his desk.

Frank heard me coming and spun around in his chair. "What's up Alex?"

"A Douglass High student matches our Jane Doe. Her name's Karla Charles."

"Matches?" He raised an eyebrow.

"Yeah, she matches the description."

"You sure?" he asked.

"Yeah, she was out Friday and hasn't showed up today."

"And, you think it's her?"

"I don't know. I spoke to a Ms. Hollis, and the girl she's talking about, her mom's a teacher at the school, and-"

"Slow down, Alex ... did you tell her, or did she tell you what the girl looks like?"

"I asked her to describe the girl. I'm telling you Frank, it's her."

He stared at me for a moment. "Okay," he reluctantly replied, "grab your list of nearby schools in case we're wrong. Oh, and run down to procurement and grab a car."

"We riding together, right?"

"Yeah," he replied. "Pull around and meet me out front."

I smiled and held my fist up like we'd cracked the entire case. "See ya in a minute, boss!"

"Alright, alright, just calm down," said Frank.

I gave him a thumbs-up and took off running like a kid in a toy store. I grabbed my bag from my desk and hightailed it down to procurement. I walked up and banged my fist a few times on top of the counter. "Hey," I yelled to the man in the back, "I need a car!"

"Hey, you need to call first next time!" he said rudely, reluctantly approaching the counter. "What's your name?"

"Alex Southerland," I replied.

"Tom," he responded. "Let me have a look at your I.D." He held his hand out and I gave him my badge. He set it on his computer keyboard and typed my information into the system. "Say's here your name's Denise A-"

"Yeah, the 'A' stands for Alexandria ... everybody calls me Alex though."

"How long?" he asked.

"Huh?" I gave him a puzzled look.

"No, not how long has everybody called you Alex. How long do you need the damn vehicle?"

"Oh shit, just today, sorry," I said, snickering. Tom had a really dry personality, but he was funny as hell to me.

"Who you work for Special Agent Denise Southerland?" he asked.

"Alex," I corrected. "I work for David Chandler now, I just started-"

He laughed loudly. "Zombie Squad!"

"Does this mean you're going to treat me nice now, Tom?"

"Hell no, I can't stand Chandler!" He said, chuckling. "Seriously, I'm just givin' you a hard time. I got a requisition pending for you from last week. Damn thing came down from way up high from the zombie man himself."

"Last week, huh? When did it come in, Friday?"

"Nope, last Monday," he replied.

"Really? But I didn't start until Friday ... that's odd."

"Yep, you need a car because you're pretty much on call at this point."

"You're kidding, right?"

"They didn't tell you?" he asked.

"No, they neglected to mention that, Tom."

"Figures," he replied. "Here, sign right down there on the X. This is an indefinite requisition for a SUV."

"But I drive my personal car-"

Tom shrugged. "Hey, do what you want. Probably be easier just to take the company car home though."

"Can I do that?" I asked, right before scribbling my most unreadable signature on the form.

"Well, if you don't, and you have a situation where you need to process a crime scene, Dave'll be standing there looking over your shoulder, and probably treat you like an idiot for not having the proper gear. Hey, it's your funeral. I just work here."

I giggled a little. "I appreciate the heads up."

"Here you go." He gave me the keys.

"You're too sweet," I said.

He laughed. "Yeah, right. Remember, the name's Tom. Just yell if you have any problems with your vehicle. You know where to go now, right?"

"Out in the garage?"

He nodded. "Yep, but I can get one of my guys to bring it down."

"No, no, that's okay, I'll find it. Thanks, Tom."

"My pleasure," he replied. "Come back and see us now."

I smiled. "Absolutely. Thanks again, buddy."

I took the elevator down and went out to the parking garage. I checked the number on the keys and located the space where the vehicle was parked. I could tell by the keyless entry remote the vehicle was a GM, but I couldn't believe my eyes when I finally saw it. My man Tom hooked a sister up with a brand spankin' new Denali. It was big, black and shiny. "Damn, I'm moving on up baby!" I unlocked the doors, climbed up in the driver seat and started the motor. The truck had everything, including the kitchen sink. I backed out of the space and pulled around to the front of the building to wait on Frank. I parked in the tow away zone and entered the school's address in the GPS to pass the time.

As soon as I got everything set, Frank was knocking on the passenger window. It took me a second to find the right button. Finally, I unlocked the doors, and Frank climbed in.

"Nice wheels," he said. "...Denali!" He strapped on his seatbelt and pointed straight ahead as if to say, *home James!* I shifted into drive and pulled off.

That truck was sweet as homemade yams, a goddamn wet dream. It literally cruised down the road on a cushion of air. Believe me when I say it was nothing like my Mustang, which rode a bit like an old 1980's skateboard. The Denali was hot.

Out on the freeway, I settled into the soft leather driver seat, which at the time was deliberately hugging my ass, teasing me, saying, *faster, drive faster, Alex!* Well, who on this earth can argue with the voice of reason? Certainly not me, so I stepped on the gas. I wanted to see what that big fucker could do. I'm proud to report it did not disappoint. The engine hummed as we blasted up to 90 MPH, my natural cruising speed.

"You looking to give me a stroke?" Frank asked, grabbing hold of his armrest.

"Just getting use to her, Frank."

"Well, hurry up and get it out of your system!" he exclaimed.

I laughed. "I just want to get there so we can get this over with, you know?"

"I understand you're excited," he said, "but take a deep breath and take it easy. We all want this guy badly, but you gotta go slow, be patient, and don't take anything or anyone too personal, not even David."

"Am I that transparent?"

"Look Alex, David's just being David. I've worked with him for years. He pushes your buttons and gets into your head to see how you respond. He wants to know how far you'll let him go without you pushing back, and how you measure up under pressure."

"Fine, but isn't that a little counterproductive?" I turned my blinker on and moved over into the fast lane to pass a few slowpokes.

"Well, that's what I thought at first," Frank said. "Thing is, this job requires a person with a unique personality. David tests your limits because he wants to put you right in the middle of the action. But, if you can't handle a few snide remarks, then you're just not cut out for this line of work. Go find you a nice school crosswalk and leave the rest of us real cops to the advanced stuff. Truth is, we've had transfer after transfer, but nobody sticks around. They just can't handle it. He hates rookies, and ain't too fond of women in the line of fire."

"But I thought he liked me, right?"

Frank laughed loudly. "David doesn't like anybody."

"So, why'd he pull me from Anti-Piracy?"

"All in due time," he replied. "All in due time."

It was right at 10 a.m. when we pulled up in front of the school. We checked the parking lot and looked around a bit outside before venturing in.

"So, what's the plan, Frank? How do we do this?"

"It's your world Alex, I'm just visiting. You found it, you work it. I'm here to see how you handle yourself and report back to David, no pressure." He smiled.

"Real funny, Frank."

By then, we'd made our way up to the front of the school.

"After you," Frank said, holding the door open.

The main office was on the right. We walked inside and up to the counter. There were a few ladies seated at desks on the other side. "May I help you?" asked one of the women.

I held up my badge. "FBI ma'am. I spoke with Ms. Hollis about an hour ago."

"One moment please." She picked up the phone and dialed an extension. "Mary, the FBI's here to see you." She hung up. "She'll be right out. Just have a seat over there."

"Thank you," I replied.

Frank and I sat down and waited. After about five minutes, the back door opened, and a middle-aged black woman walked out. She had medium length curly hair and was very professionally dressed. Her entire look was definitely on purpose. Not a single thread was out of place.

"Mary Hollis," she greeted.

I stood up and shook her hand, Frank followed suit.

"Hi, I'm Special Agent Southerland, and this is my partner Special Agent Morris. Thank you for seeing us on such short notice."

"No problem," Mary replied, "but I'm not sure exactly what I can help you with."

"Well, like I said over the phone, I need your help identifying a young woman that may be enrolled here." I pulled out a photo of my Jane Doe and handed it to her. "Do you recognize her?" I asked.

She held the picture up with one hand and covered her mouth with the other. "Oh my god", she mumbled.

"Is it-"

Mary nodded. "It looks like her, but it's hard to say." She seemed very disturbed by the photo. "I think it's Karla Charles. Her mother, Shannon Charles, teaches Biology."

"We'll need to talk to Mrs. Charles," I told her. "Is she available?"

She turned to the girl at the desk. "Barbara?"

"I'll page her," Barbara said. She snatched up the phone and dialed into the PA system. "Ms. Charles to the front desk ... Ms. Charles to the front desk, please."

Suddenly, I got anxious. I'd been preparing for this very moment since I first saw that girl lying dead on the floor, but the minute I realized it was actually going to happen, everything started falling apart. I knew what I had to do, but I had neglected to figure out in my mind how to tell this woman her baby girl was dead. I started hoping maybe it really wasn't Karla after all, but I knew better. Frank picked up on the fact I was getting jittery. As soon as Charles walked into the office, he took over. *Thank God.* I was so relieved, I just climbed into the back seat and let Frank do all the driving.

Charles walked right past us up to the counter. Looking at her, she could've been the same girl in that picture. They almost looked like twins. That convinced me even more it was her daughter.

"What's going on ladies?" she asked.

Mary pointed at us. "These officers need to speak with you," she said.

Frank immediately sprang into action. "How are you today Mrs. Charles?" he asked softly.

"Ms. Charles," she corrected. "What's this all about?"

Frank looked right and then left. Everyone, including me, was staring, waiting to see her reaction when he dropped the bad news, so he decided to opt for some privacy.

"Ms. Charles, I think it'd be better if we talked outside."

"I'm sorry, but I'm right in the middle of class. Can this wait?"

"No ma'am," Frank replied. "It's important we speak with you now ... this way please." Without giving her the opportunity to respond, he walked over and opened up the door.

Ms. Charles reluctantly followed Frank, and I trailed close behind. We walked out the office and through the front of the school. Outside, the three of us stood together under the awning in a brief moment of silence. The suspense was killing me, but so was Ms. Charles. She was a tiny thing, but she was fly as hell. She had long blond hair, perfectly arched eyebrows, an immaculate manicure, and more makeup than the law allowed. She wore a skirt that looked a little short from where I was standing, and she had on some very nice shoes that were definitely designer. Oh, and of course I'm no expert, but her boob job looked like a 90210 plastic surgeon signed his name around the nipples, I'm talking real Hollywood quality, no doubt. I'll give it to her, she was hot. I mean, who the hell wouldn't wanna take Biology from her? She probably drove all the boys in her class crazy. I don't know what high school teachers are supposed to look like nowadays, but I'm pretty sure Shannon Charles wasn't it.

"Can I see some ID?" Ms. Charles asked.

Frank and I both held up our badges. "I'm Special Agent Frank Morris with the FBI. This is my partner Special Agent Southerland."

Ms. Charles asked, "Am I in some kind of trouble, Agent Morris?"

"Frank, please, call me Frank," he told her. "When was the last time you saw your daughter?"

"Karla?" She frowns. "God, what on earth has she done now?" she asked, nervously.

"What makes you think she's done something Ms. Charles?"

"Shannon, just call me Shannon."

Frank smiled. "Shannon, has your daughter been in any kind of trouble before?"

"Nothing serious," she replied. "You know teenager stuff, but nothing bad at all."

"Do you have any idea where Karla might be now?"

"No ... umm ... we had an argument on the way home Friday. She jumped out the car and ran off. I thought she might have stayed with a friend. She's done that before, you know. I called, but she won't answer her phone ... is everything okay?"

"Ma'am, could you take a look at this photo please?" Frank nodded at me.

Before I could even get the picture out, Shannon fell to pieces. She'd been acting a little odd the entire time, but soon as I went for the photo that was all she wrote. It was like she already knew Karla was dead, and our being there was part of one big stage play she'd been rehearsing for days.

"Oh God," she cried, "please don't take my baby away from me like this!" She started waving her arms and trembling all over.

Frank put his arms around her and held her tight. She pressed her head against his chest and cried there folded up in his arms for nearly a minute.

"I understand how you feel," Frank said, rubbing her back gently, "but, right now we need to help her. I need for you to take a look at this photo. Can you do that for me?"

She stepped back and wiped her eyes. I didn't want to make any sudden moves, so I waited until she calmed down a little, and then I slowly held up the photo. She took one look and her knees buckled. She was out cold. Luckily, Frank was close enough to catch her before she hit the ground.

"Help me get her inside!" Frank yelled.

I grabbed her legs and we carried her back into the school.

"She collapsed!" Frank yelled as we busted through the office door. "We need the school nurse, hurry!"

"This way," said Barbara. She hustled over and opened the back door for us.

We carried Shannon down the hall into a small room back near the principal's office. We took her inside and put her down on the bed. Barbara got hold of the school nurse, who rushed in and immediately went to work, checking Shannon's pulse and other vital signs. Shannon seemed to be okay. The nurse told us to give her some time, so we waited patiently until she came to.

It took a long time for Shannon to regain consciousness, too long. We were just about ready to call an ambulance, but then she finally came to.

"Shannon are you okay?" asked the nurse, helping her sit up on the bed.

"Yes," Shannon whispered. She looked up at me. "May I see that picture again? Please, just once more?"

I handed it to her. She looked closely at the picture, and then put it directly over her heart. She started crying again. Frank sat down on the bed next to her and handed her a few tissues.

"Can y'all give us a minute?" Frank asked, looking back at the crowd that had gathered around.

"Come on everyone," said a woman in the back. "Shannon don't worry about your class, you know I always keep my eye on everything. Take care of your family. I'll deal with the rest. You get home as soon as you can. Come on everyone."

They filed out of the little dimly lit room, leaving us alone with Shannon, who out of nowhere smiled a rather odd smile. "That's our Principal, Cynthia Brock. She's...."

"She seems nice," Frank replied.

Shannon dropped her head and started crying again.

"I'm sorry," Frank said, shaking his head. "I really am."

"She's dead, isn't she? I can tell from the picture that she's dead. What happened? How did she die?"

I was about to tell her, but Frank cut me off.

"We're not sure yet," Frank said. "We're still investigating. Shannon, can you remember anything about last Friday? Anything you think may help us figure out what happened?"

"She wanted to spend the night at a friend's house, but I told her she couldn't. I found something in her drawer a few weeks ago, and she's been on punishment ever since. She's been so irritable lately ... sometimes, she just acts out for no reason at all. She thought I'd be lax with the punishment. Usually I am, but this time, I stuck to my guns ... I loved her so much."

Frank touched her hand. "Shannon, if you don't mind me asking ... what did you find in Karla's drawer?"

"Marijuana," answered Shannon.

"She ever come home high?"

"Yes," she said, nodding, "once, but it was a while back."

Frank asked, "Do you know who she might've stayed with Friday?"

"No, I don't really know any of her friends." She sniffled, staring at the photo teary-eyed. "Yeah, that's my Karla ... I know it's her, I can tell ... a mother can tell, you know? She's been gone since Friday ... I just knew something happened."

Frank gave her another tissue, which she used to blow her nose. "How did she die?" she asked. "What happened to her?"

Frank nodded at me, so I spoke up saying, "She had an asthma attack ma'am."

"What?" She looked surprised, like that was the last thing she expected to hear. She shook her head. "That doesn't make sense, are you sure?" she asked.

"Yes Ma'am, it was an asthma attack," Frank confirmed. "Unfortunately, she didn't have her medicine with her."

Shannon shook her head. "I don't understand she always has her inhaler. How could she have an attack like that?"

"Well, she wasn't able to get to the inhaler in time," Frank said.

"But, if she died of natural cause, then why are you here?"

"There were some circumstances surrounding her death that may tie this incident to another ongoing investigation," Frank said.

Shannon looked confused. "I don't understand-"

"Shannon, we're still investigating," said Frank, "but it's possible someone may have been with her when she died. We need your help determining what happened last Friday night between-"

"Can I see her?" she asked.

"Well, I don't think that's-"

"Please Frank, let me see her, let me say goodbye to her, please! It's all I have left ... please Frank, I'm begging you!"

Frank sighed. "Okay ... Okay." He nodded and asked, "Are you strong enough to walk now?"

"I believe so," said Shannon.

Frank stood up and helped her off the bed onto her feet. She still looked a little weak in the knees, so I hung close in case she lost her footing again.

"We'll take you down to the station," Frank said. "Fulton County police will need you to identify the body, and they'll take your statement. After that, we may have to talk to you again ... are you feeling up to all that?"

"Yes, I think so."

"Are you sure?" Frank asked. "We can do this later if you need some time."

"No, I'm fine," Shannon responded. "I need to see her."

"Okay ... well, do you need anything before we leave?" asked Frank.

"Just my purse," Shannon replied. "It's in my classroom in the desk drawer."

"Is it locked?" he asked.

"Yes." She took a keychain from her pocket and held up a key.

Frank leaned over to me. "Grab the purse and pull the car around," he said softly. "We'll meet you out front."

I nodded and took the keys. I left the nurse's room and sprinted down the hallway to look for Shannon's classroom. I turned the corner and heard the principal's voice a few doors down. I assumed she was in there talking to Shannon's class, so I followed the sound of her voice.

When I got to the classroom, the door was open, so I walked on in. I saw the principal leaning against the edge of the desk talking to the students. The entire class looked at me, but Principal Brock didn't look back in my direction at all. She didn't skip a beat. She just continued talking, so I ignored her and did my thing.

I wasn't exactly paying attention to what Principal Brock was saying, but I could've sworn I heard her say something really odd. Frank and Shannon were waiting on me though, so I just dismissed it and moved on.

I unlocked the drawer and grabbed Shannon's Coach bag. With all that was going on, I didn't have time to process everything, but I couldn't help but wonder about that bag. *A real Coach? How the hell does a school teacher afford a bag like that? Hell, I'd be afraid some lil badass hoodlum might stab me for it. I don't have much, but I know the difference between a $400 bag and some shit Tyrone sells you out the back of his rusty-ass '91 Chevy Blazer.* Shannon had the real thing. However, time was wasting, so again I ignored every impulse that something fishy was going on and got back on the clock.

I locked up the drawer and left the room. Then, I backtracked down the hall to the front of the school. Frank and Shannon were already getting close to the door, so I hustled to the truck and pulled right up front near the curb. I got out and opened the back-passenger side door. Frank and Shannon made their way down the walkway, and he helped her up into the truck.

"Put your seatbelt on," Frank said.

Shannon complied.

Frank closed her door. Then, he climbed into the front passenger seat. "Let's go," he said softly.

I put the truck in gear, and then circled around the lot and drove out through the back.

Frank continued talking to Shannon on the way to the police station. He spoke in a very kind, understanding tone. No matter what he said, he was professional and courteous. Frank was no doubt a pro. I kept quiet as I drove, paying close attention to the master, as he did his cop thing. Watching him work his magic, I knew I was way out of my depth, but I was picking up a lot in terms of how to deal with difficult situations on the job. *Lord knows I can use some help in that arena.*

It took about 30 minutes to make our way to the police station. Once we arrived, we all went inside and met the two investigators, who'd just been assigned Karla's case. Homicide Detectives Walsh and Goodman introduced themselves, gave their condolences, and were kind enough to take us down to Karla Charles' body. Detective Walsh told us to take all the time we needed, but said they needed to talk to Shannon in order to rule her out as a suspect. Then, they courteously waited outside to give us some privacy.

Being in that room with Shannon, watching everything unfold was impossible to say the least. Can you imagine having to identify the remains of your only child? Just watching it was seriously disturbing. I lack the words to express the emotional horror and stress I experienced. Karla wasn't even my daughter. Hell, I don't even have kids, but I still felt pain inside.

I watched Shannon scream and cry as if she was being torn apart, piece-by-piece, and then put back together, only for it to start all over again. She stood there, sobbing with her hands and face pressed against the glass, staring at the dead body of her little girl. I felt sad for both her and Karla.

After a while, Walsh and Goodman came back in for Shannon, but she didn't want to move away from that window, and I knew exactly how she felt. Frank and I lent a hand and, eventually, were able to get her to calm down a little. At that point, they took her upstairs to an interview room.

Frank managed to disappear while Walsh and Goodman were in the interview room talking to Shannon. I'm not sure where the hell he went, but I dared not leave. I was overwhelmed with curiosity. Damn that *innocent until proven guilty* shit. My gut said Shannon was holding out on us, and I wanted to know what it was she was hiding. I thought about going into the observation room, but I didn't want to step on anybody's toes, so I just hung back, grabbed some coffee and waited.

Walsh and Goodman talked to Shannon for more than two hours. I waited impatiently, pacing back and forth in the hallway. Finally, Frank showed back up with a folder stuck under his arm. His timing was impeccable. He got back right before the detectives finished up with Shannon. I wasn't sure what he was up to, but he seemed to be working some kind of plan, so I just kicked back and watched the show.

The detectives came out of the room together and closed the door. Shannon was still inside. I thought they were just going to take her statement, but I don't think it takes two hours to do that. When they finally got out of there, they both were rubbing their heads, and they had the exact same confused look on their face.

"Okay ... Walsh, Goodman ... what's the deal?" Frank asked.

Walsh shook his head. "Man, we got nothing."

Frank looked at them both, and then checked his watch. "Nothing? You got nothing at all? All that time you were in there? Hell, you guys had her for over two hours! Okay look, talk to me, what's going on?"

I was kind of surprised but impressed at the same time. Frank's demeanor was unexpected to say the least. Suddenly, he had this commanding presence and was talking like he was their superior. The thing is, they didn't give him any shit about it either. They showed nothing but respect for Frank.

"We took her statement ... I suspected she wouldn't be able to give us anything useful, but..."

"But, what Walsh?"

He smiled a sheepish grin and shook his head. "Nothing."

Frank chuckled. "What is this, kindergarten cop? Come on, man!"

Goodman finally spoke up. "There's something odd going on with this lady. I've seen a lot of mothers lose a child, but everything ain't adding up with this one."

"Walsh?" Frank asked.

He shook his head. "Yeah, it's not so much what she said, but how she said it, you know? It's how she's responding to all of this that's throwin' me for a loop. Listen, it's officially your case ... you want her?"

"You're officially off the hook gents," Frank replied, smiling big. "Here's my card ... send me a copy of your report, capeesh?"

"No problem," said Walsh. "If it's all the same with you, we're going to listen in on the other side. You need anything else, just holler."

"Thanks, I'll let you know." Frank turned to me and said, "Go on in and keep her quiet. I'll be back in a second." Then, he took off again.

I reluctantly opened the door and drug myself into the little interview room. Shannon didn't look up at me. In fact, she didn't move at all, she seemed to be stuck in a trance. Honestly, I was glad she wasn't talking because I had no clue where to start. I didn't know the right thing to say, but she looked so sad. I had to say something. Talking to her really wasn't a big deal, but doing it without crying? That was a whole nother issue.

"Shannon, can I get you anything," I asked, "coffee maybe?"

"No, thank you," she replied.

"Please bear with us we're going to get started in just a moment."

"I don't understand," said Shannon. "Why would anyone do this? Why'd they take her from me?"

That was a really good question, one I didn't have an answer for, but I had a few whoppers of my own. For example, I don't have the foggiest idea why, in situations like this, I just can't shut my fucking mouth. Why is that? Here's another—why the fuck do I even care? It's just a job, right? I know I should've stuck with offering refreshments, but as always, I can't just leave well enough alone. I had to go opening my big mouth.

"Shannon, I know this is hard on you, but we need your help."

"The officers said she was murdered," Shannon said, "but you told me she had an asthma attack, so which is it?"

"Yes." I nodded, "cause of death was an asthma attack. We're sure of it."

She started to get angry. "I don't understand what's going on around here! I wanna know the truth, and goddammit I wanna know right now!"

Out of nowhere, Frank busts through the door. He walks right up to Shannon and starts slamming gruesome crime scene photos down on the table in front of her one-by-one.

"Oh God, why are you doing this to me?" she cried, shaking her head violently.

Frank snatched back the chair beside her and plopped down in it. "Look, you're the one who's gonna start telling the truth around here, and you're gonna do it right now! Only child? Give me a break, what kind of mother doesn't know where her child is for three or four days?"

"How dare you!" she exclaimed, "I loved her ... you just don't understand, I-"

"Hey, don't give me that bullshit lady!" Frank interrupted. "Did you kill her? DID YOU KILL KARLA?"

"I want my lawyer!" Shannon yelled.

Frank slammed his fist down on the table and pointed his finger in her face. "FUCK A LAWYER, DAMMIT, DID YOU KILL HER?"

"NO! I loved her with all my heart!"

"That's right you 'loved' her, past tense. You already knew she was dead when we showed up today, didn't you? That's why you're sitting here not cooperating with my detectives. You spent the last two hours jerkin' their chain. Meanwhile your daughter is rotting down in a cold, dark basement! Look at the photos! Look at 'em!" Frank picked the worst in the bunch, the shot of Karla's many stab wounds, and pushed it right in front of her face. "Look at it, Shannon!" he yelled. "Look at what he did to your little girl!"

She closed her eyes and dropped her head, whimpering, "No, no, no!"

"Look at it goddammit! You tell me if she looked like she was loved. Somebody scared your baby to death and then carved her up like a turkey! You say you loved her, prove it … enough of this shit, you're gonna help us, and you're gonna help right now!"

Shannon smashed her face down onto the table, smearing her teardrops all over the photographs.

I just stood there with my head cocked to the side and my mouth open. I was taken aback because Frank was off the chain, I mean that man was fierce. A couple of hours ago, you would've mistaken him for a choirboy, but suddenly, he's a force to be reckoned with. One minute he's your friendly neighborhood Agent, next thing he's kickin' soccer moms in the spleen. It was most impressive.

Frank took a break from yelling, and the three of us sat in silence for the next few minutes. I wondered what was going through Shannon's mind. She didn't say a word the entire time. She just sat there with her face pressed against that picture, a picture of a bloody, mutilated body that used to be her little girl.

To be honest, I started feeling sorry for Shannon. Maybe Frank was being too hard on her. After all, she'd just lost her daughter. Like I say, I could tell she's holding back, but whatever it was, it couldn't be that bad, unless she actually had something to do with Karla's death.

Shannon seemed so sweet. I had trouble imagining her swatting a fly. However, Frank seemed to know something I didn't, and he wasn't playing around with her at all. I could tell by the look on his face he was going somewhere with all of it, but where? No way in hell Shannon killed Karla. We all just watched her fall to pieces over and over again, right? Nobody's that good an actor.

We sat and watched her cry for a few more minutes. Then finally, Frank broke his silence.

"Shannon, Karla will never rest until we find the man who did this. It's a game to him, and so far, he's winning. This maniac's killed before, and he's not gonna stop unless we find him right now. I know you're hurting, I know how it feels, but now is not the time to be weak … now's the time to be stronger than ever. Lives are at stake here, and more than just Karla's."

Shannon looked up at him. I thought she was going to say something, but she held back again.

"Look, my detectives know something's not right," said Frank. "I know something's not right, and guess what, Shannon, so do you. I think you want to tell me something, but maybe you're afraid what might happen. We can protect you-"

Soon as he said that, Shannon went berserk. She cried out loudly, pulling at her hair and banging her elbows and fists on the table. We couldn't understand anything she was saying, like she was speaking in tongues. She started trembling all over, and her hands were shaking badly. Frank touched her arm and she froze. She sat up straight in her chair in complete stillness as if she'd just been possessed by a ghost.

"It's hard you know," she said, sniffling. "It's hard giving them everything they need. They need so much."

"I know," Frank responded, being careful not to push her too far. "Trust me I know, I got three daughters myself. Takes a lot to take care of them."

Shannon confessed, "I didn't want her to get hurt."

"I understand," said Frank, "but we need to know what happened. I need you to tell me something Shannon ... I can't help you if you don't talk to me."

"I taught for fifteen years—FIFTEEN YEARS—but it was never enough. I could never make enough money to take care of us. I tried so hard when her father left, but I just couldn't do it on a teacher's salary. I couldn't find a way to make it all work. I've had two jobs before. I tried to budget and sell stuff, but ... she just needed so much, you know?"

"Tell me what happened to Karla, Shannon," said Frank.

"I just did it a few times at first," she explained.

Frank raised an eyebrow. "Did what?" he asked.

"We were gonna get kicked out of our home," Shannon said, softly. "I didn't want to lose my daughter. They would've taken her away from me. I swear I didn't plan on doing it again, I swear."

"Shannon, I don't follow you," said Frank.

I was paying attention and taking notes, but I didn't follow her crazy ass either.

"I've been working as an escort for the past five years," she confessed.

Holy shit! I didn't see that one coming! I was trippin', but Frank seemed hardly astonished.

Frank gave Shannon a stern look. "An escort?"

"Yes," she answered.

"Was there any sex involved?" Frank asked.

"...Yes."

"Go on," Frank told her.

"I tried to keep her away from it, but I'm not exactly 18 anymore. I'm 42 years old, and a lot of the newer clients they ... well, they wanted someone...." She swallowed hard and then wiped her tears. She took a deep breath, looked up at Frank and smiled. "They didn't want me. They wanted someone younger."

Frank said, "So, you made your daughter join the family business?"

"That's not fair!" she exclaimed.

"Life's not fair!" Frank got cranked up again. "Look lady, you pimped your little girl out, and now she's dead. What'd you expect me to say?"

"No ... no, I didn't!" she yelled, shaking her head. "She wanted to ... she wanted to help me," she stuttered, "and ... I, I didn't want her to, but-"

"But you let her do it anyway, right?" Frank interrupted.

She sighed, heavily. "Yes."

Frank tapped the table with his right hand. "Tell me what happened."

"Nothing happened. I just-"

"BULLSHIT!" Frank shouted, "tell me about the little boys!"

Shannon's jaw dropped and she nearly turned green. "I didn't know, I swear!" she said. "I didn't know anyone was taping me-"

"You got greedy, didn't you?"

Shannon shook her head. "No, I swear, I only wanted-"

"GET OUTTA HERE!" exclaimed Frank. "YOU GOT GREEDY! It wasn't enough that you were letting filthy old men molest your little girl, you had to embarrass her by screwing her classmates for money too. And, when she found out about it you shut her up permanently didn't you?"

"No!" she cried, "we had a fight. I wanted her to stop, but she didn't want to. She showed me the pictures, threw them all over the kitchen table. Said if I made her stop, she would tell. I didn't know she was taping me with them. I never meant to hurt her ... I loved her, I just, I just didn't know what else to do, I-"

"YOU COULD'VE GOTTEN HELP!" yelled Frank at the top of his lungs. "You didn't have to turn Karla into a whore! What on earth were you thinking? That was your daughter! That was your only little girl! What the hell were you thinking?"

"I don't know," she confessed. "I wasn't thinking. Since her dad left, it's like we've done everything together. We had to make the decisions together, you know? I tried to hide it from her for so long, but when she found out what I was doing, she didn't want me to do it alone. She was so sweet."

"Now, she's dead!" Frank wasn't giving her a break at all. "You practically killed her!"

"You just don't understand," she cried.

"Oh yeah, I understand!" Frank exclaimed. "I understand people just like you, Shannon. You blame the whole world for your bad luck when it's you, who made the decision to put the people you love in harm's way. You knew what you were doing. You're sick! You made your daughter do it, so you wouldn't feel bad about yourself! You didn't want to be the only one!"

"She's all I had," she mumbled. "I don't have anything left."

"You might as well have killed your little girl yourself!" Frank screamed. "You didn't beat her, you didn't stab her, you didn't cut her up like that, but if you hadn't exposed her to this sick, twisted life, she would've been home and not out in danger—not laid up, tied to a cross, cold, alone and murdered. You got one last chance to do right by Karla now 'cause you sure as hell didn't protect her while she was alive. Now, I need some information ... you gonna give me what I need, or what?"

She pulled her hair back out of her face. "I don't know what to do."

"Well, you got options," said Frank. "You asked for a lawyer, so I'm obligated. I can call one in here right now, and you can take your chances. We'll charge you with negligent homicide and statutory rape. You'll do time, 20 to 25. On the other hand, you play ball with us, and I'll put in a word with the D.A. You still go down for the child molestation, but you'll be out in 3 to 5."

She sat still in complete silence. All of a sudden, she was just dead to the world.

Frank slammed both his hands down on the table, and she sprung to attention. "Focus Shannon!" he yelled. "What's it gonna be?"

"Alright." She nodded. "Alright ... yes ... I'll do it ... I'll do whatever you need me to!"

Frank reached across and grabbed a notepad from the other side of the table. He slid it and a pen down to Shannon. "I need your client list," he said, "I want the whole thing, all the names of the kids you've been with at school and every sick bastard that put his hands on Karla."

Shannon didn't say a word. She picked the pen up and began to spill her sins all over the page like an evildoer on judgment day. As I watched her write the list, all I could think about was what she said. How she wasn't able to make it just working a job. How she didn't see any other way out. Talk about your decisions changing you from the inside out. Shannon actually seemed to be a good person, all things considered. I could only imagine just how much she had to change in order to go off and do something like this. Degrading or not, I mean regardless of how you feel about prostitution, anybody could see Shannon had been running on empty long before Karla was murdered.

I think back to when I wandered off the straight and narrow. It's a trip because the first time you do something you know is wrong, it's like downing a bottle of poison. You feel dirty and sick afterwards; however, it gets a helluva lot easier with each new dose. Next thing you know, you're doing all kinds of things you know you shouldn't, but it's too late to turn back.

Shannon went from basic survival to maximum greed all in an instant. And, for what? At the end of the day, her daughter's dead, she's got a prison sentence and maybe even the promise of eternal damnation. I'm not a Bible scholar, but I'm pretty sure there's some commandment, or at least a parable, about not pimpin' your own damn daughter.

Honestly, I'm still impressed with Frank's performance. He yelled quite a bit, but he always maintained control of the situation. He was cool as an iceberg all day long. I knew something was up when he sent me in that room by myself. After he busted through the door, the drama was on, and I could barely keep still in my seat. Even as we sat there, watching Shannon write name after name, I was still trippin'. How'd Frank know? I mean, just who the hell told him? And, how'd he put it all together so fast?

I had no idea we'd make this much progress so quickly. I so badly wanted to say, *gotcha bitch!* I felt like jumping up on the table and screaming it at the top of my lungs. I was about to bust. Frank was very observant, always paying attention to everything and everyone. He picked up on my restlessness and got me the hell out of there fast.

"Shannon, you keep writing," said Frank, "we'll be back in a few."

I followed Frank out into the hallway around the corner into the adjacent observation room. Walsh and Goodman had been watching on the other side of the see-through mirror. They'd been taking notes the whole time, and a camera positioned near the window had recorded everything. It was still running.

"Agent Morris, how'd you know?" asked Detective Walsh.

"Call me Frank. I got suspicious when she first said she loved Karla. I know folks, who lost a child ten years ago still talk about them in the present. Have birthday parties and everything. You never stop loving your kids, and you don't talk about them in past tense especially if you think they're still alive." Frank pulled out his PDA. "It was more than just that though. Remember, she told us they had an argument on the way home Friday. She made it sound like they were both at school, but the lady in the office said Karla was out, remember?"

"Yeah, she sure did," I replied.

"My gut told me something was wrong," said Frank. "I couldn't put my finger on it, but I followed my instincts. While you two were in with Shannon, I had Karen run over to the school and search Karla's locker. She found a memory card with this on it." Frank held up his PDA. It was a picture of Shannon having sex with two young boys. "I knew we had her on this, but I had no idea about the daughter." Frank dropped his head a little and squeezed the bridge of his nose. "I'm gonna need weeks of therapy."

"You got that fuckin' right," said Goodman. "I never seen anything like this before in my life."

"So, what do we have here guys, a mother daughter tag team?" I asked. "Two prostitutes, no pimp? No protection or management...? Does that make sense?"

They started scratching their heads and making funny faces at me.

"What, you think they had help?" Frank asked.

"Let me see that picture again...."

Frank gave me his PDA.

I pointed at the photo and smiled. "Look, this picture was taken in the nurse's station at the school," I said.

Frank squinted a little. "How can you tell that?"

"Photographic memory," I replied.

Frank asked, "Okay, so what?"

I blew my hair out of my face. "So, they're getting' freak-nasty in the nurse's station, and you telling me nobody knew? Nobody ever walked in on them, ever?"

Frank almost laughed. "Freak-nasty? Jesus Christ, Alex! Thug passion, freak nasty ... the hell you get this stuff from?"

"Sorry boss," I said smiling big. "I'm just saying somebody had to know what was going on. Maybe someone let them operate out of the school...?" I threw my hands up, "Okay, why are you guys looking at me like that?"

"You may actually be on to something," said Walsh.

"Maybe," Frank said, "but, who? One of the women in the office? A lady pimp? Come on now."

I thought for a second. "Why can't it be a woman? What about the principal?"

"Alex, what the-"

"But Frank, I think I-"

"Before you even go there, why would she let us search the girl's locker without a warrant?" asked Frank.

"Wait, she let us do the search without a warrant?" I asked.

Frank nodded, "Yep."

"It's a public school, right?"

"Fourth Amendment ... kids have reasonable expectations for privacy too. Public school or not, we still need a warrant."

"Hmm ... well, maybe she knew nothing was in there ... or at least nothing that would incriminate her. Maybe she took the pictures, shit I don't know. Look, all I'm saying is ... wait, hold on ... yeah, while I was getting Shannon's purse, I heard the principal say Shannon wouldn't be coming back as in never."

"She said that?" asked Goodman.

"Yeah, I'm telling you she-"

"Hey, let's keep the conspiracy theories to a minimum," Frank interrupted. "Unless you guys are gonna look into the principal, we need to stay focused on the johns."

"Hey man, no disrespect, Frank," said Walsh, "but a girl's dead here. If we seriously think there might be something shady going on with the principal, we have to check it out."

"Okay, here's the deal guys," said Frank, "FBI's not gonna charge Shannon. It's a local crime, so the ball's in your court. We need that client list though, and we might have to talk to some of the boys. We can do our thing without bumping into your guys, but I need to know if you get anywhere with the principal situation. Can you do that without a bunch of red tape?"

"I can probably work with you," Walsh replied. "This maniac you're chasing, how's the investigation really going?"

"At this point, it's fragile, but we suspect he'll kill again soon. We can't let that happen."

Walsh scratched his chin and thought for a moment. Then, he said, "If I put this through to my captain, we'll be stuck in paper and politics for the next month. No offense, but the Bureau moves slow on everything."

"None taken," Frank replied.

"I'll personally keep you posted on our progress just make sure you get that son-of-a-bitch."

"Alright, let's do it," said Frank. "Give him your card, Alex."

I gave both detectives a card, and we all shook hands. Then, Frank, Walsh, and Goodman went back into the interview room. I stayed behind and watched from the other side of the glass. By the time they got back in there, Shannon had finished making her list.

Frank picked up the pad. "This it?"

"Yes," she responded, softly.

In the brief amount of time Frank and I were talking to Walsh and Goodman, she'd written more than three pages of names.

"You remember Detectives Walsh and Goodman?"

"Yes, Frank."

"I've assured them you'll cooperate fully with their investigation. You're gonna have to sign a confession."

"I understand."

"Shannon ... may I give you a piece of advice?"

"Yes."

"I know you're a smart lady," said Frank, "and maybe, just maybe, you and your daughter were alone on this thing. But, if you had help from anybody, and I mean anybody, even if you're afraid, you need to tell these guys. They're the only ones who can help you now, understand?"

Shannon nodded.

Frank walked over and opened the door to leave. He had her list of names with him.

"Frank!" yelled Shannon.

He stopped but didn't turn around.

"Please find the man, who did this to my daughter," she said.

Frank didn't respond. He walked on out the room and closed the door.

When Frank came back into the observation room, we both just stood there, watching and listening to Shannon spill the beans. At that point, Walsh and Goodman's job was apple pie. All they had to do was just listen to Shannon ramble and give her an occasional prod. She sat at that table, covered in shame from head to toe, giving up the juicy details of her evil deeds.

Shannon's list seemed to be the missing piece of the puzzle. I couldn't help but repeat, *gotcha bitch*, over and over again in my mind. If I could've gone on the radio or TV to announce it, I sure as hell would've. Can you imagine that? Me in a news conference yelling, *gotcha bitch*, and laughing? I think cops should be allowed to gloat in public, but hey, what do I know. I was confident we had what we needed to move forward. Even Frank thought we had enough to pick up a good trail. There was no point hanging around. Frank didn't want to interrupt the flow of Walsh and Goodman's chat with Shannon, so he left a copy of her list with their lieutenant, and we got ready to leave the station.

"You alright?" asked Frank.

"Is it always like this?"

"Hell no," Frank replied, shaking his head. "I'm with Goodman. I've never seen anything like this before."

"Guess you weren't kidding about that therapy, huh?" I asked.

"Don't get me started ... look Alex, what do we have here?"

"A list of possible suspects?"

"Yeah, maybe," Frank responded. "Honestly, I don't know ... come on."

"Wait, we're not gonna search her home? I thought we-"

He shook his head. "I doubt we'll get anything, but don't worry, Walsh is on the case."

"You trust him?"

"Not really," he replied. "I don't know the guy, but Pam trusts him. Says he's a standup guy, so we'll give him some room to work, and see if he can pull a rabbit out of his hat."

I'm not sure what was sicker, the fact that Shannon put her daughter out on the corner or the fact that part of me was having trouble seeing how what she did was so wrong. The more I thought about it, the worse I felt about myself. It's crazy, I'd only been on the job a couple days, and I was already doing a morality check, sizing myself up. The messed-up thing was, no matter how I looked at it, I keep coming back to the same conclusion—I'm a bad person. While I tried to untangle myself, Frank made a call back to the office.

"Hey Boss," said Frank, with his phone pressed against his ear. "...Yeah, we just got lucky man ... I don't know, but we're on the way back now. Get Karen and Dimitri ready, we need to cross-reference a list of names with the players we've identified ... alright, we'll see you in a few." Frank hung up the phone.

"What players?" I asked.

"Classified," Frank retorted.

"Okay, you know what, I'm just gonna go get the damn car!" I exclaimed.

Frank chuckled softly. "Come on Alex let's get outta here."

Small talk aside, Frank was pretty distant on the way out. I don't blame him though. I think we both left a piece of ourselves back in that interview room.

We slowly made our way to the front of the police station. Frank stopped at the front desk to talk to one of the officers, but I didn't wait for him. I kept moving towards the two big glass doors in the front of the building.

I walked outside and pushed my way through a crowd of cops standing around shootin' the shit. I spoke to a couple of them. They were very friendly, cracking jokes and laughing. In fact, fighting crime seemed to be the last thing on their minds.

I walked to the parking lot, got in the truck and cranked up. After a few minutes, Frank came out and got in. Then, we drove back to the office.

When we stepped back through the Z-Squad doors, David and Karen were standing there waiting on us.

"You know, I think you guys are making this whole thing up," said David.

"It was some freaky shit, Boss," Frank said, shaking his head. "World's first mother-daughter, teacher-student prostitution, slash rape ring."

David and Karen both looked at me.

145

"Don't look at me," I said, "I'm just the rookie in training, remember?"

"Let me get this straight," Karen said, "you two get a bug up your ass to go out and hit a bunch of schools, and it just so happens you luck up and uncover all this?"

"Something like that," Frank replied.

"Well, I hope it wasn't a big fuckin' waste of time people," David said.

"Where's Dimitri?" asked Frank.

"He's already plugged in," Karen replied.

I still didn't know what the hell they were talking about. "Plugged into what?" I asked.

Karen almost answered, "The internet, we actually-"

David all but punched her in the arm. "That's-"

"Let me guess," I interrupted, "classified, right?"

"I like her," David chuckled. He pointed to the back of the room. "Go, go, go!"

Frank gave Shannon's list to Karen.

"If you'll excuse me," said Karen. She ran back to the mysterious computer room. The door had a security keypad located on the right side. I watched as she punched in a four-digit access code. Three... five... two... nine. Then, she pressed the enter key, the door unlocked, and she went inside.

I turned my attention back to David and Frank, who were talking about me as if I wasn't standing right there in front of them.

"How'd she do out there?" asked David.

"Not bad for a greenhorn on the first day," Frank replied.

I spoke up. "Second day."

David laughed and teased saying, "You mean you actually count Friday when you damn near threw up all over my crime scene?"

I rolled my eyes. "That was a lot to spring on a girl all at once, you know?"

I laughed a little, but Frank laughed a whole lot.

"Don't worry," Frank said, "you're doing good Alex. Much better than the last couple of guys."

"Could've fooled me!" exclaimed David. "Frank, you stick to sniffing up child molesters' crotches and let me handle the team development, got it?"

"Whatever you say, boss," Frank replied.

David was so rude and condescending—no, he was a fuckin' asshole. And, what the fuck does that even mean, sniffing somebody's crotch? *What an idiot.*

"By the way, good work today young man," David said, squeezing Frank's shoulder.

I just listened to his trifflin' ass.

"You catch this bastard and you got that vacation you been talking about, capeesh?"

"Thanks, boss." Frank smiled.

At that point, Karen was back out of the room. She walked up and gave the list back to Frank.

"That was fast," Frank said.

"Sorry, nothing."

"Guess we gotta do this the old fashion way." Frank sighed. "Look, I think I've had all I can stand for one day. I'm going home to the wife. Boss, we'll turn up the heat tomorrow and get all this stuff taken care of. We should have something concrete by the end of the week. Alex, why don't you take off and we'll pick this up in the morning."

"Okay, see you guys tomorrow."

"Later, Alex," said Karen.

"Bye, Karen. Good night David," I said, soft and sweet with a big Cheshire Cat grin.

"I like this kid," David said. He turned to Karen, "Ain't she cute as a button?"

Karen giggled. "Oh, stop it," she said, slapping the back of his hand as if to say, *behave!*

I rolled my eyes at David and left the office. I got downstairs and suddenly, I found myself smack-dab in the middle of a moral dilemma. I had a tough decision to make—drive my old Mustang or take the brand spanking new Denali home. I was completely torn and didn't know what to do. It's amazing how quickly you change your mind about something when the next best thing comes along, kinda like relationships. Me and my Stang had years of nothing but good times, so she deserved respect. Then again, maybe she deserves a break more.

I walked up to her from behind and put my hand on her tail. "Sorry babe, but you'll be okay, I promise. Hell, you're in an FBI parking garage. Believe me when I say there's no safer place on the planet, alright?"

Satisfied I'd explained the situation thoroughly, I climbed up in the Denali and drove off without looking back.

As soon as I got home, I jumped straight into the shower. After all I'd seen and heard that day, I felt dirtier than a pig in mud. I washed and scrubbed every inch of my body and then stood under the blazing hot water for as long as I could stand the heat. I stood there in the shower, leaned against the tile wall, thinking about Karla Charles and her troubled, soon-to-be incarcerated mother. I wondered if they were any different from me and my mother, and honestly, I still don't have the answer.

I'm sure Shannon will do some hard time, but I don't buy the idea of Karla being completely innocent. I don't mean to speak ill of the dead, but come on, do you really think Karla resisted much with all the money, popularity, and God knows what else on the table? Maybe she was actually committed to her mother. Maybe she was a naïve little kid who didn't know any better. I'm not sure. I just find it hard to believe she was blindly following orders. If memory serves me, and it usually does, my mother was always on some shit, but whatever she wanted, good or bad, if I didn't want to do it, or I thought it was wrong, it didn't get done. Even when the consequences of my decision involved a two-hour-long ass whooping, it was still my decision to make, and I made it; not my mother. Despite the fact I can't bring myself to give Karla a free pass, what happened to her was beyond anything she ever deserved, and I was starting to get pissed.

By now, I imagine you have an idea of how I feel about sex, hookin' and everything in between, right? Basically, I'm proud to say I'm a pretty free spirit, but even with all my vices, there's one thing that sends me ova the edge. When people fuck with kids, I lose it. No matter the situation, that shit's uncalled for. I tell you what I would do with a mothafucka that- "Hey, wait ... was that the door?" I turned the shower off and grabbed a towel. Then, I snuck into the hallway and peeked around the corner. How about that, it's Bill coming home early yet again.

I walked softly into the living room and stood by the sofa. That negro didn't even realize I was standing there watching his trifflin' ass.

"Oh, most definitely," he whispered, grinning and damn near tongue kissing his cell phone. "You know it ... uh, huh, I'mo be there I wouldn't miss it for the-"

"Be where Bill?"

He looked up at me and immediately wiped that stupid shit-eating grin off his face. He was straight busted.

"Oh, uh, hey let me call you back later man." He hung up the phone. "Hey babe," he said, walking over with his arms wide.

I pushed my hand out and stopped him. "I'm wet," I said.

Bill gave up without a fight. He walked over and put his bag down near the table. "I didn't know you were here," he said.

"Really...?" I replied.

I watched him fumble around like a blithering idiot, trying to compose himself. Men are pitiful, or maybe Bill was just pitiful. I knew he was stickin' his dick in some fat moocow. Hell, if men don't get it at home, they're getting it somewhere. I just wanted him to be a real man and stop pussyfooting' around. *Shit just tell a bitch wassup!* I was about to snap, but then I remembered my promise to straighten up my act.

"Baby, you want me to fix you something?" I asked with a smile.

"What?" He seemed surprised.

"Well, you just got home baby ... I'm sure you're hungry, right?"

He ran up to me with a spring in his step and kissed me right on the lips. "Fuck that ... I'mo fix you something," he mumbled as he tongue-kissed me.

"Oh, fo' real?" I giggled, pushing away.

"Yep, anything you want for dinner, baby."

I reached up with both hands and ran my fingers through my wet hair, shaking my booty just enough for my towel to loosen up. After a few clever gyrations, it dropped to the floor, exposing every inch of me from head to toe. Bill gazed at my glistening wet body and immediately started breathing hard. I moved in close, reaching my arms around and locking my fingers behind his neck. I wanted him out of his clothes, so I figured I'd get them all wet, leaving him no choice. I pressed my dripping body against him. Bill couldn't resist my advances this time. I had him trapped in my little love net.

"I love you," he said between kisses.

"Bill, you know what I want for dinner?"

"What baby?"

"I want something, thick juicy and hard in my mouth." I licked my lips, and asked "You think you can make that happen for mamma?"

Bill squeezed my booty with certain authority. "That's a tall order," he whispered, "but, I think I might be the man for the job."

I love how Bill makes me feel, especially the way he talks to me. It's not like with Malik and all those other fools. Bill's tone of voice makes me feel like a real woman, like he truly loves me. And, to think I'd been actin' like a horse's ass for weeks, months even. Bill had been putting up with my shit for so long, but he was still there with me, still by my side. I knew he was mad. Hell, I'd said and done some pretty bad things, but that day, I decided to make it all up to him.

My man had been working hard, and I could tell he was frustrated, so I was going to give him something real nice to relax his nerves. I grabbed his shirt and pulled him closer into me. He graciously accepted my invitation and shoved me back against the wall.

"Bill...."

"Yes baby?" He kissed my neck and squeezed my tits.

I whispered, "I need you inside me right now."

His eyes lit up like a kid's on Christmas morning. He ripped off his shirt, and I spun us around, pushing with all my might until his back hit the wall.

I dropped to my knees and unbuckled his belt. "I want it," I moaned, pulling his pants down and massaging him through his boxers. Then, I pulled them down too, exposing his swollen member. I moved in close and looked up, staring into his eyes as I circled the head of his rock-hard cock with my tongue. It was very nice, hard, and straight. With my right hand, I grabbed around his balls and pulled him deep into my throat.

"Fuck!" Bill growled, grabbing my hair and pushing himself balls-deep into my hot, wet mouth. He all but suffocated me, and I loved every minute of it.

I swallowed him whole, and then pulled it back out of my mouth and spit along the top. I squeezed and stroked it hard, rubbing my spit in along the shaft with the palms of my hands. I put it back in my mouth and did everything I knew to make him cum. I felt like a porno star down there on my knees, head bobbing back and forth, with every inch of his cock disappearing into my mouth and then reappearing. It was delicious.

I didn't realize how much I missed Bill—the way he felt, how he smelled, and how he tasted. Pleasuring him like that reminded me just how much I'll always need him.

Bill started thrusting his hips, hitting the back of my throat hard as I came forward. He was turning me on so bad. I pushed his swollen member to the side and took his balls in my mouth, one-by-one, and then both at the same time. I licked and sucked, smacking my lips all around on his heavy sack while I jerked him off like crazy. I was trying to squeeze the love juice right out of him. I gently tugged at his balls with my teeth, all the while spitting and moaning. He shivered, and then pushed my head away, which meant he almost came. That was the last thing I wanted. I wasn't ready for that. I needed to feel him inside me first.

"Not yet baby," I teased, tightening my grip on his balls.

"Come on." He pulled me up off the floor, and I followed him back to the bedroom.

As soon as I stepped foot into the room, Bill flung me onto the bed and buried his face between my legs.

"Oh fuck!" I moaned. "Yes! Right there, baby, just like that, Bill!" He circled and teased my swollen clit. "Fuck, oh my God, I'm about to cum." You could hear my juices squirting onto his busy little tongue. "Fuck me right now baby!" I yelled.

Bill didn't hesitate. It was like he'd been waiting in line 24 hours to get some. I hiked my ass up for easy access and spread the entrance of my pussy wide to receive his rock-hard cock. Bill shoved it in and went right to work, moving his hips 'round and 'round. He's not a very big man, but his body's tight, nice and muscular, and his thighs are big like tree trunks. I've been with a lot of men, but even though we look kind of mismatched at first glance, his body fits mine like a hand in a glove. That or we been together so long, it just feels natural. He was my first love, and when we make love, we fill the room with the perfect mix of lust, love, and passion.

Bill pushed me further back towards the middle of the bed, lifting my legs up high over my head to remind me who's boss. "That's right, baby you been a bad girl," he said. "I'mo teach your sexy ass a lesson." And, then he proceeded to do just that.

The next half hour was intense and amazing. Bill rammed his tool in and out of me, hard and fast, kissing and playing with my tits the entire time. By then, I doubt he could even remember why he'd been so upset with me. One taste of my sweet stuff, and it was all over.

I crave skin-to-skin contact 24x7. I need it, and Bill knows it. I put my hands around his neck and pulled him down on top of me. I loved the way our bodies moved together with only a nice layer of sweat between us.

"Cum inside me baby!" I yelled, loud enough for people in neighboring zip codes to hear.

Bill nibbled on my ear and thrust his cock in deeper.

"Please, I want it Bill!" I begged. "I need it baby, I need it!'

He pumped and pumped, deeper with each thrust. He closed his eyes and grit his teeth. I knew he was about to explode, and I wanted to feel every drop of his warm cum deep inside my sugar walls. But then he pulled out and shot his load on my tummy like I was some young Friday night fling.

And, everything seemed to be going so well. I just sat there with my mouth wide open and stared at him. What on earth could I possibly say?

Without skipping a beat, Bill got up and walked into the bathroom. He was like *wham, bam, see you later ma'am.* He didn't even bother to say *thank you.* That nigga got his, and he was out.

I lay on the bed in disbelief as Bill ran water, brushed his teeth, and did God knows what else in the bathroom with the door closed. At that very moment, I had a much better idea of what it was like to be a real porn star. I didn't have to pretend anymore. Bill used me like he was shooting an XXX flick. I just knew the director would pop out the closet and yell, *scene!*

After a few minutes, Bill finally came out of the bathroom, with a pair of shorts on. He looked over at me, and then nonchalantly walked out of the room without saying a single word. Then, I heard the TV in the living room come on.

"I guess he's still pissed with me after all," I mumbled. I went into the bathroom and washed up. Then, I put some shorts and a top on and joined Bill in the living room. He was sitting on the sofa chillin'. I just looked at him for a minute. He had his feet kicked up on the coffee table and seemed to be having himself a good ole time, watching the sports highlights for the day.

"You okay, Bill?" I asked.

He replied, "Yeah, I'm good, why what's up?"

"Nothing, you just left, and I thought-"

"What, you wanna talk or something?" he asked sarcastically.

I didn't want to go there with him, so I just backed off. After all that good lovin', fighting was the last thing I wanted to do. I just needed us to be close. I moved over and sat down beside him on the sofa. After about a minute, he reluctantly put his arm around me, and I fell over onto his chest.

Bill and I sat quietly together and watched TV for the rest of the night. He seemed somewhat happy, and we were right up under each other, but there was a lot of distance between us. I knew he didn't trust me, but at that point it didn't matter what I said or did. I think it was just something that would take time for us to get through. There's one thing I can always bet on—forget all the drama—together, Bill and I could fix anything. I loved him and was ready to put the work in to make whatever needed to happen happen, no matter what it took. Bill was my man, and I was willing to fight for him with everything I had.

We went to bed around eleven, but there was no sweet pillow talk—no hugging or kissing. You would've thought we were some old married couple. And yes, we were back to sleeping in separate corners again. I've slept closer to roommates before, and Bill, well he might as well have slept on the floor he was so close to the edge. I knew it'd take a while to get things back on track, but I hoped it wouldn't take too long because I don't appreciate being treated like second best; especially not by my Bill.

Chapter 7

The next day, I woke up earlier than ever—4 a.m. I showered, got dressed and headed straight for the office. I got in around 6 a.m. and crept up to the fourth floor like a thief in the night, being careful not to draw any unnecessary attention to myself. *Fuck all that rookie bullshit.* I was tired of David keeping me in the dark. I decided a little snooping was in order. I tried to be as inconspicuous as possible with security; no friendly conversations or nothing. You can never be too careful up in that place, there's no telling who David had snitching for him—guards, cleaning crew, whoever. Paranoid it may be, it's always better to be safe than sorry.

The Z-Squad area was empty, and all the lights were off. Together, the screensavers and the mysterious room in the back gave the floor an odd indigo blue glow. I put my stuff down at my station and crept all the way back to the forbidden door. The keypad was backlit, which made it easy for me. All I had to do was recall Karen's code and I was in. I stared at the numbers on the pad for a moment and began digging into my memory banks. My 20/20 vision and photographic memory comes in handy whenever I need to do a little breaking and entering. Saved my life a time or two. After a few seconds, I could see the code in my mind, so I punched it into the keypad and pressed the *Enter* key. The door unlocked, and I crept inside.

I moved around in there, quiet as a church mouse, inspecting each monitor. There was a lot of stuff going on, but one screen in particular caught my attention. It was some kind of game. I moved in for a closer look, but then, I heard somebody at the door.

"Fuck me!" I whispered. There was no way my tall butt could hide in there, so I just froze, praying on everything I owned it wasn't David.

The door swung open and the skinniest, hairiest man I've ever seen walked in. I knew it had to be the mystery man, Dimitri. He looked a mess too. He was wearing tan cargo shorts, sandals, and an Aerosmith t-shirt. His hair was long and thick, kind of like a white man's fro. He had a Red Bull in one hand, a Butterfinger in the other, and a Hot Pocket hanging out of his mouth. I didn't know whether to laugh or call the Section Eight folks and tell 'em to come pick up they people. I think I startled him a little. He definitely wasn't expecting to see me.

"You shouldn't be back here!" he exclaimed, his mouth full of half-chewed Hot Pocket.

"I'm sorry, I'm the new girl ... I was just trying to see what's going on in here that's all."

"Don't touch that!" he yelled, rushing over and all but smacking my hand away from the keyboard. "You shouldn't be in here," he repeated. His breath reeked of pepperoni pizza. He bit off another chunk of his Hot Pocket and put the rest down on the table in the corner along with his other snacks. Then, he came back over, tapping his finger on the monitor in front of me.

"You're not new here," he said. "I know you. You are Southerland, and David says you are trouble, no?" His accent was very thick, Russian, maybe Ukraine, but he was definitely your standard computer geek.

"Well, I was just-"

"No need to tell untruths," he interrupted. Then, he pointed to the screen. "Look, you see this? Is murder rate stats, it show how many murders are taking place ... how many investigations ... then, see look ... you drill down to methods of kill and things like that." He walked over to another computer and used the mouse to change the active view. "You are not here ... okay?"

"My lips are sealed," I replied.

He nodded. "Good ... see, you choose player to view what they do. See this guy? Is stalking girl now. Will probably kill her soon. He is Ricky Justice, the worst. Does not just kill but do hideous things with remains."

"I don't understand," I said. "Is this a game?"

"Yes, is game. You see, you-"

Out of nowhere, someone started banging on the door, hard. We both turned around, and of course, it was David, furiously slamming his fist against the window and pointing at me. The room was soundproof, but it didn't take much to read his lips. He was all up in arms.

"I'm thinking maybe I should go now," I said. "What's your name again ... Dimitri, right?"

"Yes, Dimitri Kravchenko, I am from Russia!"

I giggled. "Nice to meet you, Dimitri."

"And same Agent Southerland," he replied, staring at David through the glass. "He looks very, very angry, no?"

"Yeah, what's new? You take it easy Dimitri."

"Goodbye Southerland," he said.

Dimitri sat down at his workstation, and I headed out to meet ole Massa Chandler on the front porch to get my ten lashings. He acted like a slave driver when it came to me. I'm sure Tony would be delighted to know I hadn't even made it a whole week in Zombie Squad without pissing David off. I thought about just hanging out in the computer room for a while, you know delay the drama as long as I could, but I knew it'd just piss him off even more, so I stepped towards the door.

I stood there for a moment watching David through the window. He was so animated like he was about to have a conniption. It was hilarious too, I mean there this man was, desperately trying to put the code in to unlock the door and get to me, but he kept botching it up. I swear he was about to spontaneously combust.

I got a kick out of watching David, but I could tell he was getting angrier by the moment. Besides, it was early. I hadn't had any coffee yet, and judging from his demeanor, neither had he. So, I did the civilized thing and opened the door for him.

David took a step back, filled his lungs full of air and went off. "Goddammit Southerland, you're gonna fucking give me a coronary!" he exclaimed.

"Good morning, David," I greeted, slyly.

"Don't give me that goddamn good morning shit!" he yelled. "What the hell are you doing here at the crack of fucking dawn anyway?"

I glanced out of the corner of my eye. I could see Dimitri kind of shrinking over at his workstation.

"I asked you a question!" David bellowed.

I smiled a sheepish grin. "I'm just trying to get a jumpstart on the day. I'm an early riser, you know?"

"You'll be early fucking retired I ever catch you in this goddamn computer room again!" David snapped. "Now get outta here!"

I walked out and shut the door. "What's the deal with this game, David?"

"Southerland, trust me, you don't wanna know," he snapped. "Just let it go. The less you know, the better off you are."

"How am I supposed to do my job if I don't know what's going on?"

"Evidently you don't know what your goddamn job is, Southerland, but I'm gonna help you out. Your job is simple, it's to do exactly what the hell I say and not give me any shit about it. Now, you're on this prostitution thing, so you need to get busy, no pun intended. I need a strong lead today, and if you and Frank don't score big, then you're gonna have to deal with me. Remember your little scrawny ass was the last to come in, and you'll be the first to fucking go if I have anything to do with it."

I tried so hard, but I just couldn't hold it anymore. "Just who do you think you're talking to? That's not even necessary, and you know what David, you got a horrible attitude."

"Really, you think so?" he asked, sarcastically.

"Yes, and you need to be more respectful, or you'll lose a lot of good people."

"You're joking, right?" He grinned.

"No, I'm serious, David."

"Think I need to be nicer, huh?"

"Definitely," I replied.

David smiled really big. "More respectful to people like you, Alex?"

"Most definitely," I responded.

"Wow, I finally get it," he announced, waving his hands like a two-bit, hustling evangelist. "I've been doing this thing all wrong. Let's try it again ... good morning Agent Southerland, would you kindly do what you do best and make some coffee for Master Chandler? Black, no cream, no sugar. Now, once you're done with that, how 'bout you muster up all the training you can remember in that thick skull of yours and go pickup my laundry."

The second I heard the word *master* come out of his mouth I hit the fucking ceiling. I wanted so bad to call that mothafucka what he really was, a racist son-of-a-bitch. Instead, I just rolled my eyes and frowned.

"Too much for a smart-ass like you to handle?" he taunted. "Get to your station and process that hooker's client list or I'll drop your smug ass like a 50-pound bag of shit."

"I don't give a-"

"Daylight's burning!" he interrupted, pointing to my desk. "Move!"

I wasn't finished, but at the same time, I'd had all I could take of him. It was hard to keep my cool the entire time. I pushed back a little, but I knew not to take it too far. Like it or not, David was the big man on campus, and he was holding all the keys, so once again I bit my tongue and walked off.

"Pleasure doing business with you," said David, laughing loudly. "Have a goodin'!"

"Yeah, yeah, go fuck your mother," I mumbled under my breath. I wanted to say it to his face, but somehow, I don't think that would've helped the situation. All I know is I was beginning to build up a serious hate-on for that bastard. It's like he went out of his way to fuck with me. He needed his old, wrinkled ass whooped, and I was the woman for the job.

Back at my desk, I slumped down in my chair and backhanded the mouse to wake my computer up. I had an electronic copy of Shannon's client list, so I went through all the names and started pulling the files. My plan was to check out each of the adults, and then see what I could find on the young boys, and girls too? Yep, little girls. Shannon did not discriminate.

By the time I finished, I'd printed out two big stacks of files. It was like "Debbie does Dallas," or I guess in this case, Shannon does the ATL. She'd been a busy little bee, literally. I sorted and read through as many files as I could over the next few hours while I waited for Frank to get in. He never got to work late, but he never had any time to spare either. I could understand why though. The man had three little girls. Getting ready in the morning, his place had to be a goddamn madhouse.

Frank walked through the door right at 8 a.m. The first thing he did was stop by my desk to mess with me. "Early to bed, early to rise?" he said.

"Yeah, sometimes I guess," I replied softly.

Frank said, "I see you already managed to piss David off again."

"Word travels fast around here. What, do you guys wake each other up in the morning just to talk about me?"

"Look, don't worry." Frank smiled. "You probably heard me say this already, but you really are holding up better than your predecessors."

"Well, thank you ... I think."

"What do you have so far on the case?" he asked.

"Not much," I responded. "I just pulled all the files for the names on the Charles list."

Frank asked, "You mean for the daughter, right?"

"Yeah, the daughter's clients plus the boys and girls the mother was doing."

"Jesus, girls too?" he asked.

I shook my head. "I'm not going there, Frank."

"Well, me neither!" he exclaimed.

"I've got them sorted as best I can," I told him. "You think we'll get anything useful out of this...? Never mind, I already know what you're going to say."

"What?" he asked.

"You doubt it, right?"

Frank laughed. "I don't know Alex ... maybe we'll get lucky two days in a row."

I sighed. "You know Frank, I can't help but think this list, aside from the kids Shannon screwed at school, it's just for the daughter. We'd probably have a ten-book series if Shannon included her customers too."

"Let me ask you something, Alex...."

I spun around all the way in my chair and gave him my full attention. "What's up?"

"You think the mother should go to jail?" he asked.

"Hey, that's not fair, I-"

"Come on rookie," Frank encouraged.

I thought for a moment. "Well, she broke the law and-"

"That's not what I asked," he interrupted. "Do you think what she did was wrong?"

"Truthfully?"

"Of course, truthfully, Alex."

"The legal age of consent in Georgia is 16. I mean, if the kids are gonna do it, nowadays they probably have it all planned out by 10 or 13. I also think that ... well ... nah, forget about it."

"Go on," Frank prodded.

"Well, I just think prostitution should be a woman's prerogative. If I wanna sell my body, then whose business is it other than mine and the people I serve?"

"So, what you're saying is the cops are about to put away an innocent woman, who should be walking the streets, even after what she did?"

Frank had to have known what a loaded question that was before he asked it. I responded cautiously because I wasn't sure where he was coming from.

"There are some that might argue it's a misuse of valuable tax dollars," I replied.

"So, I guess marijuana should be legalized too?" he asked.

"Is this some kind of test to determine whether I stay with the team or not?"

Frank burst into laughter. "Just wanna see where your head's at rookie, that's all."

"Well, you ever hear of anybody overdosing on weed?"

Frank responded, "No, I can't say I have, but don't you think it's illegal for a reason?"

"I think aspirin is more dangerous than weed," I replied. "I mean, don't get me wrong, in terms of Shannon Charles, she put herself and her daughter at risk, but I don't see the daughter as an innocent. She made her choice too, right?"

Frank tilted his head to the side. "Maybe."

"All I'm saying is we all make bad choices, and we have to live with 'em. We have to suffer the consequences. Nobody ever gripes about the choices that turn out good, whether by design or sheer luck. I don't mean to be insensitive, but Karla chose wrong, and she ended up dead as a result of the choices she made, not her mother's."

"Interesting point of view," said Frank.

I went on, saying, "Karla could've stopped. The mother said she tried to get her to stop, but she wouldn't. I think she got caught up in the attention and money. What do you think, Frank?"

"I think children are precious gifts," he replied, like a superior court judge handing down a 20-year sentence to a negligent mother. "They are loaned to us, for temporary care, and I think parents will be held accountable, for all eternity, for the way in which they carry out that duty."

I gave him a sheepish grin. I didn't want to go there with Frank. I could tell from the wrinkles forming on his forehead I was hitting a Jesus-freak nerve, so I changed the subject fast.

"So, what's the plan today?" I asked. "Wanna talk to the Uncle Festers or the dumb jocks first?"

Frank chuckled a little, but then he looked at the stack of files on my desk in complete dismay. "Tell you what, why don't you call Detective Walsh and find out who the girl was with Friday. It must've been a big deal to keep her out of school. We'll start there and see what we can turn up. You can go through these files as you have time. Maybe we can get you some extra help. How does that sound?"

"Sounds like a plan to me," I said.

"Alright, I'll check back in with you later," Frank said. "Let me see if I can get back there and calm David down a little."

I giggled. "Yeah, take him an espresso or something."

Frank smiled and walked away.

I picked up the phone and gave Walsh a call.

"Fulton County Police Department," answered an officer.

"Detective Walsh, Homicide, please," I asked.

"Hold on, I'll transfer you."

Walsh wasn't in, so I left him a voicemail. I didn't have anything else major to do, so I spent the rest of the morning reading through some of the files I'd printed.

Most of the men who'd been with Karla were model citizens, married with kids, a good job, the whole shebang. That girl had to have some kind of magical, pixy-dust pussy to make them risk all that. I looked at each file carefully, but the whole time, all I kept thinking about was motive. Why would any of them want to kill her? True, they were taking a big risk fucking an underage girl, and I realize they had a lot to lose, but killing her presented an even bigger risk. My gut said none of them had anything to do with her death.

Time flew by, and before I knew, it was already one in the afternoon. Walsh hadn't called me back yet. In fact, nothing was really going on, so I decided to take a break. I went down to the canteen to grab a diet Coke. When I came back, I noticed I had a voicemail. I checked my messages. Detective Walsh returned my call while I was away from my desk. He left his mobile number, so I wrote it down on my pad and called him back.

"Yeah this is Walsh," he answered.

"Detective, this is Special Agent Southerland, FBI." *I like saying that.*

"What's up Southerland?" he asked.

"Call me Alex."

Walsh replied, "Okay, cool ... so, what's up?"

"Quick question ... did you find out who Karla Charles was with last Friday?"

"Yeah, hang on ... let me see ... ... hey, you still there?" he asked.

"Yeah, go ahead."

"John Lee," he said. "Sick bastard's rich as Bill Gates. Chinese dude. Owns several businesses all over the U.S. and China. They spent the day in a suite at the Marriott downtown."

"Friday, right?"

"Yeah," replied Walsh.

"You follow up with him yet?" I asked.

"We did," Walsh said. "According to Lee, they left the hotel around eight. His story checks out for the most part, but he doesn't have an alibi."

"Stupid question ... are you charging him?"

"Be a waste of time," he replied. "He's protected up."

"Diplomatic immunity?" I asked.

"You got it," he replied. "And since he's cooperating, we're not pushing the issue."

I cleared my throat. "So, what you're saying is, we got nothing?"

Walsh said, "Look, I pulled in a lot of officers to help out on this thing. We're trying to turn up something as fast as we can, but we ain't got nothin' credible just yet. Sorry."

"You think it's a dead end?" I asked.

"I hate to say it, but yeah," responded Walsh. "We talked to every adult on the list, but some of these guys write paychecks down here, if you get what I'm saying. Best I can do is get some of them to testify against the mother. They claim she set everything up and handled all the money."

"And, what about the principal?"

Walsh said, "Nothing there at all, plus she's been a big help so far. I don't think there's a bad bone in that woman's body."

I asked, "You sure?"

"Pretty sure, Alex."

"Okay, so what about the boys?"

"Basically, the whole sports program," he replied.

I sighed heavily. "Seriously?"

Walsh said, "Yep, the basketball team, football team, track team, couple of cheerleaders, it's ridiculous. I don't think we have a suspect out of this group though. Most of these young folks were at a game Friday night, and they all went out to eat afterwards. Their stories check out, and, either way, there's not a whole lot we can do with 'em. Hell, I wouldn't want to drag them into this anyway. I don't think they're to blame. Not trying to be shrewd, but who wouldn't spend their lunch money to get with a hot Biology teacher and her daughter?"

"Ain't that the truth, man!" I exclaimed.

"Besides, some of the boys are sitting on scholarships for college next year," Walsh said.

"Well, we don't wanna screw that up. All right listen, if you turn up anything call me on my cell. You got the number?"

"Yeah, I still got your card," replied Walsh. "Mind if I just check in with you periodically?"

"Not a problem, Walsh, thanks man."

"Alright Alex, you take it easy out there."

"You too." I picked up another line and called over to Frank's desk.

"What's up Alex?" he answered.

"Frank, the cops didn't get anything out of Shannon's list."

"Nothing at all?" he asked.

"Nope. I was sure they'd turn up a good lead with that list ... now we're back to square one. Only thing he had we might want to pursue is Karla Charles was supposedly with this Chinese businessman named John Lee down at the Marriott all day Friday. I'm thinking maybe we should go check it out, unless you think it's a bad idea."

"Hmm ... what time did they leave?" Frank asked.

"Walsh said about eight that evening."

Frank asked, "Time of death was between six and nine, right?"

"Yeah, I believe so, Frank."

"Does his alibi check out?"

"He doesn't have one," I responded.

Frank paused for a second. "So, is this guy a suspect, or what?"

"Nope, Walsh won't touch it," I said. "Says he's protected up the wazoo. If Lee's telling the truth, then the girl had to meet somebody else at the hotel or someplace nearby, which means somebody had to see something."

Frank got quiet again. "Well, it's after one now, and I've got something going on ... think you can handle this Lee thing by yourself?"

"What, check out the hotel?" I asked.

"Yep."

"If you think I'm ready, I mean-"

"Of course," he replied. "Just check with the staff. Be discreet. Try to find out what the manager knows. Oh, and get a copy of the security tapes please."

"Okay, I'm on it," I replied.

"Hey, Alex...."

"Yeah Frank?"

"Stay out of trouble ... think you can do that for me?"

I smiled. "Wise sir, if I see trouble, I'll run for my life."

"You got your badge?" he asked.

"I do."

"And your gun?"

"Yes, Frank."

"You remember how to use that damn thing?" he asked, raising an eyebrow.

"Like riding a bike."

"Alright, be careful out there," Frank warned, "and call me if you need me."

"Okay." I hung up the phone.

I must say I was a little surprised to be gaining Frank's trust so fast. An assignment like Lee had to be a big deal for a rookie. Or, was it? Come to think of it, they were probably just trying to get me out of the way, but hey, I didn't care. The sun was shining bright, and I was rollin' a brand-new GMC Denali. Most importantly though, I was finally free from that ball and chain the Bureau called a workstation.

I went downstairs and ran out to the parking garage. I got in the truck and pulled around to check on my lil pony. She was still parked in the same spot, untouched far as I could tell. I don't know what I was worried about, she looked just fine. She was covered in dust, but she was still black and glossy for the most part. I didn't drive too close to her because I didn't want to make her jealous. She's a sensitive girl, you know.

I pulled out of the parking garage and made a left off Century Parkway onto Clairmont Rd. I took Clairmont down and merged onto I-85, following it south until it split. Then, I merged onto I-75 and eventually exited 14th Street. The hotel was right around the corner. Of course, I knew exactly where it was because I'd just been up in there the other night, showing my ass, literally. I wasn't worried in terms of the case because the girl was dead the day before I showed up, so it's not like I'd be a suspect, but knowing my luck the hotel staff will be passing around copies of the video of me in that damn elevator. David would have a field day with that shit.

I pulled up to the front of the hotel and parked. I got out and walked inside the lobby.

"Welcome to the Atlanta Marriott," greeted the girl behind the desk. "Are you checking in?"

"No, actually, I need to speak to the manager."

"Uh, one moment." She picked up the phone and dialed an extension. "Mr. Brooks, there's someone here to see you ... okay I will." She hung up. "He'll be right out," she said, smiling.

"Thank you."

I took a few steps away from the desk towards the middle of the lobby. I didn't have to wait long. The manager came out in no time.

"What's up Haley?" he asked. "Somebody need to see me?"

Haley pointed to me. He looked up and then came out through the door on the right. "Hi, Jason Brooks," he greeted. We shook hands. "You need to see me?"

"Yes, Mr. Brooks."

"How may I help you?" he asked.

I showed him my badge. "I'm Alex Southerland with the FBI Atlanta field office. I was hoping I could ask you a few questions."

He shifted his weight from one foot to the other. "Sure."

"Were you on duty this past Friday?" I asked.

"Yes, during the day," he replied.

I looked around. The lobby was busy. "Is there somewhere we can talk?" I asked.

"Absolutely," he replied. "Come on in."

I followed him back to his office, and we sat down at his desk to talk. I took out a picture of Karla and handed it to him.

"Do you remember seeing this girl?" I asked.

He took a minute to study the picture. "As a matter of fact, I do. She came in about ... well, I don't know, maybe ten or eleven in the morning."

I asked, "Was she with anyone?"

"No, she was alone," he said. "She didn't check in or anything, just headed straight for the elevators."

"You see her again later that day?"

"No, I didn't," he replied.

"What time did you leave to go home?" I asked.

"About 5:30."

"You ever seen her before Friday, Mr. Brooks?"

"Jason," he corrected, "and no, I don't think so."

"How about this woman?" I gave him a picture of Karla's mother. He studied it for a moment, and then shook his head.

"No, I don't remember seeing her, but of course we do a lot of business. Lots of people come through here. Hmm ... no, I can't be sure, but she really looks a lot like the first girl only older."

"Jason, is it okay if I talk to your staff?"

He replied, "Sure. May I ask what's going on?"

"The young girl in the first photo's dead. The other woman is her mother. We're just trying to piece together a timeline of events."

"Oh my God," he gasped. "I'm sorry, I didn't know. If there's anything I can do to help, please let me know. Here..." he gave me one of his business cards. "Just call my extension."

"Thank you ... you know, there is one thing you might be able to help with...."

"Sure, anything," he responded.

"I need the security tapes from Friday," I said.

"I'm sorry, but you'll have to get with corporate on that," he replied. "Here let me see that card again...."

I gave him the card, and he wrote some information on the back.

"Call this number and ask for Donnie," said Jason. "He may not be able to get the videotapes, but he can probably point you in the right direction with corporate security."

"Jason, you've been very helpful."

"Let me know if there's anything else you need," he said. "You know your way back?"

"Yes, thanks." I left his office and wandered around for a while stopping any staff member I encountered to show them Karla's photo. Unfortunately, no one seemed to know anything, so I walked back around to the girl at the front desk.

"It was Haley, right?" I asked.

"Yes, how may I help you?" Her voice was just as sweet and bubbly as before.

"A man named John Lee stayed here last Friday. Can you tell me when he checked in?"

"I'm sorry," she replied, "but for security reasons, I can't give that kind of information out about our guests." She continued smiling.

I held up my badge. "I'm Special Agent Southerland with the FBI. It'd be a big help to our investigation."

"Oh, I'm sorry," Haley said. "Boy, do I feel stupid."

"How would you know?" I asked.

She chuckled. "Right, umm … give me a second, let me check the system." She moved over to the computer and searched for Mr. Lee's reservation. After a moment, she touched her finger to the screen and said, "Looks like he didn't check in or out."

"How's that possible?"

"I'm not sure," she answered, "but sometimes people have special arrangements with the hotel. They may keep a room for an extended stay, and so they're invoiced directly by corporate. I'm sorry, but Jason would have to help you with that."

"Tell you what Haley, can you at least check to see who cleaned the room Friday? I'd like to talk to them if possible."

She said, "I can probably check the schedule, but … oh, I can tell you who took the room service up. Would that help?"

"They ordered room service?"

"Yes," she responded, "a very big order of champagne, oysters, caviar, sparkling water, everything."

"Good deal. Who took it up?" I asked.

"Number 134 … let's see … um … yeah, Jamarr Keyes. Hey, I know Jamarr!"

"Is he working today?"

She replied, "I just saw him back in the kitchen not too long ago."

"Thanks Haley."

"No problem," she said. "Just let me know if I can be of any more help."

"Will do ... oh, where's the kitchen?"

Haley pointed to the right. "Go all the way down the hall and turn right ... then you'll go through the dining area, and the kitchen's straight back."

"Thanks, you're awesome Haley."

"No problem," she replied. "Have a nice day."

I left the lobby and walked past the elevators around the corner. I entered the main dining room and went through the double doors in the back. The kitchen was crowded, wall-to-wall with servers, cooks and other hotel staff. They were all so busy, nobody even noticed me.

"Jamarr Keyes?" I yelled. "Jamarr Keyes...? Anybody seen Jamarr?" I walked over to a cook and tapped him on the shoulder. "Hey, where's Jamarr?"

"Jamarr Keyes?" He had a really odd accent.

I nodded.

"Yes, Jamarr Keyes, he over there." The cook pointed to a young black man standing halfway across the room. He was kind of tall and had a low, faded haircut, which seemed to accentuate his extremely big ears. Like several other of the staff members, he was wearing a maroon Marriott uniform.

"Thanks Cookie," I said, giggling, but he didn't respond, he just frowned his face all up. Personally, I thought that was some good old-fashion witty banter, not to mention just plain funny, but he didn't seem to like it one bit. He looked at me as if I'd insulted the Virgin Mary. Some people have no sense of humor whatsoever. I just dismissed Cookie's grumpy, funny talkin' ass and walked over to Dumbo. I kid you not, with those ears, that boy could float off with a good breeze.

"You Jamarr Keyes?" I asked

He looked up and smiled. "Yeah, I'm Jamarr ... who are you?"

"Can we talk for a minute?"

"Yeah, we can talk out back," he said, "give me a second ... hey Esteban?"

"What? I'm busy dog!" yelled a young man a few tables over.

"Take this room service up for me," said Jamarr.

Esteban, a short Latino man with a thin mustache and spiked hair, walked over to us. "Hey, who's your friend dog? Si mamacita ... ramera atractiva!"

Spanish people kill me, automatically assuming you don't speak the language. I knew I was a sexy bitch, but why entertain an imbecile? It wasn't even worth my time, besides I had work to do.

"Yo, what I tell you before, stay out my business man," Jamarr said. "Just hook me up, I got your back."

"You owe me holmes," said Esteban, picking up the tray off Jamarr's table. "Man, you owe me big time, look at all that there."

I could feel Esteban's eyes raping me. He checked out every inch of me from head-to-toe. I thought he was going to trip up over his own two feet walking backwards carrying that tray. I wasn't even showing that much body either, I mean no cleavage or nothing. I guess he was just using his vivid imagination. Esteban was a trip, actin' like he had x-ray vision with his little pint-sized ass.

"Sorry 'bout that," Jamarr said. "Aye, yo Hector ... I got a visitor man ... I'mo step out back for a minute."

"You got that room service?" asked Hector.

Jamarr replied, "I got it covered man."

"Okay," said Hector.

"Come on." Jamarr led the way past the refrigerators, and we walked out through the back-delivery door. Outside, there were boxes and crates of God knows what all over the place. It was hot as hell in that kitchen. Jamarr was sweating a little bit, so he wiped his face with a handkerchief.

"So, you a cop?" Jamarr asked.

"What makes you say that?"

He smiled. "You move like a cop."

I nodded as if to say, *you got me.*

"Name's Alex, I'm with the FBI." I pulled out the picture of Karla and showed it to him. "You seen this girl before?"

"Hell yeah, I saw her come in here last week ... Thursday, no Friday I believe. Man, she fine as hell. So, what's up? She in trouble or something?"

"Unfortunately, she's dead," I replied.

"Oh snap," exclaimed Jamarr, "you serious?"

"I'm afraid so."

He paused for a minute. "Yeah, I seen her when I took some room service up to a suite on the top floor, regular customer, old Asian dude-"

"Mr. Lee?"

Jamarr looked up for a second. "Uh ... yeah, yeah Mr. Lee's suite."

"So, she was up there in his room?" I asked.

"Man was she!" Jamarr's eyes lit up. "She was up in there wit' nothing on but a G-string. I mean she was off the chain, know what I'm sayin? I hung around on the top floor for a minute to see what was poppin'. Don't get me wrong, I usually don't be trippin' like that, but man, she was finer than a mug. She went out to the ice machine like that too, titties was all out and everything, no offense."

"None taken ... didn't you think it was a little strange, her being out in the open like that?"

Jamarr chuckled. "Lady, I walk into a lot of strange stuff here, I'm just a brotha trying to make a dollar outta 15 cents. What these rich white folks do is they business, you feel me?"

"I believe I do ... so, tell me about the girl."

"Fine as hell," he said, "big tipper too, she gave me 50 bucks just for bringing up the food."

"You talk to her at all?" I asked.

"Nah, not really," he replied, "she just kind of shoved the money at me and went right for the food. I saw her again later that evening leaving the hotel. I was out front waiting on my ride, and I saw her, but I don't think she noticed me. Man, she looked good with her clothes on or off fo' show. Awe damn ... my bad ... is that a bad thing to say about a dead person?"

"I doubt it, Jamarr. Did she leave with Mr. Lee?"

"No ma'am," he replied. "She left with this big black dude."

"What time was that?"

"Uh ... I say about 8 p.m., maybe 10 after, I'm not sure."

"Can you describe the man she left with?"

Jamarr said, "Yeah, he was tall, maybe about six-three, six-four, built kinda like a boxer. Typical looking brother, ball head, goatee, and oh yeah he was driving this fly whip, that joint was off the hook."

"Really? What kind of car was it?"

"Brand new BMW M5," Jamarr said. "Rims was like whoa!"

"You get a license plate?"

He thought for a second, and then said, "Think it was from the west coast, Arizona or Cali."

"But you didn't get the number?" I asked.

Jamarr frowned. "Come on, how I'm 'posed to know to get that man's tag number?"

"Don't worry 'bout it," I said, chuckling softly. "Listen now, this is important ... you're sure the girl didn't leave with Mr. Lee?"

"Positive," he replied, "and matter of fact, I don't even think Mr. Lee was here Friday. I never saw him the whole time I was working. Then again, that probably don't mean nothing. I stay pretty busy while I'm here."

"Okay thanks, Jamarr." I touched his arm and said, "You've been a big help."

He started cheesin'. "You know, I wanted to be a cop."

"It's never too late man."

Jamarr shook his head. "Is for me."

"How's that?" I asked.

"I got mixed up in some credit card fraud down in Florida," he explained. "My so-called friends at the time pinned it all on me and made out with the money. I pretty much blew my chances to do anything major."

"So, whatcha gonna do?" I asked.

"Not sure," he replied. "Maybe get back in school ... try being a chef, somethin' like dat."

"There's good money in it Jamarr. You could end up having your own place. We definitely need more good brothers in the restaurant game."

"No doubt," he said, still smiling. "We'll see what happens, nah-mean? Look, I'm bout to blaze one before I get back in there." He took a cigarette from his pocket. "You mind?"

"Not at all, we're done here. Thanks again for your help."

"Good luck," he said.

I gave him a nod. "Same to you man, see you 'round."

Jamarr fired up his cigarette, and I walked around to the front of the hotel. I got in the truck and wrote down a few notes while they were still fresh on my mind. Then, I drove straight to the office.

Back on the Z-Squad floor, I stopped by Frank's desk to check with him.

"Hey, Frank."

He spun around in his chair. "Back already? That was fast."

"Yeah, I didn't get much down there, but I got a quick question for you."

Frank said, "Shoot."

"The manager said I had to get with corporate on the security tapes. How exactly am I supposed to do that?"

Frank laughed. "Pick up the phone and call 'em."

"And, they're just gonna give me the tapes?"

Frank's left eyebrow shot up to the ceiling. "You are FBI last time I checked, right?"

I frowned and Frank laughed at me like he usually does. "Don't worry about it," he said. "I'll take care of it."

I asked, "Can I watch?"

"Hell yeah," Frank replied. "You got a contact number for me?"

"You know it. Here...." I took the business card Jason gave me out of my pocket and handed it to Frank.

"Name and number's on the back," I said.

Frank put his phone on speaker and made the call. After a few rings, someone answered.

"Marriott International, this is Donnie, how may I help you?"

"Donnie, just the man I'm looking for. Listen, it's Frank Morris, FBI Atlanta, how you doin'?"

"Fine thanks for asking Mr. Morris."

"Call me Frank."

"Frank, what can I help you with today?" asked Donnie.

"Listen, one of my Agents just got back from checking out the Atlanta Marriott. We've got an ongoing investigation, and we need some video surveillance from this past weekend. Your guy in Atlanta told us we needed to speak to you first though."

"You said this is for an investigation?" Donnie asked.

"Yeah, a girl was murdered Friday night and we have reason to believe she visited your hotel. We need to check the surveillance tapes."

Donnie responded, "I understand, but you'll have to make a request like that through corporate security. I can submit it for you though."

"That'd be good, but listen I need a serious rush on it ... how long you think it'll take?"

"Couple of days maybe," he said, "but it could take up to two weeks."

"Where are you located, Donnie?" Frank asked.

"I'm in D.C.," he replied.

"You'll be able to send them down to me?"

"Yes," responded Donnie, "but can you fax something up to me in writing?"

"No problem Donnie, I'll get you some C.Y.A. I'm putting one of my agents on the line to get your info. I'll have something faxed up to you in just a few. It'll have my contact info on it, so if you have any trouble, give me a call first, alright?"

"Certainly, Frank," he replied.

"Donnie, I gotta go, but here's my gal."

I reached over and picked up the phone. I introduced myself and took down Donnie's info. He gave me his phone number, fax and email address. We finished talking and hung up the phone.

"Hang on Alex, let me go ahead and type something up real quick," Frank said. He opened up Microsoft Word and typed a brief memo, requesting video surveillance footage from the Atlanta Marriott for the entire weekend unfortunately. I wish I could've edited his note and made the request for Friday only, but he printed it on the spot and handed it to me. "Here fax this to him."

I was just about to walk away, but Frank stopped me.

"What are you working on now?" he asked.

"Nothing yet, I just got back."

"Have you done your UNAX and Sensitivity Training?"

"Not this year," I replied.

He looked at me and shook his head. "What was Tony doing with you guys down there?"

"It's not his fault. I was gonna get it done. I just hadn't gotten around to it. Besides, the deadline isn't for another few weeks, right?"

Frank shook his head. "Well, go ahead and get it out of the way, and then you can break for the day."

"Okay, cool. 'Preciate it, Frank."

"Not a problem," he responded. "Thanks for being a good sport, Alex."

I smirked a little and walked off. I felt more like an intern than a good sport. I knew they were just sending me on a bunch of bullshit jobs to occupy my time. I can see it now, David yelling at the top of his shriveled-up lungs, "Keep Alex busy, and keep her out of my hair!" Guess I had to pay my dues first, but I wanted some real action. I wanted to get into the game so badly I could taste it.

Speaking of games, I was still thinking about the one Dimitri was playing back in the computer room. I mean, what's the deal with that? Surely, the FBI doesn't pay good agents to sit around and play games all day. Did the game have something to do with the case, or what? I had so many questions, but no answers. I knew if I pushed the issue, David probably would just bust me back down to Anti-Piracy. For the most part, my career was hanging on by a thread, so that was the last thing I needed. True, my curiosity was getting the better of me, but I didn't want to piss David off again, so I kept my mouth shut.

I faxed Frank's request up to Donnie, and then sat down at my desk to complete my training.

It took about an hour for me to page through that boring UNAX training. UNAX stands for Unauthorized Access. Government employees are required to go through it every year along with some sensitivity training, sexual harassment, diversity, and stuff like that. Obviously, David doesn't pay attention to the sensitivity part. Anyway, all you really have to do is just read through the sections and then pass a third grade-level quiz at the end of each one. Thing is, even if you fail, you still show up as having completed the training, so what's the point?

I did my best to read that mess, but it nearly put me to sleep. I finally finished up and logged out of the system. Then, I got my stuff together and headed out. I saw Karen standing near the exit.

"You doing okay?" she asked, seeming a little concerned for some reason.

"Yeah, I'm fine Karen. I'm learning a lot."

"Well, I hear you're doing a great job," she said.

"Really?"

She smiled. "Yes, keep up the good work, and let me know if you need anything."

"Thanks Karen." I smiled too. "I'm leaving for the day, so I guess I'll see you guys tomorrow."

"Okay, bye now," she said.

I immediately left the office. I got in the truck and drove straight home. I was so tired, but I made excellent time getting in. So, there I was home early again for the second day in a row. I was beginning to make a career out of it, and evidently, so was Bill. His truck was out front when I pulled up.

I parked and went upstairs. I figured I'd announce myself before walking in because I didn't want Bill to be surprised or have to act funny, you know ending mysterious phone calls prematurely and all. Deep down, I knew Bill was up to something, and it made me mad as hell, but what could I do? I figured he probably been seeing somebody for a while, but for the moment, we were getting along, and I didn't want to mess that up over some petty bullshit. Whatever he was up to, I probably deserved it anyway. If it was indeed another woman, I knew it was just a fling. Bill and I had been together since high school, and no tramp on the planet could come between us. I unlocked the door to the apartment and walked in.

"Hey babe, I'm home!" I yelled.

"Hey lady!" Bill walked out of the bedroom and gave me a big hug and kiss. "You're home early again. How was your day?"

"Pretty good actually. I think I'm getting used to my new job. I did some fieldwork today by myself. It was cool for the most part."

"Fantastic," he responded.

"Wanna go out tonight, Bill?"

"Nah babe, I gotta get back to work. Gotta get our production numbers up by tomorrow, so we're looking at pulling an all nighter. You gonna be alright home by yourself?"

"Yeah, I'll be fine," I said.

"Hey, I didn't hear you pull up," Bill said. "Something wrong with the car?"

"Car's fine," I replied. "They gave me a truck to drive for work, so I left the Mustang in the garage."

"Oh, I see now. You'll take the white man's car, but not the car I give you?"

"Don't start, Bill. That was a long time ago."

"I'm just joking," he said, unconvincingly. "Need me to drive you back up there to get the Mustang?"

"No that's okay. It's probably safer up there than it is out here at the apartment. These sorry negroes 'round here be done stole my damn stereo if I left it here all day every day unattended."

"Well that was pretty racist." Bill laughed at me.

I guess me being protective of my Stang was amusing to him. I rolled my eyes. "Whatever, you know what I'm saying. At least it's locked in the garage at work, and somebody's paying attention to it while I'm not there. I don't think anyone's brave enough to try and break into it parked in an FBI lot."

"Hey, whatever happened to that guy you use to talk to in high school?" he asked.

"Who you talking 'bout, Bill?"

"I dunno, that guy from the other school," he responded. I shook my head. "You mean Malik?"

"Yeah, what happened to him?" Bill asked.

"Not sure. I helped him out about a year ago. He'd gotten into some trouble and called around looking for me. He said he had some information that could help on one of my cases. His tip actually panned out, so the judge gave him parole."

"You talk to him recently?" he asked.

"Uh ... no ... where's all this coming from Bill?"

"Just curious," he replied. "Hey look, I gotta go. I'll see you later tonight."

"Okay." I kissed him. "Be careful baby."

"See ya," he said.

After Bill left, I picked up the phone and called Theresa.

"Hello," she answered.

"T...."

"Hey babe."

"What you up to?" I asked.

"About to leave," she said, "got myself a hot date, you know what I'm saying gurl? Gonna be an all nighter tonight big bay-bay!"

"What you say? All nighter...?" I had a really bad thought for a second, but it was so ridiculous I just dismissed it. "Oh well ... alright, that's cool T. I don't wanna interrupt your flow. I was just calling to say hey, nothin' serious."

"I got a few minutes," said Theresa, "what's up?"

"Nothing ... hey, who's this mystery man anyway, and when do I get to meet him?"

"Why you all up in mine?" she snapped. "You ain't got enough men's lives to wreck, so you wanna fuck wit' mine too now?"

"Forget I asked ... how's Mom doing?"

"Good, she asked about you," Theresa said.

"Really?" I asked.

"Don't get too excited, she was like, "Is Denise still running around pissin' in the jungle like a little monkey?"" Theresa laughed hard, snorting as she cackled at my expense.

I sighed heavily. "Whatever."

"So, when you gonna get off your high horse and go see your momma?" she asked.

"When she starts acting like a momma! She's the one calling me a monkey and-"

"Alex, she loves you," Theresa interrupted. "Stop being a bitch or I'm tellin' you, you'll lose everybody close to you. You need to grow up and be the bigger woman with her and Bill. Shit it's bitches like me running 'round, lookin' for a good man. Betta watch your back out there gurl."

I chuckled. "Well, you want 'em you can have 'em. Besides, I'm tired of having to be the bigger woman. Why can't somebody else take care of me for a change?"

"Gurl yo' ass is cursed, I can't fuck witcha!" She giggled.

"You know what T, I don't want to judge you, but-"

"But, what?" she asked.

"Well, you're supposed to be all holier than thou, right? But, you know, you be cussin' up a storm, so what' up wit' that?"

"Fuck you bitch!" she exclaimed. "You coming to church Sunday?"

"Goodbye Theresa."

"Love ya babe," she replied.

I hung up and laughed. She was the craziest little thing on the planet. I went into the bedroom and changed into some biking shorts. I put on a matching sports bra and some socks. Then, I sat on the edge of the bed to lace up my favorite running shoes. Disguised as a mere mortal in my athletic gear, I stepped outside and locked up the apartment to go for a jog.

I just stood out in the breezeway on the top floor for a minute, looking out over the rail. The sky was like this beautiful work of art. It's funny, I'd just come in, but didn't even notice how amazing it was. The weather was nice too. The sun was shining bright, and it was good and warm. The temperature was almost 85 degrees, but there was a steady breeze blowing, which made it extremely nice. Usually, I have to jog in the gym, so being outside during the daytime was a refreshing change. I stretched for a few minutes, and then set my Walkman. Then, I put my headphones on, took a deep breath, and shot off down the stairs.

We lived right in the middle of the city, but our apartment complex was sitting on a small park that had a nature trail running through it. It may sound lame but being out there to me was kinda like frolicking nude through a field of fresh spring flowers; I mean no worries at all.

The trail itself for the most part was nice and flat, and there were spots along the way with plenty of shade in case you need to take a break. Personally, I don't need no stinking break. I work hard to keep my body in shape, and once I start running, there's no stopping me. Yeah, I said it, I got a bangin' body, and I like to flaunt it as often as possible. I'm taller than most girls, and even though I'm a little thin, I'm still thick in all the right places—hips, thighs, calves, and of course, now I'm no Pamela Anderson, but I got enough up top to stop traffic.

Out past the cars, I started out slow, just to loosen up a bit. I cut through the parking lot and got onto the trail. As usual, the basketball court was packed. I jogged by damn near in slow motion to give the boys some inspiration. "Play nice now, boys!" I yelled.

They stopped right in the middle of their game to watch me go by. "Hey!" they all replied, in unison.

I waved, and they waved back. I liked to see them out playing together. It's good for them to be outside. It's much better than playing video games or watching porn on cable. Sometimes, I actually sit down on a bench and just watch them play. Some of them can really ball too, even a few of the little ones. The thing I like about it is it's not just a bunch of black kids. Everybody falls victim to the stereotype, thinking black folks are the only ones who can play ball. I know I'm guilty of it myself sometimes, but I always see white kids out there, Mexicans, and Asians too. And they don't seem to care about color one bit. All they care about was having fun without all the bullshit the world likes to put us through. I promise you can learn a lot from a bunch of kids. Some of the residents get pissed with the boys. They call the office and complain, saying they make too much noise, but I don't mind. They're all cuties to me.

I kept moving past the pool area and into the woods. By then, I was up to a nice pace. I always feel good running the trail, but it also gave me a chance to be nosey and see what other people were up to. There were houses lined up along the fence on the far right. A lot of people were sitting on their decks, relaxing, and their kids were out playing in the yard. It was a sight for sore eyes.

With Journey blasting in my ear, I felt like I could spread my wings and fly away. I've always enjoyed running. Track was one of the few things my mother allowed me to do in school. I'm guessing I was good at it because I had so much practice running away from her psycho ass. I ain't Flo-Jo, but I can do my thang.

I ran both track and cross-country in high school and college. I loved every minute of it too, but running isn't for everybody. It's serious business, not for the faint of heart. It's always been one of my passions, but it's also how I partially paid for college. I had academic scholarships, but I took the track ones too. I loved running and I decided early on that nobody was going to take that away from me, not my mother or sister, and definitely not Bill. Running was my release, my therapy, that and boxing. What can I say, some people do Pilates, some people yoga, but me, I run and hit people in the face to put my mind at ease.

I hadn't been out running for a minute. I was so wrapped up in all of my issues with Bill and work, I'd forgot to take time out for myself. I couldn't keep living like that though, it just wasn't healthy. So, that day, I made a promise to block aside time every single day to run, even if the rapture was coming. Amazingly enough, the minute I said that, I had what some might call a moment of clarity. In fact, I think I actually found my center, if there is such a thing, right there on that trail, running and sweating. For the first time in a while, I actually started thinking clearly.

I've been wondering about how to make a positive change in my life forever, but never sorted out the how part of it. But, that day, I had an epiphany. I can't exactly put it into words, but it's kinda like when you play an arcade game and you figure out how to get an extra man. At that point, your entire strategy changes. You can afford to take more risks because you got an extra life. Well, that's how I felt that day, like somehow, I got an extra life. I felt like I could open up, trust more and let the people I care about get closer to me—stop pushing them away so much. Truth is, me keeping everything close to the vest hadn't gotten me very far up to that point, so why not try something different.

I feel like I learned a lot on the trail that day and, even though I may not be able to articulate it, I had it right in my mind. It made plenty of sense. Now, it was time to put it to good use in my own game of life. After all the drama and foolishness, I think I was finally ready for the next level.

Chapter 8

After a few attitude adjustments, my life was actually finally starting to change for the better. The weeks ahead were far better than those prior. My daily jogging routine turned out to be just what the doctor ordered. Refocusing on making me a better person seemed to be doing the trick. I calmed down a whole lot. After a while, I think I found peace in just about every part of my life. I wasn't angry all the time anymore, and I didn't look for opportunities to bump heads with other people. Maybe I was maturing, growing up a little. *Can you imagine that?*

Believe it or not, my relationship with Bill got much better too. We were actually good again. Speaking of relationships, David and I got way better too. I realized he wasn't the rude, mean old racist bastard I'd sized him up to be. David has an extremely rare, sick sense of humor. If you don't know him, he'll rub you the wrong way, but Tony was right, he was one of the best, and probably the most honest man I've ever known. David tells it like it is. I know it sounds like I'm kissing his ass, but it's true, he's one of the good guys, and smart too.

Hanging around David, I learned just how intelligent he really was. He was a legend in the field, and the most resourceful man on the planet. He had to have been a fuckin' Eagle Scout or something. He touched people all around the country too as if he had some kind of weird power over them. Most would say they hate him, but when he called in a favor, they did exactly what he wanted to the letter, no hesitations, and no questions asked.

Soon as I let my guard down with David, I quickly realized he and I had quite a bit in common. He made me laugh. Just looking at him sometimes tripped me out, the way he'd raise an eyebrow and smirk when he heard someone say something stupid, or when he saw a half-dressed woman. That man kept me in stitches.

David was not what you'd expect to see for a Bureau man either. His hair was long and grey, so was his goatee, oh and don't get me started on the mustache. It covered his entire mouth. When he talked, nothing on his entire head moved except his facial hair like Yosemite Sam.

I swear David was always flirting with the women in the office and just about everywhere we went. He was like the dirty old uncle at the family barbeque, sitting on a park bench looking at the young girls run around in their tight little booty shorts. He would say some wild shit to women too, but it didn't seem to bother them. They'd probably slap a 20-year-old in the face if he'd said half the shit David blurted out. But nope, they all graciously accepted every form of flattery he had to dish out, no matter how sick it sounded.

David was off the chain, but I think it was all a cover really. I imagine he'd just as soon die before ever admitting it, but I think all his smartass behavior was how, emotionally, he dealt with the mountain of evil the job brought into his life.

After all the arguments we had when I first started, I finally got David. Now, I understand exactly where he's coming from, and it didn't take long for me to start acting a fool right alongside him. Sometimes, we'd go to the mall or out to the park to clear our minds, but we'd just end up talking about people. Billy the choirboy would've given me some long, drawn-out speech about how you shouldn't make fun of people and bad karma, blah, blah, blah, but not David. He always rose to the occasion. We'd take an extended lunch just to talk bad about people and their clothes, shoes, even their pets. It was the highlight of my day.

Weeks passed and I got a helluva lot smarter about the job. Karen and Frank put in countless hours of their personal time showing me the ropes. They threw more on my plate than they thought I could handle, but I ate it all up and came back for seconds. Most of it was grunt work anyway, so it didn't take much effort to get it all done.

After about a month, I'd stacked up a mountain of wins with the team, but none of them seemed to be paying off. Our team worked hard, day in and day out, but our killer was still at large. We exhausted nearly every resource trying to track him down. Unfortunately, we weren't getting any closer to catching him. We were all frustrated, but that didn't stop us from keeping at it. The very thought of slapping the cuffs on that bastard just fueled our fire and made us work even harder.

I talked to Detective James Walsh often. I called him Jimmy. He was one cool cat. I couldn't imagine him ever hurting a fly, but he was just as anxious as we were to catch that sicko. I think he would've gone into vigilante mode if he were willing to do some dirt, you know, bend the law a little to get his man. It was a Federal case, but I knew how he felt, so I shared as much as I could without getting into trouble.

Several months passed, and everything in my life was settling into a good space. By then, I'd forgotten the old days, my wild life, and my constant foolishness. I even managed to cage up that psycho blonde slut that kept me in hell for so many years. She'd served her purpose and helped me get through the rough times, but nowadays she caused a lot more trouble than she was worth. She may be my maker and my master, but at this point, I am more like a runaway slave. I just can't listen to her anymore.

Of it all, the best thing was Bill genuinely seemed happy with me, and you know what, for the first time in a while, I was happy too. Everything seemed to be on track, even work. Well, it was going as good as it could. David complained a lot less and everybody was so supportive of me. It was all good.

Jimmy kept me up to speed on the Shannon Charles case. Turns out a lot of people actually sympathized with her, even the judge. Members of the community really dug in, giving her money and food, and all kinds of support. The state dropped the negligent homicide charges, but her clandestine activities with the boys came to light, and one of the parents pressed charges. The D.A. ended up charging Shannon with one count of child molestation, but the boy's testimony didn't help the state's case at all. Shannon's defense attorney was savvy too. He argued she was what's called a *situational pedophile*. The jury seemed to accept the idea her low wages, single parent situation, and other circumstances caused her to do what she, as a good citizen, never would have done. Shannon was found guilty, but only sentenced to parole and community service. However, she can never be alone with another child again, and of course, the school fired her. Jimmy says he thinks she's working at a local bridal store now.

I'm glad for Shannon, glad she didn't go to prison. If she really loved her daughter like she claimed, then losing her the way she did was probably more punishment than the system could ever dish out. At the same time though, I couldn't help but wonder if she wasn't a blond-haired, blue-eyed white woman, would she have gotten off so easily, or would the judge have thrown the book at her? It's not that I'm obsessed with race, but there's no doubt about it, white people in America are privileged.

I'm not that old, but I've had firsthand experience with racism. I'm extremely fair-skinned. At first glance, you might think I'm a white woman if you don't know any better. Growing up, I was even lighter, but most of my friends were black as the day's long. Hanging around them, I saw disparate treatment at its worst. We were always getting into shit, like most kids I suspect, but when we got in trouble, I always made it out unscathed. My friends, on the other hand, they constantly got the short end of the stick, even though, most of the time, I was the one getting everybody in trouble in the first place. I used to think it was funny. I'd laugh and tease my friends about how they got in trouble and I didn't. Now I realize I was getting a pass because of my pale skin. I guess people just thought I was a confused little white girl, so they'd send me home before they set the little bad niggers straight.

Sometimes, I wonder what my fate would've been if I were a few shades darker. Do I even have to ask? Sad part is, none of that's really changed. True the preferential treatment has become a lot more subtle, but it's still prevalent. I'm embarrassed to say my white-looking skin gets me into certain places and allows me to hear things the average negro ain't privy to. I guess life's funny like that. It breaks my heart, but I don't think it'll ever change, especially down here in the south. I just try to use my bright skin to do what I can for my people. Most of them don't see it that way, but I really do. Hell, most black folks get pissed when I claim to be black. Seriously, I get it coming and going from both sides of the fence, but it's all good.

Time really seemed to shift into high gear as soon as I got adjusted to Z-Squad life. Months flew by. Detective Walsh and I stayed in touch, but we soon forgot about Shannon Charles. We couldn't forget about her daughter Karla though. For me, remembering how she looked, and how she smelled that night, kept me focused on the task at hand— catching the killer.

After a while, I officially graduated from rookie status, and was finally beginning to come into my own with the team. I thought I'd never say it, but Z-Squad wasn't so bad after all. We were starting to act like a little pseudo family too, doing all kinds of things together like drinks after work, cookouts, bowling, you know the good stuff. I even started bringing Bill around them and boy did they like him. Karen thought he was just the cleanest-shaven, best-looking young man she'd ever seen. All I constantly heard from her was, "Alex, Bill's the kind of man a girl like you needs."

We continued working the same case, chasing our mystery killer. Each time we thought we were getting warm, something weird happened and suddenly we realized just how cold we were. Whoever he was, he was playing us big time. No one was willing to admit it, but we were pretty much at his mercy. The whole situation seemed hopeless to me, and from the looks of the other guys, they didn't see the light at the end of the tunnel either. I figured this asshole would walk through the door and turn himself in before we ever caught him.

Despite our best efforts to stop the killer, he murdered two more girls for a total of six. Like Karla Charles, they were both high school students, but these two were seniors. The actual murders were more like the first three though. It was definitely the same crime scene, only far more refined. Frank says our guy's evolving. I tend to agree. It would seem his skills were growing with each new kill. He was getting better attacking, and apparently had become a bona fide expert in avoiding capture.

I imagined our guy was sitting somewhere eating ice cream, watching the news and laughing at both the police and the FBI. It seemed we were powerless to stop him. All we could do at that point was stay on the trail and try to raise awareness in the community.

We kept collecting odd clues, but nothing worthwhile, nothing that made sense. Of course, Frank and I continued working together as partners. The FBI likes to put a junior agent with a senior, which is their idea of mentoring. With Frank and me, it wasn't an official deal, but he was definitely my Sensei. He taught me the tricks of the trade, and I soaked up everything I could.

When I wasn't working with Frank, I was hanging around David, picking up good detective vibes from the master. I never thought I'd say it, but we actually became good friends. More than that, we were like two peas in a pod. David couldn't keep his comments about other people to himself, and I was getting more and more vocal with my opinion. The pair of us was one big lawsuit waiting to happen, but I felt good when I was with him. I didn't have to be phony. I could let my hair down and just be myself.

The papers on my desk were stacking up pretty high, but all of it was related to the same big case. Every once in a while, I'd see Dimitri running across the floor with a hot pocket in his mouth. He'd smile at me, nod his head, and go right back into his computer room. For the longest, I wondered what was going on in there, but at that point, I'd given up trying to figure it out.

Life was great, and I was seeing things clearer than ever before. When I looked back on how I used to be, I saw a completely different person. It was as if I'd been reincarnated. I'd changed from a filthy caterpillar into a graceful, slightly pretty moth. Yes, I know what you're thinking, but I ain't beautiful butterfly material just yet. I'm trying to give myself room to grow.

I think the thing that tripped me out most about my transformation was how I went from hating the sound of my alarm clock to not being able to sleep at night for wanting to get back to work. It got to the point where my mind never stopped running. I was up the entire night thinking about all kinds of things.

No doubt about it, I was becoming a certified insomniac fast. I couldn't help it either. I tried hard, but just couldn't seem to get to sleep. Eventually, Bill got tired of me keeping my lamp on at night, but it didn't matter to me. I still did my thing laying there in bed, working inside the depths of my mind. Thing is, my life was finally good, so I think I was trying to make up for a lot of lost time. All night long, I'd think about what to do the next day to keep Bill happy— breakfast, back rub, whatever he wanted. I also thought about the cases we were working. Most importantly though, I kept perfecting my strategy on how to ignore Blondie and keep the old Alex buried in a deep dark hole. Long as I kept that up, I knew I'd be just fine. As far as the no sleep thing was concerned, I figured a little extra makeup around the eyes would keep the questions at bay, and I'll sleep when I'm dead.

Chapter 9

We continued to pursue our suspect like white on rice, on a paper plate, in a snowstorm as David would say, with no results I might add. One day, I was sitting at my desk, reading a local police case file of a murder we thought may have involved our guy. After reviewing the file, it was clear the cases weren't related, not even close, but we had to go through the motions anyway. You just never know what you may turn up. I had a few other files to go over, but I was at a stopping point, so I got ready to go on break. Naturally, before I could get my butt out the chair, the phone rang. Nobody ever calls till I'm ready to go on break.

"FBI Atlanta, Southerland," I answered.

"Alex?" came a voice.

"Hey, what's up David?"

"Come see me," he demanded.

"Now?"

"You got something better to do?" he asked. "Of course, now!"

"Alright, give me a sec." I hung up the phone and secured my workstation. Then, I walked back into David's office and closed the door. Frank was already in there. He and David were seated at the conference table.

"I'm about to go on break," I said. "You need me to take care of something first?"

"No," David replied, "have a seat, Alex."

I pulled a chair back from the table and sat down. "What's up guys? Something wrong?" I asked.

David replied, "Well, what's up is Frank thinks you're ready ... says he'd bet his Falcons tickets you're good to go."

"Ready for what?" I asked.

"Ready to be a part of this team," he replied, "but I disagree."

"I'm sorry you feel that way, David. I thought I was already a member of the team. I mean, I try my best to pull my weight around here, but you've got a birds-eye view on the situation, so-"

"Shut up kid," David interrupted. "I'm trying to say I think you're too damn good for this team."

I leaned back and squinted at him, shaking my head. "I don't understand."

David said, "You're here because those assholes over in C.I. were too chicken-shit and didn't wanna take a chance on you."

"It's cool, I like being here," I said.

"Get over it!" exclaimed David. "You've done more than we could've asked for. Zombie Squad doesn't have any friends up north, half the folks down here hate us, and the other half puts up with us 'cause they don't have a choice. Somebody's gotta do this job. Look around kid. You're the only one down here under 40. This ain't where you launch a career. It's where you end up once you've pissed off the right person. You got no future down here."

"So, what are you kicking me out already?" I asked. "What if I don't wanna go? I mean Frank, we're making progress and-"

"It's not up for discussion, Alex," Frank said.

I sighed and rubbed my forehead. "Look, I just got the hang of things, I can't-"

"Sure, you can," David interrupted, "and you will. Look, this thing's been decided way above your pay grade, so don't try to fight it. As much as I hate to say it, you're sharp, one of the best young agents we've had down here. Frank constantly brings it to my attention. I can't hold you back anymore, even if I wanted to."

"What are you talking about, David?"

"The reason you're here is because I did Tony Crane a favor," David revealed. "The recommendation was to fire you and downsize you with the rest of the cutbacks in Anti-Piracy. See, people don't care much about cybercrimes, and they care even less about stolen movies. Hell, if the Bureau wasn't getting pressure from the public on these murders, we'd probably be out on our ass too. That's why Tony ended up going to Washington, so he could put something more promising together. When he came to me, we'd already been through a few newbies, and we needed an extra hand. I promised him we'd put you to work, so we let you do a few things that wouldn't get in the way of the investigation. Hell, I figured you'd run for the hills on that first dead body, but you didn't, and you been working hard ever since. You got heart kid. You deserve better than this. We gotta clear this current case off the log one way or the other, but we can't get deep enough inside. I think it's high time we put you on the playing field. Understand though, as soon as we catch this guy, or if it looks like it's a lost cause, you're outta here."

I didn't know whether to say thanks or cry. "So where am I supposed to go?"

"Crane's already moved from D.C. to New York," said David. "Evidently, he's made a serious name for himself up there. The Director put him in charge of Kidnapping and Recovery for New York City. He's pulled some strings to get you on his team. I shouldn't have to tell you this is one hell of an opportunity, a real opportunity, not like Z-Squad. You should thank him for this ... I promise you, he's done more than you can ever imagine."

I leaned my head back and took a deep breath. It was a very emotional moment for me. Seriously, I felt like crying. Aside from Bill and that little funny looking girl, Sasha, in grade school, I never had any real friends. The way my family treated me, I can't say I ever had a real family. Bill's the only one who ever tried to do right by me, but now things are different. Z-Squad was my family, and I didn't want to leave them.

I covered my mouth and tried my best to hold back the tears. I couldn't let them see me fall apart, but all I could think of is how much I'd miss being with all of them. I took another deep long breath and sat up tall in my chair. At times like this, my daddy would say, "Toughen up Pork Chop and get the job done right first 'cause trust me, you'll have plenty of time to cry later." So once again, I followed his advice. It never let me down before.

"So, what's it gonna be?" asked David.

"Fine," I said. "If it's gotta be that way, then fine. I'll do it, but I know you've been keeping me in the dark, and if I'm going to help you catch this fucker, I need to know everything."

"That's my girl," David said, nodding. "Take it away, Frank."

Frank asked, "Alex, you ever heard of a game called Death Peddler?"

"Yeah, it's a PlayStation game, right?"

"Well, yes, but it started as a computer game," Frank replied, "the PC version was on the market way before the console. Since it uses the PC architecture, it's far more advanced than the console game, and a lot of people have come up with cracks and cheats."

"I'm not following you, Frank."

"The game can be rigged," said David.

"Exactly," Frank concurred. "See Alex, in the game you're a serial killer. You just run around killing people, and the objective is to make it through without ever getting caught. The A.I. in the game runs the beat cops, detectives, and other law enforcement agents, who are constantly trying to capture you, 24 hours a day and 7 days a week, whether you play or not. The game is extremely realistic and violent."

I nodded. "Yeah, I remember there was a big deal about it in the news. Parents wanted the game pulled from the shelves."

"They got it done too," Frank said, "but, developers from CrimNal Labs, leaked a multiplayer version out on the net along with their API for loading custom profiles, extra methods of kill, weapons and transportation, everything. They even got it hooked into a satellite image service, so now the environment looks as real as real can be. CrimNal lost the legal battle to keep Death Peddler in retail stores, but they grew to be one of the most popular developers on the market as a result of that game. Their other titles sell out on release day. The games they put out now aren't as sick and bloody as Death Peddler, but they damn sure push the limits, and the kids love it."

"Got it, but I still don't follow you," I said. "What does this have to do with the case?"

"There's a direct link," said David.

"So, what are you saying our guy's a Death Peddler?"

"It would seem that way," Frank replied. "We've tracked a player whose methods and behavior online match our guy's M.O. He kills the same way every time."

"Crucifix?" I asked.

"Bingo," Frank replied. "There's no pattern of how he chooses his victims either. He's completely random in the game, same as our killer in real life, but we just don't buy it. There's gotta be some kind of a connection to the victims, we just can't see it from the outside looking in."

I ran my fingers through my hair and asked, "So why don't we get a warrant for the CrimNal servers?"

"Wouldn't help." Frank sighed. "The game's gone completely underground. CrimNal won't cooperate either. Despite our threats, they got lots of money, plenty of lawyers, and our lawyers won't touch this with a 10-foot pole. They're claiming it's a serious liability slash civil liberties issue. Since they're actually not running the game, there's not a lot we can do to force their hand. Wherever the current version of the game is being hosted, we can't find it and no judge is willing to give us the authority to track the source. They all claim it'd be a violation of privacy."

I sighed. "So, once again, we got nothing?"

"Best we've been able to do is solicit help from some of the players. They've shared as much information as they're willing to share, but we're getting nowhere fast."

"So, Dimitri's playing the game back there?" I asked.

Frank shook his head. "No, none of us have the ... how do you say it-"

"We're too goddamn old," David interrupted. "They'd smell us coming a mile away!"

Frank laughed. "David's right. Dimitri just monitors the net and tracks activity. We're hoping he can use the statistics to try and identify patterns of behavior, or anything solid we can move on. He's also good enough to hack the system without being detected. We've been able to get a few good leads that way."

"So, you think our guy, playing the game, turned him into a real-life killer?" I asked.

"You bet your sweet lil ass," David replied. "This radical gaming engine, or whatever these techno-punks call it, is designed to produce one thing, a pack of wild, heartless, sick fucking idiots."

Frank nodded, "There's no doubt, we think this game's produced a stealth-killer. This guy's a ghost. Calls himself John Constantine."

"Charming," I said. "So, what happens if everybody playing decides to go on a killing spree for real like this John Constantine character?"

"It's highly unlikely, but it's possible," Frank said, shaking his head. "If that happened, it'd result in a catastrophic breakdown of basic law and order. People would be scared out of their minds, and if we fail to contain it, they'd lose confidence in law enforcement. We'd see a meltdown all around the country, I mean complete chaos. Bottom line, there's no scenario on the books to deal with something like that. If Constantine manages to get rock star status, and word got out he's killing for real, I'm convinced we'd see a ton of copycats out there. Whether they're as skilled as him or not, this game's like a drug to these kids, and eventually, they'll want to taste the real thing at least once. Innocent people would die for no reason at all. We gotta stop this guy and send a message before it gets to that point."

"Okay, so what can I do to help?" I asked.

Frank replied, "We need a new Death Peddler, somebody young, someone who can blend into the environment without raising suspicion. That's where you come in. We need you to get in there and generate a good lead for the team. I want you to spend the next few weeks learning the game."

"Wait, what makes you think I can do what you guys can't?"

David smirked. "You're young, dumb and stupid just like those other jokers. Don't worry you'll fit right in, kid."

I shot David a bird and he laughed, slapping his hands on the table.

"So, what's the situation?" I asked, giggling right along with David.

"You need to learn how to kill," Frank replied, "and you'll need a profile, kill method and all. You'll have to get extremely good working in the chat rooms too. Learn the lingo and learn the players."

"But won't they think it strange to see a girl playing some hardcore killer?"

"Nearly half the players are girls," said David. "Whatcha think about that?"

"Guess it figures," I speculated, "we can be a little on the rage side sometimes."

They both laughed.

"So kid, that's how it is ... you wanna play ball or what?"

"David, I'm here for the team ... I don't know what I'm doing, but I'll do my best. So, what's the next step?"

"Go home and get some rest," said Frank. "You'll be working 24x7 off site with Dimitri running support from here. We'll set up a private location with an internet connection and get the equipment you need shipped over. Meanwhile, you need to find an identity and get comfortable with it, name, family history, everything. Karen will help you with that. I gotta warn you though, these guys out here are good. They watch us as much or more than we watch them. If they smell a rat, they'll cut bait and set up elsewhere, so you'll have to go deep undercover on this one. We'll have everything in place by tomorrow. Any questions?"

"Yeah Frank, what do you mean when you say a private location?"

"You can't do this from home kid," David said, shaking his head.

"But ... but, what about Bill?"

"Like I said, you do this and you gotta go deep undercover until we get our man," said Frank. "We've been working this thing from every angle. This is the only way we're going to get close enough to this Constantine character. Unfortunately, you have to do this alone, and no one can know, not Bill, not your sister, not anyone."

I sat quiet for a moment. They were right. We were at a dead end on the case. I was just as passionate as they were, and I wanted to do my part, but I just got things back on track with Bill. I knew if I went undercover, I wouldn't be able to resurface until we caught the killer. That could be weeks, months, maybe even years.

David tapped his knuckles on the table. "So, what's it going to be, kid?"

"You're asking a lot David," I responded. "I need time to process all this."

"I'm sorry Pork Chop, but that's the way it is," he replied.

My eyebrows shot up to the ceiling. "Huh...? What'd you just say?"

"I said I'm sorry kid," he replied.

"No, what did you just call me?" I asked. "Did you just call me Pork Chop?"

David threw his hands up. "What's your point?"

"Nothing ... it's just my dad used to call me that."

He and Frank gave each other a stupid look for a split second. Then, they both turned back to me at the same time.

What are these two nuts up to?

"Look Alex, stay focused," David said. "I know it's a bum rap, but I promise you, if we don't make this work, that sick bastard's just gonna go on for years, killing victim after victim until he's ready to turn himself in, if that ever happens. Now, I know this sucks, and I wouldn't wish it on a broke-dick-dog, but this is the hand we've been dealt, I really am sorry kid ... tell you what ... go home and take a few days off. If you decide you don't want to do this, then, here...." David got up and walked over to his desk. He opened a drawer and took out an envelope. Then, he came back over and put it down on the table in front of me.

"What's this?" I peeked inside the envelope. There was a check and two plane tickets.

David sat back down in his seat. "That there's your relocation check along with tickets to New York, one for you and one for Bill. You decide not to do this assignment then you'll report to New York next Monday."

"Why so soon, I-"

"Look kid, it's either now or later," said David. "You go undercover then it's later. Otherwise, you leave next week for New York and start your new career. Now don't fight me on this shit, you hear me, Alex!"

I scratched my head. "And, what happens if I don't go undercover?"

"We already got a green light on this operation," Frank said. "We're moving ahead one way or another. Obviously, you're the ideal candidate. You've done undercover work in the Navy, you know computers, and you've closed quite a few Anti-Piracy cases. Bottom line, you know how to track this bastard down in that environment. If you don't go in, then we gotta recruit somebody else fast, and stick 'em in that apartment. I don't wanna put this kind of pressure on you, but you also know what it's like to be a rookie in Z-Squad. We went through nearly a dozen agents before you got here. Putting a newbie in that apartment is gonna be a helluva risk for all of us, and we can't afford to make any mistakes this time. Alex, you have to look deep inside and-"

"Choice is yours," David interrupted. "Karen will give you everything you need before Friday. It's real simple. If you show up at the apartment this weekend, rest easy knowing we're watching everything that moves. We'll protect you. If you don't show, then it's been a pleasure working with you, kid."

"Thank you, sir." I stood up and stuffed the envelope in my pocket.

"Get out of here," David commanded.

Frank jumped up and gave me a hug. "It's been good Alex."

They both acted like they already knew I wasn't going to do the undercover assignment. If I didn't know better, I'd say they were betting I wouldn't, and guess what, they were right not to count on me. I loved my new family, but there was no point in me lying about it. I never liked working serials. Besides, we didn't have a snowball's chance in hell of even getting close to our guy. That son-of-a-bitch was way smarter than all of us put together. I didn't want to say it aloud, but there was no way in hell we would ever catch him. I didn't have an option before, but at this point, I figured I'd just let it be somebody else's problem. I didn't know what was in store for me in New York, but it had to be better than all the depressing shit I'd been stuck with for the past few years. Plain and simple, I was ready to put my past where it belonged, behind me.

I walked to the door, getting ready to leave David's office for what would turn out to be the last time.

"Oh, and kid...."

"Yes?" I turned back towards them.

David paused for a second. "You do this, and you leave your credentials at home, got it?"

"Yeah, I got it," I replied.

David gave me a nod and said, "Good luck, Alex."

I walked out and ran straight to the supply room. I grabbed a medium sized moving box from the top shelf and high-tailed it back to my desk to collect my things. I cleared that joint completely out, even the lonely picture of Bill I had reluctantly put on my desk. After I finished packing, there was no evidence I was ever there. I left that fucker just as clean and clear as the day I joined the team. In my mind, I'd already made my decision.

No offense, but to hell with Z-Squad. I was getting the fuck out of Dodge. I saw Karen on my way out but played it cool. I didn't want her to know I wasn't coming back at all. I figured I'd visit them once I came back to get my furniture and stuff moved up north.

"Hey Karen, I'm about to leave."

"David told me about your new assignment," she said. "I'm putting together a care package for you, and I'll get with you as soon as possible on it. Actually, just look for an email from me, it'll have everything you need, okay?"

"Yeah, okay Karen."

"Everything alright?" she asked.

"Yeah," I said, smiling. "Everything's fine."

"Well, good luck," said Karen. "Be safe and call me if you need to."

"Thank you, sweetie." I gave her a hug, and then walked out of there happy as a lark, skipping down the hall straight to the elevators. I went down to the parking garage, put my little box of stuff in the trunk of my Stang, and ran back inside to see Tom.

When I got to the procurement window, it looked like Tom was just about to go on break. I'm not sure if I was happier about leaving or actually catching him right before his break the way everybody always gets me. "Hang on a sec I gotta turn this car back in Tom."

"No, you don't," he said.

"Yes, I do, I'm going to New York!" I smiled proudly.

"Oh, I doubt that," Tom replied.

"Seriously, I got a transfer to-"

"Yeah, I heard," he interrupted, "but, you're not going. Your mouth's saying one thing, but I know you're not a quitter. You hang on to that Denali. I had my guys remove all the government plates and markings a few minutes ago."

"But-"

"No buts!" exclaimed Tom. "VIN's been re-registered. You decide to stay, and you'll need that truck. You decide to go to New York instead and you can FedEx the keys back to me."

"Whatever man," I said laughing. "Fine, I like driving the Denali anyway! Seriously though, here...." I put the keys down on the counter and waved. "Take care, buddy!"

"Wait a minute!" Tom tried to come after me, but I took off.

I ran straight back down to my baby and hopped in. She was doing just fine, all except the excessive amount of spider webs inside. *YEESH!* It was weird too because I had the windows rolled up the whole time. *Ewe, I hate spider webs they are nasty!* I picked the web off my face and out of my hair. Then, I got ready to crank up. I pressed the clutch all the way down and turned the key, and wouldn't you know, the starter just clicked and clicked and then clicked some more. "Dammit!" I got out and looked around. There were a couple of guys standing near the door talking, so I solicited their assistance.

"Hey guys!" I waved, turning on my feminine charm. "Can you help a girl out?"

They both ran over.

"Car won't start?" asked the short one.

"Yeah, can you give me a jump?"

"You got cables?" he asked.

I replied, "No."

"Is it an automatic?" he asked.

"Please!" I frowned.

"Oh, excuse me. Come on Mike, we can push this thing back. Why don't you get in and steer, Miss?"

He didn't have to ask me twice. I climbed in, put the car in neutral and released the handbrake. They walked around to the front and pushed. My car's pretty light and I ain't exactly chunky, so they didn't have a problem rolling it out of the space. I straightened the wheel, and they circled around to the rear.

"You ready?" yelled Mike.

I gave him a thumbs-up and took my foot off the brake.

They counted to three and then pushed from behind, running and shoving until the car got up to a good brisk roll. I shifted into second gear and popped the clutch. The car shook and shuttered for a few seconds, but then the motor roared. I pulled up a little and stopped. Then, I pressed the gas a couple of times and rolled the driver side window down. I stuck my hand out and waved, and the short guy sprinted up.

"Nice Mustang," he said, leaning into the window.

"Thank you." I smiled, feeling proud about my baby.

"Those eighteens?" he asked.

"Yep!" I exclaimed.

He had one of those *goddamn I'm fuckin' impressed* looks on his face. "I see you got it lowered too," he said. "Is the motor still factory?"

"Please! I got a cool air intake, headers, Flow Master catback, a chip, 355 gear, a roll cage, oh and a Tremec 5-speed." I rarely get a chance to use that sentence, so I was amped up to say the least.

He stepped back and stared at both me and the car for a brief moment. "I don't know what to say!" He laughed, and said, "You got issues."

I smiled. "Why, thank you very much!"

"You better let it run a while before you take off," he warned.

"Don't worry, I got this! By the way, thanks for your help. I heard the other guy's name is Mike, but I didn't catch yours."

"Jeff, I work up in IT"

"Thanks Jeff from IT," I said in a flirtatious tone. "Name's Alex." I stuck my arm out the window and we shook hands.

"You're welcome," he replied. "You take it easy out there, Speed Racer."

I giggled a little and tapped the gas a few more times. Then, I put on my seat belt and he stepped back.

"Later Jeff. Tell Mike I said thanks."

"Will do," he responded.

He waved and I drove off. I arrived home, still high off the thought of living in New York, the Big Apple—shopping, shows and true crime. What a combination. Bill was already home again. I'm not sure how he was getting so much time off or what the hell he was doing, but I didn't care. I was so excited, I ran right up to him, kissed him on the lips, and gave him the good news.

"Hey baby, guess what ... we're going to New York!" I screamed joyously and triumphantly. But, to no avail, Mr. Bill didn't share my sentiment.

"New York?" he asked. "What are you talking about?"

"New York, you know the Big Apple, and-"

"I know what New York is," he interrupted, "but I don't know what you mean when you say we're going to New York. What, you need a vacation or something?"

"No silly, I got a transfer to the New York Field office."

Bill frowned. "Man, you trippin', right?"

"What...? No, I'm serious, it's a really big opportunity and-"

"Yeah, for you," he said, breaking free of my little bear hug, "but what's in New York for me?"

"Well, I got a lot more money on my relocation check than we probably need to get up there ... maybe you can use part of it to rent a place and finally start your own shop."

"I can start a shop right here in Atlanta," Bill snapped. "I don't need to go to no damn New York to do that."

I could tell he was getting irritated, but I didn't know why, so I figured I'd be straight up and ask. "Bill, why are you getting upset, baby? I thought you of all people would be happy for us."

"You mean happy for you!" he exclaimed. "IT'S ALWAYS ABOUT YOU, DENISE!"

"Denise? Whoa, why you gotta be hollerin' at me like that, Bill?"

"Cause I'm sick of your shit!" he yelled.

I crossed my arms. "So, what are you saying, you don't want me to go?"

Bill replied, "I'm saying I ain't going to no fuckin' New York. Ain't shit up there for me, and ... and ... I tell you what, if you decide you gone go anyway, then you can go without me, and you can forget about us!"

I didn't know what to say. I just looked at him. He was acting like a goddamn spoiled brat. I could see if he had some reservations and wanted to discuss them. Hell, I had some reservations myself, but that wasn't going to stop me from going and seeing what was up there for me. Maybe it was too much for him to process all of a sudden, but I figured we could talk and work it out.

"Bill let's just look at this thing from both sides. Now, I-"

"NO!" Bill yelled. "Fuck you if you think I'm going anywhere with you. Why don't you call the international man of mystery, Malik? Maybe he'll go up there witcha, 'cause it ain't gone be me."

"Bill, what the fuck you talking about? I ain't seein' no damn Malik or anybody else for that matter."

"Whatever!" he exclaimed.

I walked over and tried to grab his hand, but he fought me. I'd never seen him like that before.

"Bill, I don't understand why you wanna stay down here so bad anyway."

"I got family here," he said, angrily.

"You barely talk to your family!"

"Just 'cause they blood don't make 'em family," he responded. "Look, you ain't got no rings on yo' finger." He pulled away and threw his hands up. "You wanna go, go, but don't be expecting me to follow yo' ass around the country wit' all yo' bullshit."

I shook my head. "Yo know what? We'll talk about this later." I walked towards the bedroom.

"We ain't talking 'bout a goddamn thang later," yelled Bill. "Don't ask me for shit, I'm out!" He left the apartment, slamming the front door like a raging lunatic.

What the fuck was that about? I didn't want to nag and irritate him, but he was trippin'. I called his cell to see if he would actually be straight up with me and tell me what the hell was going on.

"Fuck you want?" he answered.

"Bill, stop being so nasty."

"Oh, you think I'm being nasty? Watch me!"

I asked. "What's your problem with New York?"

"I told you I don't want to talk about this shit Denise, so stop trying to make me!"

"I thought you loved me, Bill."

"Oh, now you trippin' ... kiss my ass Denise!"

"Is all that necessary?"

"Yeah," he replied, "because you just gone keep pushing me on this muthafuckin' shit till I give in, and I ain't doing it this time. You so much like your mother, it don't make no sense. That's why y'all don't get along."

"The fuck you talkin' about Bill?"

"I'm saying I'll go to hell before I follow your lying ass up there."

"How the fuck you gone call me a liar? It ain't like you tell the truth every minute of the day Bill. You know what, I may not be the best woman in the world, but I don't have to put up with this shit from you."

"THEN DO WHAT YOU GOTTA DO!" he yelled.

"FUCK YOU OLE SORRY ASS NIGGA!"

He yelled, "SHIT, FUCK YOU TOO BITCH!"

I was totally shocked. I just hung up the phone. All the years we'd been together, Bill never called me a bitch, at least not to my face. My feelings were so hurt. I went into the bedroom, fell across the bed and cried. Obviously, Bill had been taking lessons from my mother on how to manipulate me and make me feel bad about the best thing to ever happen in my life, because that's exactly what he just did. He didn't even congratulate me, or my promotion, or anything. He just went right into how he wasn't going to New York with me. And, he called me a bitch to my face. How could he even think about doing something like that?

I couldn't imagine why Bill was so hell bent on staying in Atlanta anyway. He didn't talk to his people, and there was no way my folks liked him that much. Then again, maybe I was wrong about that. When we go to church, I sit on one side and he sits over there with them. Maybe they're closer than I think—closer than he's willing to admit. Bill claims he can't stand my folks, but he sure spends a lot of time around them. Maybe they finally found a way to get rid of me permanently. I bet if I hang around one day after church, I'll see what's really going on. Or maybe not. Maybe I should just pack my bags and bounce.

I wiped my tears. "Fuck Bill! I'm going to New York one way or another."

I pulled myself together, got up off the bed and immediately started making travel plans. I logged onto the web to make a hotel reservation and rent a car up in New York for the next two weeks. I figured I'd go up, get settled in, find an apartment, and then move my stuff up later. Despite Bill's hateful tirade, I was still extremely excited about moving, so I tired myself out looking up information about the city. Later on, I ate dinner, watched some TV, and finally went to bed.

Bill didn't get back home until late, and when he finally did, he slept on the sofa. The next day, he was out before I woke up. He must've really been pissed. I don't think I ever seen him leave that early for anything, especially not work. Bill had been working at the GM plant in Doraville for years, so he could pretty much work any schedule he wanted, and it was never an early one. I guess he just had to hurry up and get away from me. I still didn't understand what his problem was. For a while it seemed like we were cool, but then he just nutted up out of nowhere. And, why the hell was he talking about Malik? How'd he even know anything about him other than his name? Maybe somebody's been talking to him and feeding him information, but who? My sister? No way in hell. Theresa's my girl, she loves me. I know she'd never betray me like that.

I didn't give it another thought. As far as I could tell, Bill was just fishin' anyway. I ain't paying his ass no attention. He's acting like he couldn't stand me anyway. If I leave, I'm sure he'd get over it. Me being gone meant he could have some more time to be alone with that other bitch, so he didn't have to sneak around anymore. I figured it didn't matter anyway. A few months and he'd be tired of her. He'd be begging to come up to New York with me.

I had the whole New York thing planned out in my mind, and I was set to go, but later that day, the unspeakable happened. I was lying on the sofa watching the news, and low and behold, they reported another murder. Right there on the screen, right before my eyes was our next victim, victim number seven. The news wouldn't give any details, but in my heart, I knew it was our guy.

"Jesus, what's the point of all this if you can't do some good? It just can't be like this, can it?"

I was torn. I didn't know what to do. Last thing I wanted was to hang around Atlanta, but I couldn't leave in good conscious without helping David take this guy down. Suddenly, I got really interested in the case again.

I grabbed my laptop and checked my email. There was a new message from Karen in my inbox. She'd sent my cover ID over. In it was my new name, copies of legal documents, protocols and the location of the apartment, everything I needed to do the job. I wanted to do the right thing, but I still wasn't sure about it all. I had to take my time and make the right choice, so I figured I'd sleep on it a few days.

Turns out a few days thinking on a critical, life-changing decision is no time at all. Friday morning rolled around faster than the speed of light. I can't even remember what the hell I was doing the days prior. All I knew was the weekend was coming, and I had to make a decision fast. To make things even more complicated, through some miracle I still don't comprehend, Bill and I were back on speaking terms. When I walked into the kitchen Friday morning, he was sitting at the table eating breakfast.

"Morning babe," he greeted.

"Bill ... baby, we need to talk about-"

"Yeah I know," he interrupted. "Look I'm sorry baby ... I just ... you know, I'm doing well at the plant, we got a church here, and I-"

"No, Bill, YOU GOT A CHURCH! See, that's what I'm talking about, I go along with whatever you want, even if I end up looking like a dumbass, sitting on the other side of the church while my man is hugged up with my family. I always cater to you, but you hate everything about what I want. It's like anything I need always seems to be low on your priority list. You don't like my job, you don't like my friends, and you supposedly don't like my family, so what's left?"

"You're right," he said. "Look I'm sorry. I really am."

"I have to leave now Bill, and I won't be back for a while."

"What...?"

"Yeah, I'll be gone for a few months, maybe more."

Bill sighed. "Where, New York?"

"No, Bill, not New York. I had two options, stay here and do undercover work away from home or go to New York and be with you. You've chosen for me, so I don't know what to tell you."

"Alex, I didn't know. Where will you be?" he asked.

"I can't tell you that," I replied, "but I'll be in the local area. I didn't want to be away from you like this. That's why I thought New York, or any change in scenery might be good for us, but I understand where you're coming from now."

"What's that supposed to mean, Alex?"

I kissed him on his forehead. "I'll be back in a few months. I'll try to check in with you, but I can't promise anything."

Bill said, "Don't worry about it baby, I'm here, and I ain't going nowhere." He jumped up and hugged me so tight, I could barely breathe. "I love you ... I promise, I ain't going nowhere ... you do what you gotta do, and I'll start looking for a place up in New York, okay?"

I pushed him away. "Don't patronize me, Bill."

He shook his head. "No, I'm serious. Do what you gotta do here, and once you're ready, we'll go ahead and move. Can you do it like that?"

Bill didn't know I'd already made up my mind. I had already made travel plans too. New York was happening with or without him, whether I decided to go undercover or not.

"I don't know Bill ... I guess once I finish with this undercover assignment, I'll ask David and see if they'll still let me go up to New York."

"Good, it's settled then." He kissed me.

"Bill, you can't tell anybody what I'm doing right now, okay?"

"I know, I know," he replied. "Look it'll be just like you're back in the Navy. I made it then, I'll make it now. I just want you to be safe whatever you're doing ... promise me that."

I tilted my head and smiled. "I promise baby."

"Okay." He kissed me again and held me for a long time.

"I love you," I told him.

"I love you too, Alex."

I smiled. "Alright, I gotta go now."

Bill walked me to the door and gave me one last kiss goodbye. I was kinda suspicious about his sudden change in attitude. He seemed to be coming around a lot faster than expected, which worried me for some reason, but I didn't have time for that. Once again, I had to put all my personal drama out of my mind and get focused on the job at hand. I left the apartment, walking slowly down the stairs and out to the car. I hopped in, cranked up, and pulled out of the apartment complex. I stopped right outside the gate for a minute to collect my thoughts and make sure I had all my bases covered. Then, I pulled out onto Northside Drive and headed for the expressway.

The apartment Karen set up was in Cobb County. I had the address and knew how to get there, but I needed to ditch my Mustang first, so I drove back to the office. I all but snuck into that place, hoping Tom wasn't there. I was sure if he saw me, he'd be gloating, and I didn't want to hear his mouth. I took the elevator up to procurement. Naturally, Tom was standing there like he'd been waiting for me to come back all along. The moment he saw me he started smiling uncontrollably. The Denali keys were sitting right on top of his desk.

I stood there at the window, rolling my eyes and tapping my nails on the counter. Tom picked up the keys and came out of the office to greet me personally. He was a short man, kind of stocky, with brown hair and grey eyes. He was one of the few guys I knew who carried a real live pocket protector. I didn't even know they still made those things, but that joker had it loaded up with pens, pencils, a little knife and all sorts of nifty gadgets.

"Southerland, I hate to say it-"

"Then, don't." I smiled.

He shook his head. "When will you young folks learn? I take it you saw the news report? Couldn't do it could you? Couldn't leave, huh?"

"Are you going to look after my baby?"

"Don't sass me," said Tom. "Give me the keys, and I'll have one of my guys clean it up inside and out."

"Thanks!" We traded keys.

"You're welcome," said Tom. "Like I said before, we took the gear out of the Denali, and it's gassed up and ready to go."

"Seriously, Tom ... thanks man."

"Don't mention it," he replied. "Listen Southerland, I heard about what they put you up to. You and I both know it's no walk in the park."

"Yeah, I know, Tom."

"You be careful out there," he warned. "Oh, and if you have trouble with the truck, just-"

"Just let you know, right?" I interrupted.

"No, we marked a local garage on the GPS. Take it there. We got agents in place, and you can trust them."

We shook hands.

"Take care Tom."

"I'll see you around ... good luck, and I'll try not to put too many miles on the Mustang."

I waved my finger at him and warned, "You better not," I said, giggling again. Tom was the cutest little thing in the whole world.

"Be good," he said.

"You too buddy."

I went back down to the garage and climbed in the Denali. I pulled up the file Karen sent to my handheld and reviewed it. My cover was Alexis Bowden, upper crust suburban white girl gone wild. According to the file, I'd been in and out of the system on several counts of petty cybercrimes, including defacing websites. There were a few outstanding warrants for parking tickets, and evidently, I was sitting on a trust fund with enough cash to use as taxidermy stuffing for Godzilla.

Karen did really good with my cover. Alexis was the perfect alias, far enough from my real name to make for good cover, but close enough so I didn't say, *Alexis, who the fuck's Alexis?* Working undercover can be a bitch sometimes. Using aliases is easier said than done. I remember blowing an operation in Brazil because I forgot who I was one day. Man, we barely made it out of there alive.

I finished reviewing the file and put my PDA down. I cranked up, pulled out of the lot and headed straight to my new undercover hideout.

The apartment was off of South Cobb Drive in Smyrna, nestled deep in the woods off the main street. It was setup almost like my real apartment only it was a two bedroom instead of one, and it was much newer, extremely nice. The carpet was flawless, and the appliances were beyond high-tech. The place was already furnished, and there was a TV in the living room. I walked back into the master bedroom, and it was just as nice as the rest of the apartment. The bed was decent too. I know because I spent several minutes jumping up and down on top of it.

Karen was a trip. When she puts some shit together, she puts some shit together. How the fuck does a stiff ass white woman from Russia know what young black people rock? Amazing that woman is. She had a closet full of little hoochie momma clothes all in my size, designer stuff too. That shit was straight hip-hop. Who knew she had it in her? Bravo Karen, bravo! I walked back out of the master and over to the other bedroom. There was a desk and chair in there, but nothing else. I assumed that's where the computer would go.

I doubled back and checked the fridge and pantry. Everything was stocked up, so I was set. Karen even had toiletries and stuff for me in the bathroom. It wasn't everything I liked to use, but it's the thought that counts. After checking the bathroom, I walked out on the deck and looked around. I spotted a tiny little camera hidden up in the ceiling fan. If you weren't looking for it, there's no way you would've seen it. "Well, David said they'd be watching," I whispered

I went back inside and inspected everything else. The only other cameras I found were up in the entryway light fixture and the ceiling directly outside the front door. Thank God, they didn't have a camera in every room. As much as I like showing my body off, I don't even wanna think about those old geezers watching me, jacking off. I could just see David saying, *hey Frank, look at that rack. Yeah, that's what I'm talking about man.* And, don't think for a second that I'm exaggerating either. You get a few drinks in those boys, and whoa momma, they're worse than me, which is pretty damn bad. It's probably why we all get along so well. Shoot, those two jokers would be talking about my ass just like I talk about everybody else. And yes, I do talk about both men and women. I don't discriminate. Yes, I look at other women, and no, I'm not gay. I just like to look at women's bodies. My sister says it's crass, but I simply ignore her lame ass. By the way, I talk about her too, especially when she goes on a binge and that little tummy starts poking out like it is right about now. Theresa's looking pretty fat these days.

I finished checking out the front, and then went back inside. I locked the front door and just lounged in the living room. After a few minutes, I got a call on my cell.

"Hello," I answered.

"Thank you," came a voice over the phone.

It was David. "You know, this is bullshit man!" I laughed.

"Eyes are up. Perimeter only. Computers are coming in ten. When my guy gets there, lose the cell phone."

"Copy that," I replied. I hung up and powered down my phone.

The deliveryman showed up in exactly ten minutes, just like David said he would. I signed for the shipment and the guy unpacked everything for me. I thought I was going to have to spend the night reading instructions, but evidently, the deliveryman's the computer technician too. He immediately started setting everything up and checking it to make sure it was all good. While he was working, I casually walked over and slipped my phone into his bag. Then, I looked over his shoulder while he set up the desktop, monitor system, and laser printer. After that, he hooked up the internet and hit a few websites. It only took him about 30 minutes to get everything set up, and I was good to go.

"Okay Ms. Bowden, we're done here," he said with a smile. We shook hands and he slipped me a new phone on the sly.

"Thank you, Sir." I wanted to giggle so badly. I love that CIA, spy shit.

The man packed his things, and I walked him to the door. I locked up the apartment after he left and ran back into the computer room to have a look at my new system, which just so happened to be mind-blowing. I had a multi-monitor display and a PC tower big as the Trojan horse. I shook the mouse and each of the screens came alive one-by-one starting from the center.

"Damn, that's fuckin' hot!" I exclaimed.

On the desk, I found a small box the technician left behind. I grabbed it and sat down, Indian-style, on the floor. I opened the package and dumped the contents out onto the carpet. Credit cards fell out along with a wad of cash, multiple IDs, checks, everything Alexis Bowden needed to be a good, or bad, citizen. I got up off the floor, climbed behind the keyboard, and tried to get a head start on learning about the Death Peddler game. With that monster of a PC running, I had all I needed right at my fingertips. Who knew work could be so easy? But, like David always said, daylight's burning, so I didn't waste any time gloating about the situation.

Dimitri sent instructions on how to find a mirror site and download the RAR files for the installation program for the Death Peddler game. I navigated to the site and used the login information he gave me. I downloaded the game along with several patches, upgrades and hacks like unlimited ammo, customized killer profiles, the whole nine yards. I hopped offline and mounted the game to a virtual drive. The install file was huge. It took forever to load, even on my wonderful new gaming box. After about 30 minutes, finally, it was on.

Getting into the game action was like stealing candy from a baby it was so easy, even without all the extras loaded. You can just start by logging on anonymously and watching the action. You can also set views to show activities of the police, the serial killers, or both, and man was that educational.

It pains me to report that some people are just sick in the head. The entire game was disturbing to say the least. And I thought I was bad. Whoever came up with Death Peddler needed to have their ass sent straight to hell. The graphics were so amazing, I was surprised the real-time uplink via the web didn't slow the action down. It didn't, not one bit. The sex, violence, and realistic graphics put you right in the middle of what I could only describe as maximum carnage on fast-forward. You know how some games have a plot or purpose? Not Death Peddler. It was just a vicious, bloody battle between good and evil, one in which no one could predict the victor. I think that's what made it fascinating to so many people, me included. I literally watched for hours on end. I spent the entire first week, sitting at the computer, eating take out and watching all the sick scenarios unfold from the minds of a bunch of idiot kids. They should have their little juvenile delinquent asses in school somewhere instead of playing this game all day long.

Following the action was like watching a soap opera gone bad only on cable TV instead of network television. There were no rules. I witnessed random rapes and murders, not to mention players torturing everything from people to cows. Those jokers were bombing, maiming, decapitating, and generally engaging in all types of sadistic acts.

One day, I was in the forum and saw a thread about some dumbass trying to go on a killing spree at the White House. Needless to say, U.S. Secret Service put a stop to that real fast. He's dead now. The Secret Service module is aggressive, relentless and unforgiving. Those agents will kill you on general principle. They don't ask any questions, they don't even read you your rights. It's just BANG, BANG, and you're done for. When you die in the game, your profile is permanently disabled. Most players who get killed try to build another one, but their behavior rarely changes. The same is true for real serial killers. They may dress differently, or try to act brand new, but at the core, their spots rarely change. To me, they'll always just be a bunch of filthy bastards.

I spent every waking moment of the day studying the Death Peddler world, paying close attention to how players play and communicate with each other. The only time I took a break was when I needed to satisfy basic needs—liquor, bathroom, food and water, more liquor, jogging, more liquor, and of course the occasional grocery store run for more liquor, in that particular order. No excuses but drinking helped me pass the time, plus I fill up and take in a lot less calories than ordering a pizza every time I get hungry.

With all the idle time on my hands, and the drinking, it didn't take long to get sucked into Death Peddler. By the end of the month, I knew almost every player, and I was keeping a log of their activity. I paid special attention to our man, John Constantine, whenever I could track him. He was clever, definitely some kind of a computer hacker, as good as Dimitri or maybe better. When he didn't want to be seen, he was nowhere to be found, just like that.

I watched Constantine carefully. He was suspect number one, but I wanted to surveil him a while before jumping into the game. After seeing his fourth kill, I was convinced Frank and David were right. Constantine's methods were identical to our serial killer's. He was an evil fucker, murdering with no rhyme, no reason, and, as far as I could tell, no remorse. When I saw him kill in the game, I reenacted the scene with Karla Charles in my mind, which made it a lot more real for me, and it helped me focus. I hated that son-of-a-bitch, but deep down in some dark corner of my heart, he fascinated me.

When I first talked about this thing with Frank and David, I had no clue what it really was all about. Honestly, I thought it was just another stupid kid's game. Boy was I naïve. Keep in mind now, I was merely a spectator at that point, but I'd fallen head over heels in love with the game. It was invigorating. Just thinking about playing made me feel superior. Those other players thought they were doing something, but they had no clue how sick and twisted Alexis Bowden could be. *Just wait! Wait till I register! Fear me! Fear me!*

Eventually, I dedicated one of my monitors to movies, so I could watch a few action flicks while I studied the game. I figured it was a good way to pass the time, so that's what I did. I watched countless hours of movies, and pretty much lived like a hermit. It was a good thing I kept my daily running sessions up or I would've been one big, fat bitch by the time I got out of there. I'd be shopping for weight-loss pills with Theresa.

I joke a lot, but working undercover is like riding a bike. It comes back to you when you need it. Unfortunately, it brings about all your old bad habits that make you credible too. At least before when I was undercover, I was out doing something just about every day. But on this case, I had a whole lot of idle time on my hands unexpectedly, and I really didn't know how to handle that. After a while, it was starting to wear me down. I thought about Bill a lot, what he was doing, and if he was okay. It sounds silly, but sometimes I wondered about stupid stuff like whether he'd eaten dinner, or if he washed his clothes. He's a grown-ass man. *Yeesh, what the heck's wrong with me!* I think I just really missed my boo. I hated we couldn't talk. Sure, I knew what was at stake, and I didn't want to blow my cover or let David down, but I had to find a way to sneak back home and see Bill, even if it was just through binoculars. I think that would've made me feel a lot better. At the end of the day, I just wanted to see his handsome smiling face.

In my newfound solitude, I began to regret all the times I ran off with someone else instead of staying home with Bill. Guess you don't miss your water until the well runs dry. If I thought working Anti-Piracy sucked, being away from the only boyfriend I ever loved was cruel and unusual punishment.

I was homesick, but I knew the only way to get back to civilization was to catch Constantine. Despite our piss poor progress to date, I was confident we'd get him. I just hoped, for my sake, it was sooner than later.

Chapter 10

Weeks passed, and I continued my daily routine of movies, jogging, drinking, and Death Peddler spectating. One day, I was in the living room watching a Ben Kingsley movie. Ever since "Sexy Beast", I been down with the King. He was one mean fuckin' bastard in that movie, and I loved it. I think I used to act like his character in a lot of ways. I was mad all the time, pissin' everybody off, saying whatever I wanted, and just generally starting a whole bunch of shit. Yeah, I can definitely relate. Anyway, my favorite scene in that movie is when he's in the kitchen, kicking that man's cabinets. Oh, and when he's like "No, no, no, no, no! No, no, no, no, no!" and then cracks the fat guy over the head with a beer bottle. Good Lawd, I was in hysterics. I bet it's hard for you to imagine how a sweet, innocent girl like me could get excited over a movie like that. Okay, maybe it's not that hard, but hey I don't hit people over the head without some kind of warning, or at least making sure they see it coming. Anyhow, I was watching this other movie where Ben was playing a serial killer that killed other serial killers, and right then, it hit me. I knew exactly how to get started on Death Peddler with a standing ovation.

I jumped online and sent Dimitri an encrypted email with a special request. As always, he was on the case. Dimitri was my genie in a magic lamp, and he was quick on his feet too. It took less than an hour for him to grant my wish. As usual, he sent the hacks with the kind of crystal-clear instructions even a drunk could follow. Not saying I was drunk the entire time, but.... *Bygones!* So, anyway, I logged onto the remote portal and FTP'd my special package to a mirror server. It was password protected, so only I could use the features, which was good because it gave me a serious edge. Once I had everything uploaded, I took the first big leap towards becoming a Death Peddler—I created a new profile.

Turns out, coming up with a cool name was the hardest thing to do. I sat there in front of my computer in deep thought, pondering long and hard about my screen name. I wanted to come up with a good one that stood out, so I grabbed a legal pad and jotted down a bunch of possibles. Once I filled up a page, I'd go back to the top and cross out all the ones I didn't like. Finally, I settled in on one that seemed to suit me—General Maximus Decimus Meridius, Gladiator, killer of all killers. Mmm, Russell Crowe was so fucking hot in that movie, swinging his big sword with his little sexy Aussie ass. Basically, I loved that movie, and I liked the way Russell said the name with extreme conviction. Amazingly enough, no one else had that username, or any variation of it, so it was perfect!

I set up everything and activated my profile. Once inside the game, the first thing I did was introduce myself to the local police department by sending an anonymous fax. It was a borderline cheap parlor trick, but no one had thought of it before, so I definitely got noticed. Tipping off the police was risky as hell, but it was a bold move that soon came to be coveted by players everywhere. I actually started a new trend. After that, a bunch of fools tried to follow in my footsteps, but most ended up getting caught or killed. After laughing at all my new copycats, the next thing I did was completely customize my character. I made sure my little killer was stacked—long jet-black hair, huge tits, a muscular, athletic build, agility, and stamina. I put her in all black military BDUs and gave her some camo face paint. She was one bad bitch, ready for some good ole fashion killin'.

I spent a lot of time getting used to the controls. They were fairly complicated. You have to keep a cheat sheet next to the keyboard to move around the city. Thank God, I was able to use a joystick too, or I guess a joypad is the proper term. That thing really made life easy, and I could use it along with the keyboard commands. After a few days playing around, I finally got down to some serious business.

My first kill was special to me, a low-level player named Johnny25. I watched him for a while and took note as he stalked his third victim. I tracked him silently like a true hunter, and it got to the point where I could actually tell when he was ready to strike. I watched him that entire day as he got organized. I knew he was going for it too because of how he acted the entire time he cased his victim's place. It's like he had to stop himself from going right in without a plan. I could tell he was hungry and ready to kill again. I waited patiently, watching him until the perfect window of opportunity arose. Then, I sprang into action. I trailed him back to his apartment. While he gathered supplies, I high-tailed it back to his victim and did some prep work of my own. I used chloroform to put his victim to sleep. Then, I went to work, setting my trap. After I got everything just right, I moved back into the woods behind the house and waited for Johnny25. I waited ... and waited ... and then, waited some more. Finally, he showed up.

Johnny25 broke into the home through the basement door. Once inside, he moved directly upstairs. The victim was in the kitchen cooking, clueless to my earlier breech, and certainly not expecting some strange man in her home. I watched her every move through my thermal binoculars.

Upstairs, Johnny25 didn't hesitate. He immediately took the woman down. He raped her right on the kitchen table and was getting ready to slit her throat when he received my instant message, which read, "Death smiles at us all. All a man can do is smile back."

Without skipping a beat, Johnny25 took off running, trying his damndest to get the hell out of there. I waited a couple of seconds and watched as he stumbled back down through the basement. He got the door open and was moving fast. He actually made it about five paces out the house before I remote-detonated the explosives I'd planted all over the house.

The blast from the C-4 was enough to take out the entire property, everything, including poor ole Johnny25. I splattered his ass all over the yard. I also took the liberty of planting mini-cams around the interior and exterior of the home earlier just to capture the carnage from multiple angles. It was too clever for words. I replayed the video a few times for my own amusement, and then started a new thread in the forum to stream a copy of the footage.

Not a single soul inside the community took my treachery well. Evidently, I'd broken some unspoken, carnal rule of Death Peddler. Oh, the private messages I received ranged from, "Why, why, why did you do it?" to "Die Gladiator, die!" Even the moderators were disgusted with me. They banned me from the forum and tried to remove my Death Peddler profile permanently but couldn't thanks to Dimitri's hacks. No matter what they tried, I just kept coming back like the Terminator.

I learned a lot working with Z-Squad, but one thing in particular was, I found out Dimitri's a lot more than just a computer geek. He's a real-life great hacker, one of the most notorious. He caught a Federal case, was charged with several counts of industrial espionage, and ended up serving his sentence under David's rule. I guess dealing with David, unfortunate as it can be sometimes, beats a 20-year stretch in a federal penitentiary any day.

Dimitri was really good, no joke. The hack he wrote for me was of a special nature, a virus capable of entering the network through the mirror site, replicating itself and finding its way to the primary host. Not only did it allow me to break all the rules, but I was able to override the folks who were trying to override me. They repeatedly booted me off the system. They even took the servers offline to reset the community, but to no avail, it didn't stop me. I was on a roll.

I continued my violent killing spree, taking out serial killer after serial killer. For the meticulous planners, I used explosives, and for the impulse killers, a high-powered, silenced sniper rifle with a thermal scope, courtesy of none other than the infamous Dimitri. I could take out a pigeon a mile away with that thing.

I quickly became a legend in the community and not in a good way. Thankfully, Dimitri had things set, so I couldn't be tracked. With a single command, I could make it, so no one could view my profile or my current activity. I was a ghost, the digital grim reaper, and no serial killer was safe.

By week's end, there were at least ten different threads created in my honor. All the players were miserable, but it didn't stop anyone from doing their thing. Death Peddler was the new age drug, and everybody who knew about it was addicted, even me, because how long can you pretend to be something you're not before you really are? Between you and me, I was hooked after the first kill.

Word got around fast about the "Killer of Killers", and I had a lot of haters out there, but some of the players actually welcomed the idea of Gladiator. They saw me as a challenge. They thought they could outsmart me. Boy, were they wrong. The Death Peddler community continued to go through changes as I delivered my promise, death to all serial killers. Even the computer driven police were starting to pick up on the fact they had some help from the inside. I was their unofficial vigilante, and I hunted my prey relentlessly, all day long and twice at night.

Unfortunately, my boldness pushed Constantine further underground. He was nowhere to be found, and if he was out there, he was being careful not to be seen. I suspected he either wasn't playing at all or was blocking me from seeing what he was up to the same way I was blocking everyone else. I soon found it to be the latter.

At first, I thought I'd lost Constantine forever, but then one day, I finally found him. *I got you now! You're slippin' boy!* He was in a residential community in Gwinnett County, Georgia, stalking his next victims, a family of four. It was him, John Constantine in the flesh, so to speak. I didn't have time to prep, no explosives, and I couldn't get in position for a good shot with my rifle. No, this kill would have to be up close and personal.

I watched him a while to see if he was serious. When I realized he was doing more than just window-shopping, I flipped through my inventory, and activated my Desert Eagle .50. Then, I switched into crouch mode and quietly followed him into the home.

Constantine was quick on his feet. By the time I got inside, he'd already killed the father and kids. He was just about to finish the woman off with his classic crucifix scene.

"I got your ass now, you sick mothafucka!" I exclaimed.

By then I'd completely forgotten I was there just to track and befriend him, not kill him. I typed up my standard message and got ready to hit the send button. I leaned my character back against the wall in the next room and waited until Constantine tied the woman to the cross. My plan was simple, wait until he started killing the woman, run in, aim and fire before he could do anything. I was just about to message him when, all of a sudden, my monitors went blank.

"What the fuck?" I moved my mouse around a few times, but nothing happened. I hit several keys, but again, nothing. Then, I looked under the desk to make sure I still had power. I did. "What the hell's going on?"

Suddenly, a message popped up in the middle screen. It read, "I see you."

There was a command prompt with a flashing cursor. Somebody wanted to chat, and I was willing to bet it was Mr. Constantine himself, so I responded.

"You've been busy," I typed and pressed the Enter key.

He wrote back, "I will kill you, bitch!"

My screens flickered back on and I saw the woman crucified on the floor. John Constantine had done his business right under my nose and then fled the scene. He was gone without a trace. I checked everywhere, but I was wasting my time, and I could hear police sirens, so I got out of there.

"Damn, I fucked up! Shit!" Maybe I hadn't found him after all. Maybe he drew me in, so I'd start playing his game. Maybe he'd found a way to track me after all. "How the hell did he take over my computer like that?" I ripped my network cable out of the router and checked the system logs, but I didn't see anything out of the ordinary. Just to be on the safe side, I left my network cable unplugged and took a break.

I walked into the bathroom and looked in the mirror. I was a mess. I'd been at it nonstop for weeks, away from home and away from Bill. I was homesick more than ever, and to be honest, I think I was starting to go a little crazy. I looked like a straight psycho. I'd worn the same clothes damn near three days in a row, and my hair looked like I'd been riding a roller coaster all day. No matter how bad I looked though, aside from getting back home to Bill, the only thing I thought about was which unlucky fuck I planned to kill next.

Murder had become second nature to me. I guess it always had been. Maybe my old buddy Lt. Riggs was right when he called me a natural born killer. He used to say, "Girls don't belong out here, but I know your game sailor. I know why you're here. You seem nice and civilized on the outside, but inside you're a hateful whore, a cold-hearted, evil bitch, and I'll be goddamned if I ever turn my back to you." That's one helluva thing to say about somebody, but I never denied it. I embraced it. Hell, I thought if everyone believed I was a sick crazy bitch, they'd stop messing with me, but they didn't, which made me act even worse. Like I say, you just can't let people abuse you. I'd suffered enough abuse at the hands of my own mother. It'll never happen again.

Riggs swore he had my number. I always thought he was just a sexist, egotistical pig, but the way I played Death Peddler, I dunno, maybe he was right about me. I played like the evil cold-hearted bitch he claimed I was and taking those assholes down didn't bother me one bit either. I just wish I could've found a player that slightly resembled Riggs. That would've been the icing on the cake. Damn a rifle and some explosives, I'd take my time, cut that son-of-a-bitch up, piece-by-piece, and eat his heart with some fava beans.

Day after day, I sunk deeper into my digital monster. I started drinking even more heavily than before. At first it was just a few drinks a day, but it quickly escalated to me finishing as many bottles as I could keep down. I was spending a fortune on that shit. I thought I had it all together, but I didn't. I had lost control yet again, and I couldn't stop myself this time. The walls I put up to keep that sick bitch Blondie at bay fell apart at the foundation, and I was back to the old me, the real me.

Full of liquor and rage, I made my fellow serial killers pay the ultimate price for everything I hated about life. I unleashed hell on them. It got so bad I nearly forgot the reason I'd gone undercover. I totally stopped thinking about the case. Hell, finding Constantine was like searching for a needle in a stack of needles anyway, so I just stopped trying at all. Instead, I focused all my energy on putting the fear of God into the other players. I was eating less, playing more, and drinking like a wino. Everything was a blur, and unfortunately, for me there was no turning back. I'd already crossed the razor thin line between reality and fantasy.

The weekend rolled around fast. It was Saturday night, and I'd been ruthlessly killing all week long. As usual, I'd been drinking all evening, which meant I was in a great mood. Plus, I was logged in and up to no good. I'd just finished killing some simpleton, and I wanted to keep playing, but I had to stop because I was so horny, it felt like I was going to implode. All I could think about was dick. I needed some bad, but unfortunately, that wasn't an option. Bill was off limits and bringing a man back to all that shit would've been just plain weird—too many questions to answer. Besides, David was still watching. Only thing I could do was find a suitable alternative, toys.

I put my little Gladiator to sleep and searched the web to see what was in the area. I found an adult shop nearby, literally right up the street. I figured that was the way to go, so I waited until it got dark outside and got ready to leave. I changed out of my sweats and threw on a thin black dress with some sandals. Then, I grabbed my keys, took some cash from the dresser, and grabbed a bottle of Hennessy on my way out.

I went outside and hopped in the truck. I knew I was already tipsy because I couldn't figure out how to put the key in at first. Finally, I found the ignition, cranked up and took off.

I was swerving all over the road up South Cobb Drive, but I didn't care. At every red light, I'd sip a little Hennessy. Soon as the light turned green, I drove and then sipped, and then drove and sipped some more. After a while, I was sipping more than driving. I'm sure there's some clinical term for when you know you're doing something wrong, but you keep right on in the moment. That's exactly what I was doing. It was obvious I had serious problems, but as far as I was concerned, the reward far outweighed the risk. I felt good, and I was about to feel a whole lot better real soon.

I kept driving north until I reached the corner of South Cobb and Windy Hill Road. The store was up on the right just after the intersection. I pulled into the lot and parked. I didn't even bother turning the truck off. I wanted to get in and get out quick. I ran up to the door and stumbled inside like a strung-out dope-fiend at a crack house. I walked right up to the counter.

"Dildos?" I whispered desperately.

The man behind the counter laughed. "Over there," he said softly, pointing to the far back wall.

I spun around and rushed over to grab one, but there were literally hundreds to choose from. "Dammit!"

"You okay back there?" asked the store attendant.

"Shut up ... just shut the fuck up!" I slurred, "tryin' to fuckin' concentrate back here."

If dick is what you need, that store had it all—two headed, hypoallergenic, strap-on, dishwasher safe, rotating, powered, small, and big. Hell, they even had one as big around as my thigh. I need to meet the stupid ass who'd stick that thing between her legs. No way in hell that shit sold. Then again, it was on the shelf, so I guess somebody wanted it.

I paced back and forth for a while, stopping occasionally to read the back of any package that caught my eye. I was getting more impatient by the moment, but then a double penetration vibrator nearly reached out and grabbed me. I picked up the package and read the back. According to the description, it was the first strapless dildo, which was more than enough marketing jargon for me, I was sold. It was made of silicone and the entire thing was jet black. It looked slick and sexy. My kind of play thing.

God, I was so frustrated, if slim-Jim up front wasn't looking so shady, I would've ripped that dildo open, shoved it in, and turned that bad boy on high right there in the middle of the store. Obviously, that was a bad idea. Besides, the floor was nasty as hell, so I rushed back to the counter, gripping the little package tightly in my arms.

The cashier was grinning from ear to ear. "Great choice," he said. "May I also suggest some bacterial toy cleaner or some personal lubricant?"

I didn't wanna hear anything he had to say. I just wanted to check out and leave. "Whatever," I snapped, pushing the package across the counter. "Just put it all in a bag."

He rang everything up. "That'll be $101.81."

I didn't even trip about the price. Hell, I wasn't paying for it, Alexis Bowden was. I took some cash out of my pocket and slammed it down on the counter. He carefully placed my items into a bag, and then picked the money up to sort it.

"Here," he said, holding up a 20-dollar bill, "you gave me too much."

"Keep it!" I yelled, snatching the bag off the counter and breaking for the door.

"Miss, your receipt!" he shouted.

I didn't slow down for a second. I busted out the door and ran straight for the truck. Thank goodness it was still out there. A brand-new SUV, running with the keys in the ignition in that neighborhood was like a box of free glazed doughnuts on the counter at a weight-loss center. Not sure what I'd do if some jackass drove off with it, but I sure as shit would come up with some bullshit story for the report, I promise you that. Yes, even when I'm drunk and horny as hell, OPR stays at the forefront of my mind. *They're not gonna catch me slippin'!*

I climbed back into the driver seat, shut the door and ripped open the package. I was going out of my mind I was so horny, I couldn't wait to get home. I needed instant pleasure, and I was in luck. My dildo came with a tiny silver vibrator you insert into the base. I took a big gulp of Hennessy, switched on the little vibrator, and pressed it up between my thighs.

"Oh, fuck!" I moaned, slamming my head back into the headrest and shutting my eyes tight. "Damn, that shit feels so good!"

I played with myself until I came, but that wasn't enough either. I wanted more. I wanted to feel the real thing. I thought about climbing into the back seat, but then I changed my mind. I didn't want to be all cramped up like a cheap date. I wanted to treat myself real nice.

I pulled the truck in gear and wheeled out of the parking lot, blasting down South Cobb, pleasuring my clit and drinking Hennessy until my vision was blurry from all the alcohol and orgasms. Luckily, there were no cops out, or I would have been up shit-creek without a paddle. I'm pretty sure I ran a few red lights.

I made it back to the apartment in record speed, safely I might add, no crashes, and no run-ins with the law. Lord knows how I got my proxy card for the gate to work. It seemed a lot more complicated than usual. I fumbled around for a while, but eventually got in.

As soon as the gate opened, I stepped on the gas and slung the Denali around to my building. The tires squealed as I damn near parked sideways in a space. I got out and stumbled up the stairs as fast as possible with my little pleasure bag in tow. My pussy was throbbing and aching for more attention. By then, Blondie was steadily sweet-talking me. She told me she wanted me bad. She said I was powerless to resist her charms, and she was right. I told her I was sorry for turning away from her for so long, and she welcomed me home with open arms.

Once inside the apartment, I grabbed a few bottles of whatever I had left in the kitchen, and then ran back to the computer room where I planned to put on a fantastic show for my master. I turned off the lights, put some porn on and ripped off my clothes. I felt sexy all over. I couldn't keep my hands off myself. I spread out a blanket down on the floor and got ready for a night in with the girls.

I drank as much as I could stand while I assembled my big black shiny cock. I was already dripping wet, but a little extra lubricant never hurt anyone, so I smeared some all over my new toy. Then, I got down on my back, rubbed my pussy, and pushed that big black cock deep inside.

"Oh God!" I screamed, ramming it in and out of my little love tunnel. It was hard to believe how amazing it felt inside me. I couldn't wait to feel it in my ass too. I wanted it in both holes at the same time, so I spread my cheeks and pushed the smaller bulb deep inside my tight little asshole. "Oh, wait ... almost forgot the vibrator." As soon as I switched it on, little shocks of pleasure zipped up and down my spine.

"Fuck!" I moaned, wiggling my ass, pushing and pulling that shiny smooth thing in and out in a perfect rhythm.

It was so easy to play with that little toy. Each stroke brought me closer to the next explosive orgasm. It was pure ecstasy. I pleasured myself and drank all night, showing Blondie how I could work it in multiple positions until I passed out spread-eagle on the middle of the floor.

I woke up around 3 a.m. on a cold, wet blanket, my new toy by my side. I was so drunk I couldn't see straight. All I knew was I had to pee badly. I dragged myself up and took off running, or at least I was trying to run, but fell down several times on the way to the bathroom. I was so pitiful it was ridiculous. I finally got in there and kept trying to pull down my panties, but obviously, I couldn't because I wasn't wearing any. I was butt naked. Eventually, I realized my error, and just in time, because as soon as I sat down, it was like a damn flood. I sat there for the longest, slumped over, peeing for dear life. I felt like I was going to throw up too, but I managed to hold it down.

I finished using the bathroom and stumbled back into the computer room. My head was spinning along with the room and my new dildo. I'd left it on, and it was still buzzing around on the floor, so I reached down and turned it off.

I was all messed up. I think it was safe to say I was beyond the legal limit. Somehow, under the influence just didn't quite describe it. I was completely shit-faced. I literally kept counting my fingers, coming up short. I was desperately trying to figure out what happened to the 11th one when I noticed something strange on my computer.

I stumbled over and put my face right up to the middle screen. I couldn't believe what I saw. My Gladiator was asleep, but my profile or better yet, my computer, was being hacked.

"Mothafucka!" I slurred.

It took a minute for the light bulb to go off in my head, but I soon realized it was my lucky day. I was being hacked by none other than John Constantine himself. He was hard at work, paging through my profile and making edits to the code. I watched for a moment, waiting to see what he was really up to. I decided not to do anything until he uploaded something, which from the looks of things he was getting ready to make his move.

My patience paid off. Before long, Constantine started pushing over one helluva hack. I was surprised he connected peer-to-peer, but I wasn't complaining because his system was wide open. No matter how good Constantine was, he was getting sloppy. I had him by the short and curlies, and it was time for me to tighten my grip and yank down hard. I shook my head and tried to focus, but it didn't work, so I smacked my forehead with the palm of my hand until I convinced myself I wasn't drunk anymore. I rubbed my eyes and pulled out my old Anti-Piracy hat. I plopped down in my chair, sat up straight and went to work.

Since Constantine was so exposed, I figured I'd trace his IP address, but it wasn't an easy task. I pulled every trick in the book, racing against time, hoping he wouldn't disconnect until I finished. I sent my final trace package and it was running ... 50%, 75%, 95% ... finally, it was done.

"Gotcha bitch!" I yelled.

I could see everything—his IP address, service provider and all. He was registered to a location in Atlanta. I couldn't risk logging onto the FBI's database from the apartment, so I copied the address down on a piece of paper, so I could follow up on it later. I was still very drunk, but I kept shaking myself awake. "Coffee ... yeah, I just need some coffee."

I got up to go put on a fresh pot, but then I noticed an image slowly loading on my screen. It was fuzzy at first. I couldn't make it out. But, after a few seconds, it cleared up completely. I squinted hard and moved in for a closer look. "Fuck me!"

I ransacked my closet and got dressed, falling all over the place like a wasted bum. I managed to get a t-shirt, some jeans, and sneakers on. Then, I grabbed my keys and ran out to the truck. I got in and peeled out of the apartment complex.

Out on the freeway I broke damn near every traffic law on the planet, racing to get to Northside Drive. I was so drunk the truck seemed to have a mind of its own. I wasn't even wearing my seatbelt. It took everything I had to keep from slamming into somebody else's car, but I actually made it to my real apartment in one piece. *Thank you Jesus I'll never drink again!* I pulled around back and parked.

Unfortunately, parking in the back meant more stairs, and I was barely standing, but I had no time to fool around. I drug myself up the stairs, stopping several times along the way to keep from blacking out or throwing up. My head was scrambled, and my legs burned with each step.

"Somebody, please help me," I yelled, still working my way up, but it seemed no one was around.

It took me forever, but I finally reached the top floor. I walked down the breezeway and around the corner to my apartment. I was worn out. My lungs were on fire and no matter what I just couldn't catch my breath. I tried to open the door, but it was locked, and I didn't have my keys, so I knocked as hard as I could, which in my condition, wasn't very hard at all.

"Bill," I whispered, my face pressed against the door. I knocked again. "Bill, open up, it's me." I was so frightened and scared. I just knew someone was in there, and I didn't have my gun or anything, not even a goddamn pocketknife.

I knocked a few more times and finally realized the door wasn't locked after all. I was pulling instead of pushing. "Fuck!" I turned the doorknob again and pushed the door open.

The apartment was pitch-black. Bill startled me. He was standing right in the middle of the living room, but he wasn't moving. I didn't know what the hell was going on, but he seemed completely out of it.

"Bill, you okay?" I whispered, panting and gasping for air.

He reached out for me, but then he just fell backwards onto the floor. I dropped to my knees and crawled over to see if he was okay. I elevated his head and checked his pulse. He was breathing, definitely alive, but he was out cold.

"Bill, wake up!" I shook him and rubbed his head, "Bill, please wake up!" I cried. I tried everything, I even slapped him a few times, but he didn't respond. "SOMEBODY HELP!" I screamed. "PLEASE SOMEBODY CALL 911!" But then, I heard footsteps behind me, moving fast. *How the hell did I let somebody sneak up on me?*

No sooner than the thought ran through my mind, I heard a sound that made me think my head was a baseball traveling 101 MPH towards a pissed off Barry Bonds with a loaded bat. I tried to turn around, but with all the booze in my system, my reaction time was shot to hell. My assailant was swinging for the fence. He struck me with a blow that nearly took my head clean off. I fell over beside Bill on the floor. I was rattled, but not quite out. I looked up and saw a shadowy figure standing over me. He realized I was still conscious, so he swung again, but I managed to block it with my forearm.

"Help!" I screamed.

He looked confused like he wanted to swing again, but he was too close to get another good one in, so he abandoned his club and moved into punching range. I tried my best to fight him off, but I was injured, drunk as hell and too damn slow. I couldn't defend myself or Bill. The man attacking me was small, but he was strong as a bull. He smashed my face several times with a closed fist, knocking me unconscious with the final blow. Just before I blacked out, I heard him say, "Goodbye Gladiator."

I woke up days later in a bed that was not my own, my head feeling four sizes too big for my body. When I moved, it was like someone was trimming the inside of my skull with a gas-powered weed-whacker. I looked to my left and saw Bill in a chair beside me, holding my hand. He'd grown a little scruffy beard. "Relax," he said, squeezing my hand.

I had trouble speaking at first. "Where ... where am I?" I stuttered. My throat was dry, and I felt completely out of it. I wasn't sure what was going on.

"You're at the hospital," Bill replied.

"God, my head hurts." I coughed a few times. "What happened?" I tried to sit up, but then I realized I was handcuffed to the bed. I tugged at the restraints. "Bill, what the hell is going on?"

"Look, just take it easy Alex. A lot of people are saying things I know can't be true ... I don't really know what the deal is."

"What are you talking about? And, why the hell am I chained to the bed?"

Bill shook his head. "I don't know what's going on, but ... all I know is something's not right. We have to figure it all out, but I-"

The door swung open and Bill got quiet. I could see several officers standing out in the hallway guarding my room. At that point, it was clear something bad happened, but what? Last thing I remembered was driving home.

Out of nowhere, David walked in. He did not look happy at all. He was all frowned up, and it wasn't the usual frown either. I could tell he was beyond pissed. "Can you give us a minute, Bill?" he asked with zero emotion.

"Sure David." Bill squeezed my hand again. "I'll be right outside, Alex."

Bill walked out and David closed the door behind him. Then, David came over and sat down on the edge of the bed. He rubbed his forehead and scratched his chin.

"Well, I just don't know what to say, kid," he said. I could hear frustration in his voice.

"What's going on, David?"

"You tell me? I put you on this case, and you get overzealous, jump the gun on Constantine. Then, you start getting sloppy. You go into some kind of drunken rage, putting everybody at risk ... not to mention you lost the best lead we ever had."

"Wait, what the hell are you talking about? No, I was trying to ... Umm ... I can't remember, it's like an address or something ... shit ... yeah, I traced his IP-"

"We been to that house already," said David in a tone he'd never used with me before. "There's nothing there, Alex, nothing at that address. Your apartment was a disaster. Your blood alcohol level was .18." He shook his head. "You fled the scene, and crashed the Denali-"

"Wait, I don't understand, I-"

"Do I even need to tell you that you're off this case?" David snapped. "Probably out of the damn Bureau too. Soon as you get outta here today, you'll be held at the Atlanta Field office while OPR conducts their investigation."

I didn't know what to say, I just kept my mouth shut.

David said, "I'll do what I can, Alex, but if she doesn't pull through-"

"Pull through...? Who?"

"Your sister!" he responded, angrily.

"What?" I was so confused.

David sighed. "Your sister was there the night you broke protocol. Don't you remember?"

I squinted hard, tugging at my restraints. "What are you talking about David? Am I under arrest?"

"I'm talking about your sister! You were drunk out of your mind, and you attacked her."

"NO!" I exclaimed.

David became even more agitated. Whatever allegedly happened, he seemed like he just knew I was guilty. "I've said too much already," he said solemnly. "Karen and Frank will take you into custody." He stood up.

"David, I swear I didn't do anything," I cried. "I don't know what happened, but I know it didn't go down like that, I swear!"

He looked back at me. "I hope to God you're right, kid."

"What about Theresa?" I yelled.

David didn't respond. He just walked out the door. I heard him tell the officers outside to make sure nobody got back in my room, not even Bill.

I was devastated. There were no words I could say, I just cried. I cried all afternoon. All I wanted to do is see my little sister, Theresa, and make sure she was okay. I just didn't get it. Why the hell would I try to beat her up, even if I was drunk? I love my sister, and I'd never do anything to hurt her. I sat there in that bed and sobbed until I ran out of tears.

The nurse came in periodically to check on me. She was sweet, but I didn't feel like talking to her, or anyone else for that matter. Each time she tried to start a conversation, it just made me cry worse. Eventually, she gave up. After that, she just came in at the top of each hour to check on me, but she didn't say anything.

Towards the afternoon, she came back in, but this time, she wasn't just checking on me. Something was up. She pulled up a chair and sat down.

"They're ready for you now," said the nurse. "Do you feel well enough to leave? I'm just asking 'cause you can stay here as long as you need. You still got a nasty bump on your head. I won't let them take you if you're not well."

"I swear I didn't do anything wrong!" I exclaimed.

"Baby, I don't have nothing to do with all that." She took a cool wet towel and wiped the sweat off my face.

"I just need someone to know the truth," I whispered.

"You know the truth," she said softly. "Listen, there's one thing I know baby, God don't put nothing on us so big we can't handle. The tests we go through in life only make us stronger. All you have to do is make sure your heart is in the right place." She smiled. "You do that, and the truth will come to light, you hear me?"

I nodded.

"Now, open up ... you take this, it'll help you with that headache of yours."

She put some pills in my mouth and helped me sit up for a drink. I sipped the water and swallowed the pills. "Thank you."

"You be strong Miss," she said.

The nurse left the room, and then Karen walked in. She was a sight to see. I looked at her and smiled.

"Hey Karen!" My voice was still weak. I spoke again, but she didn't respond. She just walked over and uncuffed me from the bed.

"You got five minutes to get dressed," she said.

"Karen, I-"

She frowned. "Look, I don't wanna be here anymore than you, so don't make this difficult, just put your shit on, and let's go."

I sat up on the edge of the bed. "Karen, I promise I didn't-"

"Save it!" She walked over to the closet and pulled out my clothes. I could only assume it was what I came in wearing, because the t-shirt still had blood on it.

Karen tossed my clothes down on the bed beside me. She acted like she didn't even want to come near me. "I'll be outside," she said. Then, she walked out and slammed the door.

"Well I be dammed, Karen's trippin! Just what the hell is going on?" Despite my pain, I sprung up and quickly got dressed. I walked over to the door and opened it, but the cops outside panicked. They acted like they were going to tase me, so I backed up and waited.

I saw Karen sign something, maybe a prisoner release form. She gave the clipboard to one of the officers, and then waved me into the hall. She pulled my arms behind my back and cuffed me. Then, she proceeded to push me out through the front of the hospital like a perp. It was so embarrassing.

Karen walked me out to a Ford Crown Victoria parked near the curb. I noticed Frank sitting in the driver seat. Karen put me in the back. She didn't even uncuff me.

"Keep your mouth shut," warned Karen. "This'll be over soon." She slammed my door, and then got into the front passenger seat.

Frank turned around and looked at me. I could tell by the expression on his face he wanted to say something, but he didn't. He just turned back around, pulled the car into gear and drove off. We went straight to the office—no stops.

They processed me just like a detainee and locked me in a holding room. It was horrible. I don't think I'd ever been in one of those little rooms before. All it had was a raggedy cot, a sink and a toilet. I didn't even have a mirror. The entire situation was screwed up, but I had a feeling it would get worse.

And where was Blondie? Nowhere to be found. Suddenly, she'd completely disappeared, and I realized whatever I was facing, I had to do it alone.

It felt like my life was quickly coming to an end. I had no clue what evidence they had on me, but it was obviously enough to treat me like a two-bit criminal. None of it made any sense to me though. If all I was guilty of was getting drunk and beating up my sister, then what the fuck was I doing locked up? They weren't telling me everything. I guess it didn't matter. Whatever happened, I was caged up like an animal for it.

I thought, *if I have to go to prison, I hope they give me solitary confinement*. But, knowing my luck, I'd get stuck in a tiny, cramped cell with a big girl name Bertha, who makes me her prison-bitch. I'd rather they just kill me and put me out of my misery.

I stayed in that little holding room for days, passing the time by working out, doing push-ups, sit-ups, squats and lunges, as many as I could pump out. In the morning, I'd brush my teeth, wash up, and get right back to exercising. Something told me I needed to get ready for the fight of my life.

After a while, my mind was beginning to clear up, but I seemed to have lost some of my short-term memory. There was something important I needed to remember, and it was a life and death situation, but whatever it was, I'd temporarily lost it.

I thought back to the night I broke cover and went home, as much as I could remember, but none of it added up. No matter how I did the math, each time I came to the same conclusion—I didn't do anything wrong.

Whatever I was charged with, somebody set me up, but who? I must've been on to something, but it didn't matter at that point. I was in custody, locked up in a cell with no way out and no way to clear my name. I didn't even know what I was in for.

I remember David saying something back at the hospital, but I can't seem to focus long enough to remember. I just knew somebody wanted me out of the game—off the case. I have to admit, they did one helluva job. I was locked up, and the killer was free, still at large, and still taking lives. It wasn't supposed to be like this.

Chapter 11

I did everything I could to pass the time, but I couldn't get used to being caged up like an animal. It was poisonous to my system like kryptonite to Superman. I started losing track of the days, and it seemed the chances of me seeing daylight again were slim to none. The good news about the lockup was the guards were always on schedule, to the millisecond, with food. The door would swing open every morning at 8 a.m. for breakfast, then at noon for lunch, and again at 5 p.m. for dinner. The bad news is the food sucked something awful. I guess that was part of the torture program—feed me dog food and eventually I'll break and start singing like a bird.

I doubt dying couldn't be much worse than sitting there all day long, alone, doing absolutely nothing. Solitary confinement was mentally draining. At the end of each day, it felt like I'd been running the Peachtree backwards, blindfolded, wearing high-heel, steel-toed boots. If I thought I was losing it before, incarceration really did the trick. They kept me in there so long I actually started thinking I was guilty of something. The only thing that stopped me from believing that was is that I had no clue what crime I committed. Can't be guilty if there's no charge, right? Either way, I had to get out of there.

One day, I was lying on my bunk, waiting for the trash they called dinner to show up. It was about 10 minutes to 5 p.m. when the door swung open.

"Oh, what a magical treat, dinner's early," I mumbled. I rolled over towards the door, but to my surprise, it wasn't the guards bringing dinner. I had a visitor; a woman.

"Come with me," she said.

I sprung up and followed her out. I didn't give a damn what she wanted, anything was better than staying in that little fuckin' room.

We walked down the hall to the showers. "Take your clothes off," she ordered. "Go ahead ... we can talk while you get cleaned up."

I felt like a POW, and I stunk something awful. I desperately needed to be clean, so I cooperated and got undressed.

I stepped into the shower and turned the hot water on full blast. I'd forgotten how good running water feels. All that hovering over the sink, splashing water up on yourself to wash up is for the birds. A girl needed a shower.

The woman handed me a package of soap, which I immediately tore open and used to lather myself up. I made sure I covered every nook and cranny. I was so filthy, and there was no telling when I'd get more shower privileges. *Shit, I'm already sounding like a goddamn inmate.*

"I'm Doctor Linda Stephens," said the woman. "I'm a psychiatrist with the Office of Professional Responsibility."

I looked up but didn't respond. Suddenly, I realized what was going on. She wasn't there to help me. She was OPR, which meant I was jumping out of the frying pan and into the fire. I should've just stayed in my cell.

"Can I call you Alex?" Stephens asked.

I shrugged my shoulders. Hell, she was watching me shower, so I didn't give a shit what that dyke called me as long as she kept her distance.

"Good, I'll call you Alex. Listen, Alex, we're conducting an inquiry regarding your recent actions in the field, understand?"

I didn't say a word.

"It's okay," she said. "You don't have to talk to me right now, you can just listen. The results of our preliminary investigation are inconclusive. So, my job is to determine if you did anything inappropriate while you were engaged in your undercover assignment."

I rolled my eyes at her.

"I understand how you feel, Alex, but what this means is the Disciplinary Review Board will rely solely on the results of my assessment. If I determine you acted within the guidelines, you're in the clear. But, if I believe for a second you had a hand in all this, then you'll be charged, and I'll testify against you in Federal court."

By then, I was finished washing, and was just letting the water run over me as I sized up little Ms. Shrink in the depths of my mind. I had her number. She was probably on the review board herself. That or she was trying to make a name for herself, looking to get a promotion off my blackass. Either way, the one thing I knew for sure was she wasn't playing on my team. I'd seen her type before back in the Navy. See, I know how they operate. She'll read me the riot act, and then make like she's my only friend in the world, my white knight in shining armor. That way, she can coax me into saying something she could use against me or anyone else she's trying to make a case against. I could tell she was a clever one, but I had no intentions of giving her the satisfaction of trapping me. I knew exactly how to deal with her.

I guess I was taking too long because the good doctor stepped into the shower, reached around me and turned the water off. That broad was a trip. She got her blouse wet too. I think she was more of a psycho than a psychiatrist.

"Do you understand what I'm saying to you?" she asked sternly.

I walked past her and grabbed a towel. "Am I being charged? If so, then I'd like to know what the charge is."

"Alex, I operate on the merit system," she responded. "You cooperate with me, and I'll reward you. You get the information you want as soon as I start getting the information I need. If you work with me instead of against me, this'll all go really fast, understand?"

I was really starting to get pissed. But then I realized that's exactly what she wanted me to do, get frustrated and let my guard down so she could trick me into saying something. I had to keep my emotions under control, so I just internalized it and put on some deodorant and powder.

"How long is this gonna take?" I asked.

"That's completely up to you, Alex."

I said, "So, basically I'm your prisoner?"

"No," she replied.

"So, I can go?" I asked.

Stephens shook her head. "You've been released into my custody. You'll stay here until the evaluation is complete. You're confined to holding when we're not in session. We'll conduct our sessions in my office. Or, if you'd like to be more comfortable, you can stay with me during the evaluation. You'll have to be fitted with a tracer though."

"This is bullshit!" I exclaimed. "Fuck you!"

"I take it that means you prefer to stay here?" she asked. I didn't respond.

"Like I said, it's okay if you don't want to talk to me," she said callously. "Shame what happened to your sister."

"What are you talking about?" I asked.

"I'll ask the questions here!" she shouted.

"Fuck off bitch!" I turned my back to her and started drying my hair with a towel.

She walked away and returned with an FBI t-shirt and jogging pants. She put them on the counter along with some socks and slippers.

"Put those on, and let's go," she ordered.

I tore open the packages, checked out the t-shirt and pants to make sure they fit, and then got dressed. After, I followed her back out into the hallway. We walked down to her office, which was on the administrative side of the building. I'd never been down there before. I followed her into her office and looked around for a moment.

"Have a seat," said Dr. Stephens, pointing to a little black leather sofa directly across from her desk.

I chuckled. "You gotta be kiddin' me."

She smiled. "Go ahead Alex, it really is quite comfortable."

I sat down and kicked my feet up. She seemed to disapprove, but I didn't care. "You're right, doc, it is quite comfortable. But this isn't your office is it?"

"Why do you say that?" she asked.

"Am I right?" I smiled.

"Yes, you are right. I'm just using this space to conduct our sessions. Does that make you feel uncomfortable?"

"Nope."

"Good." She smiled and stared at me for a moment.

"So, how does this work?"

"Well." She paused briefly. "I'd like to start by telling you what we've found so far."

"Okay shoot."

"Interesting choice of words," she retorted. "We found a lot of contraband in your undercover apartment."

I grinned from ear-to-ear.

Stephens thumbed through some documents. "Let's see here ... yes, mostly sex toys, open containers, pornography, and things like that."

I started giggling. Something about the way she said *pornography* was just hilarious to me.

Dr. Stephens continued laying it all out. "We suspect you drank to the point of severe intoxication at which time you decided to blow your cover and go home to your boyfriend William C. Jackson ... Bill I believe is what you call him, correct?"

I didn't respond.

"When you showed up at the apartment, you found Bill with another woman-"

"Get outta here, doc!" I laughed.

"You saw them together and you got angry," she said. "You knocked him out, and then you went into the bedroom only to discover the woman he was in bed with was your sister, Theresa Southerland."

By then, I'd stopped laughing and started paying attention.

Stephens continued, saying, "In a drunken rage, you drew your firearm and fired three rounds. One struck the wall, one went into the headboard and the last hit your sister. The bullet lodged into her chest cavity." She looked right in my eyes. "You seem to be following me now. Good."

I shook my head, and a tear streamed down my cheek.

"You left the apartment in your government issued GMC Denali," she told me. "You were extremely intoxicated, still drinking and completely out of control. You crashed your truck into a telephone pole. Your blood alcohol level far exceeded the legal limit, and you were unconscious when they found you. In addition to having alcohol poisoning, you were in a coma for two days. You're lucky to still be alive."

"Is my sister okay?" I asked, crying.

"We'll get to that in a minute," she replied.

"Fuck you." I sprung up off the couch. "I wanna know now!"

She wrote something on her pad.

"Don't fuck with me lady, 'cause I'll-"

"Do you want to go to prison?" Stephens asked. "Do you, Alex? Because that's where you're headed. You keep it up and I'll have no choice but to report what I know so far, which by the way isn't very good. On the other hand, you cooperate and you're free and clear, back in the field and on your way to New York to a new job and a new beginning ... don't you want that for yourself?"

I plopped back down on the sofa. I put my elbows on my knees and buried my face in my hands.

"Are you okay to continue?" she asked. "Do you need some water?"

"No, I'm fine," I mumbled.

"If our time together is not successful, you'll be charged with assault with a deadly weapon, obstructing a Federal investigation, and maybe even homicide. You and I have a lot to talk about. Are you ready to continue or do you need more time?"

"Let's just get this shit over with lady."

"Good then," she replied. "Let's start with your family ... tell me about your mother?"

I looked up and gave her the evil eye. "Nothing to tell."

"Do you love her?" she asked.

"What does this have to do with whatever happened?"

"I need to establish a baseline," said Stephens, "and how you feel about your mother will help me to do just that ... perhaps you need more time?"

"No ... I mean ... you know, she ... she's a mom."

"What was she like growing up?" she asked.

"Tough ... she was very hard on me."

Stephens rubbed her chin. "Why do you think she was so hard on you?" she asked.

"My mother's Jamaican, very proud. She met my father in Jamaica and she came back with him to America. She had big plans, but they didn't work out, so she took it out on me, constantly."

"And your father, he's a white man?" she asked.

"You have my file."

"Yes, I do Alex, but I'd like to hear from you. Was that difficult for you growing up?"

"What?"

She responded, "Your parents being an interracial couple."

"I didn't notice until ... well, she was the only one, who ever seemed to have a problem with it."

"You mean your mother?" she asked.

"Yes."

"Alex, what would she say about it?" she asked.

"Lots of stuff ... I believe she loved him, but she just gave him so much shit...."

"Go ahead Alex," Stephens encouraged. "Anything you say will be kept in strict confidence."

"I just think maybe she was racist. I guess to some degree we're all a little racist at times though."

"Interesting," said Stephens as she wrote something else down. "So, you think she gave you a hard time because of your complexion?"

"Absolutely."

She looked over the rim of her glasses. "What makes you think so?"

I shrugged my shoulders. "She told me."

"What did she say to you, Alex?"

"Basically, she was ashamed of me, and no one would accept a half-breed like me without me having some kind of credentials, you know a prestigious career."

"How did that make you feel?" asked Stephens.

"Didn't bother me really," I responded, "I just knew that's how she was."

Stephens paused for a minute and flipped through some more papers on her desk. "I pulled your medical history," she confessed. "Seems when you were seven years old you were treated at the hospital for a number of serious injuries. Do you remember that?"

"That was a long time ago."

Stephens kept bringing up ancient history. "According to the records, you were treated for a broken arm, several broken ribs, and a broken eye socket. What happened?"

"I fell down the stairs," I snapped.

"Was there abuse in the home?" she asked. "Did your father abuse you or your siblings?"

I laughed loud as hell. It was almost impossible for me to take her seriously. She didn't know what the fuck she was talking about. I just shook my head.

Stephens said, "Alright then Alex ... tell me, how you felt when you learned your father had been killed on the job?"

Now that shit just set me off. My face turned beet red and I saw myself getting up off that couch, walking over and punching that bitch in the fucking throat. I think she could see it too, so she backed off and moved on.

She cleared her throat. "Okay, we'll come back to that ... I want to talk about your schooling for a moment. You graduated early ... how'd you feel about that?"

I calmed down and tried to answer her question. "I didn't feel anything. It was just school. College was harder, but I made it through."

"Did you want to go to college?" she asked.

"Of course."

"Why did you pursue a degree in Criminal Justice?" she asked.

"My mother wanted me to be an attorney. I didn't know what I wanted, so it seemed like a good compromise at the time."

Again, she wrote in her pad. "But you didn't want to be an attorney?"

"I was young," I replied, "I didn't know much of anything at that point."

She smiled. "Did you find it difficult to fit in with the older students?"

"At first, but after a few frat parties ... well, you get the picture."

"Yes, I do, Alex."

We continued talking for the rest of the afternoon. Stephens asked question after question about my childhood and school life. Most of it was standard shrink bullshit, so it was irritating to say the least, but hey what else did I have to do. It was that or back to my cage, so I put up with it as long as possible.

The next few days were just as boring and uneventful as the first. Dr. Stephens would ask a stupid question, and I'd give her the driest most boring response I could conjure up. However, the fourth day was different. Sparks began to fly the moment my ass hit the couch.

"I want to talk about the time you spent in the Navy," said Dr. Stephens. "More specifically your Special Operations time in South America."

"That's classified," I retorted.

"Not from me, not anymore." She held up a tri-folded document. "This is a writ from the U.S. Attorney General, granting me access to your entire file, including all your military records. I've already reviewed your file in detail. It says you were a part of an operation to bring down a number of cocaine traffickers in Rio de Janeiro."

I instantly got heated. "You're talking about sensitive, classified information, lady. I don't know what you did to get access to my file, but this is highly inappropriate, and-"

"The Navy offered to release these files to me!" she exclaimed.

"What?" I sat up straight on the couch.

She nodded. "Yes, it seems they too are concerned a highly trained naval officer might be taking out innocent civilians."

"That's not fair!" I pointed at her.

"It turns out you're a little more than an Intelligence Officer, aren't you?" asked Stephens.

My jaw dropped. "What are you talking about, lady?"

She replied, "You know how to hurt people, don't you? You know how to kill, how to torture."

"You're full of shit!"

"I talked to Lieutenant Riggs," said Stephens.

"What?"

"Lieutenant Riggs ... you know the Seal Team Leader you worked with down there? He told me you were a killer ... a wild woman were his exact words."

I shook my head. "You don't know anything about me."

"Alex, Lieutenant Riggs says you took down targets without authorization."

"He ordered me to take out those targets because the mission was compromised. He had orders from the-"

"Riggs remembers it differently," interrupted Stephens.

"Fuck him! He's a goddamn liar! I trained with them, and when they needed more than just intel support, I did what I could to help. Jesus Christ, what are you trying to get at?"

She sighed. "What about the favelas in Rocinha and Copacabana?"

"Look, those poor people had no-"

She smacked her fist down on the desk. "Look, I'm not talking about those poor people. I'm talking about what you did down there on behalf of the U.S. government! You posed as a prostitute, you snorted cocaine, you came back with a drug problem, and-"

"NO! That's not what the file says, and you know it. I was in Rocinha a hell of a lot longer than I was supposed to be, and I had to do coke to maintain my cover. You of all people should know anytime that happens to an undercover agent in the field, you have to go through a program. You're trying to make this out to be something it's not. We did some good down there."

"Do you really believe that?" she asked. "Tell you what don't answer that, let's move on ... what steps have you taken to deal with your addictions?"

"The fuck you talking 'bout, lady? I told you I don't do drugs!"

"Say I believe you," she responded, "say you don't have a drug problem ... obviously you're an alcoholic and you seem to be unable to control your libido, for lack of a better expression."

"What I do in my personal life is my business, so you can kiss my-"

Stephens interrupted me, yelling, "When you spiral out of control and put other agents and civilians in danger it's no longer your business! You're in the public eye, and you're going to have to deal with it because OPR is going to deal with you, like it or not."

I sat up and pointed my finger at her again. "Look here you fuckin' OPR puppet, I don't have to tell you shit!"

She stood up. "No, what you have to do is convince me you're ready to go back in the field. Make no mistake I'll put you on permanent medical if I feel you're not cooperating."

I laughed loudly. "All you shrinks are full of shit."

"Excuse me!" exclaimed Stephens. She put her hands on her hips.

"You told me you'd either clear me or bring me up on charges. Now, you're saying you'll put me on medical. You don't have any authority, do you? You're just fucking with me, trying to make me say something you can use against me with the review panel."

"You don't even realize the slippery slope you're on, do you Alex? I'm here to help you, but you have to be willing to accept my help."

"I tell you how you can help me, you can go fuck yourself, shrinky. I've bled for my country. You got no right to be judging me! We saved lives down there and here at home too. You don't like how we operated, that's your problem not mine. I suggest you write your fucking representative."

"Do you understand why you're here?" she asked.

"Preliminary investigations over, I'm innocent, but you're looking to prove your usefulness. I wonder, what happens when I get up, walk out this door, and go the fuck home."

"We're getting off track here," she said. She sat back down, took off her glasses and set them on the desk. "Why do you feel the need to do drugs, drink, or have promiscuous sex without positive social interaction?"

"Promiscuous sex, what the fu...?" You know what doctor...? See, the drug lords down in Brazil caged me up and turned me into a crack-whore. Didn't Riggs tell you that's what he used to call me all the time, crack-whore. Ever since I broke out of my cage at the zoo, I just can't help myself. In fact, you're looking kind of tasty to me right now." I licked my lips and winked at her. "Let me ask you something doctor, would you consider this to be negative social interaction or a psychiatric cluster-fuck?"

"I think that's enough for today." She closed my file and started organizing her desk.

"No doc, turn around, and bend over for me ... let me see that ass, baby. I betcha wear a thong, don't you? You a nasty girl, doc? Come on, shake it momma shake that little bony ass!"

She picked up the phone and called for security. When they came in, I was still showing my blackass.

"I'll bang that pussy out, sexy mami chula!" I yelled.

"Come on Southerland," said one of the guards, "don't make us do this the hard way."

I stood up and said, "See ya tomorrow, sexy!"

The guards escorted me back to my room, and I spent the night working out. After I finished exercising, I entertained myself, singing songs and dancing until I finally wore myself out and fell asleep.

The next day, we started our session early. I sat on the couch and stared Dr. Stephens down until she was ready to deal with me.

"You seem a bit on edge today, Alex," she said. "Would you like to talk about it?"

"Sorry doc, I had a rough night, too much partying." I smiled.

"What kept you up?" she asked.

"Ya know I'm glad you asked. I kept imagining you in a tight-fitting sheer blouse with no bra. Your nipples were hard, and I had my hand up-"

Stephens threw her hands up. "Okay, okay, enough ... you win!" I crossed my arms and grinned. She wrote something else down in her little notebook. "Perhaps I went too far yesterday. I can admit when I'm wrong. Will you accept my apology?"

"Don't judge me," I said. "Our troops go all over the world and sometimes they have to do unspeakable things to maintain the freedom you and people like you take for granted everyday. Don't you dare look down on me!"

"You're right," she said, "it was irresponsible of me to bring up your past in that way. It won't happen again, okay?"

"Fine."

"Thank you, Alex," Stephens said. "I feel like we're making progress, like we're on the same page now, so why don't we discuss more recent events? Tell me about the night your sister was shot."

I paused for a moment. I rubbed my head and sighed. "I just, I was ... I don't know. I guess if I ever had a real addiction it was playing that damn Death Peddler game."

"How so?" she asked.

"I felt powerful when I played. I planned out every little detail of my attacks, and I really got into taking those other serial killers out."

"So, you enjoyed killing?" she asked.

"I've lived my entire life taking orders or trying to please other people. Killing in that game made me feel like I was finally in control of something and watching the aftermath in the forums only added fuel to the fire."

"But you've killed before in real life," said Stephens.

"I thought we weren't gonna talk about that!" I snapped.

She sighed heavily. "I'm just saying you have taken a life before. Is that why you liked playing this game?"

"No, it was different. With the game, I was able to kill, and the entire community talked about it. It wasn't like some bullshit suicide mission, where the only folks who knew what happened were the same people loyal to the cover-up."

"I see," said Stephens. "The night you went back home, had you killed in the game that day?"

"Several times," I responded.

"Were you angry or upset about something?" she asked.

"No," I said, shaking my head, "I felt good ... I drank a little and-" She looked at me over the rim of her glasses. "Okay, I drank a lot, and I masturbated for a very long time that day. I wasn't upset at all. In fact, I couldn't have been happier.

She held her pen up to her lips. "Do you masturbate often?"

"If you weren't boring me to death, I'd be masturbating right now."

She cleared her throat. My response seemed to make her very uncomfortable. "What made you break protocol and return home?"

"The man we were investigating was hacking my computer. I saw him, so I traced the source. I found his IP address and was getting ready to move on it, but then he loaded a picture onto my screen."

"What did you see in the picture?" she asked.

"It was a picture of my apartment, my real apartment. Someone took a picture of Bill on the sofa sleeping, and there was a gun pointed to his head."

"Why didn't you call for backup?" she asked.

"I don't know. I was-"

"You were extremely intoxicated," Stephens reminded. "Is that why you didn't call for backup?"

"Like I said, I don't know," I replied, "I just got dressed and drove home as fast as I could."

"Alex, how do you think the killer knew your identity, or where you lived?"

"I don't know," I responded.

She said, "So, you walked in and saw your boyfriend in the bedroom. What happened next?"

"No, he wasn't in the bedroom. When I saw Bill, he was standing in the living room. It was dark, but I could still see him, and I knew something was wrong. He just didn't look right."

"What do you mean?" she asked.

"It's hard to describe, but he looked lifeless."

"Where was he at that time?" she asked.

"Where? He was in the living room."

Stephens looked really confused. "No, you found him in the bed with your sister, right? Did you break into the apartment and surprise them?"

"Why do you keep talking about the bedroom, I didn't...." I paused for a second and thought hard. Then, I nearly fell off the sofa. "Oh my God!" I finally remembered what I'd forgotten. I was so stupid. I should have seen it all along. Dr. Stephens said it the other day. Hell, she just said it a minute ago, but I guess I didn't want to hear it. I'd blocked it out of my mind, but now it was clear to me. Bill had been fucking my sister, Theresa, for months, maybe even longer. All the nights he was working late, the weekends he was supposedly on the job, and all that going out with his friends—the entire time, he was laid up with that fuckin' cow. How could she do that to me, my own sister. I thought she loved me.

I felt like my heart melted and drained down into my stomach. I knew Bill was full of shit. He had such an abrupt change of heart when I told him I'd be gone for a while. He just wanted me to leave, so he could get that stanky bitch up in my house. I would've given Bill a pass if he was fucking anybody other than Theresa. I mean, I had my share of issues, but fucking my sister? What kind of man does some shit like that? My mind exploded like I had total recall of 20 years all in an instant. My thoughts were wandering all over the place.

"Alex...? Alex...!"

"I'm sorry, Doctor Stephens, what did you say?"

"I need you to stay focused here, Alex," she said. "Did it make you angry to find your boyfriend and your sister in bed together?"

"Bill and I had been having some problems. I thought he'd been with someone else, but we were trying to straighten things out. When I told him I wanted to move to New York, he blew up, but then he came back a few days later and seemed to be okay with it. I thought we were fine, but maybe this explains why he was so eager to change his mind about me leaving. How could I be so stupid?"

"When you graduated from the Academy, you were issued a Glock 23 handgun, correct?"

"No."

"Alex, the file says-"

"I opted for the Glock 22," I interrupted.

She quickly rechecked my file. "You're right I'm sorry," she said. "So, your standard issue Glock 22 40 caliber ... where is it?"

"I don't know," I replied. "David made me leave it at home when I started the undercover assignment, and-"

"Would it surprise you to know that the bullets they took from the crime scene were 40 caliber?"

"Yes," I responded.

Stephens paused for a moment. "Ballistics confirms they were fired from your weapon. This Glock 22 ... it's been in your possession since you started with the Bureau, correct?"

"Well, obviously, whoever broke into the apartment-"

"Let's save that for now," interrupted Stephens. She sat up in her chair, and in a condescending tone said, "According to Dimitri's report, you killed quite a bit in this Death Peddler game, or simulation, or whatever it is. Earlier you said when you played this game and did all this killing, you felt you were finally in control of your life. You were trying to make a point and show the other players how powerful you were, right? Would you agree with that assessment?"

"Maybe ... Yeah, I guess so."

"Then, what point were you making when you opened fire on your sister?" she asked.

"What...? Wait, no, I never even knew she was there until I talked to David in the hospital. Even then, I didn't know what happened. When I got to the apartment, I opened the door, Bill was standing in the middle of the living room, but then he just fell out. After that, I got hit from behind and that's all I remember ... look, I need to lie down."

I felt like my heart had been broken up and stomped on by a big man wearing cleats. I could barely breathe. I stretched out across the sofa and cried.

"Would you like some water?" asked Stephens.

"No," I whimpered.

"Can you continue?" She seemed genuinely concerned for me.

"Yes," I sniffled, wiping my tears.

"Can you remember anything else about that night?" she asked.

"No, I'm sorry."

"Let's go back to earlier that day, Alex. You drank quite a bit of alcohol."

"Yes."

"Hmm," she responded, "so you drink on the job a lot?"

"Never."

"But you did that day?" she asked.

I sighed. "Yes."

"Why?" she asked.

That was a good question, one I was afraid to answer. Maybe she was right about everything. After all, I did have a condition. Most FBI agents were full of courage and valor, but I ran on alcohol and sex. Dr. Stephen's hit a nerve, so I just clammed up.

I spent the rest of the day half-ass listening to the good doctor yap. She desperately tried to dig deeper into my life, as if her success depended on her ability to pick it apart. While she poked her big nose around in almost every part of my life, I did some scrutinizing of my own. I didn't like it, but it had to be done.

After a few more sessions, I started to let my guard down. I felt a lot more comfortable talking to Dr. Stephens. Perhaps for the first time in my life, I finally accepted I truly did have a problem. I took it seriously. It wasn't just a joke anymore. Sure, I've said it in the past, and I always talked about getting help, but never actually took the steps to make it happen.

Talking with Dr. Stephens, it seemed I was beginning to make some major progress, but it was still too early to tell. In our sessions, we continued talking about a lot of things. I shared the intimate details of my sorry little life, and Stephens eventually returned the favor, revealing a few personal things about herself.

One day, Dr. Stephens finally gave me the news I'd wanted to hear since I'd been taken into custody. "Our time together is finished," she said. "My evaluation is complete, and you're free to go. You've been reinstated."

"Don't play with me," I responded. "Are you serious?"

She smiled. "Yes, I submitted my report to the review board, and they've cleared you for duty with provisions. You are to report to New York at your earliest convenience. However, you must continue your sessions with a therapist for the first year or as long as OPR deems necessary."

I was on the edge of my seat. "So, all I have to do is go see another shrink up there?"

"That's correct, Alex."

"Honestly doc, I didn't think we were doing too good."

"That's why I'm the doctor and you're the patient." She smiled.

"So, that's it?" I asked.

"Yes." She wrote down a note in her pad.

"No final words...? Nothing?"

"I always make good on my promises, Alex. Your sister is recovering just fine. I spoke with her yesterday."

I asked, "How is she really?"

"Physically, she's stable, but mentally, she's not doing so well. She honestly believes you attacked her."

"Did you tell her what really happened?"

"I did," she replied. "However, I believe your sister suffers from post-traumatic stress disorder brought on by the attack. Right now, she believes what she wants about that night. On the other hand, your boyfriend Bill's statement is consistent with yours. You had no gunshot residue on your hands when you were taken into custody, and overall, the evidence supports the theory someone else was in your apartment. As for your sister, she'll need ongoing treatment, perhaps Critical Incident Stress Management, in order to cope with all of this. In my professional opinion, it's going to take some time for her to heal both physically and mentally."

I sat quiet for a moment. "Thank you for telling me," I said.

Dr. Stephens smiled, but only for a brief moment. "Alex, there is one more thing...."

"What?" I asked.

"Your sister was with child at the time of the incident. Unfortunately, the doctors were unable to save the baby ... Alex ... Bill was the father. I'm sorry to be the one to tell you, but as a friend, I thought you should know."

I didn't know what to say. If that wasn't the nail in the coffin, I don't know what was. Right then, all I could see was red. Bill and Theresa were making a fool out of me the entire time. It was my fault though because there were plenty of warning signs, but I didn't pay them any attention. I may not have trusted Bill, but I trusted Theresa. I should've seen it coming. How many times did Theresa talk about how she'd be lovin' Bill down if he were her man or how she hated me for this and that? I guess when someone says they hate you, for whatever reason, even if they're family, believe them. It was hard to imagine how they could stoop so low. Then again, Theresa's a fucking snake and Bill's got less backbone than a dead earthworm. All it probably took was just one whiff of strange pussy from a familiar trick to get Bill to turn on me. *I hate that bastard, and when I get out of here-.*

"May I offer some advice?" Stephens broke my train of thought.

I nodded.

"You're young," she said, "young and gifted. You've had a lot to deal with in a very short period of time, perhaps more than you were ready for. In my professional opinion, during difficult times in your life, I believe you overcompensate by closing yourself off to others. Anytime they get close to you, you push them away. Maybe you're only at your best when everything around you is in complete chaos. I know this can be hard to hear, but you're on a destructive path, and you just can't keep going like this. I believe there is hope for you. I think you have to find a way to make a positive change in your life. I hope your new therapist can help you with that. In the interim, don't let circumstances change who you are, or you'll inhibit your ability to make good, sound decisions. I can prescribe some medication to help with the anxiety if you like."

"No thanks, Doc ...I don't have anxiety ... just family problems."

She frowned a little. "Well, if you need me, look me up, okay?"

I walked over and shook her hand. "Thanks for everything."

"You're welcome." She smiled. Then, she opened her bottom right drawer and placed my belongings on top of her desk. She had my badge, gun, cell phone, and car keys all in plastic evidence bags. I gathered everything up and walked out of the office.

There were several messages on my phone, so I checked them as I walked towards the elevators. It was midday, and the office was busy as ever. My coworkers looked at me as if they'd seen a ghost or were looking at a mental patient. I was still wearing the FBI sweats and slippers. I nodded at a few people I knew but didn't stop to talk. I dialed in the pin for my voicemail and went through my messages while I waited for the elevator. There were a few hang-ups, but Malik actually left me a message:

"Yo Alex, they got me crossed up down here on some bullshit charge. Look man, I can help you with your case," he whispered. *"I know who Karla Charles saw after she left the hotel. Yo, I swear, you help me, I'll give you everything ... I'm tellin' you I know who the killer is, man, come on! I'm down in Fulton County lockup man, I gotta get outta here ... Red, you gotta help-"*

I heard a voice in the background tell him his time was up, and the call disconnected.

"Damn Malik, what the fuck man?" I was off the case, so there was nothing I could do. Only option was to go see David, but I had a feeling he wouldn't listen to me. I paced around a while, and then finally got up enough nerve to go down to Z-Squad. I ran down the hall through the doors and onto the floor.

Frank was standing there holding a bunch of papers. He looked up at me and smiled like never before. "Alex, you okay?"

"Yeah I'm fine."

Karen heard us talking. She jumped up and ran over, hugging my neck tightly. "Alex you're back!"

"I'm sorry," I said.

"Me too. We thought ... I just..."

"Karen don't worry about it," I shook my head. "I just made some bad calls, but I'm better now."

"We were worried about you," Frank said. "OPR wouldn't let us talk to you until the investigation was done. I...." He smiled. "It's good to see you."

"Good to see you too, buddy ... how's David?"

Frank shook his head. "You know ... what can I say, he's still David."

"He's pissed we got so close without an arrest," Karen said.

I sighed. "Look, I gotta talk to him."

"That's going to be kind of tough right now," she replied.

"Listen, I've got a CI from an old Anti-Piracy case," I told her. "He's locked up in Fulton County, but he claims to know the identity of the serial killer. His name is Christopher Young. He calls himself Malik, now I know-"

"What the hell's going on out here!" yelled David, stampeding straight for us.

Karen and Frank moved back out of the way.

David looked mad enough to bite a crowbar in half. I could hear it in his voice. He stormed right up to me and started yelling.

"THE FUCK YOU DOING DOWN HERE?" He put his finger in my face and continued yelling, "You're off this case! You're not cleared to be down here, so you need to get the hell off my goddamn floor! Maybe you'll give those assholes in New York more respect."

"David, look I'm sorry, but I-"

"DON'T!" he snapped.

"But-"

"I SAID DON'T!" he exclaimed.

I reached around him and touched Frank on the shoulder. "Fulton County," I whispered.

Frank nodded and we shook hands. Karen gave me another hug and I was just about to leave when Dimitri came busting out of the computer room. We all watched as he ran up to me like a kid about to meet his long-lost sibling.

"Good trace!" he exclaimed. "Will miss you."

"Thank you, Dimitri."

Without skipping a beat, he spun around and ran back into his little room.

Dimitri was weird, but he was my boy, the super digital pimp. He was down for whatever.

David looked like he wanted to laugh at Dimitri, all of us did, but the situation was way too tense. David shook his head and pointed towards the door.

"Good bye David," I said. I tried to grab his hand, but he folded up his arms. He didn't want me to touch him. Honestly, I think he was just putting on a show. Of course, he was pissed off and disappointed, but I knew he still cared for me. The thing is, David's old school, all about protocol. I'd taken advantage of him, betrayed his trust, and the worst part is I let the team down when they needed me most. David gave me the cold shoulder, but I understand he had to save face and uphold his reputation. We started out rough, I mean extremely rough, but I'd grown to love that little old man. He had my heart, and I was definitely going to miss being around him.

I left the office and went out to the parking garage. Out of all the things Stephens said, one thing was really bugging me. She said something to the tune of I destroy everything in my path—relationships, opportunities, everything ...well, everything except my Mustang. The entire world could piss on me all at once, but she was my faithful, black stallion, and she was still waiting for me in the garage right where I'd parked her. She was there for me the whole time, even though I'd left her for that flashy piece of shit Denali. When I saw her, I could tell she wanted to show me how cute she was. As promised, Tom cleaned her up and she was sparkling.

"Hey my Black Beauty," I whispered. She was the only thing left on the planet that still loved me. The car was unlocked, and the keys were in the ignition, so I got in and cranked up. I drove straight home.

I wasn't sure what to expect back at the apartment, but when I got there, the place was dark and completely deserted. That son-of-a-jackal Bill had already moved all his stuff out. I took the home phone off the charger and sat down on the sofa. After a few deep breaths, I called Bill's cell phone.

"Alex," he answered, "you okay?"

"Save it Bill! How could you do this shit to me?"

"Alex, I love you ... look, we haven't been right for a long time-"

"That's not true!" I cried. "I been trying to do better."

"I care about you-"

"Bullshit!" I interrupted. "All this fuckin' time, you been with her?"

"I didn't want it to happen like this," he said.

"How long, Bill?"

"What?" he asked.

"How long you been fuckin' my little sister in our bed, you muthafuckin' son-of-a-bitch? That's some low-down dirty shit! Did my momma set this up? What, she supervised and stood over the bed while you got that stanky bitch pregnant? You got her pregnant Bill! My sister! You got my own fuckin' sister pregnant, you sick bastard!"

"Baby, I...."

As soon as he called me baby, I started yelling at the top of my lungs. "FUCK YOU BILL, DON'T CALL ME BABY! I HATE YOU NIGGA, FUCK YOU!"

"You don't mean that," he said. "Look, this has been tough for everybody, why don't we-"

"NOT TOUGH ENOUGH FOR YOU! YOU GOT WHAT YOU WANTED. YOU MADE A FOOL OUT OF ME AND TOOK AWAY THE ONLY FAMILY I HAD LEFT."

"Alex ... I need you to understand it wasn't like that," he pleaded. "I didn't mean for this to happen. You and I were having issues and Theresa was there ... she was there for me, and now I ... well, she needs me now."

"Yeah, I'm sure her pussy was real comforting, go to hell!"

"Wait, I-"

"What Bill? What on earth could you possibly say to me now?"

"Nothing, I just want you to know I-"

"Exactly!" I exclaimed. "Nothing! GO FUCK YOURSELF ASSHOLE!"

I slung the phone across the room as hard as I could throw it, smashing it up against the wall and shattering it into little pieces. I was so angry it felt like I couldn't breathe. My life was a complete mess, and, as usual, nobody gave a tinker's damn about anything other than what they wanted.

Bill called my cell several times after that, but I just kept pressing the ignore button and sent his call straight to voicemail. I sat down on the sofa in total silence. I didn't cry. I didn't utter a single word. I just tried to compose myself.

The blinds were shut, and the lights were off. I sat there in the dark by myself on that sofa until after 8 p.m. By then, I think I'd gotten over being hurt. At that point, I was just pissed. I didn't want to get up, but I didn't have any choice because I had to pee. I ran into the bathroom and sat down on the toilet, still holding my cell phone as it continued ringing. I think Bill called at least three more times while I was in there. He sent a few text messages too, but I didn't even read them. Far as I was concerned, Bill, Theresa, my entire family, were all dead to me now, everyone except my little brother Chris. I just hoped he'd grow up to be a strong young man and see past all their bullshit. Maybe he and I could have a relationship then.

After I finished and washed my hands, I just stood there in the bathroom, staring at myself in the mirror. I do that a lot. Yes, I'm quite vain. You can say what you want. Call me a liar, or even a narcissistic raging lunatic, but you couldn't tell me I don't look good. *I know I'm fine as hell. Bill's the one who's gonna be missing me.* I think I got my confidence from Dad. No matter how bad things were going, he always felt good about the way he looked.

I just stood there in the mirror, gazing at myself. I did look good even though I'd just been released from captivity. But, I'm not sure I was really thinking about my appearance. I think I was actually searching for something. What I was searching for, honestly, I don't know, but whatever it was, I realized soon I wasn't finding it in the bathroom, so I decided to drop the issue and move on.

I took a quick shower and combed my hair. I was going to just sit and mope around the house, but then I decided the world didn't revolve around my family or my sorry ass ex-boyfriend for that matter. I'd been stuck up in a cell for God knows how long and was stressed the fuck out. I needed a goddamn drink, so instead of wallowing in my life's pain, I decided to go out and get drunk out of my mind.

Chapter 12

The night was hot and muggy, and the moon was barely visible, giving the clouds a nice glow from above. The forecast called for scattered showers and thunderstorms, and by the looks of it, the weatherman was finally right—it was definitely going to rain. I'd rather be drunk than drenched any day, so I figured I'd get my butt in somebody's bar before it started pouring down. I hopped in the car and took off down Northside in search for a proper watering hole. I wasn't picky about where I drank as long as I didn't have to put up with a bunch of hillbilly shit.

Halfway down the road, I got the eerie feeling I was being followed, so I slowed down a bit and kept my eyes on the rearview mirror. Usually, I'm right on the money when it comes to stuff like that, but I never saw anything out of the ordinary, so I just dropped it. If someone was following me, I'm sure it was just OPR keeping tabs on me anyway. They claimed I was in the clear, but when you get in their crosshairs, you're never off the hook. Those overzealous bastards are just about as bad as the serial killers we chase. They poke, poke, and poke until they turn up some kind of dirt on you. Shit, ride anybody's back long enough, and you'll eventually get something. We're all human.

I didn't drive too far up the road. After a few miles, I noticed a place called Manettie's. I'd seen it before, but never stopped in. From the outside, it seemed to be cool, and it was always packed, so I gave it a try.

The Manettie's parking lot was full, so I parked around back. I got out of the car and walked to the front of the building. Inside the lights were dim and the music was blasting. Turns out, it was actually a sports bar, so I was feeling that because the game was on. I stood there, scoping out the place for a minute, but then out of nowhere it hit me. The pain I'd fought so hard to get rid of, the very thing that got me locked up in the first place, it wasn't a thing—it was a she, and she was Blondie. She'd abandoned me when it looked like I was going to prison for life, but now she was back and stronger than ever. Initially, I'd set out to get drunk that night, but when she showed back up, she brought with her the familiar thirst, and it was over- powering.

A buddy of mine back in the service once told me if you drink long enough, you'll find death at the bottom of a shot glass. I'm not sure if he meant it this way, but that night I wanted to drown myself in booze until my heart stopped beating. I just should've taped a warning sign to my chest that read, *Do NOT revive*, in case the paramedics got any bright ideas. I was at rock bottom. When I say *all time low*, I mean it. I didn't have anything else left to live for.

Manettie's was busy as hell, and there weren't any tables available. In my condition, I couldn't wait, so I walked up to the bar and sat down. The music was insanely loud and there were games playing on almost every screen up on the wall behind the bar. It was definitely my kind of place. Not too loud for you to talk to a close friend, but loud enough to pretend not to hear some asshole's retarded pickup line.

So, there we were again. I was back in the same situation I'd been in many times before, fucked in the ass by everybody I knew without even so much as a peck on the cheek. I realize now my mother was actually right, and they were all just treating me how I deserved. Like she said, a half-breed like me would never amount to anything. Only two things that were consistently good in my life remained, my car and my ability to get a strong glass of whatever's getting poured at the time. So, without further delay, I flagged down the bartender and proceeded to get my drank on.

"Whatcha drinking tonight, sweetie?" he asked.

"Whisky if you got it!" I shouted.

He asked, "On the rocks?"

"No, the ice gets in the way of my drinking!"

He smiled. Then, he put down a small napkin on the bar in front of me, followed by a shot glass. He poured a single, but I gulped it down before he had a chance to pull the bottle away.

"Hit me again," I waved, "and make it a double ... and get me a beer too."

He looked at me a little strange, but I gave him the evil eye, so he played it smart and got back to pouring. "Name's Brent," he yelled. "What kind of beer can I get you?"

"Heineken, and keep it coming, Brent."

He smiled again. I guess I was amusing to him. "Coming right up," he said.

A few hours passed and I'd gone through several more beers and God knows how many shots. I sat alone at the bar trying to wash the horrible taste of my life out my mouth. Judging from my blurred vision, I'd say it was working. One more shot, and my pain started to dissipate. I couldn't feel a thing, but I wasn't slowing down either. Even with all that time off the bottle, I hadn't lost my touch. I could still drink a frat brother under the table.

I ate a few peanuts and continued to watch the basketball game, synchronizing my incremental intoxication program with each new play on the court. Every time they took a shot, so did I. Around 10:30 p.m., a tall, redheaded woman walked over and climbed up on the stool beside me.

"Who's winning?" she asked.

I really didn't want to be bothered, but I think the booze made me a lot friendlier than usual. I slowly looked over at her. "Detroit by two."

"I love basketball ... what's your name?" She was the bubbliest little white woman I ever met.

"Alex."

"Hi Alex," she said and smiled, reaching for my hand. "I'm Cynthia."

"Nice to meet you Cynthia." My speech was slurred.

"Bartender," Cynthia yelled, waiving Brent back over, "I'll have what Alex here's having."

"Come here a lot?" I asked.

"No, it's my first time, how about you?" asked Cynthia.

"Me too," I said, offering a fake smile.

"I just had to get away from all the bullshit," she said. "Fuckin' men, you know what I'm saying?"

"You said it right Cindy, fuckin' men!" I raised my glass in the air and then took another gulp.

"No, it's Cynthia!" She corrected.

"Sorry, I'm terrible with, um... um..."

She smiled and waited as long as she could, but then finally helped me out. "Names?"

"Yep, that's the one!" I squinted and stared at her face. I didn't want to be rude, but something about her seemed vaguely familiar. "We met before?" I asked.

"Just now," she said laughing loudly.

"Right..." I giggled and then burped like an old man. "Oh, excuse me."

Brent poured her drink and she took a sip. "God, that's strong!" She covered her mouth, coughing from the burn of the hard liquor.

I couldn't help but laugh at her. "So, you having trouble with your man?"

"Just men in general," said Cynthia, "always running their mouths about shit they shouldn't ... and, don't even get me started on the money situation. I swear they're a bunch of bitchy little girls!"

"I'll drink to that." I held my beer up and took another big gulp. "Yeah, my old man ran out on me wit' that cunt of a sister of mine ... I hate them mothafuckas."

She raised her shot glass and smiled. "Fuck all those motherfuckers!" she said. Then, she took another sip. "Let me buy you a drink, Alex."

"Nah," I replied slowly, "I'm done, I'm about to-"

"Oh, come on ... bartender!" yelled Cynthia, "get me and my new friend Alex another round on me! This one's for the girls! First round of many, yay!"

She was a trip. After that next round of shots, I completely gave in to her suggestion, and we took turns buying. We drank and laughed and talked about everything from sports, to men and shopping.

Once the game was over, I was pretty much done for, but Cynthia wanted to buy one last round and toast to all the sorry ass men across the planet, my kind of toast. Naturally, I agreed.

While Cynthia was placing our order, my cell phone rang. I fumbled around for a second and finally got it up to my ear. "Hello?"

"Alex!" came a frantic sounding voice.

"Who dis is?" I asked, giggling. I was so amusing myself.

"It's David."

"Oh, yeah," I slurred, "hi Davie, how you doin' buddy?"

"You alright?" he asked.

"Yup," I slowly replied.

"Alex, are you drunk?"

"I think so." I laughed.

David asked, "Can you talk?"

"Yup." I giggled again, leaning over onto the bar.

"Listen, you were right. Your CI's story checked out. The girl, Karla Charles, she left the hotel with him. Remember the security tapes you and Frank requested?"

"I don't think I can remember my name right about now."

David seemed concerned about something, but I found it a little hard to focus.

"We checked the security tapes from the hotel tonight after talking to your CI," David said. "Karla Charles walked out of the hotel with him, but the video shows her jumping out of his car and getting into someone else's. Alex, Karla left the parking lot with the killer."

"I know whatcha mean," I replied. "This parking lot was full when I got here too, wait, you here...?" I looked all around. "Fuck you at man? I don't see you."

"Stay with me Alex!" he exclaimed. "The killer's the principal ... no, it's not really the principal, the real principal's dead. The woman at the school stole the principal's identity. She's been running prostitutes using teachers and kids from schools in the area. Your CI's been running dope for the Chinese businessman, Lee, who lets him use the suite at the Marriott to setup the deals for the principal. The principal had this autistic boy go out and crucify any girl that wandered off the reservation. That's why the murders seemed random. That little bastard can hardly speak, but he can hack the NSA and kill with the best of 'em. We got him in custody now. Alex, you there?"

"Yeah Frank," I slurred.

"No, it's David. Look, the girl and mother stole a bunch of money from the principal. She had the girl killed to force the mother to give up the money ... hello ... hello, Alex?"

"I'm glad it all worked out for you ... I gotta go to New Jersey now."

I looked over my shoulder and saw Cynthia putting some cash down on the bar.

"Listen Alex, your CI's gonna testify in exchange for immunity. We got a warrant for the principal's home and office, but she's nowhere to be found. Your CI believes she might be coming after you ... Alex, you gettin' all this?"

"Huh?" Nothing David said was registering.

"She knows who you are!" he said slowly. "The boy's John Constantine. He hacked your computer and was able to find out where you live. Where are you now?"

I looked down at the book of matches on the bar. "Manettie's?" I slowly enunciated.

"I know the place," David said. "I'm on the road about ten minutes away. Look, don't talk to anyone. Meet me around back. I'll pick you up and get you to a safe house."

Have you ever been drunk out of your mind, I mean totally wasted, but then something crazy happens and you're instantly sober? Well, all of a sudden, I noticed Cynthia pushing up on me, breathing heavily down the back of my neck. I thought it was just some kind of drunken lesbo action, until I felt something cold, round, and hard pressed against my side. There's no mistaking that feeling. It was the barrel of a gun. I may've been shit-faced, but suddenly I got completely sober real fast.

"It's silenced," she whispered softly, her lips damn near inside my ear. "You scream, and I'll drop you right here. Stupid drunk bitch, nobody will even notice until I'm long gone. Now, hang up the phone and slide it to me, slowly."

"David, I ... shit ... I gotta go." I hung up the phone and gave it to her.

She put my phone in her coat pocket and nudged me. "Get down," she said.

I hopped down off my stool and stepped away from the bar. She immediately started pushing me towards the back door. "Move it!" she ordered.

"Okay, okay."

I walked slowly down the hall with her right on my tail, poking that gun in my side every step of the way. My feet were so heavy I could barely walk, and it seemed like it was taking forever to get to the back door. *So, this is how it's gonna end...? Shit, I need another drink!*

As we passed the bathrooms, a guy walked out of the men's room. "Excuse me ladies," he said.

I tried to signal him with my eyes, but he looked just about as drunk as I was. Damn an eye signal, I don't think he would've noticed a bright red flare with the lights off. Men are so stupid.

Cynthia pushed me out through the back door. It was dark as hell because there were only a couple of lights working out there, and they were on opposite sides of the parking lot. We walked out to the lot and she continued pushing me around with her gun. I could be wrong, but I don't think she was working any kind of plan. She was all over the place, literally, like she had to build up the nerve to kill me, and then decide how she was going to do it. She also seemed to forget where she parked. That or she was completely wasted too. I dunno she seemed to have a lot more control over her actions than I did.

We got halfway across the parking lot when she stopped and circled around, waving the gun in my face.

"You gone die tonight whore!" exclaimed Cynthia.

I tried to reason with her as best I could. "Look lady, I don't know anything. I don't have anything to do with what you did or nothing. They fired me, so I don't even care what you do!"

"Shut up!" she yelled. Then, she pulled out a fist full of her own hair.

"This bitch is crazy!" I mumbled.

"Just shut your fucking mouth!" She aimed the gun at my head.

I put my hands up as high as I could, which in my condition was about shoulder height. "Look, please, I-"

"Shut up!" She ran up and smacked my head several times with the butt of her gun until I dropped to the ground. "I said shut the fuck up!" she screamed.

I put my hand on my head and pulled back a bloody palm. I felt woozy. She grabbed me under the arm and we both struggled to get me back on my feet. Then, the strangest thing happened. She ripped off her hair and threw it on the ground. I almost threw up, but then I realized she'd been wearing a wig. I looked closely at her face.

"Hey, wait a minute, I know you!" I exclaimed. When she sat down at the bar, I knew I'd seen her before. I thought back to the day we first talked to Karla Charles' mother at the school, and suddenly I remembered she's the helpful principal that pretended to care so much about Shannon's well-being; the very principal, who said Shannon wouldn't be coming back; the same principal, who allowed us to search Karla's locker without a warrant. I was right. She'd been playing us the whole time. Probably planted the evidence Karen found in Karla's locker. And David just told me over the phone about this bitch, but it didn't register until she took that big ass rug off her head. It was definitely her, and she had revenge in her eyes.

I could tell Cynthia wanted to end my life, and there wasn't a damn thing I could do about it. I was a fly caught in that black widow's web, and she was moving in for the kill.

"Give me your keys!" Cynthia demanded.

I tipped my head to the side. "What?"

She pressed the gun to my temple and got right in my face. "I SAID GIVE ME YOUR FUCKIN' CAR KEYS BITCH! Don't make me kill you right out here in the open, I WILL DO IT!"

Slowly, I pulled my keys out of my pocket and held them up.

Cynthia snatched my keys away and pulled me up off the ground. Then, she started pushing me forward again. "WALK TO THE CAR, SOUTHERLAND." She kept rambling as we slowly crept back to my Mustang. "You two assholes think you can make a fool out of me, huh? I want my fucking money! If I can't get my fucking money, then somebody's gotta die, and it looks like it's gonna be you tonight! I swear you make one fuckin' move and I'll execute your ass! Right here, right now!"

We reached the car and she used the keyless-entry remote to unlock the doors. The parking lamps flashed twice. She shoved me around to the driver side and opened the door. Then, out of nowhere, I saw headlights from an oncoming car. They were blindingly bright. I was drunk and banged up, but I could still tell they were Crown lights, and the car they were attached to was barreling right towards us. It came to a screeching halt about ten feet away. The driver side door flung open and a man jumped out. He quickly drew his weapon and took aim at Cynthia using the car door as cover.

"FBI, freeze!" he yelled. It was David. He'd made it just in the nick of time. A minute later and I would've been gone forever.

"David she's got a gun!" I yelled.

"It's okay kid, I'm here," he responded.

Cynthia grabbed me from behind and spun me around into a one-arm chokehold. "DON'T FUCKIN' MOVE OR I'LL BLAST THIS WHORE!" She pressed the gun to the side of my head. "I SWEAR I'LL KILL THIS BITCH DEAD, I GOT NOTHIN' TO LOSE!"

"Put the gun down lady," David ordered. "We know everything about the girls, the teachers, and the boy too."

"FUCK YOU PIG YOU DON'T KNOW SHIT!" She pressed the gun harder against my head, grinding the silencer into my temple.

David circled around the car door and started advancing on us.

"STOP!" she yelled. "Don't come any closer goddammit! I'll do it. I'll kill this pretty bitch. Be a shame too, I could get top dollar for her." She licked my shoulder and laughed like a crazed maniac.

Suddenly, the parking lot lit up and the ground shook beneath us as thunder roared through the sky. Lightning flashed again, and I felt a few raindrops on my face. Then, the sky opened up, dumping buckets of rain on top of our heads. I was instantly soaking wet, but that was the least of my concerns. I was at the wrong end of a killer with a handgun.

We stood there in the back-parking lot of Manettie's in a stalemate for what seemed to be an eternity. Cynthia and David were drawing down on each other like a showdown from an old Clint Eastwood movie, only instead of watching it on TV, I was right in the line of fire.

"BACKUP'S ON THE WAY!" David yelled. "You got nowhere to go." He kept moving forward.

"I said stay back!" She raised her gun and pistol-whipped me.

I fell facedown into a puddle near the curb. She leaned over me and held the gun with both hands. I rolled over and looked up at her. This time, her finger was on the trigger. She was dead serious.

"GET BACK OR I'LL KILL THIS GODDAMN BITCH RIGHT NOW! I'LL DO IT MAN!"

I pulled myself up. "PLEASE SHOOT THIS BITCH, DAVID!" I yelled. "PLEASE!"

"SHUT UP," she yelled, kicking at me. "If you don't shut the fuck up...." She pulled back the hammer on the gun. She didn't have to finish her sentence. I got the point.

"Okay, alright," David said, raising his gun in the air. "Look, we can work this out ... just tell me what you need ... you let her go, and everybody backs off. You'll be on your way, nice and easy."

"I don't believe you!" she screamed. "Put the gun down first!"

I shook my head, crying like a baby. "Please David just shoot her," I whimpered.

"SHUT UP BITCH! SHUT THE FUCK UP!"

She swung again and hit me so hard my brain shook inside my head. For a split second, I lost my hearing. My vision was blurry then. All I could see was raindrops and stars.

"Okay, wait!" David leaned down, keeping his eyes focused on her gun. "Hey, don't look at her, look at me, okay ... that's it ... look, I'm putting it down ... please don't do that again."

"Put it down now!" she commanded.

David reassured her, saying, "I'm putting it down, okay?"

"SLOWLY COP! DO IT SLOW, OR I'LL SPLATTER HER FUCKIN' BRAINS ALL OVER THIS PARKING LOT!"

"No need for that," David replied. "Just calm down." He squatted slowly and dropped his gun on the ground. Then he put his hands in the air and stood back up.

"KICK IT AWAY COP!" she ordered, growing more unstable by the moment.

David complied, kicking his gun over to the curb. "Okay now ... I'm unarmed."

I could hear the dispatcher on his radio. Backup was one minute out. "I'm just gonna reach for my radio, alright ... don't shoot! Don't shoot! I'm just gonna tell them to stay back, okay? That was the deal. We stay back, you go on your way, okay ... don't worry, Cynthia, we're gonna get what you need, just let the girl go."

"I WANT MY FUCKIN' MONEY!" she yelled.

"We're gonna get you your money," David reassured, "just give me a second here."

David held the radio up to his lips and depressed the talk button. Something told me to look up at Cynthia. She wasn't aiming at me anymore. Her gun was trained on David. I felt paralyzed, frozen in time. Everything was moving in slow motion. I could tell by the look in her eyes she was about to shoot, and so could David. He went for his backup and drew down on her like the fastest gun in the west.

I don't know what I was thinking, but I was trying to stop her. I didn't care if I got killed in the process. I was ready to die. I lunged up at Cynthia, trying to bite her or do anything I could to stop her from shooting David, but I was so weak and drunk I just got in the way, and David couldn't get a clear shot.

Cynthia elbowed me back down to the ground and fired three times at David. The silencer muffled the blasts. She hit him with each shot. David doubled over, and his body started twitching. Then he got completely still. Blood spilled out and mixed in with the rainwater running along the ground.

"DAVID NO!" I hollered, scuffling to get over to him, but Cynthia caught me from behind. She smacked me in the back of the head with the gun, and I almost blacked out. She was tall and thin, but she hit hard as hell.

Cynthia grabbed me by the arms and started pulling me. I kicked and screamed the entire way as she dragged me back to the car. She got in through the driver side, pulling me into the car, still pointing the gun in my face as she climbed over to the passenger seat. I was down on my knees with my head stuck inside the door.

"Come on, get in bitch!" she demanded.

I climbed up and slid down into the driver seat. I was crying and still very drunk, it was so hard to see, and the rainwater in my eyes didn't help either.

"SHUT THE FUCKING DOOR!" she yelled, holding my right wrist with her left hand and pointing the gun at me with the other.

I closed the door and wiped the rain and tears from my eyes.

Cynthia handed me the keys. "Drive bitch!" She sat back and leaned against the passenger door, still pointing the gun at my head. "I said drive!"

"I CAN'T!" I exclaimed.

She damn near jumped on top of me, breathing erratically like a sick lunatic. "YOU BETTER DRIVE RIGHT FUCKIN' NOW!" she yelled, spitting all over the right side of my face.

"I'm drunk!" I screamed. "I can't drive like this with a gun pointed to my head!"

She lowered the pistol and pressed it against my side. "FINE, NOW DRIVE!"

"OKAY, SHIT!" I started the motor and shifted into first. I fastened my seatbelt, let the hand brake down and spun the wheel hard right to turn the car around. I drove through the parking lot, being careful to avoid David's body. As we drove past, I saw him move. He was still alive. He still had a fighting chance. I prayed backup would arrive in time to save him.

"Hurry up, move!" Cynthia commanded.

I pulled down to the edge of the parking lot and stopped, looking in my rearview at David's body.

"Make a left," she ordered.

I reluctantly turned into traffic. "Look, I don't know what's going on, but you shouldn't have done that. He's a Federal-"

"You don't know what's going on?" she yelled. "LIE AGAIN BITCH! SAY ONE MORE GODDAMN THING LIKE THAT AND I'LL BLOW YOUR FUCKING HEAD OFF RIGHT WHERE WE STAND! You and that dumb nigger tried to make a fool out of me. I know you had something to do with that little whore and her momma taking my money. What did you think, I wouldn't find out?" She pressed the gun harder into my side. "You think I'm stupid? Nobody steals my money."

"You killed her?" I asked.

"Bitch please, I didn't kill her, but I killed her stupid-ass momma. I didn't have time to get that little fucking gimp to make a crucifix, so I shot her and dumped her body in the park. I bet you thought you were hot shit getting that close, huh?"

"What the hell are you talking about?" I asked.

Cynthia reached over and yanked my hair so hard I nearly swerved off the road. "I'm talking about my fuckin' life bitch." She shoved my head back, and then returned to her position back against the passenger door. "I'm a teacher! I teach my girls how to survive and how to take what's theirs. I watched you that night," she said. "I saw you with him. He loves you any ass can see that. That cold-hearted motherfucker would've slit your throat if you were any other bitch."

"The fuck you talking about?" I asked.

"Marriott hotel ... "come inside me baby, come inside me!"" she taunted in a silly voice.

I squinted. "Malik...?"

"That's right bitch, Malik or whatever the hell that nigger calls himself. You think you're special, but you're not. You're just a stupid, cheap slut. He rams that huge black cock of his inside me every chance I give him. I told him to recruit you, but all he could manage to do was fuck you like the dumb whore you are. He's weak and pathetic, and so are you. I should've killed you that night. I hope you really got off because that's the last cock you'll ever see. Both of you are just like that little retarded bastard, Walter. He's a worthless piece of shit, and never would've amounted to anything if it weren't for me. His parents didn't know what to do with him, but I did. I gave him life. I taught him how to hate, how to murder, and how to keep you dumb fucking cops guessing and chasing a ghost. Serial killer, I mean just how fucking stupid are you people? His only problem was playing that stupid game. He should've killed you like I told him too, but it doesn't matter ... soon as I'm done with you two niggers, that little retard's gonna have an accident. There, over there, get onto the highway now!"

I made a right at the light onto the I-75 South ramp. I merged into traffic on the highway and got over a few lanes to the left.

"Did y'all fuck each other on top of my money?" she asked, belligerently.

"I never touched your money!"

"Shut up!" she yelled again. "You thought you were the shit stealing from me, huh? You take my money and get in the way of me disciplining my girls, so now I'm going to have to fuck you up!"

I just continued driving as she monologued.

"Soon as I find his ass, I'll kill that nigger too!" she declared. "Matter of fact let me call him right now and tell him how I plan to dump your body on the side of the fuckin' highway. Then, I'll wait for him to show up and shove this gun up his asshole and pull the trigger. You're going to watch me kill that big dumb nigger. I'm gonna kill him right in front of your face, and there's nothing you can do about it, bitch! FBI give me a fuckin' break. You're just a dumb fucking cunt!"

I dared not tell her Malik was sitting in jail. She would've killed me the moment I said it.

"Look lady, honestly I don't know anything about-"

"Shut up and pull over into the emergency lane."

I turned my hazard lights on and moved one lane over to the right.

"I SAID PULL OVER BITCH!" exclaimed Cynthia. "Steal my money and try to make me look like an idiot ... Malik took from me, so I'm gonna take something from him. I'm gonna blow your brains all over this goddamn highway, now pull over ... let me call this dumb nigger now." She took her cell phone out her purse. She held the phone up high so she could see the display and keep an eye on me at the same time. She put the phone on speaker. It rang, but of course, Malik didn't answer. "Didn't I say pull over? You deaf now bitch? PULL OVER!"

A million thoughts were running through my head, but I knew I had to do something fast. If she got away, they'd never catch her again. She'd just assume a new identity and find another spot to set up operations. She had to be stopped. It was just me and her. I had to act fast.

No matter what, I knew Cynthia was going to kill me, and maybe earlier in the night, I really wanted to die, but once it was clear it was about to happen, it didn't seem to make as much sense as before. Besides, if I was going to die, it'd be by my hands, not hers.

I said a quick prayer and tightened my grip on the steering wheel and gearshift. Then, I popped the clutch, slammed into third gear and smashed the accelerator to the floor. The front-end jumped as the rear wheels spun us up to 90 MPH.

"The fuck you doing bitch?" she yelled. "Slow down or I'll shoot!"

I hit the clutch again and jerked the car into fourth gear. The wheels chirped as I popped up off the clutch and stomped the accelerator back down to the floor. You could feel the G-forces as I gunned it up to over 100 MPH, swerving back and forth to avoid traffic while still accelerating. We were flying. I pushed it up to 120 MPH ... 140 ... 150. The engine roared like a 757 jet on take-off, and Cynthia was going berserk.

"STOP, STOP OR I'LL FUCKIN' SHOOT!" she threatened.

"YOU KILL ME AND WE BOTH DIE, BITCH!" I hit fifth gear and pressed the gas pedal down hard, as far as it would go. I continued accelerating. We flew right past a cop whose cruiser was parked sideways on the shoulder. I don't know how fast we were going when we passed him. The speedometer needle was just hanging all the way down on the right, but we were still picking up speed. I looked up in my rearview and saw he turned his blue lights on. He pulled off into traffic after us.

"STOP!" she yelled. Then, the inside of the car illuminated with a bright light.

It took a second for the pain to kick in, but once it did, I realized that bright light was the muzzle flash from her pistol. She shot me right in the thigh. It was totally unexpected.

"FUCK!" I cried, taking my foot off the gas and grabbing my thigh around the gunshot wound. It felt like my leg had been ripped open from the inside out. I turned and looked at her. The barrel of the gun was still smoking, but that time it was pointed right in my face. Her hands were shaking, but I knew she meant business.

"Dare me!" she exclaimed. "I'll do it, I'll kill you right now and take my chances. I told you before I got nothing to lose!"

I started sweating badly. Blood was splattered all over the steering wheel and gearshift. My hands were wet and sticky. We slowed back down to 80 MPH, and the cop finally caught up to us.

Cynthia yelled, "I'M TELLING YOU BITCH, PULL OVER! I got nothing to lose!"

"Yeah, you keep saying that," I winced in agony, my leg throbbing. I shook my head and just said, "Fuck it!"

Without thinking, I slammed my head back against the headrest and slung the wheel to the right as hard and fast as I could spin it. The highway was so slick from the fresh rain mixing with oil on the blacktop, we hydroplaned, and the car catapulted into the air. I immediately let go of the steering wheel to keep from breaking my arms when we slammed back down. The car flipped once in the air, and then it crashed into the road and rolled over repeatedly. Each time we flipped, the gun went off, but I wasn't worried. I figured the crash would be enough to kill us both anyway.

I watched in slow motion as my beautiful black Pony got ripped to shreds all around me. Parts were flying everywhere. My airbag deployed and everything except the doors got torn off—the hood, fenders, rear hatch and side mirrors too. To be honest, I wasn't scared at all. I didn't even close my eyes. I just figured it was my time to go.

We flipped several more times before coming to rest on all four tires, sideways in the center lane. Suddenly, I could see the bright lights, swooping in and surrounding my twisted body. I was drawn to them. I could feel my spirit leaving, floating up to heaven off the wings of my forgiving, extremely merciful and sympathetic angel—the one who had enough pity on my mortal soul to spare me from eternal damnation. *No more pain Alex, it's all over*, I thought. You know, I always thought the light would be pure white, but it wasn't ... actually, it was electric blue ... uh, and it wasn't off in the distance either... matter of fact, it was spinning around me in a flashing D.O.T. pattern... *Awe shit, goddammit that's just the lights from the fuckin' police car!* "CAN I GET SOME HELP IN HERE?" I yelled.

Somehow, by the grace of God, I was still alive. Believe it or not, so was my car. The motor was still running, squeaking and clunking on its last leg. It gave new meaning to, "Ford Tough." There was smoke everywhere, outside and inside the car, and I smelled gasoline. I could hear tires screeching all around us as motorists swerved to avoid hitting the debris and twisted heap of metal that used to be my car. With a crash like that, I owe my life to that damn weird racing seatbelt—that and the roll cage is probably the only reason I survived. *Thank you, Patrick, you performance part installing geek! I could just kiss you right about now!*

Evidently, the good Lord saw fit to spare me that night, but Cynthia, or whatever her name was, she wasn't so lucky. The only glass still intact was the windshield, and her body was folded up like a pretzel right between it and the dashboard. The gun was still in her grip. While the car was tumbling down the highway, she managed to shoot herself several times, including once in the head. There was blood, brain fragments, and hair all over the top of the dashboard. It was a gruesome sight, but a comforting one. Believe me, the world is a much better place without that bitch walking the streets at night.

The cop had pulled back a little when he saw the car flip out of control. He kept his distance until we landed, which was good for me because if not, he probably would've slammed right into us. I'm not sure I would've survived two crashes.

The officer rolled up slowly, shining his spotlight up into the back of the car. He stopped his cruiser a safe distance back, and then got out. I could see him in the unbroken half of my review mirror as he approached us, slowly and cautiously. He radioed for backup and a rescue ambulance as he walked around to my side of the car.

"EVERYBODY OKAY IN THERE?" yelled the officer as he drew near.

I used whatever strength I had left to reach up and turn off the motor. I turned the key, but it didn't stop. I would've laughed, but it felt like my chest plate had been shattered. That airbag knocked the wind out of me. The engine finally died after a few seconds.

The cop walked up and peaked inside. "Miss are you hurt?" he asked.

"No, I'm swell," I said coughing, my face covered in blood from all of Cynthia's pistol whipping and all the cuts and scrapes from the accident.

The cop shined his flashlight over at the corpse to my right. Every ounce of her blood was splattered all around inside the car. The seats, carpet, ceiling, and dashboard were all soaked in demon blood. The cop looked confused like he was trying to sort out in his mind what happened, but after a few seconds, he just gave up.

"I'm gonna get you out of there, just hold on," he said.

He tried to open my door, but it was jammed. "The frame must be bent," he said, reaching in to unbuckle my seatbelt. He pushed the release button on my 5-point harness and tugged at the seatbelt a few times on all sides, but it was stuck too. By then, the motor seemed to be smoldering. He quickly took out his pocketknife and carefully cut each one of the belt straps to free me. Then, he reached in and pulled me out through the driver side window. It hurt like hell, and it took a minute, but he finally got me out of there and leaned me up against the car.

"Can you walk?" he asked.

"I think so."

"Come on," he said, "this thing could catch fire."

I put my arm around his neck, and he helped me hobble back to his police cruiser. I was clinching my wounded thigh the whole way. Talk about pain, it felt like all my blood was draining by the pint out the hole in my leg. I sat down in the back of his car with the door open, and the officer took a quick look at my leg.

"I think you're going to be okay," he told me. He reached in his pocket and took out a handkerchief. "You need to put pressure on the wound," he said, pressing the cloth against my thigh.

"SHIT THAT HURTS!" I shrieked.

He told me, "Hold it right there with both hands, alright?"

I nodded. Then I took hold of the cloth and pressed down on my leg as hard as I could without passing out. I rested my head against the backseat and closed my eyes. I was all messed up, literally.

"Paramedics are on the way," said the officer. "Don't go anywhere, I'll be right back." He took off.

I was in a lot of pain, but it didn't stop me from being nosey. I watched the officer through the back window. He went back to where my car first flipped. There was a ton of debris in the road, so he put down flares to warn oncoming drivers. He lined them up one-by-one, past his cruiser, and all the way leading up to the actual wreckage. Then, he took his flashlight out and started waving it around to bring the highway back into order.

After a few minutes, more cops showed up and blocked off two lanes. Then a fire truck and ambulance arrived. The other officers secured the scene while the cop, who pulled me out the car came back to talk.

"Look, I know you're injured," the Officer said, "but I got a dead body and a gun up there ... I need to know what happened. You and your friend been doing some drinking tonight? Maybe had an argument or something?"

I shook my head. "That woman is a suspect in multiple murder investigations. What's your name officer?"

He replied, "Holt, Jacob Holt ... third precinct."

"Officer Holt, I'm Special Agent Alex Southerland, FBI. The woman up there shot a Federal agent, and then took me hostage. I need you to get a hold of Special Agent Frank Morris in the Atlanta field office."

"Okay," Holt responded, "you stay put and let these guys check you out."

"I ain't going nowhere, Jacob," I replied.

He waved the medics over.

The paramedics helped me up out the back of the police car and into the ambulance. One of them cut up the side of my jeans. He wiped away the blood and took a close look at my wound.

"It went through the back!" he yelled to his partner.

He rolled me over on my side and went to work on my leg while his partner took care of the scrapes on my face and the big gash on my head. He put some kind of ointment on me that set my entire head on fire, but I was lucky to be alive, so I didn't complain. I just sucked it up and let it burn. Compared to Cynthia's fate, it could've been a whole lot worse.

"You need some stitches up here." The paramedic pointed to my head where Cynthia smacked me around with her gun. He prepared a syringe, pulled up my sleeve and swabbed my arm. "Wait, have you been drinking tonight?" he asked. He must've smelled the alcohol on my breath.

"Yes ... like a lot."

He immediately put the syringe away. "I can't give you anything right now, but we'll get you to the hospital soon. I know it hurts, but just try to relax, okay?"

I gave him a slow thumbs up and closed my eyes. My head was ringing like a bell tower at high noon.

The paramedics finished treating my injuries and strapped me down in the bed, so we could leave for the ER. I just lay there in the back of the ambulance trying to keep still. My head was throbbing, and my leg didn't feel any better. I was cold, so I asked the medic to put a blanket over me. He did. He was very kind. It didn't take long for Frank and the rest of the crew to show up.

"You okay?" asked Karen, climbing up into the ambulance with me. Frank got in too.

"I'll live," I replied. "You see her?"

"Yeah we saw her," Frank said.

"That her?" I asked.

He nodded. "Yeah, it's definitely her."

"Don't worry about anything," Karen said. "You did good, baby."

I tried to smile, but it hurt too much. Who knew life could be so good and so fucked up at the same time?

"Where's David?" I asked. "Is he ok?"

"He's on the way to the hospital," Karen said. "He was wearing his vest, but he took a bullet in the side. We won't know how bad it is until they get him in surgery."

I started crying. "He was trying to save me ... I'm so stupid."

"Don't do that!" Karen said. "David was doing what he does best, his job. Don't worry about him, he's a tough old bastard, and he'll be just fine."

"Promise?" I asked, my eyes full of tears.

"I promise sweetie, now you take it easy. Frank and I are gonna get out here and process this scene before the cops screw up all the evidence. We'll make sure they take you to the same hospital David's headed to, okay?"

"I love you," I said.

Karen smiled really big. "We love you too sweetie, now you hold on."

Frank touched my hand. "Everything'll be alright," he said, a big smile on his face. "You did good, kid. I'll be at the hospital soon as I can get there. You want me to call Bill?"

I thought about it a second and then frowned. "No, not Bill. Just promise me you'll come, Frank ... promise!"

"No worries," he said. "I'll be there ... I'll see you real soon, kid."

I nodded and then they exited through the rear of the ambulance.

After about a minute or so, one of the medics climbed back in with me and shut the doors. "We need to get you to the hospital now, Miss," he said. "You still doing alright?"

"I think so."

"Good, just hang on." He checked my vitals and then banged on the front wall a couple of times with a closed fist.

I could see my car through the side door of the ambulance as we drove off. It looked like it had been through a junkyard compactor. It was a big heap of twisted metal sitting in the middle of the highway.

"So long Black Beauty," I whispered.

"What's that?" asked the EMT.

"Nothing."

On the way to the hospital, the paramedic seemed concerned about the extent of my head injuries. He continued talking to me, and kept a watchful eye on my vitals, making sure I didn't lose consciousness. As soon as we pulled up to the hospital, they rushed me inside the ER where the nurses and doctors asked me a bunch of questions.

"How fast were you going when you crashed?" they asked. "Were you wearing your seatbelt? Did you hit your head inside the vehicle?"

I guess I answered everything to their satisfaction because they immediately rolled me into a room where a young man started an IV and went to work treating my bullet hole and stitching up my head wounds. He seemed very concerned about the amount of swelling on my head, so he called in Dr. Makesh, the resident neurologist.

I told Dr. Makesh I was fine, but he said they needed to run tests to be sure. He ordered a CAT Scan to look for any sign of swelling or bleeding in my brain.

The nurse rolled my bed into another room for the test. Once everything was done, they moved me down to ICU. After a couple of hours, the doctor came back in to talk to me.

"Agent Southerland, I'm Dr. Makesh. Remember me?" He smiled. Makesh was an Indian man with a short haircut, and very kind eyes. He was extremely well dressed. He rolled over a little black chair and sat down beside my bed. "How are you feeling now?" he asked.

"My head hurts, I'm sorry, what was your name?"

"I'm Dr. Makesh, remember?" he asked.

"Oh, yes, you came in before."

"That's right. Here, let me have a look at you..." He leaned in close, lightly touching around the top of my head. "Your CT results came back and everything's just fine. It looks like the swelling's already going down. I don't think you're in any danger here, but you still have a good bit of alcohol in your system. I'd like to keep you overnight for observation, alright?"

"Do I have a choice?" I asked.

Makesh smiled. "You're going to be just fine, Ms. Southerland."

I hated hospitals, but I didn't argue with him because it felt like a woolly mammoth spent the night pouncing up and down on my head.

Makesh finished checking me out and said, "Can I ask you a question?"

"What?"

"If I get a wheelchair in here, you think you might feel like seeing someone?"

"Who?"

"ASAC David Chandler is here in ICU," said Makesh. "He's out of surgery and awake now ... he's asking for you."

I sat up in the bed. "Yes, OUCH!"

"Hold on there, take it easy," said Makesh. He reached over and helped me lay back down. "Rest a few minutes, I'll be back soon."

"Thank you, doctor."

He smiled. "Anytime."

Sure enough, after about ten minutes, Makesh showed back up with a wheelchair. He pulled my covers off and picked me up. He was strong. He gently sat me up in the chair being careful not to bump my leg. Then, he put one of the blankets over me. "Come on let's go," he said softly.

Makesh rolled me down to a room on the other side of the floor. Then, he spun the wheelchair around, opened the door, and pulled me inside. David was lying there in the bed with a bunch of wires hooked up to him. I could tell he was in rough shape, he was swollen up pretty bad, but he was still alive. Karen was right. He was a tough ole bastard.

"Agent Chandler look what I have for you," said Makesh.

David leaned his head up and smiled. "Southerland," he whispered.

Makesh rolled me up right beside the bed.

"Agent Chandler, now I don't want you to get too excited with this gorgeous young lady in your bed." He smiled. "I'll leave you two alone for a while ... just press the red button up there if you need us." He walked out and closed the door.

"You look like shit," David said, his voice weak and raspy.

"David, I love you. I'm sorry I-"

"Shut up kid. I got something I need to tell you."

I touched his hand and he turned it over and held mine tightly.

"I lied to you," he confessed.

I shook my head a little. "What are you talking about David?"

"I lied," he repeated. "Pretended not to know you and gave you a hard time. I didn't tell anybody. I'm sorry, but-"

"What are you saying?"

"It wasn't an accident you ended up here with me in Z-Squad, I knew your dad."

"What?"

"Crane and I both knew him," he said. "We worked cases together. We were there with him when he died."

My jaw dropped, and a tear built up in my eye. "You're hurt David, it's all the medicine ... you don't know what you're talking about, just hush and rest ... please."

David described my dad to the letter. "Blonde hair, thick mustache, tough little fucker," he said. "Sheriff's Department."

"Yeah, but I don't understand, I-"

"We were there on the raid with him when that kid shot him. It was a joint task force, guns and drugs." David coughed. "Crane and I were partners. We were right there with him. Before he died, he made us promise to take care of you. I, I thought I'd broken that promise tonight. I had to see you before..." He coughed again and suddenly broke out into a cold sweat. I took the edge of my blanket and wiped his forehead. "God dammit, I was so afraid she hurt you," said David.

"It's okay ... I'm alright, now take it easy. You gotta rest to heal." I started crying.

"We been there the whole time," said David, "watching, trying to protect you. Tony sent you the magazine, you remember that?"

I nodded, "With the FBI lady?"

"That's the one, kid." He smiled. "We been looking after you. I didn't want you on this case. I was afraid you might get hurt ... I was right."

"No David, I'm okay, I'm fine," I sniffled.

He laid his head back against the pillow, closed his eyes, and tried to clear his throat. "You made an old man happy tonight," he said. "I can rest now. I want you to go to New York, and I want you to give 'em hell, you hear me!" He started coughing again, only this time it was a wet cough. It didn't sound right to me.

"David...?"

"Give them fuckin' hell kid," he coughed and coughed, and coughed again. Then, he started spitting up blood.

"Oh shit, David!" I jumped up and wiped his mouth. "NURSE! NURSE!" I screamed, frantically pressing the emergency button near the headboard. "NURSE, SOMEBODY GET IN HERE NOW!"

Within seconds, two nurses came running in along with Dr. Makesh.

"Get her back to her room!" Makesh ordered.

"No, David, I love you!" I screamed, fighting with the nurse for her to let me go. "David, I love you!"

The nurse forced me back down in the wheelchair and rolled me towards the door. I screamed at the top of my lungs, but David never responded.

I fought to stay inside that room. I even tried to grab hold of the door handle with both hands, but I was too weak. The nurse easily overpowered me. Out in the hallway, I continued yelling at her. "LET ME GO, BITCH! DON'T LET HIM DIE LIKE THIS GODDAMMIT!"

"You have to calm down ma'am," she said. "Everything will be just fine."

Back in my room, I was too burned out to fight her, but that didn't stop me from giving orders just like David would've. "LEAVE ME HERE! YOU NEED TO GO HELP HIM!"

"Hush now sweetie," said the nurse.

She put me back in bed, and then checked my blood pressure. It was high—140 over 90. "Here, this will help you relax." She gave me a shot in the arm, and after that, I was out like a light bulb.

Chapter 13

That night was the last time I saw David alive. The 22-caliber bullet that pierced the side of his vest bounced around inside his chest cavity, just barely missing his heart and lodging up inside his throat. The doctors operated and were able to remove the bullet, but the damage was irreparable. David didn't have a snowball's chance in hell of making it through the night. He knew it, and so did Dr. Makesh. Before leaving the hospital, Makesh told me David's dying wish was to lay eyes on me one last time. Hearing that made me so sad I cried. I truly appreciated everything David had done for me. When I say I love him, I really mean it. I was devastated he was gone, but at least I got the chance to see him before he died. Dr. Makesh didn't have to do what he did, but I thank God every single day that he gave me a chance to see David before he died. Unlike with my dad, I actually had the chance to tell David I loved him. I hope he heard me. I think he did.

Even today, I still second-guess my actions leading up to that night. I'll always be conflicted about the whole thing. On the one hand, if I hadn't done what I did, we probably never would have caught the killers, but on the other hand, my Davie would still be alive.

The days following David's death were impossible to cope with, almost as bad as the night I watched him die. David and I had a lot in common. Like me, he was a loner, no real family and not many friends outside of Z-Squad. Hell, Frank had to see about his affairs. I was supposed to leave for New York immediately, but I decided to hang around and help Frank with the funeral arrangements. It was important to me that everything was done right. We at least owed David that.

Tony called as soon as he heard the news. He was hurt, probably a lot more than he let on over the phone. Unfortunately, he couldn't make the funeral. He was completely tied up with his new responsibilities. He just sent flowers down along with his sincerest condolences.

Frank told me Tony and David had been best friends for some time, and after a bit of snooping around on my own, I verified they both knew my father. What David said was true. I felt horrible David was dead. It was all my fault, and Tony not being able to make the funeral made me feel even worse. I wish I knew David sooner. I wish we could've had more time together and been closer, but it's too late now.

Believe it or not, FBI Director Mullen actually came down from D.C. the day before the funeral. He asked me how things were going, and I told him all was good, but I think he could tell I was lying. I was glad he was there though. For the most part, I was worried he'd be the only other person, besides the Z-Squad folks, to show up. That was no way to send David off, but what could I do? I thought about asking Mullen to make some calls or something for me, but I decided not to. I didn't have the heart to tell him nobody cared about one of the Bureau's most valued agents.

Frank asked me to do the eulogy, and of course, I agreed. I spent the night before the funeral jotting down my thoughts. I wanted to make sure what I said was meaningful, you know, something that honored David properly. It took me a while to get it all down on paper, and it was a bit draining too. I was tired when I finally finished. It was late as hell, but as usual, I couldn't get to sleep. I hadn't slept since David died. Since then, my mind had been moving 1,000 MPH nonstop. I can rarely think straight anymore, and there's no such thing as rest for me nowadays. I used to joke about staying up all night or having insomnia, but now that I actually have it, it's no laughing matter. That night, I couldn't even drink myself to sleep. I just lay in the bed gazing up at the ceiling.

When the morning came, I got up and did absolutely nothing. Everything was already set for the funeral, so all we had to do was show up in black to say goodbye to our old friend one last time. I just tried to pass the time, so I did some busy work around the apartment.

The funeral was at 1 p.m. at Westview Cemetery, so I planned to leave the house at about 12:15. I hadn't eaten anything all morning. I was hungry, but I couldn't bring myself to eat. I just wanted to get to the funeral and get it over with. Problem was, I didn't have transportation. My Mustang was literally in pieces, so I needed a ride to the funeral, but I dared not call Bill. He would've taken me, but I had enough to deal with already, and seeing him would've just complicated things. He would've just wanted to talk about him and me there and back, and I wasn't feeling that at all. Besides, based on how I was feeling, if Bill said the wrong thing, we'd end up having two funerals instead of one.

I called Frank, and he stopped by to pick me up on the way. I was extremely grateful to him because I really needed to be around someone who cared about David being gone more than their own problems.

We left on time, and there wasn't much traffic, so we arrived a few minutes early. Everyone I expected to attend was there—Director Mullen and his wife, Pam Reece from the morgue, and the entire Z-Squad team, but there were also a few stragglers I didn't know. The funeral was held in the memorial hall. Everything was beautiful, and we started right on time. They played some music, and then Chandler's priest got up to say a few words. Once he finished, they called me up to do the eulogy.

I hobbled up to the front, gripping my little walking cane, and stood behind the podium. I was struggling to maintain my composure. There weren't many people in there, so I wasn't nervous or anything, just heartbroken. I had to work up to a point where I could open my mouth without crying, but by the time I finally built up enough strength to go through with it, the doors in the back of the hall flew open.

Rays of sun poured in from the doors, and dark shadows fled in all directions as sunlight covered nearly every square inch of the memorial hall. I focused and looked outside but couldn't believe my eyes. There was a mob of people lined up as far as the eye could see, all the way back to the road. One-by-one, they entered the hall, circling down front and paying their respects to David. They brought flowers too and put them down all around his casket.

I stood in awe, watching for over 30 minutes as people filled the memorial hall to capacity. Once all the seats were taken, they stood in the aisles, and others gathered around the doors and windows, looking in from outside.

I was completely moved. Turns out, damn near the entire Bureau from Atlanta to D.C. showed up, plus people from the community, including family members of victims David had helped over the years. His daughter showed up too. Hell, I never even knew he had a daughter, but he did, and she came to honor him. I had no way to count, but there could have been more than 1,000 people, old and young, that showed up to pay their respects.

Once everyone settled down, it was time for me to speak, but all I could do is look down and stare at my notes. I tried to start, but after seeing all those people there for David, my emotions got the best of me. I parted my lips and was just going to say something, but then I heard someone talking loudly all the way in the back.

"Excuse me," said the man, pushing his way through the crowd. "Pardon me."

I watched as he made his way up to the front. It didn't dawn on me until he was standing a few feet away that it was Tony. He'd made it. I immediately burst into tears.

Tony walked up to the casket and leaned in close to David's body. I stood there with my mouth wide open and watched Tony whisper something to David. I don't know what he said, but a tear streamed down his cheek.

By then, everyone was emotional, and I'd completely lost it. Tony looked up and smiled. He gave me a quick nod and said, "It's okay Alex ... go ahead."

I wanted to, I really did, but after seeing Tony, unexpectedly, I just couldn't. I was too choked up. I stood there, crying and sobbing like a baby, embarrassing myself in front of all those people. I tried to grab the microphone, but my hands were shaking too much. I just couldn't pull it together.

Tony ran up to the podium and put his arm around me. "It's okay," he whispered, pulling me close and squeezing me tight, "Shhh ... it's okay, Alex."

"I can't do it Tony, I just can't," I whispered. "I'm sorry, I miss him."

"Me too," he said, nodding slowly. "I miss him too. Here, let me help you...." Tony tilted the microphone up to his lips. Then, he cleared his throat and said, "We've come together today to honor David Chandler...." He sighed deeply and paused for a moment. Then, he continued saying, "To say goodbye to the David Chandler many of you have known for a lifetime and whom I've come to know over the past 20 years. In that time, I came to know David Chandler, know him as an FBI agent, as a husband and father, and as a humble servant to the public. It seems almost impossible for one man to have touched so many lives in so many different ways. Ladies and gentlemen, when you find a great man, one who is kind and genuine, a man who is honest in everything he does ... a man who would give his life for each and every one of us here today, you just want to take a piece of him with you wherever you go. There's one thing we can all say ... we all took a big piece of David, but he still had a lot more to give. In my time with the Bureau, I've watched the distinguished David Chandler touch many of you through his tireless work, and as I stand here today, there's no doubt in my mind he rests in a much better place. The FBI notes it has been a matter of privilege to experience his contributions to the Bureau and the community. We thank God for holding David Chandler in his hands, and we ask Him to look after him with loving care, for he was without doubt the best of us. We will hold David close to our hearts, until the day when we meet again and come to be close to him once more ... may God bless all of you, and may God bless David Chandler."

Everyone jumped to their feet and clapped. We all wept as we followed the pallbearers to the gravesite. The Priest prayed once more, and then they lowered David's casket into the ground, right beside his wife Sara, who'd died eight years prior.

As they covered David's casket with dirt, I watched, looking all around to see the expressions on everyone's faces. There was no question in my mind. One way or another, they all genuinely cared a great deal about my Davie. They too were sad to see him go. And, at that very moment, I was the saddest I'd been for a long time. But, after a few minutes, my sorrow left, and suddenly I wasn't afraid for David anymore. I wasn't afraid for me either. Seeing all those people and sharing their pain, I realized how tough life must've been for David. I couldn't imagine how hard it was for him to go out every single day, faced with all those people, their stories, and their pain. With that in mind, I was just happy for David; happy he could finally be at peace.

After the funeral, I hung around Atlanta for a few more days. I had some unfinished business to attend to. I needed to visit an old friend. I went to go see Malik in the Fulton County lockup right before the authorities released him. He was in a holding cell, waiting for a Federal judge to sign an order to grant his immunity and set him free.

I hated Malik for the mess he'd made. He was partly to blame for what happened to those girls and David too. I confided in Frank about my situation with Malik. He pretty much had the story already though. See, Frank's one of those anal-retentive investigators. He'd already watched the rest of the surveillance tapes from the hotel, and of course after seeing me prancing around half naked, he put two and two together. Evidently, in addition to the cameras in the elevators, there were cameras on each floor, so he really got the whole story, up close and personal. I told Frank I was going to go see Malik. He made me promise, I mean pinky-swear and take a blood oath, I wouldn't do anything stupid.

"Don't screw your career up over that dumbass," Frank said.

He seemed to be under the impression it made a difference Malik helped us get the autistic boy into custody and find the woman behind the murders. I didn't share his sentiment. Malik's half-ass attempt to help towards the end was just him trying to save his own ass and score a get out of jail free card. Besides, what happened to all Cynthia's money? Somebody took it, and I bet on everything I own it was that mothafucka, Malik. For me, it didn't matter what he did after the fact, he should've never done the fuckin' shit he did in the first place. He knew he was wrong.

When I used to look at Malik, all I saw was hot, steamy, wild ass sex to the point I didn't bother to look at the man behind the big dick. But I was starting to see things clearer, and nothing made me angrier than the fact he'd walk away a free man after all the shit he did. Yeah, Malik may have had immunity from the police, but not from me.

I walked into the lockup and asked the guard if I could see the prisoner. He kindly obliged. I'm pretty sure he could tell what I was thinking by the look on my face. He wouldn't even look me in the eye, like he wanted no part of what he suspected was about to go down. As I waited for them to unlock the cell, I took a brief moment to recall Einstein's Theory of Relativity for Frank's sake. He'd made me promise not to do anything stupid, so I wanted to be as smart as a whip when I got in there with Malik. As soon as the cell door opened, I hobbled in on my little walking cane and proceeded to unleash hell.

"Red!" yelled Malik. He looked up and smiled, reaching for me, his hands still cuffed.

I didn't say a word. I leaned back, gripped my cane like a golf club, and then smashed the end of it straight up into his balls, Tiger Woods style. It was a perfect shot.

"DOUBLE FUCKIN' BOGEY," I yelled, gritting my teeth.

"FUCKIN' BITCH!" He doubled over onto his knees. "GOTDAMN ... MOTHAFUCKA, MY NUTS! AWE HELL NAW, SOMEBODY GET IN HERE!" He rolled around on the floor in agony, screaming at the top of his lungs, holding his balls. I circled around him slowly, hopping from leg to leg.

"Not so bad now, huh?" I took a real good deep breath, and then I leaned over and hit him again, this time on the crown of his big fucking skull.

"Shit, G ... get her off me man!" he stuttered, blood streaming down his face.

The guards didn't budge. They just stood outside with their backs turned while I whaled on Malik's ass.

Everyone in the department knew Malik had a hand in a bunch of little girls being pimped and murdered, and they knew he was getting off scot-free. I think they would've done the deed themselves if not for fear of losing their jobs. But I didn't have that problem. I just didn't give a fuck anymore.

"Where you think you goin'!" I yelled as he tried to crawl away. "You big pimpin', remember?" I stepped on his left collarbone to hold him down and tried to hit him a few more times in the balls, but he kept blocking my blows with his arms. I swung until I tired myself out and started sweating profusely. Then, I stomped on his chest with my good foot and yelled, "That's for David, bitch!" I spit in his bloody face, and then hobbled back out of his cell, satisfied I'd made my point.

"Y'ALL SEE THIS SHIT MAN...?" he yelled, pressing his hand against his head. "LOOK WHAT YOU FUCKIN' DID ... DIS BITCH CRAZY! I'M PRESSING CHARGES ... GUARDS! GUARDS!"

I didn't pay him a bit of attention, and neither did the guards. They all but high-fived each other as I limped up out of there.

Kicking' Malik's ass made me feel like I'd done a real public service. I felt like a million-dollar bill. Afterwards, I promised never to intentionally engage in premeditated bad behavior again. I was a changed girl, so I pledged from that point on, all my fuck-ups would be completely spontaneous.

When I look back on all the changes I went through during that period in my life, I think I made the biggest change on the day of David's funeral. From the moment I saw his casket going into the ground, I stopped seeing things through my own eyes, and started trying to live my life for others. David taught me a lot, and maybe his death was my last lesson. Maybe it was God's way of opening my eyes and preparing me to go out and be a true servant of the people.

It may sound odd, but I believe the night David died he forged my signature in blood right above his on a contract he'd been fulfilling since before I was born. It was one of a special nature that required me to repay an awesome debt to the entire world for the rest of my life, just as David had before me. It was never his debt to pay, but he did it selflessly, without a single complaint, and with no regrets. It'll be almost impossible to fill his shoes, but I'm willing to accept the challenge with all my heart and all my soul.

David Chandler, you watched over me, constantly encouraging me to change my life for the better, and I love you for that. I'll always keep you in my heart, right next to my father, and I will never, ever let you go. Rest in peace old friend.

* 9 7 8 1 7 3 3 4 6 5 6 0 1 *